FRIENDS OR FOES

-

KJ Graham

ISBN: 1500181633
ISBN 13: 9781500181635
Library of Congress Control Number: 2014911140
CreateSpace Independent Publishing Platform
North Charleston, South Carolina

Table of Contents

CHAPTER ONE

The Doctor

I watched as the gull swooped on the unsuspecting beachcomber, trying to steal his lunch. For October, at the far end of the Blackwaterfoot Beach, it was an unusually busy day. As well as the beachcomber, there were two gentlemen who looked like they had just fallen off the front page of a winter catalogue, also a woman walking her German shepherd. For Arran in October, that was positively a crowd. Arran was usually a very quiet island in the winter, as all that remained on the island were the locals and hundreds of empty holiday homes. Situated on the west coast of Scotland, it nestled between the Mull of Kintyre peninsula and the Ayrshire coast, a beautiful and peaceful little island.

That was the reason I was there, but today, not so much. My mind started to wander again, and I wondered if this were some sort of battle fatigue or shell shock. I was spending a lot of my time reliving my past experiences. Was it just because I had too much time on my hands now, or was it because seven months ago I had looked a man straight in the eye and shot him dead? Not that killing him was a problem—in my career I had killed many men, but until that day, I had never had to do it face to face. Our eyes made contact just as I squeezed the trigger, and the MP5 bullet passed straight through his heart, killing him instantly. The life left his eyes, his legs buckled under him, and at that moment, I knew my career was over. The years of training couldn't prepare you for that. Enough was enough.

It was not planned. I was a member of a three-man team sent to Pakistan to terminate an Al Qaeda cell. Due to faulty Intel, the job never happened. Not a bad thing in my eyes—we were a man short, and I had been drafted into the team at the last minute, reassigned from my normal training duties. We were packing to return home when we were asked to assist the Pakistani police. An American businesswoman had been kidnapped and was being held in an office block. No American forces were in the area. I had a bad feeling about this—going in half-arsed to a job with no intel was not a good idea, especially as we had not trained as a team, and our specialty was not hostage recovery.

When we arrived on the scene, the shit had already hit the fan. The police had tried to storm the office and had lost two men, the psycho had lost the plot and was demanding a van to take them to the Afghan border, and he was promising that if not, the woman would be executed in thirty minutes' time. Gerry, the original team leader, decided we would go in blind with flash bangs. Taff, the third member of the team, was not happy. He wanted to wait for the Americans. Gerry told him to shut it and get his kit on before the American bird bought it. It had escaped Gerry's attention that I was the senior rank. I let it slide for the moment as Gerry was trained in hostage extraction.

After a quick look at the outside of the office, I managed to talk Gerry into letting me place a charge on the right-hand wall of the office. It was only stud partition, built cheaply and quickly to house the ever-growing call-centre culture of this country. It wouldn't take a lot of persuading. I was the munitions expert in the team and would go in through the wall as a backup while the other two stormed the front door of the office.

With four minutes left until the deadline, we stormed the office. Taff went in first. He took the door down and went in with flashbangs, lost his footing on an upturned desk, and went down. Gerry went in at the same time as my charge went off. I waited for a fraction of a second until the dust cleared, checked my safety was off (I was on single shot), and moved into the gap in the wall. Psycho had had some training and

2

had stayed in the leg space of a desk while the flashbangs went off. He appeared as fresh as a daisy, shooting Gerry in the neck.

As he fired, he sensed movement on his right and swung his weapon round, but he was too late. I already had my MP5 shouldered and on target. My training kicked in. Holding my breath, my brain was screaming at me to squeeze the trigger, not pull it. It was all over in a fraction of a second, but as the gunman died, I felt a part of me die with him. When Taff and I returned to Hereford, I requested to be RTU. Two months later, I was on my way back to my native Scotland a free man, with a very messed up head. It had been the straw that broke the camel's back. Since joining the Royal Engineers from school, I had lurched from one disaster to another, with only my career to keep me sane. Now my career was over, and I had nothing to look forward to, and a lot of time to do it. When there was nothing to look forward to, one tended to look back at what might have been.

Jill and I married at eighteen. We had been an item since school. She fell pregnant with a honeymoon baby, and we were off to a flying start. Then fate took a hand in my destiny, Jill died in childbirth—a brain aneurysm—I also lost my baby daughter. Jill had insisted on a home birth, and when disaster struck, there was no medical team to help my unborn daughter. By the time Jill was taken to hospital, it was all too late, a terrible weekend that would haunt me to my dying day. I had been based in Northern Ireland at the time, and after a return to Stirling to bury my family, I threw myself into my work. It was the only way to cope with the despair I felt.

Because my work was now my life, I started to gain a reputation for my bomb-disposal skills and was used by the Special Forces and MI5 in an advisory capacity. It didn't take long until I was seconded full-time into the Special Air Service and shipped back to Hereford for training, although not the training I was expecting—no Brecon Beacons for me. Yes, there was military training, but MI5, Special Branch, and SIS training was the norm. It was more about making bombs than defusing them. It was clear to me from the start that the pen-pushers in Whitehall had decided to take on the paramilitaries at their own game. The gloves were off. MI5 and SIS loved mind games. So a lot of their training was more brainwashing than training. I was shown footage of squaddies being executed, not the stuff that made the nine o'clock news. I was left in no doubt what my fate would be if I fucked up. The brainwashing worked. I returned to Ireland ready to wage war on the enemy.

I was still daydreaming when something landed at my left foot—a baseball cap. I looked up to see where it had come from. The beachcomber was heading my way, and to my surprise, it was a rather pretty if somewhat flustered girl. I grabbed the cap before it made a second bid for freedom and gave it a shake to get rid of any sand it had collected. Its owner arrived a few seconds later, somewhat out of breath, her carrier bag weighing her down as she clambered over the rocks to where I sat. "You must have collected some amount of shells. That bag looks heavy." I smiled as I pointed to the bag. There was an awkward pause.

I took it she was shy; it was as if she did not know what to say. She changed the subject. "I knew I should have bought one with a strap."

I nodded. "And a waterproof one, if that keeps coming." I pointed out to the Mull of Kintyre where heavy black clouds were forming. The low winter sun still danced on a calm sea, dazzling me and stopping me from studying the girl's features. The hills of Kintyre on the horizon were masked by approaching sheets of rain.

"Yes, you are right." She studied the sky. "Time to head for home."

I stood up. "Can I help you with your bag?"

She transferred the bag to her other side as if to stop me from reaching for it. "No, no, you have been too kind already. Thanks for saving my hat. See you later." She started to head for the car park. "I'm sure we will. It's a very small island."

Time for a coffee, I thought. I hadn't realized how cold I was until then. As I approached the car park, an old Fiesta was just leaving. I could just make out the girl from the beach through the steamed-up windows as it pulled away. She was a bit strange, I thought, but I suppose talking to a strange man on a deserted beach wasn't high on a things-to-do list for a lone female.

There were only two cars left in the car park—my Freelander and a big Vauxhall. I scanned the beach but couldn't see anyone. Looked like whoever owned it was about to get very wet. The rain was starting to spit. I fired up the Freelander and hit the heated-seat button. As I pulled out of the car park, the heavens opened. Even on full speed, the wipers were struggling to cope with the rain.

For some reason, I turned left along the coast road heading to Machrie, instead of right for home. It was late afternoon, and I wasn't ready to sit in the house for the rest of the day. About two miles further on, I came round a bend to find the little blue Fiesta in a ditch, its owner jumping up and down at the side of the road like a madwoman.

I pulled up and hit the hazard switch. No jacket...this was not going to be pleasant. The rain hit me like a wave as I stepped out. The girl took a double take. "Yes, it's me again. Is it stuck?"

"Yes, sorry to be a bother again. An idiot in a van tried to overtake me, and I ended up here."

"No problem. Can I have a go at moving it?" I jumped in and started rocking the Fiesta back and forward on the clutch. On the fifth attempt, it came free with a bang. I could feel all was not well. On further inspection, I found the left tyre was off the rim. The tyre was destroyed. Half an hour of fighting with the old jack and the spare wheel, and we were back in business. The water was running out of the bottom of my trousers and filling my trainers. All I wanted was a hot bath. "There you go. That's you sorted."

The girl smiled at me. "I am really sorry. Please come down to the cottage. It's only a quarter of a mile down the road. You will catch your death. I can dry your clothes and make some hot tea. I won't take no for an answer."

"I don't want to make a nuisance of myself. I will be fine."

The girl held out her hand. We shook hands. "My name is Kay, and I said I wouldn't accept no. Let's get out of this weather. Follow me."

Kay marched off without another word and set sail in the patched-up Fiesta. I had to put the foot down to catch her up. Just as I caught her, she veered to the left onto a farm track and headed down toward the shore. Halfway between the road and the shore sat a little white cottage. It was in a stunning location and had its own little track down to its own little private bay and jetty below a cliff face. The clouds had started to clear as quickly as they had arrived, and as I pulled up to the little fisherman's cottage, the sun cast long shadows across the beach, making the bay look like a scene from a postcard.

Kay ran into the cottage flinging her jacket off in the porch. I assumed I was meant to follow. On entering I found the porch led straight into a cozy little living room with a view of the bay. It was clear the décor had not been Kay's choice. Although clean and presentable, the two armchairs dated from the sixties and the pictures on the walls depicted fishing boats, giving the feeling that this little home had belonged to a fisherman.

Kay appeared armed with a toweling robe and hustled me into a bathroom that was straight out of the nineteen-seventies, complete with a shocking pink bathroom suite. I put up a halfhearted opposition to the idea that I hand over my clothes for drying, but she was having none of it, telling me the kettle was on and to get a move on. The robe was a touch on the small side to say the least. Having been made for a petite woman, it struggled to cover my forty-eight-inch chest, but it did smell nice, a faint hint of perfume and talc.

Kay had used the time I spent in the bathroom changing into dry clothes and filling the kettle. As I left the bathroom, Kay spotted me halfway across the living room and burst into a fit of giggles. I obviously looked worse than I felt.

"Forgive my ignorance, but I just had a thought. Here you are half-naked, wearing my bathrobe, and I don't even know your name."

I struggled with the robe. "It's Adam. I can't shake your hand again, as I am trying my best to hold your robe together." This time we both laughed. The ice had been broken, and from that point on, we started to bond as friends.

Three cups of tea later and two cycles of the tumble dryer, we had discovered a little more about each other. Kay was Dr. Kay Miller on leave from Dundee University and renting the cottage. I told almost the truth: Adam Macdonald, retired from the Royal Logistics Corps and trying to find something to do with the rest of my life, staying at an old army friend's time-share in Brodick for a month. Kay asked me to stay for tea, but I made my excuses and left. I did not want to overstay my welcome. I had not expected this. I needed to get my story right. I had almost slipped up a few times. I almost introduced myself as Mac and when asked where I had served, I had fumbled badly. I was just not used to company anymore. I took Kay's wheel with me telling her I would get it sorted for her. I knew a garage owner and would get her a good price. I lied. I just wanted the opportunity to see her again.

On the way back to Brodick, I had time to think. I did not like telling Kay lies about my past. After leaving the service, I was given advice and help by the SIS.

There were a lot of Irish people who wanted a word with me, so to speak.

After returning to Ireland from Hereford, I had been teamed up with Mary O'Conner. She was a native Northern Ireland girl who had been working with Special Branch in London until then. As soon as we met, we clicked. She was clever, brave, and very, very good-looking. She could have auditioned for Miss World if she had wanted—six feet tall, natural auburn hair, skin like satin, and all the bumps in the right places…which stood her in good stead for infiltrating the various gangs in Ireland. We were a great team. She found out where the bombing was going to occur and who was doing it. We broke in. I modified the bomb, usually so it had an accident as it was being moved or primed. It worked a treat, and that year the news reported on dozens of cases where the bomb had gone off killing the bomber. It made the terrorists look stupid, it reduced their numbers, we didn't have to pay to keep them in a jail, and best of all, it saved hundreds of lives. I justified it to myself by saying if they didn't touch the bomb they would be OK, so they died by their own hand. After some time the paramilitaries started to smell a rat, in particular the IRA. We had hit them very hard.

Trying to keep a secret in Ireland is a difficult thing to do. The guys in the army referred to me as "the Mac." When a bomber was blown up, the guys would say the Mac had called on him. It had got back to the IRA that this mythical figure called the Mac was hunting them down, which was not a bad thing. The bombing campaign started to dry up, but who knew if it was fear or a lack of bombers that caused it. The IRA tasked one of their section leaders to track me down and deal with me. They hadn't sussed that Mary was helping me, which was good, but we had to start being extra careful. The guys we were dealing with were not stupid. If they found us, there would be no mercy, not even for a woman. Mary had found out from one of her contacts that I was top of the wanted list, and that Danny Flynn, a nasty piece of work even by IRA standards, was the man tasked with finding me. Mary had the idea to go after him before he got to us. I did not like this for two reasons—one, it would put Mary in harm's way, more danger than she had ever been in before; secondly, we had no intel that said he was a bomb maker. He might have directed where a few bombs ended up, but he was never in the same place as a bomb, which neutralized my special talent.

We spent two weeks studying our target with Mary drinking at his local. He was well guarded and Mary found out no information. It was as if people close to him were too frightened to even mention his name. I again expressed my concerns to Mary, but she laughed them off, saying it was sweet that I was worried for her safety, but she was a big girl who could look after herself. Another two weeks passed, and we were getting nowhere.

Out of the blue, Mary called me and arranged to meet for a drink. This was usually what Mary did when she had info for me on a job, but this was not the case tonight. We met at the arranged time. I was unshaved, hair like a mop. The last thing you wanted to do in Ireland was look like a soldier. My cover story was that I was an out-of-work sparky from Scotland looking for work, so my dress had to fit the bill. Mary arrived looking a million dollars—her long auburn hair was tied up in a ponytail, and she was wearing spray-on jeans, which were the latest fashion and left very little to the imagination. I wondered what a beautiful girl like Mary would be doing with an out-of-work sparky from Scotland. I shared my thoughts with Mary. She blushed, gave me a pretend slap, and said I worried too much. There was an awkward pause. Then Mary said she needed to ask me something.

"I'm all ears." What Mary said next took the wind out of my sails. She admitted that she couldn't break into Flynn's inner circle and that we would struggle to catch him out. He was a cunning bastard, and she was worried that he would get to us first.

"Adam, I know you have the gear. I have seen it. We need to take him out first." Another awkward silence followed.

"You mean blow him up." She nodded, silent again. "Mary, you know if I do that, I am no better than him or any of the others we have dealt with. Mary, you know I would do anything for you, but please don't ask me to do that. The dishonorable discharge and jail would be bad enough, but to think I had turned into the very thing I have been hunting would destroy me."

She sat for a moment then gathered herself. "You're right, pet. I should have known better than to ask you. I think you are too much of a gentleman for this godforsaken country. We had better think of Plan B." At that, she got up. "I will call you when I have the solution." She gave me a saucy wink and marched out the pub door before she could be accosted by any of the local drunks.

I left the pub around eight thirty and decided to head home for an early night. I was worried about the situation we were getting ourselves into. I thought it was time to give up and get back on the trail of the bombers. Mary would have to give it a rest, if only for her safety.

At ten-fifteen the phone rang. I thought it was Mary, as it was a secure line, but to my surprise it was a male, who announced himself as Neil. "Adam, you need to get Mary O'Conner out of there now. She is in big trouble. Go now. Take her to Fourteen Elm Street. It's a safe house. Go now." The phone went dead.

Shit. I grabbed the keys to the Cortina that I had been using and shot across town. I dumped the car three streets away and half-ran, half-walked the rest of the way. My heart was pounding more from the stress than the exertion. As I approached Mary's front door, I knew something was wrong. I could see a slight chink of light from the edge of the door. It was slightly open, and Mary was too careful for that. Something was wrong. I gently pushed the door open with my arm and listened for a second. Nothing. What now? Go in, not knowing if an intruder were present, or stand in the doorway, a perfect target for a sniper? A quick check downstairs found nothing. The rooms seemed untouched. I moved slowly up the stairs, trying not to let them creak and announce my arrival—still silence, only my heartbeat in my ears, which by now was almost deafening. Hopefully, Mary was in bed asleep. I would need to be careful. If I startled her, I might end up (as the Americans say) a victim of friendly fire, or as we say, a total balls-up. Only one room left to check—the bathroom. The door was ajar. I popped my head round the corner.

It took a fraction of a second for my brain to register what I saw. Carnage was probably the best word to describe it. Horror was the first emotion, then despair. My legs folded under me, and I slid down the wall in the far corner of the room. I was a physical and mental wreck. The videos at Hereford were U-certificate compared to the scene in the bathroom. Poor Mary had been in the bath when the execution squad had burst into the room. She had taken a round in the chest and one to the head. Not happy with this, they then proceeded to cut out her tongue and use it to write "traitor" on the bathroom wall in her own blood. Her tongue had been left in the soap dish.

I don't now how long I sat there before any kind of sense returned to my brain. It could have been minutes—it felt like hours. With some effort, I managed to get my shaky legs to support me. I had to wipe the tears from my eyes before trying to negotiate the stairs. Back to the car was as far as I could make. I sat in the car for hours in a type of self-induced trance. It was the siren that brought me back to Earth. Who was this Neil character? How did he know Mary was in trouble? I couldn't think straight.

It had taken her death for me to realize that I had fallen in love with her, and it was all too late. My despair turned slowly to rage, then to a terrible cold fury. Flynn would die for this, and it wasn't going to be pretty. Mary would get her last wish. If I died trying, then so be it.

We had a weapons store at a unit in a local business park. Funnily enough, the PIRA took protection money for looking after the business park and making sure no harm came to its clients. If they only knew who was paying them, they would have thrown up in their ski masks. I filled a holdall with equipment, pressure pad, wire, detonators, a small amount of C4, and Mary's spare Beretta Tomcat. It might come in handy, and it was small and easy to hide. A tool kit was my last item on the checklist. By the time I had sorted in my head what I was doing and got the kit ready, it was six in the morning. I was going nowhere near the house just in case Mary had talked, or in case my own team tried to lift me. That was not going to happen until Flynn was dead.

An all-out attack on Flynn was not possible and probably would fail, as he was well protected. However, Mary and I had noted a weakness in his protection. Every lunchtime he would be picked up by taxi, one of the old traditional London cabs that the IRA utilized as a network of informers and drivers. Flynn had a favorite driver. Fat Pat was as his name implied—a chubby chap with a chequered past. He was suspected of driving for one of their hit teams, and anybody who messed with Pat usually ended up in hospital. On one occasion, a joy rider stole his cab, and the unfortunate youth was found in a Belfast alley minus a kneecap, courtesy of Pat's friends. I thought it was high time Pat and I got acquainted.

As I approached Pat's door, I could see through the glass panels that he was just about to leave. As his hand went for the handle, I kicked the door open. It broke his wrist and hit him square in the forehead. He collapsed backward into the hall with a groan. I marched straight in and closed the door behind me. He was still dazed and was attempting to sit up. I kicked him hard between the legs. He groaned and fell over. I pulled duct tape and cable ties from my pocket and got to work securing him and gagging him.

After a few minutes, when he started to regain his awareness, I asked him if he could understand me. I was met with a defiant stare. "I'm only going to ask you one question, Pat, and then I will leave you alone. Are you picking up Flynn at the normal time today?"

I bent down and removed the duct tape from his mouth. "You are a fucking dead man. You have no idea who you are dealing with, son."

I replaced the tape and stood up. "Tut tut. And there was me being nice to you as well. We can soon sort that though." I dragged him from the hall into his kitchen. He kicked and squirmed but was trussed up like a turkey and had no option but to give in.

His eyes watched me as I left the room; I was back in a second with a pillow from the bedroom. "Don't worry. It's not for your head." I pulled out the Beretta. His eyes widened. I placed the pillow on his left knee, then the Beretta. "I just don't want to wake up your neighbours, Pat. It's early yet. Pat, you don't know who you are dealing with. I'm finished being nice. Answer the question, or I will remove your knee-cap the Irish way."

He was starting to shake like a leaf. I again removed the tape from his mouth. "You stupid bastard. He will kill you for fun." He was starting to weep.

I pressed on. "You let me worry about that. Answer the question."

"Yes, yes, I am picking him up. I hope he blows your fucking brains out."

I hit him square on the jaw with the butt of the Beretta. Frank Bruno couldn't have done it better. He went out like a light. I tied him to the cooker and doubled the amount of tie wraps and duct tape. He wasn't going any place fast.

Pat didn't have a garage, so I had to work on the taxi at the side of the road. I pulled on a pair of overalls. I wasn't too worried about being seen, but people tend not to bother when they see somebody in overalls working on a car. They just think it's a mechanic, and that nothing sinister is going on. A few screws later and the back seat was out; the pressure device went in with Velcro tape and was wired to a timer set for four minutes, then two detonators in the C4. The C4 was tricky. I didn't want to kill him, not just yet. I took a calculated guess at the amount and finished rebuilding the seat—carefully, so as not to trigger the pressure pad. Next, I removed the door panels and cut the cables to the rear interior handles so that when my guest arrived, he would not be leaving not without my say-so. Finally, I placed a gallon of petrol under the bonnet. I didn't want it near the explosion, and the bonnet would shield it. An army-issue bulletproof vest was wedged around the back of the driver's seat between the bulkhead that separates driver and passengers. Hopefully this would stop any bullets from my guest or shrapnel hitting my back.

12

I had done a timed run this morning from Flynn's house to a bit of wasteground. It was three minutes away. I left the Cortina close by, picked up the holdall, and legged it to Fat Pat's house. We were all set.

At 12:30 p.m., I left with the taxi. I had borrowed Pat's donkey jacket and cap and was wearing a flack jacket under it, which bulked it out and gave the impression I was about the same size as Pat. I pulled up at Flynn's house at 12:45 p.m. and blasted the horn three times. I had watched Pat do this a dozen times during our surveillance.

I hoped they would take the bait. He normally just jumped in the cab, gave Pat directions, and his heavy squad met them at the restaurant.

Flynn was a careful man, changing his route and eating-place constantly, and waiting for his guys to arrive and check out the restaurant before he got there. I was going to have my hands full keeping him from bailing out when he discovered that it wasn't Pat behind the wheel. I needed to do this for four minutes. The door of his house opened. He emerged, followed by one of his heavies. This was not normal.

He walked to the cab. His heavy walked across the street to a parked Sierra, which had two occupants, and started talking to the driver. Flynn got in the back of the cab and slammed the door shut. He wasn't watching me. His attention was on the Sierra.

"Drive, Pat, while Tommy keeps those stupid MI6 bastards occupied."

I hadn't seen them sitting there. My attention had been on the Flynn house. I thanked my lucky stars Flynn had been on the ball. The last thing I needed was them tailing me. Flynn still hadn't noticed. He had his head in MI6 land.

I checked my watch. Two minutes twenty seconds until showtime , and we were making good time. Flynn leaned forward and started to give me directions, then stopped suddenly. He was looking in the rearview mirror. "Who the fuck are you? Where is Pat?" One minute ten seconds to go, and it was going to be the longest of my life.

I slipped Mary's Beretta out and sat it between my legs. "He's got tonsillitis, guvnor. He sent me instead."

He wasn't buying it one little bit. "Stop this fucking car right now."

The waste ground was on the left, and I had just passed the Cortina. "You're the boss." I indicated in and pulled onto the waste-ground. He was banging on the glass partition with a Makarov pistol and telling me to get out. I reached into my pocket and popped two earplugs in.

I heard the metallic click of the pistol being cocked. Then a white light and a heat wave hit me. I honestly didn't know if I had been shot or if the charge had been detonated. For a few seconds I think I was out. Gradually things started to come back. The taxicab had no glass left anywhere. There was a six-inch piece of shrapnel sticking through my seat back and digging into my flack jacket. Luckily, it had not penetrated it.

I kicked the driver's door open and staggered out. Flynn was in a bad way. The blast had broken his back and legs, and a spring from the seat was protruding from his groin. I thought at first he was dead, but slowly, he started moving and moaning. His gun was on the seat next to him. I removed it and tucked it into my belt. "Can you hear me, Danny boy?"

His eyes rolled in his head. Then with a groan and a huge effort, he focused and looked at me. "What have you done to me?" He was shaking badly and sweating.

"Listen to what I have to say, and save your energy. You are about to die, but you need to hear this first. The girl you killed in the bath was Mary O'Conner. She was my partner, and this is her revenge. Oh, and by the way, I'm the guy you've been looking for. They call me Mac."

I walked to the front of the car. No need to open the bonnet, the blast had done it for me. I removed the gallon of petrol and started pouring it all over the car. It splashed on Flynn and seemed to revive him. "Sweet Jesus, no, don't do it. I'm sorry about the girl. Please, I can give you the name of the guy who did it. It wasn't me. I was told to get rid of her. I was only following orders from Merlin. Please, I can give you information. I know where there is a huge arms dump. We can do a deal." I pulled out a box of matches. "Who killed her? Who is Merlin? And does he know about the arms dump?"

"Tommy Downes killed her. He was talking to the spooks. He's been to the dump. Merlin calls me. I don't know him, only his code name."

I turned away and tossed a match in the window as I turned. As I walked toward the Cortina, I heard the whoosh as the fuel vapor ignited. I shouted over my shoulder, "No deal."

Change of plan—I had been going to turn myself in at the safe house, but now this was unfinished business. I drove back to Flynn's house, found a phone box on the corner, and called his house. After only two rings, the phone was picked up.

"Is that you, Downes?"

Silence then. "Yes, who wants to know?"

I left the phone hanging and walked along the street, checking for surveillance vehicles. It was clear. I walked up to the front door and knocked on it with the butt of Flynn's gun.

"Flynn sent me. There is trouble. Let me in," I shouted, working on the assumption that they had been called by the heavies to say Flynn hadn't turned up for lunch.

The door was flung open by Downes. I immediately shot him in the left kneecap. He collapsed, and I stepped over him, ready for any of his mates who were still around. I was lucky. They had all obviously departed for the lunch patrol.

Downes was in some pain, crawling toward his handgun, which had fallen from his grip when I shot him. I kicked it along the hall, well out of reach. "Tommy, you're in a spot of bother, my friend. You have only one chance before I blow your other kneecap off and make you a cripple for life. Listen carefully. Who told you to shoot Mary, the girl in the bath—and I want the exact location of the arms dump." Just to underline my request I rolled him on his other side, cocked the Makarov, and placed it against the back of his knee. "It's your turn to speak. Do it wisely if you ever want to walk again."

He was obviously in a huge amount of pain already; he had wet himself with the shock and had started shaking badly but was holding out. I could hear sirens in the distance. This had to be quick. "Don't worry about Flynn coming after you. He met with a small accident earlier, and you are about five seconds away from your own little accident if you don't start talking."

"There is a barn with a yellow roof between Mayobridge and Warrenpoint. It has a false floor." He was silent, as if deciding whether to tell me the rest.

I rammed the pistol into his leg. "You have something else to tell me."

"Flynn ordered me to kill the girl. She was a British spy." I pulled the trigger and Tommy's kneecap exploded, leaving what was left of his leg lying at a strange angle. He screamed then lay there gasping for breath.

I bent down next to his ear. "I lied about the one chance. Sorry mate, but look on the bright side. I haven't cut your tongue out yet. If I hear of you doing anything other than winning wheelchair races, I will be back to finish the job."

I left the Makarov in the hall. I did not want to get stopped with something that could tie me to both attacks.

My first instinct was to fire up the Cortina and head for Warrenpoint, but I had started to shake like a leaf. One look in the interior mirror told the story. I was ashen grey, spattered with blood, quite a lot of it my own. There were various cuts and a chunk missing from my left ear. I needed to get cleaned up and regroup, but not at my house. There would be some awkward questions for me to answer there, and I wanted to finish the job, if only for Mary's sake. I didn't want her death to be completely in vain.

I headed south to the outskirts of the city until I found a bed and breakfast. A quick washdown with the remains of a bottle of water and my sweatshirt binned, and I was looking almost passable.

As I paid for my room, I was aware of the landlady looking at my wounds. "Is my face bad? I'm a sparky, and some idiot wired up a light the wrong way. I was checking it as it exploded in my face. I've not had a good day."

She studied me for a second as if wondering whether to believe me or not. "You're lucky it wasn't your eye, son. Go upstairs and have a shower. I will leave some plasters and things by your door."

True to her word, after my shower I opened the door to find a tray with a mug of coffee, a ham sandwich, paracetemol, and bandages.

While wolfing down the sandwich, I consulted a tourist map I had found on the dresser that showed roughly the area I was going to be searching tomorrow. I wondered how many tourists they had. It must be hard to make a living—their industry had been decimated by the troubles. My thoughts returned to the task in hand. My tools had been blown up in the taxi, so all I had at my disposal were a tourist map, a Beretta, and a Cortina with three-quarters of a tank of petrol. It would just have to do. After breakfast, the landlady talked me into doing a couple of electrical repairs. I was happy to oblige—one, it helped my cover story; and two, Nancy the landlady was a very helpful and pleasant lady. It was the least I could do.

She waved me off after handing me a packed lunch and wishing me all the best. I headed down the A1 at a steady pace and was in Newry about an hour later, then out to Mayobridge. I would start my search from here and head toward Warrenpoint.

The country was beautiful, very similar to Perthshire in Scotland— green, undulating fields bursting with every kind of crop, hedgerows full of wildlife. Unfortunately, I had not realized how many farm buildings there were in the area.

Even armed with the information I had, it was like looking for a needle in a haystack. After two hours of searching, I pulled off into a field, stopped, had some lunch, and pondered the problem. I had a shit map. I couldn't ask anyone for the fear that they would inform the IRA, and if there were indeed an arms store, guaranteed there would be IRA in the vicinity guarding it. If I did manage to find it, there would be a lot of luck involved.

I was tired. The rage that had given me an inner strength had started to recede. In its place, an empty black hole was forming. I needed to be on the move again to keep my mind working. I headed north again, back the way I had come, but more to the hills than before. Another hour of searching proved fruitless. Traveling along a lane, I could see about a quarter of a mile ahead a police car parked at the side of the road. A split-second decision sent me left along a farm track to avoid a confrontation with the local police. On my right, I could see an old corrugated iron barn. It was rusty red with a yellow roof.

My heart missed a beat. All day it was the only building I had come across with a yellow roof. Could this be the arms dump? I parked the car about half a mile away in a lay-by and legged it back to the barn. I sat in the hedgerow for twenty minutes, watching for activity around the barn, but there was none—no visible cameras or security measures.

I crawled along the hedgerow until I was halfway along the left side of the barn, then cut across the grass to the wall.

I was not about to enter from the door. There might be cameras trained on the door. It might be alarmed or booby-trapped, so it made much more sense to find another entry point. A few minutes searching found a loose and corroded side panel. I teased it open slightly and carefully inspected it for trip wires while I stayed alert for movement from within.

Once my eyes adjusted to the dim light in the building, I could see that the barn was empty except for the rusting frame of an old vintage tractor in the far corner. Another ten minutes passed as I scrutinized the interior, checking for anything out of the ordinary. I finally plucked up the courage to enter. I pulled the panel further apart and slid in quietly. The floor was covered in straw, which worried me. You could hide anything under it. For all I knew, the floor could be covered with antipersonnel mines. I moved slowly and deliberately toward the centre of the barn, my eyes on stalks, checking for any straw that looked out of place or uneven. I arrived at the centre of the barn wondering if this were the right place. Had I been deceived? Was there an arms store, or had they just been trying to save their skins?

Another detailed examination of the barn from the centre revealed no more clues. I headed for the only thing in the barn—the old Massey Fergusson in the corner. As I approached it, I could see a concrete plinth between it and the wall. This looked out of place and aroused my suspicions. I walked toward it cautiously. As I drew nearer, I could see it was in fact a stairway. I knew at that point I had struck gold.

The stairs led down fourteen steps to what I could only describe as a cold-war nuclear bunker. There were no doors, and a light switch on the right activated a row of storm lamps, revealing a corridor some fifty meters long, packed with crates, most of which were open. The first crate revealed SLR army-issue rifles. The second was much more worrying—six shoulder-mounted, Russian-made, surface-to-air missiles. The next box held Kalashnikov rifles, and the next four crates all contained Semtex. Then there were two boxes of detonators and wiring, six crates of various ammunition, and three crates of various handguns that bore the stamp of US customs. It looked as if the United States had decided that they were not the only ones who had a right to bear arms. I stopped looking at that point. I was only halfway down the corridor. It was now clear to me that this had to be the main arms store for the IRA. I had originally planned to set a booby trap, so that somebody entering the store would set off a charge, but this plan had to change. I could not take the chance of something going wrong. It had to be destroyed right now, not left in the hands of the IRA. Its destruction would bring the IRA to its knees. I had them by the balls. I got to work double quick. Within five minutes, I had charges set and timed to go off in fifteen minutes. I set a grenade with a trip wire at the foot of the stairs, three feet in front of the light switch, so they would catch the wire in the dark before they hit the light switch should they arrive before the main charge went off. Then I retraced my steps and left by the same way as I had entered.

Once out in the lane, I broke into a jog. I did not want to be close when that lot went up. I had not calculated what the effect would be, mainly because I had only checked out half the dump. Even if the other half were empty, it was still going to be a major explosion. I was ten feet from the Cortina when the shockwave hit me like a brick wall. It sucked the air from my lungs. Then the ground under my feet shook. I turned and looked. Where the barn had once stood, there was now a huge crater as if a meteor had hit Ireland. Time to get the hell out of here.

Back in Belfast, I headed straight for 14 Elm Street. I dumped the Cortina streets away, and I tucked the Beretta in my sock, just in case anything went wrong. After all, I had no idea who this Neil character was who had told me to get Mary to this address. On my arrival at the address, a middle-aged, well-dressed woman ushered me in. After telling her I was Adam Macdonald, she let me into the living room. As I looked around, I could hear her on the phone. She was speaking in an urgent but quiet voice. She obviously did not want to be overheard. I started to doze off by the fireplace. My exploits had taken their toll. It was late evening, and I was ready for bed.

Car doors slammed outside, and then the doorbell rang. The woman must have been waiting behind the door because it was answered immediately. Seconds later, the living room door sprang open, and two heavies marched in followed by a tall, thin guy, obviously the boss. I leapt out of the seat, my sleepy head clearing immediately.

I didn't know whether to shake their hands or go for the Beretta. "Macdonald, you're an arse, and you still owe me that fiver." The voice had come from the boss. I knew the voice, but my brain was still trying to place it.

Neil Andrews stepped out from between his protection detail. He was thinner than I remembered, a few more wrinkles, and still with his black curly haircut that had never changed since I met him. "Jesus Christ, Neil, what are you doing here?"

"Trying to save your sorry arse. What the hell have you been up to? The last time we met you were getting on a bus heading for uni." Neil dismissed his heavies, who left for the kitchen.

"How long have you been doing this, Neil?"

"Since I was recruited at university by MI5."

Neil had been my best mate at school. We had played rugby together, joined the chess club together, told each other of all our dreams and plans. For years, we were almost joined at the hip—until Neil had announced that he had been accepted for Oxford to study law. After that, we lost touch with each other. Knowing Neil's capabilities I had expected Neil to become a hotshot lawyer, and I didn't think that a second lieutenant would travel in the same social circles as Neil, so I never made an attempt to contact him, although I did wonder sometimes what had become of him.

Neil wasted no time with small talk. He got right down to business. He wanted to know exactly what the IRA trio had said, and what I had seen at the barn. He took notes as I described the arms haul. He grimaced as I mentioned the US customs seals and went pale when I mentioned the surface-to-air missiles. We both knew what would happen if a terrorist got to the perimeter fence of Heathrow with one of those bad boys. After an hour of me recounting my story, Neil had heard enough. "We need to get you out of here. Your days in Ireland are finished. You're a hot potato, and the IRA will leave no stone unturned until they find you. There is an informer high in British echelons of power. His code name is Merlin, and we have not tracked him or her down yet. Mary was betrayed by this person."

"Neil, Flynn mentioned that name. He did not know who it was. He only talked to him on the phone."

"We have had to destroy all of your records so the same fate does not befall you."

I thought for a second. "What about the taxi driver and Tommy Downes? They can identify me."

Neil smiled at me, not the smile I had seen so many times. This was pure, malicious glee. He had indeed changed from the person I used to know. "Adam, I don't like loose ends. They come back to haunt you. The official story is that there was an internal feud within their gang. Danny Flynn found out there was a plot against him, went to their houses, tortured them, then put a bullet through both their heads, but it was too late. They had already planted a bomb that killed him. The police are closing the case. They found Flynn's gun in the bushes at the taxi driver's home."

I was not sure what to do next. Should I ask more questions, shut up, or thank him? I didn't know this new Neil. Was I too what he called a loose end?

Neil read my thoughts. "There is a chopper waiting to take you straight back to Hereford. You will be redeployed. What you did was naughty, but the outcome was spectacular. You have probably saved thousands of lives. It hasn't gone unnoticed at higher ranks, but as long as there is an IRA presence, you are in danger. The Mac was near top of their hit list, and he's now even higher than the royals."

At the airfield, we walked to the chopper without speaking. As I went to board the chopper, Neil grabbed my arm and shouted into my ear over the noise of the engine. "Adam, don't blame yourself over Mary's death. You made sure she didn't die in vain. If it was anybody's fault, it was mine. She was my fiancée, and I sent her to look after you. Mark my words. When I find out who betrayed her, that person will die a terrible death."

Our eyes met. We were both welling up with tears, but I couldn't find any words to say. We parted with a pat on each other's back. Two weeks later I was in Australia on exchange duties with the Australian SAS, training troops on munitions and mine techniques, and promoted to the rank of captain.

***

Away in a little world of my own, I had driven round the whole perimeter road of Arran. It was late evening when I turned off the main road into the gravel drive that led to the log cabin where I was staying. A normal trip should have taken twenty minutes from Kay's little cottage, but I had taken two hours. Earlier in the day I had spent time in the local hotel gym, then the pool. This I had been doing every morning to keep myself fit, and now I was ready for bed. I went to bed happy in the knowledge that I had something to look forward to tomorrow, not just another day with my thoughts.

I was up early and straight down to the hotel via the local garage to drop Kay's wheel off for repair. The pool was off limits first thing in the morning so the resident guests could have their swim, so I headed for the gym. I followed an hour's circuit training by practice for a Taekwondo grading, a passion I had picked up during my time in Australia. Maybe now, with no distractions in my life, I could finally study for my higher grades. I had managed a red belt with black tags, but lately, my training had dropped off. With no one to train with, it was difficult to improve on my knowledge of the art. It was like playing chess by yourself. It just didn't work. I gave up and headed to the pool.

The pool was like a sheet of blue glass. The hotel had few guests this time of year, and none of them had ventured as far as the pool, so I had it all to myself. I ploughed up and down for half an hour until my arms and legs started to feel twice their weight. After a shower and shave, I checked my watch. Still too early to pick up Kay's wheel. I headed for the lounge bar and settled myself down with a large mug of coffee, a bacon roll, and the local paper, the *Arran Banner*. There was not a lot of reading in the *Banner*, mostly ads and various local meetings. The most amusing article was about a local man who had witnessed a UFO sighting conveniently as he left the bar in Blackwaterfoot in the early hours of the morning.

I chuckled to myself, wondering how many drams it had taken him before he started seeing little green men, and how much stick he was getting from his mates. Right at this minute, the local bobby was probably writing down his name in his little black book.

The morning had cleared up while I was at the hotel, and now there was hardly a cloud in the sky. It was going to be a beautiful day. The wind had picked up, and the waves that rolled into the beach were now capped with white tops. The tide was in, and the waves thundered down on the beach, reminding me of a smaller and colder version of Bondi Beach in Australia. But as yet, the beaches were deserted. Only the occasional hardy seagull had ventured out. On arrival at the garage I was happy to see the Fiesta wheel complete with new tyre sitting waiting for me at reception. I paid the bill and headed for Kay's little cottage. En route, I wondered what the good doctor would be up to this fine morning. Would she be in at all?

On arrival, I found the little blue Fiesta parked at the door. I knocked on the door, but there was no answer. A second, heavier knock brought the same result. I tried the door. It was not locked and swung open to my touch. Dr. Miller did not answer to my calls and was nowhere to be seen. A further search of the beach and outhouse proved fruitless. The keys were in the ignition of the Fiesta. I smiled to myself. I wondered if Kay had left the house and car like this in her native Dundee, how long it would have taken before she would be calling the police to report a crime. Obviously she had relaxed somewhat since arriving here. I was having a bit of a dilemma. What I should do next, leave the wheel and call back later, or hang about on the off chance she might return? What the hell, the tyre had to be put back on the car anyway, as the spare tyre was as bald as Kojak's head.

I got to work on the old Fiesta and had it jacked up in no time. Ten minutes had it changed. I was putting the spare back in the boot when I heard a voice behind me. "Not you again."

I turned round, not sure if it had been said in jest or in earnest. Kay was standing at the corner of the cottage. She was dressed in an old pair of torn blue jeans, a blue hoodie, and her trademark blue baseball cap. She had an ear-to-ear smile that lit up her face. She was indeed a lovely looking girl, not beauty queen stuff like Mary, but a natural, girl-next-door type of beauty. Her smile, to my relief, told me she had been pulling my leg with her last remark. I decided to join in the mickey-taking. "You shouldn't have bothered to get all dressed up for me."

She looked down at herself and blushed. "So it's going to be like that is it, wing commander?" She knew fine well she had chosen the wrong rank and was trying to wind me up.

"Wing commander? I'm not a pretty boy in the RAF, thank you very much."

The windup had worked. She smiled again, knowing she had won the round. She stopped the mickey-taking and became more serious. "Adam, you never did tell me your rank and job, did you?"

I thought for a second. Oh, what the hell. I was fed up with all the lies. "It's Captain Adam Macdonald, at your service, madam."

Kay was still smiling. "Well, captain, it's almost lunchtime, and I'm starving. If I promise to change, will you accompany me for lunch to the local tearoom in Machrie?"

Without waiting for a reply, she dived into the cottage, leaving the door open, presumably for me to follow her. On entering the living room, I found she had already vanished into her bedroom and, by the sounds of things, was busy getting changed for lunch. Her bedroom door was half-open, and she shouted through, "I take it that was a yes, captain."

I was busy examining the signature on one of the paintings to see if it was a famous artist. "Kay, I was only kidding. There is nothing wrong with what you are wearing. I was only pulling your leg."

"I know, Adam, but you were right. I let myself go here. Nobody normally sees you, so why bother?" Just as she said that, she stepped out of the shadow of the bedroom door. She had tied up her shoulder-length black hair in a ponytail and put on some makeup. She wore a slim-fitting black skirt that reached halfway between her knees and ankles and a black blouse with little pink flowers. A pair of black high heels finished off the outfit. She had paused for effect, studying my face for a reaction.

"Well, Dr. Miller, you scrub up well, but you are going to need a coat, or you will catch your death in that outfit at this time of year."

A ten-minute drive along the coast road brought us to an old converted farm building that was now masquerading as a restaurant-cum-arts-and-craft shop. The car park was empty, and I wondered as I pulled up if it were actually open. Kay assured me that it was open every day until three. I still had my doubts. My mind was put at rest as soon as we entered the restaurant. The smell of home cooking filled the dining room and steamed up the small panes in the refurbished windows.

A lot of money had been lavished on the old building. The stone walls were painted white to lighten the room and to make up for the small windows. The floor and roof had been replaced by new-but-authentic beams. The lighting was modern but chosen to look original. Kay had obviously been here many times and picked a window seat overlooking the beach, which was only two hundred meters away on the other side of the coast road. An older woman in her seventies appeared and after chatting to Kay for ten minutes took our order and left.

"I take it you come here a lot."

"Almost every day for the last two months. It gives me more time to spend on the beach rather than cooking and cleaning up."

The menu prices were not cheap. It stood to reason that the owner needed to recoup the cost of renovations. "It must cost you a fortune to eat here every day. The university must pay you well?"

Kay smiled. "I've got a little secret up my sleeve. The government is picking up my bill, including all expenses. So you see, it would be mad for me to cook and clean when I could be doing research."

After lunch, there was an argument about who was paying the bills for lunch and for the replacement tyre for the Fiesta. I lost on both counts but did manage to get Kay to agree that the next lunch was on me. She gave in easily on that point, which pleased me as I could now make plans to see her again.

After lunch, we walked along the pebbled beach in front of the restaurant, asking each other questions, getting to know each other a little better. I told Kay more about my army past without going into the finer detail. Kay was impressed that I had worked in Australia, but all I told her was that I was on loan to the Australian army. She seemed to accept that and didn't ask why.

I asked Kay more about her work. She explained she was a marine biologist, and she was here to write a paper on the effects of the changing Gulf Stream off the west coast of Scotland. She was very passionate about the subject and explained it in great detail, some of which I already knew, and a lot I did not. I made the mistake of asking whether it was worth all this attention and was told in no uncertain terms that the Gulf Stream had a hundred times more energy than all the man-made energy in the world, and if that force changed in any way, we should know about it, so studying it and understanding it was vital to the health of the planet. I stood corrected.

Changing the subject slightly, I asked if this was the research the government was paying her for. She was silent for a moment as if thinking how to reply. "I was told not to discuss it with anyone, but I suppose I can bend the rules for you. I'm sure you know bigger secrets coming from the army. I have been asked to take readings at specific times and specific places checking for radioactivity. They sent me a Geiger counter and instructions for using it."

It was my turn to be silent. "So why would they need you? Why not send somebody in that field of expertise?"

Kay smiled. "Adam, have you never heard the expression, never look a gift horse in the mouth?"

I thought for a few seconds. "What government department asked you to study this?"

Kay admitted she wasn't sure. A man had made contact with her at the university and had given her a laptop on which to record and send information, and an email address to send any correspondence and requests for payment, which were promptly paid into her bank account. Requests to study certain areas were also sent by email. I pointed out that this was a strange way for a government department to do business. Kay shrugged this off by saying I was out of touch, and this was the modern way to operate. I was still somewhat concerned at this latest revelation, but Kay changed the subject, probably to stop me asking any more awkward questions.

"Captain Macdonald, I have a proposition for you."

I forgot about our previous conversation for the moment. "I'm all ears, Dr. Miller. What had you in mind?"

She frowned at me. "You can get your mind out of the gutter. It's an engineering proposition. I need an engineer to rebuild my boat, and I wondered if you would be interested, as you are currently unemployed." She was back in windup mode and was trying hard to suppress a smile.

"My dear doctor, for your information, I am not unemployed. I have taken early retirement. Also, my mind was nowhere near the gutter, but I am a sucker for helping beautiful women, so please continue."

Kay blushed and seemed to be stumped for words, then regrouped. She turned and walked back toward the car. "You better come and have a look before you make a decision."

Back at the cottage, Kay headed for the outhouse. This was situated between the cottage and the beach and had served as a boathouse for many previous owners of the cottage.

Kay opened the doors and side door to let the light in. A boat lay covered with a tarpaulin. We both pulled off the tarpaulin to reveal a boat and a crate with an engine. Kay cursed. She had got mud all down the side of her black dress removing the tarpaulin. As she was dusting herself down, she asked if I knew anything about boats. I admitted I had little to do with them, but it was mechanical, so it could be fixed. Kay went to put the kettle on and change. I had a rake about the boat. In a storage compartment, I found a booklet for the boat. It was an Orkney longliner, sixteen feet long with a front cabin. Halfway down the boat, it had a driving seat and steering wheel. All the required cables and wires ran to the back of the boat, but there they lay in a pile.

A close inspection of the crate found a Johnston forty-horsepower outboard motor, brand new and by the looks of it, just delivered. I was no expert, but it looked a bit big for the little fishing boat. Kay appeared with two cups of coffee. "Well, what do you think? Can you get it seaworthy for me, Adam?"

She had changed back into her jeans but left her hair up and still wore the black blouse. My comments about her appearance had obviously hurt her pride. "Oh, I am sure we can manage something for you. Where did you get this lot from?"

Kay smiled again. "When I rented the house, the landlord told me there was a boat in the garage. I wanted to buy it from him, and he said if I paid him six months rent up-front, I could have the boat. So when I sent an email asking for the rent, I requested they send me an engine for the boat for my research. When I opened the crate, there was a note saying this was the engine for my sixteen-foot speedboat. Oops. So I don't know if it will fit."

I spent the next three days firstly gathering the tools to start fitting an engine, then in the outhouse tinkering with the project. Kay spent a lot of time handing me tools or, when it started to get dark, holding the hand lamp as the outhouse had no electricity. In truth she couldn't have done much work anyway as the weather had turned bad, and the winter storms continued nonstop for four days. The stern of the boat had been modified and strengthened to take the forty horsepower engine. The engine was suspended from the roof beams by a block and tackle. The boat was maneuvered into place on its trailer, and the engine bolted in place. A few modifications to the steering cable, and we were in business.

Our last trip on the fourth day was to the local garage to pick up a new battery and fill the fuel cell for the first sea trials.

The winds had dropped the next day, but it was still raining. The final job was to blow up the trailer tyres with a foot pump. Kay and I staggered over the stones at the top of the beach, but when the wheels hit hard-packed sand, it was a bit more maneuverable. With the trailer half-submerged, it was time to tilt the engine. The moment of truth had arrived. The first three turns of the key were fruitless. I had half-expected this as the engine first had to draw up the fuel. With every turn of the engine, Kay got more worried looking. On the fourth attempt, the engine spluttered then died. I actually thought Kay was going to cry.

On the fifth attempt the engine fired, stuttered a bit, then roared into life on a high idle. I was not quite ready for the reaction. It was as if Kay had just won the lottery. She squealed with delight, waded round the side of the boat, and flung her arms around my neck. I was grinning like a Cheshire cat as I wrapped my arms round her waist. The freezing November sea contrasted with the heat from Kay's body, and we both clung onto each other, enjoying the warmth and intimacy of the moment. I was thinking that I could get used to this when I noticed the boat starting to float away from the trailer. Grudgingly, I released my grip on Kay and dived to stop the boat making a bid for freedom.

Five minutes later, we were cruising along the coast toward Blackwaterfoot. Another ten minutes and we had both had enough. I turned the longliner round and headed back to the cottage. We were frozen to the marrow. Twenty minutes of cursing followed as we fought to get the boat first on the trailer, then get the trailer back to the out-house. Back in the cottage, we had the coal fire lit in a few minutes. We were both soaked to the skin, but neither of us had an ounce of energy left. I sat staring into the flames. Kay arrived from the bedroom with a quilt. She sat next to me and flung the quilt over both our shoulders. She was grey and shaking like a leaf. We were both on the edge of hypothermia.

We had already broken that invisible barrier between us as we hugged when the engine fired, so it felt perfectly natural when I slipped my arm around her shoulders. She responded by resting her head on my shoulder. We sat there for ages, quietly enjoying the peace and the warmth. Eventually, I broke the spell. "I have a bone to pick with you, Dr. Miller."

Kay pulled away from me slightly and looked at me quizzically.

"Where the hell was your beloved Gulf Stream today? Brass monkeys wouldn't have gone out in that water."

Kay shook her head and snuggled back into my chest. Another ten minutes passed, then Kay cleared her throat and whispered in a low voice, "Adam, you can stay here tonight if you like. Only if you want to."

A few seconds passed, neither of us breathing. "Kay, that is the best offer I have had in years—it really is, but as an officer and a gentleman, I am going to decline tonight. We both need a good night's sleep. If I stayed, I might be tempted to keep you awake, and anyway, I need to go home to think what you can do to repay me. You owe me big, lady."

I staggered to my feet and pulled Kay up. The clock on the mantelpiece said 10:38 p.m. Kay walked me to the Freelander wrapped in her quilt. I was about to get in the car when Kay spoke. "Do you think it would be acceptable for an officer and a gentleman to give a girl a goodnight kiss?"

For the second time that day, she wrapped her arms round my neck, and we kissed. I was having second thoughts about my decision to leave when she pulled away from me. "You will come round tomorrow, won't you?"

I jumped in the car and put the window down. "You try stopping me. Even the Gulf Stream couldn't stop me."

She walked away, shaking her head.

The next morning I was up early, despite my tiredness the previous night. I had woken early and couldn't get to sleep again. My mind kept coming back to Kay's mysterious deal with the alleged government. Something just did not smell right. Kay had been blinded by the financial side of the deal, and I was pretty sure no government body could just hand out money like that. Why measure radioactivity on Arran? If it was because of the nuclear subs passing on their way to Faslane, surely it would be the Ministry of Defense who would do the tests, and it wouldn't be farmed out to a freelancer.

The more I thought about it, the more I worried. On leaving the service I had been given a number to contact in the event any of my Irish friends found me. I was pretty sure it was a hotline to MI5. It might not have been Neil's number, but I was sure he wouldn't be far away. The phone was picked up on the second ring and mentioning Neil Andrews had the desired effect. I was told to hang up, and someone would call me back. The phone went dead. I got up and went to make a cup of coffee while I waited. The kettle was still boiling when the phone rang.

CHAPTER TWO
The Truth

My attempt at small talk with Neil fell on deaf ears. He wanted to know why I had called the number. I started to explain the situation with Kay. He listened without interrupting until I got to the part about the radiation on Arran.

He stopped me abruptly and asked me to hang on a second; he was back on the line within two minutes. "Adam, get yourself to Edinburgh airport for fourteen hundred hours. I will be in the Costa Coffee lounge." The phone went dead. My stomach churned. This was not good. That was not a request; that had been an order. What the hell had Kay got herself involved in?

I checked my watch. If I got the finger out, I could make the eleven o'clock boat for the mainland. My trip went smoothly. I made the boat with five minutes to spare, and at that time of year, there was no need to book. An hour spent in the coffee lounge of the big ferry gave me time to think. I wondered what job title Neil held now. When we first met in Ireland, he had been given the Northern Ireland job because nobody wanted it. He looked on the job in a different light. To him it was not a hot potato; it was a chance to prove he was a safe pair of hands. Neil always set his sights high, so who knows how far up the tree he had climbed.

The trip from the boatyard in Ardrossan to Glasgow was slow. I joined a queue of vehicles heading into Glasgow along an overcrowded A-class road. Once on the M8 motorway and clear of Glasgow, I made good time and was in Edinburgh airport for one forty-five. I settled myself down in the corner booth at Costa Coffee with a super-sized mug of coffee and surveyed the passing travelers, looking for Neil's tall, wiry frame. I did not have long to wait. Neil arrived with the obligatory two bodyguards in tow and sat down by my side.

His bodyguards took up station at either side of Costa Coffee. "Adam, I don't have a lot of time, but what I have to say could not be said over the phone, so please listen. Two years ago, one of our agents was following up a lead in Nevada. He had been gathering evidence that a private government contractor employee had stolen classified British military documents and passed them onto the Americans. In the course of his investigations, he stumbled upon something the Americans were trying to keep a secret. Before he could complete his mission, he was found out and assassinated. Before he went missing, he called to say he thought it was some type of revolutionary aircraft and that it left some type of radiation signature. His body was found in the desert four miles from Area Fifty-One. He had been shot in the head.

"Five months ago, our counterparts in Canada informed us that the secret project had been moved from Nevada to Machrihanish Air Base in Scotland, and that their top agent in Britain, who had informed them of our agent previously, had been put on alert to inform them of any interest in the base. Some quiet checks made this story plausible. A crack Navy SEAL unit was redeployed from Virginia to Machrihanish, and radio-burst emissions have been detected on the Isle of Arran for the last two months—which we suspect is a CIA cell. We needed to get someone near to the base without arousing suspicion, which brings us to Dr. Miller."

Neil leaned in. "We need to know what is going on in Scotland. The thing that caught my attention was the Canadians told me the American agent's code name—Merlin."

It was like somebody had stabbed me in the heart with a dagger made of pure ice. Our eyes met. The look in Neil's eye had not changed from that night in Ireland so many years ago. "Adam, I need to get this bastard, and I am going to need your help. I need you to go back to Arran and look after Kay Miller. I have sent for my best agent, but there is a situation to attend to first in Argentina. Sam will take over from you as soon as Argentina is sorted out."

Neil stopped speaking for the first time since he sat down. He still had the mop of dark curly hair, but he had more stress lines round his eyes since I had last seen him. "Jesus, Neil, what are you doing? That girl has no idea what danger you have put her in. She is a civilian. You can't do this. You have got your readings. Now get her out of there."

Neil shook his head. "Sorry, but the readings are inconclusive. I have already emailed Dr, Miller and told her to take readings from Machrihanish. You had better turn tail and get back across to Arran before she leaves without you."

There was no point arguing. Neil's mind was made up. I got up to leave. I started to walk away, then turned round as Neil and the bodyguards were about to leave. "Neil." They all turned at once. "If anything happens to Kay Miller, bodyguards won't save you, and that's a promise from me."

Neil stared after me as I turned and walked away. I made the last ferry back and sat in the same coffee lounge as before; the only difference was this time my brain was scrambled. Dead secret agents, spy planes, espionage, Navy SEALs, it was a scene straight out of a movie, and I was stuck right in the middle. Suddenly, it struck me I had lost all track of time. I had promised Kay I would see her today, and it was now evening, and I hadn't even spoken to her. I called her on her mobile, and she answered immediately.

"Where have you been all day? I was worried sick. I tried calling the lodge, but there was no reply. I even drove over to the lodge but the gardener said he saw you leaving this morning. I thought at first you had caught pneumonia, but when I found out you had left, I didn't know what to think."

I could tell from her voice she wasn't kidding, and I could have kicked myself for being such an idiot. "Kay, I am really sorry. I should have called you. I got caught up in something today and had to sort it out in Edinburgh. I've been on the road all day. I'm back in Brodick just now, waiting for the boat to dock. Again, I am truly sorry."

There was silence on the other end of the line. "Can I buy you dinner to make it up to you?"

Silence again. "No, you can't." My heart sank. "But I can buy yours." She was up to her old tricks again. "I will meet you at the Kinloch in a hour. Will that give you enough time to recover from your trip?"

We had the whole lounge at the Kinloch Hotel to ourselves. It was a dark, rainy Wednesday night in November, and most of Arran's population had elected to stay by the fire and watch television.

We placed our order, then sat staring out the lounge windows, which looked out on the small Blackwaterfoot Bay. We were both obviously in thoughtful moods, as neither of us had said much. I was trying to think of what to say after today's proceedings, and Kay was probably wondering how to tell me about her impending trip to the Mull of Kintyre. I decided Kay needed to know at least some of the truth. I couldn't tell her everything, but I couldn't lie to her and watch her put her life in danger.

Kay spoke first. "Well you haven't told me what you were up to today." She stopped midsentence. "I'm sorry. That was none of my business."

I stared at my feet and took a deep breath; this could be the end of our friendship. "Kay, unfortunately, it has a lot to do with your business."

Kay sat bolt upright and stared at me.

"I was worried about this deal you have with the government. I have a contact in the government, so I called him to see if he could find out a bit more about this business. He was in Edinburgh, so we had a meeting. The people asking you to do this are from the intelligence community. They are worried about the emissions coming from a prototype plane the Americans are using. That is why they have asked you to go to Machrihanish to take readings. There is a large American air base there."

Kay sat with her mouth open. She was about to say something just as our meal arrived. The waitress made sure we were happy with our order and left. Kay was still staring at me. "Your contact must be good. I only received the email this morning. Your meal is getting cold."

She was pissed at me, and she had every right to be. I had stuck my nose in her private business. "Kay, I'm sorry, but I was worried about you. I needed to warn you before you went waltzing across there and got yourself into bother." I regretted the last statement as soon as it was out.

"Adam, I am twenty-nine years old, not nine. I think I can make my own decisions, and what you have told me changes nothing. I was paid by a government department to collect data, and data I will collect, with or without you sticking your nose in. I've suddenly lost my appetite. Good night."

I tried to reason one more time with her, but it was only winding her up more. I decided to let it go for the evening and try again in the morning.

***

Outside in the car park, the two occupants in the big black Vauxhall watched Kay leave. The passenger packed away the directional mic they had been using to listen to the conversation. The driver smiled at his passenger. "The lights are goin' to be burnin' bright at the Pentagon tonight, buddy. I say we waste the bitch tonight."

The passenger shook his head. "Let's get back to the shack and call it in. We wait for orders. This is a friendly country, and we can't go wading in without authority, pal."

***

On the other side of the world in Sarmiento Park, Cordoba, Argentina, Sam's phone vibrated. There was a text. It read: "Finish business immediately. Services required urgently. Come home. N." Two minutes later, Sam's phone vibrated with a second text from an unknown caller. It read: "Get back quick. Merlin has resurfaced." And it was signed, "A friend."

***

I sat for five minutes after Kay had left, trying to plan my next move. I had hardly eaten all day, but I was no longer hungry. I paid the bill, apologized for leaving the meals, and left. Outside in the rain, a big black Vauxhall was just leaving the car park. I wandered over to the Land Rover and got in.

I sat for an hour watching the waves break from the darkness onto the beach. Just when I thought life was getting better, my old friend fate came along and slapped me in the face again.

I awoke next morning thinking my throat had been cut. I wandered through to the kitchen to make breakfast. Looking at the clock, I was startled to find I had slept until eleven o'clock. I checked my phone hopefully to see if Kay had called. She hadn't. A mug of coffee, toast and marmalade, and a banana later, and I was feeling better and up for round two with Kay. I grabbed my gear and was about to leave when a thought crossed my mind. I turned the coffee table on its side and removed Mary's Berretta, which I had taped to the underside. It was my insurance policy against unwanted Irish visitors.

The truth was, it had not left my side since Mary's death. It was the only thing I had that was hers, and I kept it as much for the memory as for the security.

The weather had cleared up, and the drive across to Kay's was a pleasant one. On arriving at the cottage, I was relieved to see the Fiesta parked in its usual position. Kay was not in the cottage, so I wandered down toward the beach. The outhouse doors were open. I walked into find Kay loading the longliner with life rafts, life jackets, a hamper, and her box of equipment. She stopped dead in her tracks when I entered the room. She looked like a naughty schoolgirl caught with her fingers in the cookie jar.

"What do you want? Or are you just checking on me for your friend in the government?"

It was my turn to shake my head. "And a good morning to you too."

She was avoiding eye contact at all costs. "Adam, just go. I don't have time for this."

I stood my ground. "Did you turn into Ellen Macarthur overnight? How do you think you are going to launch the boat and get it back into the water on the Mull of Kintyre once you have taken your readings?"

She was giving me daggers. "I will just ask some kind gentleman to give me a push."

I laughed out loud. "Your kind gentleman is probably going to be a marine giving you a one-way ticket to Guantanamo Bay." I pressed home my advantage, holding up the second life jacket. "Expecting company?"

She looked crestfallen. "That was bought for you before we fell out."

I shook my head again. "Kay, I have never fallen out with you. The only thing you can accuse me of is caring too much for you. Please listen to me. Don't do this. It is too dangerous. If it has to be done, let me go. I will get your readings, and then we can both go and look for your Gulf Stream."

Kay started to sob. "This is my entire fault. You can't get involved. It's my mess. I'll sort it."

I made a split-second decision. "No, we will sort it. You need two people to launch a loaded boat that size. We will both do it, but you have to promise me if things get rough, you will do exactly as I tell you."

Kay nodded. She put her arms around my waist and cuddled into me. "I'm sorry, Adam."

I put my fingers under her chin and gently lifted her head so we were making eye contact. "There is nothing to be sorry for. Get your kit. We need to get going. I want to be back before dark."

The longliner launched no problem, and the addition of a pair of waders was a great help in keeping dry.

***

From the top of the cliff above Kay's little cottage, an uninvited guest watched them leave for the Mull of Kintyre. He picked up a high-powered, two-way military radio. "You have two unwanted guests on their way to you. Subjects are unarmed. You are authorized to eliminate them. Please be discreet." There was a pause. "Roger that, SEAL One out."

***

The trip was going well. Then, just as we were about to round the tip of the Mull of Kintyre, disaster struck. The throttle went dead. The engine would tick over, but it would not rev.

Luckily, I found the fault quickly. Something had come adrift in the housing that held the lever next to the steering wheel. Kay, who was sheltering in the little front canopy, took the opportunity to pour hot coffee from flasks. We had learned our lessons from the last trip and were wrapped up well. Half an hour later, the throttle was back in action, but we had drifted back toward Arran. It had delayed us badly. It was already starting to get dull. The return trip would be in the dark. We passed between Sanda Island and the coast. Kay consulted the map she had been sent. About fifteen minutes later, the rocky cliffs gave way to a sandy beach. A golf course lay in the dunes directly behind the beach. Somebody was about. There was a model airplane or a microlight around somewhere, although it was out of sight at the moment it could be heard in the distance. Kay announced excitedly that we were here. We cut the engine and let the tide take us onto the beach.

We pulled the boat a little out of the water, and Kay busied herself getting the Geiger counter set up. Out of sight of Kay, I checked the magazine in the Beretta and tucked it into my belt. According to the map, one hundred meters behind the dunes lay the perimeter fence and the end of the runway.

Kay was taking her time with the Geiger counter. I bent down to try and hurry her up; I did not want to spend one second longer here than I had to.

Kay was tapping the side of the unit. She had a puzzled expression on her face. I asked what was wrong, and she said that she thought the needle was stuck. She moved back to the coastline, and the needle dropped on the scale. She looked up at me in horror, and her expression said it all.

"How bad is it?"

The colour was draining from her cheeks. "Five hundred rem. Chernobyl was six hundred rem. We need to take a couple of photos of the Geiger counter against the background of the air base, then get the hell out of here."

We clambered over the dune-covered golf course and headed for the perimeter fence at the end of the runway. Kay held the Geiger counter up while I took two pictures. Kay was bending down packing the Geiger counter away when the first little sand explosions happened on Kay's left. Kay looked at the sand puzzled. I froze for a second, but then my instincts kicked in. I dived to my left, hitting Kay with a rugby tackle. As we both fell to our left, the next volley of shots passed us, one so close I could feel the disruption in the air above my head. The shots had come from a silenced weapon, and the close grouping and accuracy meant only one thing—whoever was doing the shooting was an expert.

I grabbed Kay's hand and on my belly crawled and slithered first sideways, then back the way we had come, toward the sea, over the dunes through a bunker, hoping the sideways movement had thrown the shooter off our direction. Luckily, the daylight was almost all gone. We lay perfectly still in the edge of a bunker, listening and watching for any movement from the direction of the airfield. Kay had got the message and was staring at me with huge, tear-filled eyes. I wanted to comfort her, tell her everything would be OK, but the slightest movement or noise would bring the enemy down upon us. We had got closer to the beach than we originally thought; it was only ten feet to the edge of the dunes. Another cautious look around and I saw that everything was still. I whispered into Kay's ear to tell her to slowly move to the edge of the dune but no further. I was praying the shooter did not have night-vision goggles, or we were sitting ducks.

Halfway there, the sand and grass started kicking up on both sides of us. We both dived for the edge of the dune, falling over the edge, mercifully without being hit. We crawled along under the lip of the grass bank until we were level with the boat. Crossing that strip of sand would have been suicide.

The way the grass had been kicked up proved that there were at least two shooters. I whispered to her to stay put, not to move a muscle until I came for her. She was in a bad way, shaking like a leaf, but she got the idea. I crawled back over the edge and slowly, slowly crawled into the nearest bunker I could find. I stopped and listened. Nothing. These guys were good. I had no idea how to tackle them. They were probably Navy SEALs, which was not good. They would have all the toys, and I had a lady's Beretta.

***

Moving in a sweeping pattern, the two Navy SEALs worked methodically toward the beach. It wouldn't be long now until they flushed the intruders out onto the open sands of the beach where they would finish the job off.

Petty Officer Howie was annoyed with himself. That was the first time in his career that he had missed his target. The intruder was quick, but he would soon have his payback. He was moving too quickly. The fact that he knew his quarry was unarmed had made him overconfident. Six feet from the last bunker, a man stood up from the bunker and shot him through the chest twice at point-blank range.

***

The big sergeant's body fell forward into the bunker.

I felt like I was about to pass out. I thought for sure when I stood up that would be the end. My heart was racing. If the soldier had been wearing body armour, that would have been it. My Beretta bullets would have bounced off like rain. I turned the soldier over to examine my enemy. He could be best described as Darth Vader in camouflage. He wore the modern American battle helmet, but it had a visor grafted onto it with breathing apparatus, presumably some type of chemical warfare suit. His weapon was familiar to me. It was the snub-nose M16 with suppressor. I grabbed the rifle and two spare clips, took a quick snap of the dead soldier, and headed over the edge of the dune again. I sat still and listened again. Nothing. My nerves were at breaking point.

There was still at least one soldier out there. I told myself that at least I had a decent weapon to defend myself with. I had been issued a similar weapon during the Iraq War and had become familiar with it. I had already pushed my luck too far and decided to stay put for the moment.

***

Seaman Fernandez had heard the two shots to his left and was making his way to the area. He could not understand where they had come from. Had Howie's rifle failed? Had he used his side arm? If so, why had he not made comms?

Fernandez decided to investigate before he contacted the control. He was roughly parallel with the boat and had stopped to examine the bay. He was sick of having to wear the radiation kit. It impaired his vision and hearing. Worst of all, you could not wear body armour or night-vision equipment with it on. It was like fighting with one hand behind your back. Fernandez stood on the grassy dune above the beach, listening for any telltale noises.

***

I had loaded a new clip into the M16 and, as quietly as possible, pulled the hammer back, ready for action. I was wondering how Kay was holding up when the noise that I had previously thought was a microlight started to get louder. Something in the back of my mind was ringing alarm bells. It came back to me in a flash. It was a Predator surveillance drone, an unmanned aircraft. I had seen them in Pakistan heading over the border into Afghanistan, looking for Bin Laden's hideout.

I was just about to move forward to sneak a peek in the sky when behind me the sand crumbled and sent a little avalanche of sand down between my legs. Someone was on the banking above me. I raised the M16, praying it was not Kay come to look for me, and pulled the trigger, moving the rifle in an arc, hoping to cover a large area of banking. The bullets burst through the banking in a cloud of sand, turf, and soil.

***

All the bullets bar one missed Seaman Fernandez, but the one that hit him inflicted terrible damage. It passed through his groin, puncturing his bladder and smashing his pelvis before leaving through his side. He fell forward over the banking and started to half-turn. Another burst from the M16 finished the job. He took another three rounds in the chest and stomach and lay still, his sightless eyes staring into the star-filled northern sky.

***

My peripheral vision caught movement above me. It was the drone. If we were to have any hope of getting away from here, I had to take it out. Taking aim just in front of it, I emptied the rest of the clip. Nothing. I rammed the last clip in, pulled the hammer back, and opened up again, emptying the full clip into the air. There was silence. The Predator went into a dive and exploded on the beach twenty meters from the boat. It was time to get the hell out of here. We were going to have to take our chances that there were no other troops. I dropped the empty M16 and ran onto the beach, screaming for Kay to get in the boat. She appeared on my left from the banking and made a sprint for the boat.

I stopped, took another picture of the dead soldier in his radiation suit, then another of the downed drone. I hit the bow of the boat at full charge with my shoulder. For a fraction of a second it stuck. Then the suction of the hull on the wet sand broke, and it began to slide into the water. I screamed at Kay to get the outboard down and started. I glanced anxiously over my shoulder expecting to see half the US Marine Corps pouring over the dunes, but there was nothing.

***

Master Chief John Steiner stood in the control room, finding it hard to take in what had just happened. The CIA had just informed him of an attempted incursion of the facility. He had also been told it was a man and woman civilian who were unarmed. He had been given a direct order from the Pentagon to terminate the targets.

Because of this order, he had given the task to the two best SEALs in the unit. In the circumstances, he had not supplied backup and was horrified when the feedback from the Predator showed both his men down. Then the two-million-dollar Predator, which was supposed to be bulletproof, was shot down. He had to get this situation back under control, or he was history. His hand was trembling as he picked up the phone. "Get Phil from public relations up here now. Tell him he needs to put out a press release to say one of our search-and-rescue choppers crashed on landing. There were no casualties but the beach is off limits until crash investigators carry out an inquiry."

He then lifted a red phone. "This is Master Chief Steiner, deploy Angels One and Two please. This is a search-and-destroy mission; I repeat, this is a search-and-destroy mission. Good luck."

***

I could hardly believe our luck. We were taking huge risks. The little boat was traveling reasonably quickly on three-quarters throttle. We had been at sea for twenty minutes, and as yet, there was no sign of pursuit. We had just passed Sanda Island. Its summit stood out against the starry sky. The waters around Sanda were choppy, but for this time of year, they were remarkably good. The icy wind swirled round our heads and stung like a swarm of bees. I could not risk slowing down. I prayed that we didn't run aground; at the speed we were traveling it would have been nasty. Kay stood by my shoulder and refused point blank to sit in the forward cabin, instead electing to stare into the waves, looking for rocks. Another thirty minutes and we would be back on Arran. I followed the coast until the lights of Campbeltown came into sight, then pointed the bow of the little boat right across the sound toward the welcome sight of Arran.

Then I heard the noise. At first, I wasn't sure. It came and went with the wind, and the boat's engine note combined with the wind made it difficult to listen. I dropped the throttle to half and listened again. There it was. It faded again; then the wind brought the noise back to my ear.

A controlled panic seized me. Kay was saying something to me, but it was not registering. My mind was in overdrive, trying to work out a solution, and my stomach was trying to turn itself inside out. The noise I had heard, a distinctive heavy beat, only came from one type of aircraft. It was unmistakably an Apache attack helicopter, and the only thing that stood any kind of chance against it was a fighter jet, and as I only had a fishing boat, we were in big trouble.

I slammed the throttle to full and flung the steering back hard left. The little boat balanced on the top of a wave then fell sideways, almost going over. Only its sturdy hull design saved the day. It turned its bow into the next wave and cut through, starting to build some speed. Campbeltown was just behind me, and I considered it for a second, but American forces could be there in a matter of minutes from the air base, and I didn't fancy my chances.

The beat was constant now. The only saving grace was the chopper had followed our route instead of coming cross-country. It had given us a little more precious time to run. It had taken me five minutes to reach the Mull of Kintye coastline, and I was going as fast as the little fishing boat could go. I was only twenty feet from the shore and in great danger of running the little craft aground. I had no visual contact with the chopper, but the rotor beat was now distinctive and heading in our general direction. My head was on a swivel, trying to watch the coastline and keep an eye out for the helicopter. A few seconds later, I was alerted by Kay tugging at my sleeve. She had seen something and was trying to warn me. I followed the line of her outstretched arm and in the distance could make out the sinister shapes of two Apache helicopters skimming the surface of the water and headed in the direction of the southern tip of Arran. I thanked God I had turned back. I would have been a sitting duck in the middle of the sea. It looked as if they were going to start the search from Arran. If so, that would give me a few more precious minutes to try and think of something.

Suddenly what appeared to be a cave mouth opened up on the left. I throttled down and let the little boat trundle on. I asked Kay to keep a look out for the choppers while I tiptoed toward the mouth of the cave. On close inspection, it was not a cave but an inlet cut into the wall of a forty-foot cliff. Halfway up the cliff, a tree sprouted from the rock, its dense branches covering the inlet like a leafy quilt. I nosed the little boat into the cleft in the rock. With the bow touching the craggy stone wall, the stern just made it in by six feet. This was as good as it was going to get. I cut the engine and silence took over. I was not at all sure we were going to get away with this deception. The Apache was equipped with thermal-imaging technology, and simply hiding the boat was a long shot. Our body heat and the hot engine could be picked up at some distance.

I racked my brain for a solution. Then I had an idea. Dragging out the survival kit I had seen Kay loading into the boat, I started pulling it apart, looking for one specific item, and there it was, a thermal blanket that you would wrap a hypothermia victim into get body heat up. It was a shiny silver blanket that reflected heat. I pulled it out and spread it over the stern and engine, and Kay and I ducked under it. In theory, this would block our heat signature while the tree would block the silver reflection. It was the best I could come up with. I had seen at close hand what devastation one of these Apache helicopters was capable of. It was time to pray.

***

Major Trent Weatherby of the Missouri National Guard flew the lead Apache, code-named Angel One. His second in command, Captain Tim Sleigh, flew the second National Guard Apache, code-named Angel Two. Their original plan was to intercept the fishing boat before it made the coast of Arran. They had been briefed by Steiner on the night's events and were aware that the most likely destination for the fugitives was Arran. They were somewhat surprised when they were not able to find the craft and complete the mission. Weatherby ordered Angel Two to return to the coastline of Kintyre and to proceed north while he followed the coastline of Arran north. Hopefully the terrorists would be caught in an Apache sandwich. Major Weatherby had been given full command and control of the mission and was informed the target must be eliminated at all costs.

***

In the longliner my adrenaline levels had started to drop, and fatigue was taking its place. My right shoulder was badly bruised from my attempts at getting the boat off the beach, my face was burning with the exposure to the elements, and I was stinking of cordite from the guns. Kay wasn't in much better shape. Her lower lip was burst where she had slammed her face into the side of the boat as I did my emergency turn, and her ribs were either bruised or broken where I had rugby-tackled her to the ground when the gunfire started. Worse, her nerves were shattered. She was curled up in a ball in my lap, quietly sobbing. "Kay, we need to keep our strength up. Do we have anything hot to drink/"

This seemed to bring Kay back to life. She fumbled about in the dark, coming up with a flask of tea. It was lukewarm, and we had no sugar, but it did the job. We shared one cup as no other could be found in the dark, and drained the remains of the thermos.

Kay found some boiled sweets in her jacket pocket and shared them, four each. "Adam, what is happening? This is our country, and we are being hunted like criminals by our allies. We need to get the readings back to our government, so they can stop this madness. People in Kintyre are in danger. They need to be checked. If that radiation is as bad outside the base, people are going to start getting sick."

Kay stopped speaking. The thud of the rotor blades was getting close. I could feel Kay's grip on my arm tighten and her breathing stop. The Apache passed at a distance. I suspected it was nearer Arran. Things went quiet again, just the occasional scrape of fiberglass as the tide pushed the longliner against the stone cliff face.

"When we get back to Arran, I will call my friend. He will get this mess sorted out, but we need to get off Arran. It's not safe. They must have people on Arran. Why else did the helicopters head straight

there? They knew where we were going. You need to come with me, ,
and no arguments this time."

Kay snuggled into my side for warmth. "You won't get any arguments from me; you have proved your point." There was silence for a
second. "Adam, I'm so sorry. You have done nothing but help me, and
all I have done is argue with you and get you into real trouble."

Under the blanket, I had started to warm up and after the exertions on the beach, drowsiness had set in. "Kay, it's not your fault MI6
had not told you the whole truth. You were misled."

The blanket rustled as Kay tried to move her legs, probably to stop
cramp setting in. "MI6 were not the only ones not telling the whole
truth, I think. Royal Engineers don't normally carry on like that, do
they Captain Macdonald?"

The beat of the rotors approaching saved me from having to answer
the question. The noise steadily grew as the machine approached from
the south. This one was not going to miss us. Kay curled up in my arms
and squeezed me tightly. I closed my eyes and waited. We would soon
find out if our hiding place had worked. There was no doubt what
would happen if we were discovered. You don't send an Apache to
capture anyone—it is a pure hunter-killer.

***

In the cockpit of Angel Two, the second pilot and gunner were
looking at a very faint heat signature on the coast below. They were
about to pass when the pilot decided it was worth a second look.
Two miles away, Davie Smith and his mate Bill Johnston were on
their way back to Campbeltown from a sea-fishing trip via the dis-
tillery at Lochranza for a well-needed dram to keep the cold out.
Bill was asleep in the front cabin of the little fishing boat while
Davie contemplated more liquid refreshment at the pub when he
got home.

Angel Two hovered above the tree that was hanging out over the
coast. The two pilots were locked in conversation over the suspect heat

signature when their headsets burst into life. "Angel Two, we have located target and are engaging. Angel One out."

Davie heard the heavy beat directly in front of him, and his first thought was that it was the air-sea rescue from Prestwick out looking for somebody. That was Davie's last-ever thought. The gunner of Angel One had the longliner in his crosshairs. The two-second burst from the Apache's chain gun sent hundreds of thirty-millimeter cannon shells bursting through the cabin of the fishing boat, sending splinters of fiberglass, glass, bone, and flesh flying everywhere. A second burst finished the job, sending the little Seagull engine across the surface of the water like a skimming stone.

The radio burst into life again in the cockpit of Angel Two. "Target eliminated. Angel Two return to base. Dropping marker buoys for cleanup crews. Good job, everybody. The drinks are on me. Angel One out."

Captain Sleigh throttled up and lifted the Apache clear of the tree-tops. Swinging her nose to the south, he smiled to himself. Trent would be unlivable with now he had his first confirmed kill. He doubted if he would be able to live up to his promise of buying the drinks at the bar as he wouldn't get his head through the door.

***

The Apache had hovered above us for what were only a few minutes, but to me it seemed like hours. The downwash of the rotors brought leaves and branches down on our heads and threatened to blow away the blanket. They must have discovered us. Why else stay right above us?

At one point I thought I heard gunfire, but with the Apache above us and the sea echoing off the walls of the cliff, it might have been my imagination. As quickly as the helicopter arrived, it departed. Kay was clinging onto me so tightly, her watchstrap had cut into me, drawing blood. She was chalk white and was obviously expecting to die here in this watery grave.

"We are going to stay here awhile. This could be a ruse so we drop our guard and get careless."

She nodded but said nothing. The quiet helped us calm our nerves. The engine had cooled enough for me to take a chance and remove the blanket covering it. With our jackets on the floor of the boat and the thermal blanket over us, we were able to stretch out, and within a few minutes, we were both asleep.

***

Within fifteen minutes of the Apache attack, the fast patrol boat arrived, aided by the homing beacon in the buoy that Angel One had dropped. The patrol boat had been lurking about the area, waiting for the call. The cleanup was fast and efficient. Both the bodies were recovered, and what was left of the longliner's hull was winched on board and covered with a tarpaulin. It would be inspected fully on return to base.

***

I awoke with a start. It was grey dark, the dawn not far away. It was time to move. Kay was still asleep and whimpered in her sleep as I moved her gently to one side. Getting out of the little inlet proved much harder than it had been getting in. The only way I could make the boat move was to stand in the bow and push against the cliff. It was made worse by the waves trying to push us back in, and my damaged shoulder had now seized up, so every movement was through gritted teeth.

After ten minutes of to and fro, the little boat broke free from the inlet only to be smashed sideways into the cliff wall. The crash jolted Kay awake; her eyes were wide with terror.

"You are OK. We just kissed the cliff wall."

She calmed down, seeing that we were free from our self-enforced imprisonment. "How long until we get home? I need the toilet, a bath, and a coffee, in that order."

I thought for a second, looking at our position. The gloom was lifting, giving us an idea of our position. "Forty minutes I reckon, give or take five, but I hate to be the bearer of bad news. We need to get off

50

Arran immediately, no time for baths. Toilet, change of clothes, grab your gear, and by that time, I will be back for you."

She looked at me with a confused expression. "Back for me? Where are you going?"

"I need to go back to my cabin. I lost my phone in all the excitement last night, but I have a note of my contact's number at the cabin. I need to grab my gear and hand back the keys for the cabin." It was choppy but the little boat made good time through the icy sea.

*****

In a side hangar to the north of the main runway at Machrihanish sat the remains of the longliner. To one side, there was a small pile of articles collected from the sea. And on two trestle tables lay the bodies of the unfortunate fishermen. Master Chief Steiner and Sergeant Phil Isbeki stood surveying the carnage. Steiner had been in the middle of his breakfast when Sergeant Isbeki burst into the staff room. His face said it all. Steiner got to his feet as Isbeki was asking him to accompany him to the hangar. It was immediately apparent why he had been called. The two bodies were in their sixties and both male. They had hit the wrong target! "Shit! That asshole Weatherby has dropped us in it. Get me our guys on Arran, pronto."

*****

The little boat touched down on the beach at the cottage fifty minutes later, and it took a further ten minutes to load the boat on the trailer and drag it up to the outhouse. I left Kay shuffling to the cottage toilet cross-legged. Fifteen minutes later, I was in the cabin, clothes changed, and flinging things in bags. Unfortunately, the only thing that had survived last night's nightmare was the little compact camera. My phone, watch, and, worst of all, Mary's Beretta were all missing. I dropped the keys at the reception and headed back. To try and save time, I took the Machrie moor road, arriving at the little cottage road from the opposite direction. About quarter of a mile from the cottage, I could see a car leaving the cottage road. It was a big black Vauxhall. I gunned the Land Rover toward the cottage. The Vauxhall was gone. The Land Rover skidded to a halt in front of the cottage.

I blasted the horn. Nothing. I got out and shouted for Kay. No reply. A search of the house found nothing, and the outhouse was the same. I walked down to the little beach. She was not there. Had she been taken by the Americans? I turned and started to walk back to the little cottage when something caught my eye. The wind was blowing something about further along the beach. I started to walk toward it. As I got closer, the object got larger. I started to run. It was a body. Under my breath I was muttering the same words over and over. "Please, God. No."

I arrived at the foot of the cliff in a sprint. It was Kay's crumpled body. Her eyes stared back at me. Her face was unmarked, and there was a peaceful expression on her pretty face. The back of her skull was smashed on the rocks. She had been thrown from the cliff top. I closed her eyes. She could have been sleeping.

In a dazed stupor, I climbed the footpath to the summit of the cliff. At the top was a viewpoint with a chair, and next to the chair was Kay's trademark blue baseball cap. I looked at it—the badge was the New York Yankees. How ironic, I thought. I couldn't focus on the Mull of Kintyre. It was blotted out by my tears. I was a broken man.

CHAPTER THREE
Revenge

It wasn't self-preservation that brought me down from the cliff top. More than once I thought about joining Kay at the foot of the cliff. It was only the thought that if I did that, they would have won, that stopped me. The game would have been over, and I couldn't allow that.

So much for Neil and his mythical top agent, Sam. I checked the house. Kay's laptop was gone, along with all the documentation. Calling the police was only going to do one thing—get me locked up. I took everything that could come in handy, called along the road to the tearoom, told them there had been a terrible accident, and left. I parked the car in one of the many forestry car parks on Arran and went to sleep.

***

Al Koslowski and Brent Franklin were dismayed when they arrived at the lodge to find the target had left. A fast dash to the ferry proved fruitless, so they headed back to the girl's cottage to look for him there but drove straight past when they spotted the police car in the drive. They headed back to the shack to report their findings. They would set up surveillance on the ferry terminal in the morning. If he were trying to get off the island, this was the only way in winter.

***

Next morning, I was awake early. The car had frosted over during the night, and I could see my breath inside the car. I started the Land Rover and let it run to get some heat back in my frozen body. My shoulder was still agony, but my physical state was good compared to my mental state. I had never experienced a low like this before.

***

It was a beautiful day in Langley. The sunlight was streaming in through the large picture windows of the office of Brad Whiteford, the deputy director of the CIA and head of operations at the NCS. His office looked out over immaculately trimmed lawns and shrubs. He had been fast-tracked up the CIA ladder and was only three jobs away from his ultimate goal, CIA director. His meteoric rise had been swift thanks to the fact he had his finger in every pie and had made contacts in every civilized country, and also some not so civilized. He had become used to success, the report in front of him made grim reading. Suddenly, the day did not seem so beautiful. He kicked his shoes off, swung round, and put his feet up on the desk, using his feet as leverage to tilt back the big tan leather recliner. He thought maybe getting comfortable would make the reading more palatable. The report detailed how, at the air base in Scotland, they had lost two highly decorated SEALs and a very expensive surveillance drone.

They had then mistakenly killed two local fishermen. Thankfully, they had eliminated one of their targets, but now the second target had eluded them and was believed to be on the run on the small island of Arran. He was a very worried man, though from the outside no one would have known. He was a cool customer who rarely showed his emotions. He thought the situation through in his head. He needed to contain this situation within his department. He had been in charge of security for the SR3000. It was a joint NASA-Pentagon project, the replacement for the shuttle, which was coming to the end of its life.

The SR3000 was revolutionary. Thanks to its new fusion-powered engines, it was a breakthrough, another leap for mankind. This was as important as the discovery of the wheel—a plane that could not only fly in space but could travel in and out of the Earth's atmosphere at will. The plane used a revolutionary, fusion-powered force field that protected the hull from the effects of reentry. Anybody connected with this ground-breaking project was bound to go far.

His problems had started when his British agent informed him that MI6 were snooping around Nevada, looking for something. The problem was compounded when one of the engineers of the project reported to him that he was about to submit a report asking that the project be stopped as dangerous levels of radiation had been found after every reentry from space. There was a problem with the integrity of the force field for some hours after use. The reason the engineer was talking to him was because the report had been stolen from his motel room, and he wanted to report it.

Brad knew this would tarnish his glittering career. Being associated with a failed NASA mission helped nobody's career. He told the engineer to go back to work and say nothing until he had found the report. In due course, they had found from their contact in Britain that the MI6 agent had the report. He was dealt with accordingly, and the report retrieved. The engineer had a nasty accident the following day and died on the way to hospital.

Two weeks later the whole project was moved, at Brad's request, to a remote airfield in Scotland where he could control the situation, away from the majority of NASA engineers. If it were true about the radiation, it was close enough to Britain's nuclear submarine base for that country to take the blame if people started getting sick. His plan was working—until two of his agents based on a nearby island reported unusual activity by a stranger to the island, and it had been on a slippery slope since then.

This new stranger who had evaded every attempt to stop him was worrying. He appeared to be well trained and clever, but all database records using facial recognition from the downed drone proved negative. This man was a ghost.

He decided to give the two agents on the island forty-eight hours to find this man before he called in the cavalry. The quicker this was resolved, the better. Although his superiors knew the project had been moved for security reasons, they knew nothing else, and it would stay that way. The department he was now in charge of had the clout to do this. The National Clandestine Services department had the biggest resources within the CIA and answered to very few people. He had already filled the paperwork in explaining how the CIA drone had been shot down in Afghanistan and a SEAL team had been flown from Scotland to Afghanistan to retrieve it for the CIA. Unfortunately, they had lost two of their team under heavy fire from the Taliban. The bodies had been flown to America for burial. The girl on the island had committed suicide. The police had found a letter in her pocket, and the local air-sea rescue was still looking for the lost fishermen, aided by American rescue choppers from the base. It was all tied up nicely except for that last loose end. Who was this ghost?

***

I booked into a small hotel in Whiting Bay, on the south of the island well out of the way, and parked the Land Rover in the overspill car park at the rear, away from prying eyes. I forced myself to eat something from the breakfast menu. Over breakfast, I pondered the problem of what to do next—cut and run, head for London and Neil's office to spill the beans? Or stay here and find Kay's killers? This would be no mean feat, as I was probably going to be up against trained CIA operatives. I on the other hand had nothing, no surveillance equipment, and no weapons. After returning to my small bedroom for a shower and shave, I changed and went for a walk to clear my head. As a precaution, I wore Kay's blue baseball cap pulled down low over my eyes. My stroll took me by the local chemists, which were advertising prescription glasses in the window. I slipped in and after a wander around, checked out the choice of glasses. I soon found a pair of Clark Kent-lookalike specs. With the weakest lenses fitted, I purchased them along with two Mars bars and headed back toward the hotel, eating a Mars bar and wearing my new specs. It was on the way back, my head clearer, that I made my final decision. I had known all along, if I was being honest with myself, what I would do.

I was a proud Scotsman and to me, heading for London was like admitting defeat. I would not be chased out of my own country by criminals hiding behind the American flag. I would stay, and as my old rugby coach used to say, "The best defense is always attack." The last thing my enemies would expect was an attack.

Just opposite the hotel there was a general store that sold almost anything. As I walked past, I saw on the back wall, along with the Hula-Hoops and kites, a baseball bat set. On entering the store and after a closer inspection, I was surprised to find it was the real deal, not a kid's imitation. I bought the set, which went well with my New York Yankees baseball cap. I deposited my purchases in the boot of the Land Rover and headed for Brodick. If I were look-ing for somebody on Arran, I would be checking out the ferries. I parked the Land Rover on the outskirts of Brodick, in the drive of a lovely new bungalow that was obviously someone's holiday home. The weeds had grown up between the slabs on the drive, and no car had been parked here for months, another one of Arran's part-time inhabitants.

As I walked down the hill toward the pier, I could see the big ferry docking. I had just about timed it to perfection. I walked across the road and into the booking office. The room was empty, bar two cou-ples. I pretended to be interested in the tourist brochures, but out of the corner of my new specs, I was checking for a possible target. Neither of the two couples looked likely candidates. One couple was in their seventies, and the others were busy studying the day's papers and had never lifted their heads. Not exactly surveillance material. Outside in the car park, three cars and four vans waited to be loaded on board. There were two guys outside, an elderly gentleman with his West Highland terrier, who thought barking at the ferry would scare it away, and a fit-looking guy in his early thirties leaning against the rails, balancing on his racing cycle. He looked like he was just about to start a stage of the Tour de France. He was wearing wraparound shades and looked the most lightly character. I was conscious that I had spent enough time with the brochures and headed across to the coffee machine, then to the far corner, where I could keep an eye on both exits and still watch the car park. I had just sat down when I heard the voice, an American voice from the far corner of the car park.

***

Al Koslowski was halfway to the ticket office, heading for the toilet, when his partner shouted at him to get more coffee. Al frowned. He had been paired up with the biggest mouth in the service and wanted this assignment to end. He didn't like working with this loudmouth, gun-happy loser. The big black Vauxhall was parked behind a row of post office vans in the adjacent commercial car park.

***

As the big American approached, it all fell into place. This was one of the two guys I had seen on the beach that first day I had met Kay. They had obviously seen what she was up to. The American walked into the room and headed straight for the toilet.

I was in two minds what to do next. I could follow him in and try to break his neck, but he was tall and wiry-looking. He would give me a hard time. No, his time would come, but not now. He came back out and headed to the coffee machine. Two minutes later, he was heading back across the car park, his long legs carrying him at speed. There was something in the way he walked and carried himself. I was sure he was ex-military. His partner was a different kettle of fish—younger, louder, less disciplined. He looked like a wild card. Probably the killer of the pair. Sitting watching them, I wondered which one had flung Kay from the cliff.

The red mist had started to descend. I hated the fact I was unarmed. Without a doubt, if I still had Mary's little Beretta, I would have used it. As the big Vauxhall left the car park, it took all my strength to sit there and do nothing. They would be back for the evening ferry, and I would be ready.

***

On the way back to the shack, Al was quiet. He let Brent do the driving. Brent talked constant rubbish all the way back to the shack, but Al was not listening. Something was bugging him, something in the back of his mind, but he couldn't put a finger on it.

He forgot about it, and his mind drifted to a different problem. He wanted out of this job. He did not feel comfortable with the mission. What were they doing in a friendly country, killing an unarmed woman? He had almost walked away from the job, and only loyalty to his country forced him to comply. Brent, on the other hand, was having a ball. He actually looked like he enjoyed killing a defenseless young woman. The look on his face when he came down from the cliff had almost made Al physically sick. He had to stop himself drawing his gun and blowing Brent's brains out.

Suddenly, it clicked. He knew what was bugging him, and the realization of it sent a shiver down his spine. The man in the corner of the ticket office was wearing the same Yankees cap as the girl. It was him, and he wasn't running away—he was stalking them. Who was this stranger? The office seemed to be at a loss to identify him. He had to be somebody's agent; he was too well trained. Al decided not to share this revelation with his partner, whom he had nicknamed "Billy the Kid," for obvious reasons. This man would not pull the wool over his eyes the next time they met.

***

By the time the evening boat arrived, I had changed into dark clothing and purchased black training shoes. I would not run the risk of waiting at the pier. There was no need. I had watched the big black Vauxhall appear from Brodick's main street, and in the evening from my position behind the bank, I had watched it arrive. I would wait here for it to pass, then follow it to its destination, and kill both the occupants. Simple! Sure enough, five minutes after the boat departed, the big Vauxhall passed. I waited a few seconds, then pulled out behind it.

During my wait, I had not been idle. I had broken into the driver's light circuit and made a crude switch with some wire twisted together so I could make the light go on and off at will. The String is the road that crosses the island through a mountain pass, and following the Vauxhall was pretty simple. I kept a fair distance as I watched the big car climb the mountain pass ahead. There were few turnoffs, so it made my life easier. As we approached Blackwaterfoot, the road split two ways, and I had to get closer to see which direction the big car had taken. It turned left along the cliff-top road, heading south. I stopped at the junction and watched it climb the hill.

I waited until it was out of sight, then disconnected the headlamp and continued following my quarry. I gunned the Land Rover to catch up with the Vauxhall. It continued on for a few miles, then took a left turn onto the Ross road. I waited at the junction for a few seconds, then followed with my side lamps on. I didn't see the Vauxhall turnoff, but I could see his head lamps against the hillside, which corresponded with a little track into the trees on the left.

This was as far as the car would go. Even if it were a few miles up the track, it was obvious that the track only went to a farm or similar, and the rest would be carried out on foot. I grabbed the baseball bat and headed up the track at a steady jog. I didn't want my prey settling in for the evening. I wanted them still moving around.

***

In the car on the way back, Al had been quiet again. The whole time they were at the pier, his eyes were out on stalks. His side arm had the silencer fitted, and the safety was already off, but the man had not reappeared. As they had approached the shack, he had asked Brent if he thought they should do a drive-by. Brent looked at him, surprised. Al explained that at no point had they been alone on the road. Brent shrugged it off, saying that the last car to follow was the local cop, who he knew had only one head lamp working, and he was too stupid to tail anybody.

When they reached the road end, Brent turned off. Al still thought he should have passed the junction, then doubled back to see if anyone had followed, but he was tired, and it was too late to do anything about it. He just hoped this was the last case he had to work with this idiot.

Al had asked Brent to put out the garbage before they had left, but as usual, he had left everything at his backside. He asked again, but Billy the Kid was in the next room, busy logging onto Langley to see if they had any new instructions.

Al gave up taking to him (he was a lost cause) and headed out the back door with the rubbish. He had gone from light to pitch dark, and his night vision was minimal. As he approached the bin, he sensed movement on his left. He reacted at the speed of light, flinging himself backward, away from the movement.

***

I had aimed for his temple, but his swift movement spoiled my aim. I had put everything into the swing—all my muscle, all my pain, all my aggression, all my fury. It was now or never. The baseball bat made contact. The jarring almost took the bat from my hand, and my wrists felt like they had dislocated, but the bat had hit Al squarely across the windpipe, crushing his larynx into his spine. He collapsed. He was alive for the moment and making a terrible gurgling, rasping noise as his body tried to draw air through his shattered throat. I stepped over him and checked him for a weapon. He was unarmed. My plan started to unravel. I had counted on him carrying a weapon. I stepped into the room as the younger agent appeared through the doorway.

Rugby tactics took over I charged at him, hitting him square in the gut with my head. The momentum carried us over in a cartwheel, and we landed against the wall. My opponent regained his footing first and as I stood up sent a flying kick that was aimed at my head but luckily caught me across the chest.

The power in his kick took me by surprise and sent me backward across the room, winding me badly. My kidneys hit the worktop, and my head bounced off the cupboards. I was thrown forward again right into a spinning kick that caught me on the side of the head.

I was close to losing consciousness and hopelessly outmatched. This guy was a martial arts expert. I looked to my right. I had one chance left—if I could get him close enough. The kettle had just boiled, and I could hit him with the boiling water. Brent saw my glance and smiled. From his back, he produced a Glock and fired at the kettle, which exploded in a fountain of steam.

The bastard had been armed all along. He was just playing with me as a cat plays with a mouse. He grinned at me maliciously as he took aim at my head. There was a crack, and the gun flew from Brent's hand. He grabbed his wrist as his face contorted in agony. There was movement in the doorway and a figure in black stepped into the room, both arms extended, holding a silenced automatic pistol. The gun was aimed at Brent's head. The figure's gaze never left Brent.

"Adam, it's me. Sam." To my surprise, Sam was female. She turned her attention back to Brent. "Now, that was naughty. You don't bring a gun to a fistfight, but if it is a gunfight you want, you shall have it, sir."

Her gun kicked noiselessly, and she shot Brent between the eyes. The back of his head exploded like a watermelon, giving the far side of the kitchen a new, gruesome decoration. His body collapsed in a heap of twitching jelly. She walked across to me and extended her hand to shake mine. I was somewhat bewildered.

"It's an honour to meet you, Mac." Her eyes met mine. They were stone-cold grey, with not a flicker of emotion. I had absolutely no doubt that I was looking into the eyes of a cold-blooded killer. She was 100 percent pure assassin.

CHAPTER FOUR

Sam

S am was not one to hang about. "Adam, go outside and check the other clown is dead. Load him into the passenger seat of the Vauxhall, then get back in here and put this idiot in the boot of the Vauxhall."

I went to check the pulse of the agent outside, but there was no need. The minute I put my fingers to his neck to check for a pulse, I knew. In the cold winter evening, the body had already started to cool and was cold and clammy to the touch. I started to lift the agent from the kitchen floor when Sam reappeared from the lounge area and handed me a bin bag. "Put this over his head. I don't want him leaking all over the Vauxhall."

I made the mistake of asking what it mattered if he leaked all over the Vauxhall and was told to shut up and get on with it. Sam was busy on the computer. Brent did not have time to switch it off and was still logged on with all the passwords already logged. It was a gold mine of information. Sam downloaded files then, using a strange looking USB device, uploaded a programme onto the computer. I asked Sam what this was. "It's a toy we borrowed from the CIA, and our boffins modified it for our use. It's a very clever little virus that won't touch our computers but kills every motherboard that this terminal has logged through. Anyway, enough of the talking. Here, take this, and let's go."

She handed me a gun and four clips of ammo she had taken from the drawer. "It's a Glock seventeen. It's a good gun, better than that peashooter you were hanging onto."

I was about to argue but decided now was not the time. Sam called all the shots. I was told to follow her back toward Blackwaterfoot along the cliff road. At the highest point, she stopped the big Vauxhall and pulled the dead agent into the driver's seat. Sam pointed the big car's steering over the edge, started it up, leaned in with a foot on the brake, and selected drive. She lifted her foot off the brake, and the car glided away, slowing slightly as the tyres made contact with the grass. Then it was gone. I stayed to listen for the crash. Sam had already started walking back to the Land Rover.

We had loaded Brent into the Land Rover boot, and I expressed my concern that he would leak all over my boot. Sam smiled and told me not to worry. That smile worried me more than the bloodstained boot.

Sam's rental Corsa was parked at the Ross Road junction, some three miles from the shack. She told me to follow her back to Brodick. She parked at the shops, lifted two containers out of the boot, locked the little car, and dropped the keys down a drain. The containers went in the boot next to Brent's body. She climbed in and told me to drive to Kay's house.

On the way there, she called a number on her mobile. "Hi, is that the Sandy Beach Guesthouse? Hi, it's Mrs. Hunter. I'm just calling to check you received our reservation for tomorrow night. You did? That's lovely. See you tomorrow." She hung up and sat thinking for a few seconds. "Adam, I take it Kay's speedboat is still in working order."

It was my turn to smile. We arrived at Kay's house after ten in the evening. The little house stood out in the moonlight; the wind whipped the bushes around it. I had tears in the corners of my eyes. You could have said it was because of the cold wind, but I knew it was not.

As soon as we arrived, Sam was out shouting commands again. I was told to get the petrol out of the car and get the outhouse open and the boat out. The big doors were locked, but the hinges were badly rusted away. I was maneuvering them so the latch on the lock would come free when Sam appeared and asked what was taking so long, I told her to have some patience. I was almost there.

She took a step back, drew her silenced Glock, and fired four times through the lock. The door swung open. She marched past me into the garage. "What the hell is this piece of junk?"

I smirked. "That's your speedboat."

She glowered at me. "You're braver than I thought, crossing the sea in that bathtub. Get the Yank's body into the front seat of the Chelsea tractor, then fill the boat with fuel."

I frowned. "What are you going to do that for?" It suddenly clicked. "No, wait, not the car. It's only six months old. It cost a fortune."

She carried the fuel can to the driver's side. She was speaking in a low growl now. "Yes, it probably did, so ask yourself—do you want to get out of this, or would you rather the CIA bury you in your precious Land Rover? Get the Yank in the front, or piss off so I can do it. We need to burn the body to hide the gunshot you idiot"

***

I grudgingly moved the body and went to fuel the boat while Sam soaked the body and interior of the Land Rover in petrol. Luckily, Kay had left the ignition key in the boat. It fired first turn I left it idling tied to the trailer so it wouldn't float away. Sam was busy flinging a mixture of our clothes in a rucksack. The rest she flung in the back of the Freelander. She asked if I needed anything else.

I pulled my fake specs from the glove box. Then I found Kay's blue cap and tucked it in the rucksack. I climbed aboard the longliner while I watched Sam set fire to my pride and joy. What made it worse was I was sure the bitch enjoyed doing it.

We loaded the longliner and sailed away into the night. I was at the wheel and asked Sam where we were heading. Her answer sent a shiver down my spine. "Did I just hear you say Campbeltown? Are you insane? We can't go back over there," I screamed over the noise of the wind.

Sam must have realized I was on the edge because she seemed to back off a little. "Adam, for one they are going to send their very best after us, so we need to be on our game and that means you need to be a team player so listen up, then shut up. We are going to stay in their backyard because it's the last place they will look for us. I know and you know the faked deaths of the two Yanks in the cars won't fool the CIA, but they might give us a few precious hours to get away, so get off my back."

I wasn't happy at being spoken to like that, not after all I had been through. "Right, Mrs. James-bloody-Bond, it's your turn to listen up. There are a few things you need to know. I take it you knew Kay and I were sent across to get radiation readings, but I bet you don't know the rest of the story. The place is like Fort Knox. They knew we were coming. We had to escape, and they were not for taking prisoners. To get away I had to kill two Navy SEALs and shoot down a Predator drone. They came looking for us with Apache gunships, so you can bet your last dollar the place is going to be jumping with activity. Oh and yes, those all-important radiation readings. I don't know if you are a science boffin, but they are five hundred rem on the beach, just slightly less than Chernobyl. I bet the guesthouse you phoned earlier doesn't have to use the toaster to toast bread. It just does it by itself. I hope you booked a short stay, or do you fancy a tan from the inside out?"

Sam said nothing. She was obviously taking in what I had just told her. I set the longliner on a course for Campbeltown and the engine to half-throttle. It was going to get uncomfortable. It was windy, and the waves exploded over the bow as the little boat fought every peak and trough.

***

In London, Merlin stood at the front door of the American embassy. The young marine checked his credentials, then saluted. "They are waiting for you inside, sir. Have a nice day."

Merlin entered and was ushered into the communications room on the left. The room had various computers and radio gear and a row of phones. The end phone was off the hook and had a light flashing to say someone was on the line.

Merlin lifted it with some trepidation. He did not like Brad Whiteford. He was a thug with a suit, but Whiteford had his hooks in him deep, and he had to toe the line. "Hello, Brad. How are we this fine morning?" His knuckles were white as he gripped the phone, waiting for the reply.

"Cut the crap. Did you do as you were told?" Brad was his usual pleasant self.

"Yes, I spoke to the prime minister personally and advised him that we were in danger of causing a CIA operation to fail. As a result of this, all MI6 operatives have been ordered to stand down from any operations involving American interests." He waited for Whiteford to reply. There was silence for seconds.

"You need to find something out for me. There was an attack on two of my agents based on the Island of Arran, possibly by two MI6 agents. They have caused havoc. I can't rely on MI6 to say they have backed off. There is a team en route, but from satellite pictures, it appears we have lost two agents to them. We have lost all our satellites, and all computer transactions have been destroyed by some kind of cyber attack that corresponded with the attack on our agents. I want you to find out who these two are. We suspect the second agent is the same ghost who attacked the SR3000 project. I need to know who he is. The base commander in Scotland has a picture of him from the drone, but because of computer failure, I cannot give it to you. May I suggest you get yourself to Scotland and see if you can tie the picture of the ghost to any of your agents."

The phone went dead. After leaving the embassy, Merlin phoned his office and spoke to his secretary, saying that the meeting at the American embassy had gone well, but he was tired and was going to take a few days off and to reschedule any meetings for the following week.

After hanging up on Merlin, Brad dialed a new number and spoke to the head of the computer section of the CIA, who confirmed they were still working on the virus. They identified it as one of their own that had been given to MI6, but it had been modified, which was causing the problems. And the attack had definitely originated in Scotland.

Brad hung up and called another number. "Major, your team has full authority to eliminate the problem. I can't stress this enough, major. This is of vital importance to our country's security. Do whatever you need to. I need you on scene in twenty-four hours. I have put funds into your account."

Deep in the basement of MI6 headquarters, known as Vauxhall Cross, Neil Andrews was almost pulling out his dark curly hair. Against his better judgment, he had contacted Sam and told her to drop the Machrihanish case and return to Vauxhall Cross. He had his orders from his boss, the head of MI6, who in turn had his orders from the prime minister. The problem was he had just received two bad pieces of news. He had just found out about Kay Miller's death, and he had received a text from Sam saying she was taking some long overdue vacation time.

Which meant only one thing—she had gone AWOL. Between her and Macdonald, they were both loose cannons. They could get everybody in serious trouble, including himself.

***

We were taking much longer than expected to cross over to Campbeltown. The seas were heavy, and the longliner ploughed its way through, but it had slowed our progress drastically. Sam had sat in the little front cabin for a while, obviously deep in thought, but she had just come out and joined me at the wheel. "Adam, when we get to the guesthouse, we are booked in as Mr. and Mrs. Hunter. I have explained to the landlady we are newlyweds on our honeymoon, so we need to act the part." She rummaged around in the rucksack and produced a passport and credit card. "I have these for you. Your name is Allan Hunter, and I am Ann Hunter. I will hold onto them until we get there."

Eventually, we were approaching the Kintyre coastline, but we had been knocked off course by the weather. I estimated we were a couple of miles north of Campbeltown. Sam suddenly told me to stop the boat, shut down the engine, and give her the Glock she had given me. I sat staring at her with a puzzled expression on my face.

"We are going to swim from here after sinking the boat." She placed my Glock in a sealed bag and then put it in the rucksack.

"Are you mad? That must be at least two hundred meters to the beach. Let's just take the boat in and hide it. There is no need to kill ourselves trying to swim ashore in these conditions. You won't catch me jumping out of a perfectly good boat, thank you very much."

"That's what I thought you would say, so let me help you." The silenced Glock appeared from her side as she spoke. She fired a full clip into the floor of the boat, smashing the hull to pieces. The water started bubbling up through the shattered floor panels; she calmly packed her Glock away in a watertight bag and loaded it into the rucksack. The water was churning up through the floor like a geyser about to explode. The little boat was going down fast. I turned, ready to ask her what she thought she was playing at but only caught a glimpse of the soles of her ladies Nike trainers as she dived over the edge.

I followed her, using the side of the boat to launch me as far as possible. My plan failed miserably. As I dived, I was hit broadside by a huge wave, which took me under with it. I kicked for the surface and came up gasping for air, twenty feet north of the sinking boat but no closer to the shore. I regained my composure and kicked for the shore, putting everything into it. My shoulder ached, the freezing water stung like acid, but I ploughed on, thanking the lord I had been doing a lot of swimming to keep fit. But this was no swimming pool. It was like trying to swim in a washing machine. Every time I lifted my head to check on my bearings, the shore looked no closer.

The water seemed not so cold now, and the waves were calmer. I doubled my efforts. This was for sure the start of hypothermia—my brain was starting to close down. I knew I must get ashore soon before the drowsiness kicked in, or I was doomed. Minutes that seemed like hours passed. Then with a crack, my hand hit the stones on the seabed. I had made it. My knuckles were badly bruised, but I felt nothing. My legs and arms were numb, and my brain wasn't far behind. I collapsed on the beach. The life was drained out of me, and all I wanted to do was sleep. Sam slapped me hard across the face. The first time it was in a dream, but the second one stung, and I started to regain my senses. She was screaming at me to get my stupid arse off the beach before I froze to death. I was really starting to dislike this woman.

***

In New York, Aron Fletcher, a retired major from the 101st Airborne Division who had spent the last two years of his army career with Delta Force, was surveying the Manhattan skyline from his penthouse office overlooking Central Park. Life was good. He had taken the gamble and set up his own business, supplying security staff for dangerous parts of the world. Business was booming. There was no shortage of hellholes, and no shortage of businessmen trying to make a fast buck there or press reporting on them, and they all wanted the kind of protection he could deliver. He had just finished making the final arrangements for his team's trip to Scotland.

He went over it in his head again. His first choice was always the same, whatever the team. His best friend, Ed Holts, was his right-hand man and second-in-command. He had been the 101st's best sniper. His second choice was Areli Benesch, a fugitive and former Mossad employee. She had killed a fellow Mossad agent in a fight but had evaded capture by the Israeli government by faking her own death. She was now on hire to the highest bidder. She had been one of Mossad's rising stars before it all came crashing down around her. She was 100 percent pure spy. Third choice was German Lukas Richter, a retired GSG9 close-combat weapons instructor. In an enclosed space, he was the most lethal force Fletcher had ever seen. He did jobs on the side to help build up his pension fund. Fourth choice was Marcus Laine, a Finnish hit man who had no known military training but was most likely Europe's most successful assassin.

Brad had transferred six million dollars to his Swiss bank account from one of the CIA's offshore accounts, money that on paper had been given to NASA for research and development. Fletcher agreed to one million dollars for each of his team on the understanding that the money would only be paid into their accounts on the death of both fugitives. That left a healthy two million for his new company, and a free trip to bonny Scotland. Life was good.

***

Brad Whiteford stopped dead in his tracks as he entered his office. Sitting in his seat was the CIA director. Brad made a joke that he thought he had walked into the wrong office, but the director ignored it. "Brad, it seems we are having computer problems. My team tells me the problem originated in Scotland. Do I need to know anything about what's happening across there?"

Brad decided a half-truth would do for the moment. "Sir, I was just on my way to see you. We lost two of our guys in Scotland, and whoever did it hacked the computers. I was just in the process of sending an investigator. The computers will be back online soon, sir."

The director stood up and ambled round the desk while checking his watch. "Seems like you have a handle on the situation. Keep me informed of progress, and if you need help, call Neil Andrews at MI6. He is a good guy. He will help you find whoever did this, and it keeps the Brits in the loop. After all, it is their country. Must fly—got a lunch date with a senator."

Brad ordered coffee from his secretary then studied three folders in front of him. The first was a CIA employee who had just started, the second one was an agent under internal investigation for being drunk on duty, and the third had been with the FBI since the Mayflower landed and had one month left until he retired from his desk job in the CIA. Brad decided the new start was too much of a risk, as he would have a point to prove and no one yet knew how good he was.

The second also was too much of a risk. He could make the CIA look stupid. Sending him to the home of whisky would probably be too much temptation. No, it had to be the retiree, a last job before hanging up his spurs. He had worked in the office in various positions and had not handled his own case. He would be rusty and counting the time down, not making any waves until they handed him his check and gold watch. Brad had already sent his kill team. This investigator would only be window dressing to keep the director happy. He did not want this guy finding out too much about anything. He flicked the switch on the intercom and arranged for his secretary to call John Zelenski, brief him on his assignment, and then pack him off to Scotland.

***

I followed Sam off the beach with some difficulty. She marched ahead while I stumbled forward. I had little feeling in my feet, and the cold winter wind whipped round me like a blanket of ice. Just off the beach sat a little modern cottage. As I stumbled up the monobloc path, Sam put her elbow through the backdoor window and marched into the kitchen. I followed her in, too tired to argue and just glad to get out of that hellish wind. No one was home, and nothing worked, no lights or heating. The owner had obviously no plans to use the house at the moment, another one of the growing holiday home brigade.

The single bedroom cottage had only one double bed. Sam took charge again. "You need to get your clothes off and get under that duvet." I was still half-dazed and drowsy. My feet had started to burn from the cold, and my shoulder and hand were aching. I was sitting on the edge of the bed trying to get my shoes off with my good arm and hand when Sam walked past me completely naked. She stopped, bent down, and helped me undo my shoes. Then she climbed into the right side of the bed while I finished removing the rest of my sodden clothing and crawled into the other side of the bed. Sam turned round and snuggled into my back.

"Don't get any ideas. This is straight out of the textbook for dealing with hypothermia victims." I tried to reply, but in seconds, I was sound asleep.

I awoke the next morning to the sun streaming in through the bedroom window. Every muscle in my body ached, and it took some time for my eyes to become accustomed to the bright sunlight. Sam to my surprise was sitting on the end of the bed fully dressed. She had been up for some time and had all the wet clothes on the windowsill to dry. She was sitting, staring at me, saying nothing. It was as if she was trying to make her mind up about something. Suddenly, she broke her silence. "You are not what I was expecting. It must be hard for you to live up to your reputation. You are not at all the person Neil described. You are far too normal!"

I sat up. Sam had placed some of my clothes from the rucksack on the floor next to the bed. To my surprise, they were dry. The rucksack must have had a watertight compartment. I looked around the room. It was barren other than a bedside table with Sam's silenced Glock in pride of place on top of it.

"So is being normal a bad thing? What did you expect me to be?" Sam's grey eyes never flickered, and she continued to stare at me as I began to dress.

"I was expecting a Scottish Rambo, your typical Special Forces hard man."

I pulled my T-shirt over my head a bit too energetically, causing the pain in my shoulder to return. "Sorry to disappoint you."

Sam jumped up off the bed and crossed to the window, studying the picture-postcard view of the south end of Arran in the distance. "I wouldn't worry. Hard men are not my type. I'm far too competitive. I either want to beat them or kill them. It's just my nature, so normal is fine, just a bit puzzling."

We made the bed and cleaned up any mess we had made, then left. With any luck, the break-in would not be found for a while, and if it were, they would probably put it down to a burglary, not to fugitives on the run. We had only walked half a mile when a local bus on its way to Campbeltown stopped by our side. The driver asked if we needed a lift to town, and we accepted gladly. Sam paid the fare from the last stop, and we sat on the passenger side, surveying the coastal scenery as we headed into town.

I couldn't remember the last time I had eaten and put it to Sam that we needed food first. It didn't take much persuading. Sam was as hungry as I was, and when the bus arrived in town, we headed for the local supermarket and sat in window seats in the cafeteria. I wolfed down bacon rolls and mugs of coffee, and then polished off a jam donut, much to Sam's disgust. She nibbled on her cereal bar then downed two yogurts and a bottle of mineral water. We talked about trivial things to start with. Then I brought up the subject of her last mission. "Neil told me at our last meeting that he was sending for you, but you had unfinished business in Argentina. Can you tell me about it, or would you have to shoot me?"

Sam stopped in midswig, putting down her mineral water. Yet again her grey eyes pierced mine. It was somewhat unsettling. She was obviously deciding if she would spill the beans to me, or if she just going to shoot me anyway. She was hard to read, and that was probably why she was a good agent.

"I was sent to assassinate an army general who was whipping up support for a second invasion of the Falkland Islands." She continued to gaze at me, gauging my reaction to this revelation.

"Did you complete your mission?"

Her features were cast in stone. "I have never failed on a mission yet. He died of an alleged heart attack." She took another swig of her water and looked away across the car park.

"How did you manage that one, and how many missions have you had?"

She squirmed in her seat and looked out across the car park again. She looked like she was having a flashback to the situation. "Befriend him, get close to him, get him to drop his guard, then two drops of a chemical in his wine, and it was good night, Vienna. And to answer your second question, I've lost count. Lots of missions."

"Do you ever have to sleep with your target to gain their trust?"

Her head shot back round, and the stare she gave me was more piercing and deadlier than before. "Whatever it takes."

She got up and walked across to get the bill. I decided the last question I had asked was a step too far and decided to leave it at that for the moment. We left the supermarket. Sam went back to I'm-in-charge mode again. "We are going to walk back the way we came in, toward Torrisdale. I spotted the guesthouse on the hill on the right on the way in on the bus. We need to get in character. Remember, we are meant to be newlyweds, so you can carry the rucksack and walk with your arm around me—and try to look like you are having the time of your life.

When we get to the Sandy Beach Guesthouse, let me do all the talking. I will be the chatty bride and you will be the strong, silent type, OK?"

Ten minutes walk and we were at the white pillars of the entrance of the Sandy Beach Guesthouse. The steep, winding drive led up to a big white Victorian-style house overlooking Campbeltown Loch, with a commanding view of the town. It all looked a bit Basil Fawlty to me, but I decided to stick with Sam's wishes and keep my mouth shut.

Sam pulled the knob emblazoned with the word "Bell" and a proper bell started ringing somewhere in the house. It sounded more like there was a town crier in the house. The door flew open on the third set of chimes, and a small fat woman with rosy cheeks stood in the doorway. By the look of her, we had caught her mid-baking session. Her apron was covered in flour, and she was cleaning her hands on it as she spoke to Sam.

I stood quietly while Sam went into full Oscar mode. "Hi, I am Ann Smith—sorry, Ann Hunter. We spoke on the phone yesterday. This is my husband, Alan. Sorry about the name thing. I haven't got used to the new one yet. We are a bit early I know, but we had no choice. The nice AA man dropped us off. We had planned to do a bit of sightseeing before we got here, but when the car broke down, we had no option but to cadge a lift from the AA man."

Sam bombarded the landlady with chat, feeding her our cover story. Mrs. Hatton was an English lady who had moved up from London when her husband had taken early retirement from the Bank of England. She showed us around the house pointing out all the relevant points. We followed hand in hand, playing to the audience. We eventually ended up at the door to our bedroom suite.

Mrs. Hatton opened the door and showed us the massive room. "We keep this room free normally. It's usually only booked for special occasions, but as you poor dears have had such bad luck, and it is your honeymoon, I thought you would like to have it instead of the room you originally booked. What about your luggage? That bag you have can't be all you have, surely."

Sam slipped her arm around my waist as she spoke. "No, it's in the car, but the AA guy had no room in his van for it, so we just grabbed a few things for a couple of days until we go for the car."

I slipped my arm around Sam's waist and devilment came into my head. I placed my hand on Sam's right buttock. I could feel her body tense, but she showed no outward sign of her awkwardness. Mrs. Hatton decided she had outstayed her welcome, and as she was closing the door behind her, she announced if we wanted a meal or anything else just to call in at the kitchen.

Just as the door clicked shut, the blow hit me in the sternum. Perfectly placed below my rib cage, it winded me so badly that I was seeing stars before my eyes and had to sit down on the chair by the door to regain my composure.

"Don't ever try that again, or the next time I will break your neck. I'm going for a shower." She unpacked the Glocks and put them in the top drawer of the unit by the bed, grabbed some things from the rucksack, and headed for the en suite.

"Sam, I was only acting out the part. I am sorry if I pissed you off. I was only teasing you a bit."

There was no reply from the en suite, just the sound of the shower going on. I wandered round the room, looking out over the bay and checking out the room. To my amusement, the king-size bed was a waterbed. I collapsed on it. It gave way under my weight. Then I proceeded to bounce on it and roll on it, until the novelty wore off. Sam emerged from the en suite and started drying her hair. Then she began applying makeup with military precision.

I watched from the bed. Until then, I had taken little notice of my new partner in crime—there had been no time to study her. She was reasonably tall for a woman. I put her age at around thirty and her height at five-elevenish. She was not skinny and had a fine pair of hips, but now that I was looking at her with only a towel wrapped around her, I could see the defined muscle tone on both her arms and legs. Her physical fitness was not in question. She worked her body hard.

She did not have the raw beauty of Mary or the pretty girl-next-door looks of Kay, but she had that something you could not put your finger on, and her eyes were mesmerizing. I wondered how many men had looked into them just before they had met their fate. It was like looking into the eyes of a tiger, beautiful but deadly. Sam combed her shoulder-length blond hair into a ponytail and came round to the opposite side of the bed to sit down. I had forgotten for the moment about the waterbed and remembered only as she started to sit down.

It was too late. Expecting to sit on a firm surface, she fell backward. The whole bed sagged, and as I rolled toward the centre, we both rolled into each other. I braced myself for the next round of punches, but to my surprise, Sam actually smiled at me and rolled over onto her stomach next to me.

"You knew about the bed and said nothing. That was dirty. You are meant to be an officer and a gentleman, not trying to get me into bed."

I smiled and turned on my side, propping my head up with my hand facing Sam. "For your information, madam, I waited so long for you to come out of the shower that I forgot all about the bed until you collapsed on it. I had no devious plan to seduce you, although you do clean up rather well, and I may have to rethink that strategy."

Sam slipped under the covers and removed the towel before launching it at my head. "Go for a shower, you horrible, smelly man."

She was only joking, but I decided to comply. I had enough war wounds without her adding to them further.

CHAPTER FIVE

The Hunt

The US Air Force C130 cargo plane circled Glasgow Airport, waiting for permission to land. The navigator approached Agent Zelenski, who was sitting forward of the cargo area. He informed Zelenski that they were about to land and that a police vehicle was waiting to pick him up and take him to Arran.

John Zelenski was a naturally inquisitive person and quizzed the navigator about why they were not using their own base on the mainland and transferring him by patrol boat. The navigator explained that the base was engaged in a search-and-rescue mission for missing fishermen and wanted the base left free. The truth was that Brad Whiteford had given strict instructions that Zelenski was not to be given access to the air base at any cost. The last thing he needed was more trouble across the water.

As Zelenski's military flight touched down at Glasgow Airport, a privately chartered Gulfstream was touching down at Machrihanish air base. On board were Aron Fletcher and his team of mercenaries. The team was missing one member—Areli Benesch was not with them. She was still on her way from Hong Kong where she had been dealing with a Triad warlord who was getting too big for his boots. The Chinese were not afraid to fight fire with fire and had hired Areli to remove him, which she had accomplished with ease. She had arranged to meet up with the team in Scotland two days later than their planned arrival. Waiting for Fletcher's team were two hired black Range Rovers, both with blacked-out windows.

Waiting impatiently in one of the hangars was Merlin. He had good reason to be impatient, for his trip from London had not been in vain. On arrival he had been shown the image from the downed surveillance drone. His heart missed a beat when he saw the image. He was probably one of the few men in the world that could put a name to that face—Mac. The last time he had seen this face was many years ago, in a picture from Mary O'Conner's funeral. In the picture, an unknown man stood next to Neil Andrews. Merlin had been curious, as after all, he was who had sent her to her death. After a bit of digging about, he had found out it was a man the Irish called "the Mac." He had turned the UK upside down to try and find this Mac, but all files on him were missing. He had vanished into thin air, and until the moment the drone picture appeared, he had never been seen or heard of again.

Aron Fletcher and his team loaded both vehicles with their gear his was not the type of equipment you could get through customs, so the air base had worked out perfectly. Fletcher took a stroll through the hangar with Merlin. He gave Fletcher a note with his mobile number on it and told him to contact him if he needed any help. He then went onto the more pressing subject of "the Mac." Merlin handed over a dozen photos of Mac's face. "Listen, my good chap. This gentleman is not to be taken lightly. He was a member of the Special Forces working for MI6 in Ireland. The havoc he caused in that country was outrageous. He was a specialist in bombs and is as slippery as an eel. Be on your guard. The other person in the attack on your agents in Arran is suspected of being a woman. She tried to disguise the way she walks, but a specialist has studied the satellite images of the attack that night and is sure it is a woman. Here are some files I have collated on women working for MI6. She may or may not be one of them."

Fletcher took the files and started to walk back to the vehicles, which were now loaded and ready to ship out. He climbed on board the lead Range Rover and Merlin closed the door. "Toodle pip and happy hunting, old boy."

Both 4x4s pulled out of the base. Ed Holts drove the lead car. "Who was that asshole?"

Fletcher shook his head and smiled. "That, my good friend, is our contact in the UK, and you are right. He is an asshole." Fletcher handed out the pictures and studied the files on the woman while Ed set course for a town called Stirling, where they would spend the night before traveling to the ferry for Arran.

Fletcher was deep in thought over Merlin's warnings about this man called "the Mac." If he served in Ireland during the troubles, he must be in his late thirties, early forties. Now, if he were having to tow a girl agent around with him, he wouldn't be too much trouble when they found him. It would be over quickly, and Fletcher would be two million better off.

***

Sam was nowhere to be found when I emerged from the en suite. I had opted for the bath instead of the shower and had lost all track of time bathing my battle-scarred body. I dressed quickly and went in hunt of my newly acquired wife. She was on the front steps of the house, deep in conversation with Mrs. Hatton. When I poked my head out the door, she went back into Oscar mode. "There you are, honey. I was beginning to think you had drowned in the bath. Mrs. H has kindly said we can borrow her niece's and nephew's mountain bikes so we can go and explore, as we don't have a car."

Mrs. Hatton set sail across the front lawn like woman possessed. She had seen the local fishmonger and was waving him down, presumably to order fish for the evening meal. I seized the opportunity, took Sam's hand, and walked round the side of the house. "What is the deal with the bikes? Have you forgotten it is November? And we don't have any cycling gear."

Sam knew this was going to be a hard sell—it showed in her expression. "I want to take a look at the air base while we are here."

I stopped her midsentence. "Are you completely out of your tiny mind? No! No way, that would be suicide. I made the mistake of listening to one stupid female before and almost paid for it with my life. I was just on holiday, and now everybody is trying to kill me, including you."

Sam's face said it all. "You were on holiday? What do you mean? Are you telling me you were not assigned to this case by MI6?" She looked horrified.

"Sam, I am a member of the public, whose newly acquired girl-friend was fed misinformation by the British secret service to get her to do their dirty work for them. I am a retired soldier and Kay was a doctor of marine biology at Dundee University."

For a second, Sam's face was a picture of pure rage. Then she took control of herself and calmed down. "Adam, I am sorry. Neil gave me the impression that you were working for him. I am sorry for being a bitch. You go and put your feet up and have a coffee. I will see you for dinner." She turned and wheeled one of the bikes out of the gate.

"Wait, where you are going?"

She looked back and smiled. "I told you where I was going." And she was gone.

For a second, I stood in a dilemma. Then I was off. I ran upstairs, pulled on trainers, a fleece, my false specs, and Kay's blue baseball cap, jumped on the second mountain bike, and set out after Sam. What was I doing? This was beyond madness, but I knew I had a much better idea of the layout of the base. I left town quickly, but Sam was nowhere in sight. I changed up to top gear and got the head down. As I approached the junction on the left, busy checking the red MOD signs for Machrihanish, two black Range Rovers pulled up at the junction. The front windows were down in both cars, revealing some nasty-looking characters inside. Then, as quick as they were there, they were gone.

Something bothered me about my encounter. They didn't look the right clientele for Range Rovers, and the chances of finding two such cars on this winding country lane was remote. Another two junctions to the left, and I was in front of the civilian side of the base, called Campbeltown Air Terminal. Still, Sam was nowhere to be seen. I cycled into the car park, but she was not there. Only four cars were in the car park—a big black Vauxhall, a Land Rover with a snowplough, an old battered Chevette that had more hits than the Beatles, and a lovely old Rover 3.5 Litre. I decided to wait for a bit to see if my partner would appear.

As I sat waiting, I chuckled to myself. Whoever had parked the lovely old Rover was a brave man. The Chevette from hell was parked right against it. I could imagine some youth jumping in the old Chevette and whacking the side of the shiny black Rover. Then a voice from behind me startled me. It was Sam who had apparently cycled up from the military side of the base, the side closest to the Irish Sea.

"Do you never do what you're told, Mr. Hunter?"

I smiled and made it look to the casual observer as if we were having fun. "Sam, the big black Vauxhall is exactly the same type as the CIA agents used on Arran. Did you see anything down at the military end of the base?"

Sam had her back turned to the base, presumably so no one could read her lips. "No, but it is like Fort Knox down there. All approach roads to that big hangar have double security gates, probably automatic. There don't seem to be any personnel wandering about, which ties in with your theory about the radiation. Speaking of which, let's get out of here before we start to glow in the dark."

We started to head back to Campbeltown before the light started to fade. On the way back, Sam pointed out the lack of wildflowers around the base, then told me that when I was in the bath, she had borrowed the house computer and looked up the effects of radiation at Chernobyl, one of which was the death of wildflowers, in particular, bluebells.

We cycled along silently, each deep in our own thoughts, Sam broke the silence by bursting out in laughter. "Adam, I owe you another apology, The Land Rover I torched was actually your own car, not a pool car from the firm. No wonder you were pissed at me. By the way, did you see the two Range Rovers that left from the military side of the base, complete with some dodgy characters in them? I think we will change our plans and get out of here tomorrow."

Back at the guesthouse we just had time for a quick shower before the evening meal was served, and as expected, Mrs. Hatton had managed to catch the fishmonger and had served up homemade fish and chips. The chips were hand-cut, large and chunky; the fish was the size of a house and served with garden peas. Sam left the chips and peeled the batter off the fish, electing to only eat some fish and peas. I wondered as I nibbled at the fish what a Geiger counter would have made of the meal. We retired early to bed, which would probably have been expected of newlyweds anyway. I could sense an awkward moment coming as we began to undress. I thought I would head it off at the pass and asked Sam if she wanted me to sleep in the chair.

Sam stripped all her clothes off and slid into bed. "Adam, don't be stupid. We don't know where we will sleep tomorrow, so get in the bed. You need a good night's sleep. Don't worry. I won't touch you." She smiled, turned over on her side, and switched off her bedside lamp.

Sam shook me awake the next morning. She had been up for some time and had already crammed in a run, breakfast, and a shower. She had my breakfast on a tray and was impatient to get going. "Eat your breakfast while I tell you what we are going to do next. First we are going to catch the bus down at the terminal. It leaves at ten thirty for Glasgow. We get off at Tyndrum. We are going to join the West Highland Way and hike for a few miles to the Bridge of Orchy Hotel. I have phoned and booked two single rooms in different names. Tomorrow we will catch a train from Bridge of Orchy station to Morar."

I sat munching on my toast, trying not to get crumbs in the bed, and trying to wake up and take in the instructions that had just been barked at me.

"And what is in this Morar place that we need to cross half the world to get to?"

She had a sly smile on her face. "That you will just have to find out when you get there."

I continued munching on my toast, thinking over what Sam had just said. Sam wandered across to the wardrobe letting the dressing gown fall to the floor as she began to pull on a pair of lacy pants.

"Sam, I would appreciate it if you warned me before you wander about in the nude. It's not good for a man's blood pressure at this time of the morning, and come to think of it, it's not good for my blood pressure at any time of the day. Why are we running away up north? Why are we not calling in the cavalry? Where are Neil and his usual entourage of heavies?"

Sam's smile vanished. "Adam, I wanted to get you out of danger before I told you this. I was going to tell you yesterday, but when you told me you don't work for Neil, it threw me. On my way to help you, Neil contacted me, told me to abandon the operation, and return to headquarters for my next assignment. It was effectively signing your death warrant. I didn't want to tell you. I know you were good friends." Sam continued to dress in silence. I placed the breakfast tray on the dressing table and wandered across to the en suite. I had suddenly lost my appetite.

***

The big black Range Rover sat outside the ferry terminal building. Lukas Richter and Marcus Laine sat in the front seats surveying the latest arrivals from the ferry. Richter was used to stake-out situations, having been involved in many German police operations over the years, but Marcus Laine was a very different animal. He was normally a loner and did his best work by himself. It was only the million-dollar paycheck that kept him there. To him, sitting there waiting for the targets to fall into their hands was like a fisherman standing in the river with no rod, waiting for the salmon to jump in his pocket. Fletcher and Ed Holts had crossed over earlier that morning and were on the island looking for leads.

John Zelenski, the CIA investigator, was already one step ahead. He had been given a Strathclyde police sergeant and driver to help with his inquiries and was on his way to the shack. The local police had been told to close the farm road off but not to investigate the house until an American investigator had arrived. En route to the shack, the somewhat overweight, ruddy-faced sergeant had tried to make conversation with Zelenski, asking what department he was with. Zelenski was less than forthcoming with information, simply saying he worked for the government. When they arrived at the shack, they found it open. Zelenski surveyed the devastation in the kitchen and asked his escorts to search the place for bodies. The big sergeant marched in and looked around the room until his eyes took in the wall splattered with blood and brains.

"Jesus Christ, what happened here, then? It's worse than the Barrowlands Ballroom on a Saturday night!"

They were just finishing their search when an out-of-breath constable appeared at the door. "Sergeant, you better go and have a look. They have found a car at the foot of a cliff three miles away. The local shepherd says it has a body in it."

An hour later, Zelenski arrived at the foot of the cliff. Accompanied by his driver and the shepherd, they had zigzagged their way down to the crushed Vauxhall. The tall CIA agent's body was halfway out the window and staring at them with dull, lifeless eyes. His neck and lower jaw had been smashed and could well have been caused by the accident. Zelenski took some pictures of the scene and used a pad connected to his mobile phone to take the dead body's fingerprints. These were then sent down the line to Langley. This intrigued the constable with him. He was amazed by the gadget, and he was even more amazed when Zelenski received a text two minutes later with all the deceased driver's details. Apparently, the driver was Al Koslowski, a diplomat on vacation. Zelenski quizzed the shepherd about the road. Had any other cars in his memory ended up down here? What were the road conditions? Had he seen this car before? Had he seen anybody unusual around this area lately? All his questions were to no avail, however.

As he was speaking to the shepherd, the constable was on the radio to one of his colleagues, shaking his head in disbelief. Zelenski called him across and asked him what the problem was.

"Oh, nothing to do with this, sir. It's just that for years, nothing happens on Arran. Then all of a sudden everything goes mad. That's another body found, and what're the chances of that on a wee island? Somebody committed suicide along the coast. The local boys tell me that is the second suicide this week. It's worse than the telly."

"Right, constable, let's go. I need to see this so-called suicide because this gentleman was on vacation with a friend, and I am not a fan of coincidences."

The big police Volvo estate pulled up outside Kay's little cottage and parked behind the local bobbies' Astra. Between the house and the outhouse sat the remains of the burnt-out Land Rover. The scene was not a pretty one. The gruesome half-skeletal body of the dead man was in the driver's seat. Zelenski spoke to both the officers and asked if either had had much experience with burned bodies. The big sergeant had seen it all, so Zelenski asked him to help with the identification progress. He took a few snaps of the situation, but fingerprinting was not going to work. When he explained what he wanted the sergeant to do, the big man went pale at the thought but did as he was asked. He held open the victim's lower jaw, allowing Zelenski to take a close- up picture of the dead man's teeth. The smell of burned flesh was almost unbearable, and both men gagged as they performed their grisly task. The results took ten minutes to come back this time. Zelenski used this time to examine the surrounding area.

Meanwhile, the local constable came up to him and tried to give him his take on the situation. "Sir, if you don't mind me saying, I think you are barking up the wrong tree. This man was a friend of the lady of this house, who only last week took her own life. He obviously had feelings for her. Many witnesses say they were an item. Possibly he couldn't live without her, and that's why he took his own life, nothing to do with the American gentleman who crashed the car."

Zelenski gave him a cold stare and asked him to follow him to the burnt-out vehicle. "Well done, Sherlock, but just before you wrap this case up and head for your local pub to tell all your buddies about how you solved another case, pray tell me why the skull between the eye sockets is missing and a huge portion of the rear skull is also missing? A pattern that is consistent with a bullet between the eyes. Furthermore, constable, I am willing to wager my last pay packet that the blood and bone samples that I have just found sprayed all over a wall in the house I have just come from match this man, which also means that there is a very good chance that the terrible American driver was murdered as well."

Just then, his phone chimed to tell him he had a text. He stopped and examined his phone. "As I thought, this gentleman was Brent Franklyn, also a diplomat on leave."

Zelenski left the local police to arrange for the cleanup of the three sites he had visited. On the way back to his hotel, he went over in his head what he would be writing in his report that evening.

He knew the two dead men were CIA and had been careful not to let anybody local know this. Also, the marks on the driver's neck were not caused by the car. The damaged area was too wide and by the looks of things had occurred prior to the accident. In his opinion, they had both been killed at the house, then moved for some reason. He had also noticed that the lock to the garage door had been shot off. He had lifted the shell casings for further tests, and tomorrow he would start asking the locals a few questions.

Fletcher was passed the information that Zelenski had found out at almost the same time as Zelenski received it. He had also some luck with the picture of the man. They had stopped for fuel in Blackwaterfoot, and the kid serving the petrol recognized the man in the picture. He had served him a few times and had repaired a tyre for him. He didn't know were he was from, but he did not stay in the village, and the boy had not seen him for days. Fletcher gave the kid his mobile number and a fifty-pound note and told him if he saw him again to call the number right away and it would be worth another fifty-pound note.

***

By midafternoon, Sam and I were north of Tyndrum on the West Highland Way, about four miles south of the Bridge of Orchy Hotel, which sat next to the railway station and was a popular stop-off point for walkers on the West Highland Way.

We had bought lunch and a second rucksack in Tyndrum and had spread the load between the two rucksacks. I had said very little on the journey. Sam had tried sparking up conversation, but I was not in the mood for discussions about the beauty of our surroundings or what we were going to have for supper.

She tried a more direct approach. "Adam, I don't think Neil would abandon you like that. There must be some reason for his actions. He has stood by you many times, so it makes no sense that he was going to leave you for the wolves." Sam was watching me and waiting for a response.

I looked down at my feet as we trudged over the frozen gravel path. "If you had been at our last meeting, Sam, you would have seen a reason for leaving me to fend for myself. I tried to talk Neil out of sending Kay to get readings from the air base, but when he refused, I lost my temper and threatened Neil's life if anything happened to Kay"

Sam shook her head and studied the huge, white-capped mountain on her right. "Only you would threaten to kill the deputy director of MI6. You are a nutter, but I don't think Neil will have taken you too seriously. No, there is something going on here that we don't know yet."

I stopped walking for a second, staring at the mountainside. Just below the summit, there was movement. I pointed out to Sam the deer moving down to lower pastures for winter. Together we counted twelve deer.

"Come on. We better keep moving, or we will be late for supper. So if you were given orders to terminate this mission, why are you still here?"

Sam walked along; she was staring straight ahead, trying to think of something to say. "I am not completely sure about all the reasons, but I couldn't let one of our real-life heroes get killed knowing I had walked away from the job, and you are Neil's friend. I was kind of doing it for him too. I was curious about you, and I wanted to meet you. I had heard so much about you from Neil and Mary. I didn't tell you it was Mary who trained me when I first started, did I?"

I did not respond immediately, as I was trying to think if Mary had ever mentioned Sam. "I think you are pushing it a bit too far when you compare me to a hero. Most of the time, I was just doing my job."

The white building in the distance had to be the Bridge of Orchy Hotel. It was in the middle of nowhere. Big snowy clouds had started to form over the mountains, and even as we walked we could feel the temperature starting to drop. We were going to get to the hotel just in the nick of time. This was not a terrain you wanted to be on if it started to snow. The weather could change in the blink of an eye.

"You may not know this, Adam, but like it or not, in military circles, you are a hero. Did you know Neil blocked you from being awarded the DSO in the Gulf War? He had to do it to protect your identity after the carry-on in Ireland. Although you were never recognized for it, some people involved in the operation reckon it should have been the Victoria Cross. Adam, do you know how many DSOs were awarded during the Gulf War? Not many. Your files were destroyed, so I have only heard rumours about the mission. Care to fill me in on the details? Just to pass the time until we get to the hotel."

We could see clearly now where the trail came down to the railway and crossed over. On the other side of the rail tracks ran the main road between Stirling at one end and Fort William at the other. The hotel was situated at the roadside, opposite the railway. "Sam, we are just about there. It's a long story, so it will have to wait for another time, I'm afraid. Let's go and get cleaned up for dinner. I'm starving."

We both checked in separately, Sam opting for a drink at the bar while I checked in. Later we met in the bar for a drink.

We also decided to eat separately, Sam in the dining room while I had my meal in my room. We agreed to meet at 10:45 a.m. at the train station and grab the train to Malaig in the morning, so it would be an early night for us both.

I polished off a large sirloin steak and all the trimmings and to pass the time, busied myself with stripping the Glock and cleaning it. Whoever had owned it previously had badly neglected it.

***

Zelenski had started his investigation with the village closest to the house where the second victim was found. He had wandered around the little hamlet of Machrie and found very few people at home. He wandered up to the little farm shop and restaurant and bumped into the old lady who was just about to leave. He was happy to find she was a natural chatterbox and even happier when she confirmed she knew the girl who stayed at the cottage. She had also met her "gentleman friend," as she put it. She had been shocked when she heard that Kay

Miller had committed suicide. It was her friend who had called and asked her to call the police. But the biggest revelation was when she told him that the pair of them had been restoring a boat in the shed. Kay had called her the morning before she died to say she was taking the boat on a trip to the far side of Machrihanish to study sea life and if she wasn't back for lunch the next day, to contact the coast guard.

Zelenski thanked the old lady and left. By pure chance, his next stop was Blackwaterfoot, as the police driver needed fuel for the police car. While the driver was filling the car up, he took the time to speak to the kid blowing a tyre up at the door. He was some what flabbergasted to find that another American had been there yesterday and had asked the same questions. He was even more surprised that the other American had shown the kid a picture of a person he was looking for.

Zelenski was not the desk jockey that his boss thought. Indeed, he had only taken the desk job to appease his wife, who had suffered a nervous breakdown some years ago. Up until his transfer to the CIA desk, he had been a rather successful FBI field agent. He was no fool, and he was starting to smell something bad about this case. Not only was there somebody else investigating his case, but the details of the burnt-out Land Rover had come back with a false name and address for the owner. Also, his brother-in-law, who still worked at the FBI, had informed him that at the same time the attack on the agents in Arran happened, most of the computers at the Pentagon as well as at the FBI had failed. The shit had hit the fan, and the CIA had been told to find out what was going on. Zelenski called Langley and spoke to a member of the computer division, calling in a favour he was due.

His contact confirmed grudgingly that the virus had started from the Arran agent's computer, but he had never told him this, or Whiteford would have him shot.

Zelenski sat in the back of the police Volvo, trying to make sense of it all. He was trying to put a jigsaw puzzle together. The problem was, he was pretty sure somebody was hiding some of the pieces. If the majority of the defense computer network was hit by a cyber attack threatening the security of the nation, would you send one investigator? No. So why was he here when clearly there was another team looking who knew more than him, and why withhold the information about the cyber attack? Brad Whiteford clearly knew about it, but although it was Whiteford who had sent him, he had said nothing. Zelenski decided to set a trap to see if anybody would take the bait. He contacted Whiteford directly and informed him that he had talked to a woman who had told him the suspected fugitives had left the island by boat, and that first thing in the morning, he would go to the cottage and check to see if the boat were still there and confirm the woman's story. It was a wild guess, but Zelenski, whether right or wrong, used it to hopefully flush out whoever was behind the second search team.

At around four thirty, the big black Range Rover, its side lamps on, pulled up outside the old cottage. Aron Fletcher and Ed Holts got out and headed straight toward the old boathouse. Halfway there in the gloom, Holts stumbled on a rock in the semidarkness and almost fell. Fletcher shouted to him, "Holts, are you OK, pal?" Holts just cursed and kept going. On arrival at the boathouse, they found the doors wide open and no boat in sight. Out in the water, the top of the boat trailer was visible as the tide receded. Fletcher stared across the stretch of water to the mainland and the lights of Campbeltown.

"Jesus, we have been sitting here like dummies while they are halfway to China. Get a map and find out where that is over there. Then get Benesch on the cell and tell her to get across there and start flashing that picture to everybody who is breathing. Let's hope the trail isn't cold."

"Don't worry, Fletch. The Israeli bitch will find them. She is a true piece of work, pal." The big Range Rover left in a hurry, its occupants busily reorganizing their plans.

A few seconds after they left, high above the cottage on the bench at the cliff top, Zelenski popped out his note pad and wrote down: "Israeli woman Benesch, Yank Holts, Yank Fletch." In the darkness, he was almost invisible. He sat smiling to himself. He had just found another two pieces of the jigsaw.

Areli Benesch had hired a car using fake ID. She had been on her way from Glasgow Airport when she got the call from Holts to head for Campbeltown. She pulled into the first lay-by and reset the satnav for Campbeltown. She also took the opportunity to open the package from Fletcher that the courier had given her at the airport. It contained more fake IDs and her weapon of choice—a SIG Sauer Pro 9 mm, six spare clips of ammo, and a silencer. Also in the pack were two custom, handmade throwing knives. She felt more at home now. She always felt naked without some sort of weapon.

Two hours later, she was out in the Scottish countryside and decided to stop in a deserted lay-by to rest and grab something to eat. She walked across the heather-clad moor. About a hundred metres away sat a lonely fence post. Areli headed toward it, stretching as she went.

On arrival at the post, she took one last bite at the apple she had been eating and placed it on top of the post. Then, she fought her way back through the heather to the car. She proceeded to fit the silencer to the SIG and load a clip into the handle. She studied her surroundings, and after was sure no one was close by, she nudged the safety off and took aim at the apple. She fired once and the apple jumped in the air. Her second shot hit it in midair. Suddenly there was movement to Areli's left. She swung round and in the same movement brought the gun to bear on the target. She fired twice in rapid succession. There was an explosion of feathers, and the two grouse that had just taken flight crashed to the ground, stone dead. Areli reset the safety and removed the silencer. She was happy with the weapon. It felt good, and she felt at ease with its operation. She was still the best shot Mossad had ever trained.

***

The train arrived in Malaig just before two in the afternoon. Sam announced we were here, which was not a surprise, as this was the end of the line. We disembarked and wandered out of the station. Sam seemed to be trying to make up her mind about the next move. Suddenly she was off across the road to the local petrol station. She vanished into the office and a few minutes later appeared with who was presumably the owner-cum-mechanic-cum-salesman. He was a balding, chubby gentleman decked out in blue overalls that had never seen a drop of oil. Sam walked him across to the old Land Rover that sat on the forecourt. As she passed me, she winked at me mischievously.

The old pile of junk had a for-sale sign on the windscreen that proclaimed it had tax and was MOT'd. Sam set about trying to get the price down, and to my horror, she agreed if the sales gent agreed to fill the tank with fuel, she would give him two thousand pounds cash for it, as we had a long journey in front of us.

She added her husband had always wanted a Land Rover. The sales gent caught my eye at that point and smiled at me, I was forced to return the smile, pretending I was over the moon at my wife's gift. The salesman scurried off to count the cash and get the logbook before we could change our minds. Sam gave the salesman a big kiss when he reappeared and tossed me the keys. We filled the tank, and we were off. The fuel gauge didn't work. I could see the road under the throttle pedal and the wheezy petrol engine was only slightly faster than a farm tractor, but the worst thing by far was the smell—a mixture of hot gearbox oil and cow shit.

CHAPTER SIX
The Glass House

Sam started to give me directions and after a few miles started rummaging through her rucksack. We had just passed Morar, and the next sign proclaimed Arisaig, two miles. She told me to slow down and take the unmarked left turn. This was easier said than done, as the brakes on the old girl were worse than the bodywork. The road turned through three hundred and sixty degrees and passed under the main road, through a tunnel. The single-track road climbed steadily for a mile and a half until a house came into view on the horizon. Sam told me go straight up to the house. As we got closer, it began to get more and more impressive. It was a very large two-story building, facing out to sea and perched on top of the hill overlooking the islands of Rum, Eigg, and Muck, with beautiful, white sandy beaches below. The front of the house was made completely of black smoked glass. Even the balcony and garage doors were smoked glass. This had to be a millionaire's pad, but as we pulled up, Sam pressed a button on a remote she had been searching for, and one of the garage doors glided smoothly inward. I nosed the old Land Rover into the spacious garage. Parked in the next bay was a silver BMW M5. As I switched the old girl off, the door silently closed behind me. I was speechless. Surely this wasn't Sam's, but there was no way it was a safe house either.

Sam climbed a wrought-iron spiral staircase in the corner of the garage and shouted down to me if I didn't fancy the stairs, there was a lift in the far corner. Sam was loving this and was taking great pleasure in adding to my amazement. I decided to take the lift and ended up in a spacious black marble kitchen, I estimated the kitchen alone would have given you no change from a hundred grand. As I was examining the kitchen, there was a swishing noise, and the wall opposite the lift started folding away, revealing a open-plan, sunken living room with bespoke black-leather suites built into the walls, all facing outward for a view of the islands.

Even in late November, the view was breathtaking. I could only imagine what it would be like on a beautiful summer's day. And just to add to the effect, the smoked glass balcony outside was three steps down so it did not impede the view.

"My god, Sam, this house must have cost a fortune to build. It must be in the millions."

Sam wandered across and handed me a glass filled with a dark-looking liquid. "It's vodka and cola, just a better brand than you had at the hotel, and yes, you are right. It was millions, seventeen million to be precise. Cheers."

I wandered around trying to take in my surroundings while Sam bombarded me with facts and figures about the German-designed HUF house we were standing in. A view from the rear window showed banks of solar panels set into the ground to the rear of the house, which were only visible from above. Further back and to the right, two wind turbines rotated. Sam explained that the house was completely self-sufficient. An underground bunker below the wind turbines contained the electrical storage area, which was also fed by the solar panels. This in turn powered the house.

Sam led me on a tour of the house. Upstairs was a living area, eating area, and two double bedrooms with en suites. Downstairs was the double garage / hall, a full-sized gym, a utility room, and a bathroom. The basement had been cut from pure stone and contained an office, a sauna, and a large storage room. The next room Sam was obviously very proud of. It had originally been a ten-pin bowling alley that had run the length of the house, but the bowling apparatus had been removed, and in its place was an all-singing, all-dancing, computer-controlled shooting range. She explained that the room had been fully soundproofed. The solid stone walls surrounding it helped to absorb the noise. Sam admitted this was the only room in the house that she had designed.

We were both in need of food, so our next stop was the kitchen. A search through Sam's fridge and cupboard proved one thing—Sam was a better shot than a cook. Sam went for a bath while I tried to rustle up some sort of meal. Most of the food was in tins, but there were some frozen items in the fridge.

Portions of chicken looked like the best option, and an hour later we sat down to my version of sweet-and-sour chicken and noodles. It lacked a few ingredients that I did not have, but it was passable, and we washed it down with more of the very potent vodka. We retired to the lounge. It was pitch black outside. Sam clicked a button and blinds sped along the windows noiselessly from either side. To my amusement, they were located between the three layers of triple glazing, and when they reached each other, they pivoted round, closing off the darkness completely.

Sam commented that this was her kind of blind, as it didn't have to be dusted. My comment was that was fine, but if it packed in, I wouldn't like the bill to strip out the window for repairs.

"Do you like the vodka, Adam?" Sam stared into her glass as she spoke. Again it was as if she were trying to decide whether to tell me something. "Adam, you are the only person I have ever shown this house to. No one, not even MI6, knows that it exists. It has no communications from it, so it cannot be traced. I come here when I need to get out of the rat race, and I knew I could come here if I ever need to vanish. Up until today, however, I have never needed to use it for that. We should be relatively safe here for the moment." Again she stared into her glass. There was a silence for a few seconds.

"Sam, how did you come by the house? You said you only designed the shooting range, so who did the rest?"

"I don't know why I am telling you all this, but I suppose I have started, so you better hear it all. The vodka that you are drinking belonged to the original owner of this house. She was the wife of a Russian drug lord, and the house was built to front a new Russian drug enterprise. The Russian market was getting too competitive, so a new venture was set up, bringing drugs into Britain. Russian trawlers would drop shipments of drugs in Iceland, and the drug lords bought a fleet of Icelandic fishing boats to transport and land their shipments of drugs at various ports on the west coast of Scotland under the guise of fishing. This house was the storage and distribution centre for Scotland. The drugs were then shipped to London for distribution; this was a problem more for MI5 than us, until Interpol tipped us off that the Russians had started using the route to get KGB agents into the UK. I was given the assignment to eliminate the wife and bodyguards while one of my colleagues went to Russia to eliminate the drug lord. There was to be no come-back on the government, so it had to look like an accident. The drug lord was hit by a lorry, which left his wife. She also had a car accident, and unfortunately, it got a bit messy. I shot out the rear tyres of her Mercedes as her bodyguard was taking a bend at speed. He lost control, but instead of flying off the road as planned, the car crossed onto the wrong side of the road just as a fuel tanker started to pull out from a lay-by."

Sam was visibly shaking. She was having problems continuing with her story. She looked up into my eyes, and I saw that her eyes were filling up with tears. "Adam, why did he have to pull out that second? I could do nothing. It was too late. They all died in the explosion. They wouldn't have known about it. I had to make it look like an accident, but why did he pull out? A few more seconds was all it needed. I followed my orders. Can you see, Adam? I had to do it, and you can't plan everything. It was an accident."

With some effort she managed to pull herself together. She took a large slurp from the vodka. "The tanker driver was only twenty-nine. He had his eight-year-old son with him, and he left a wife and two-month-old daughter. I hate this fucking job sometimes." Sam stood up, came across to where I was sitting, and sat next to me, wrapping her arms around me.

I was unsure what to say or do. I had never thought I would see this side of Sam. She was a hard nut, and I was finding it hard to believe there was a human being hidden behind the assassin's mask.

"Sorry, Adam, but I need a cuddle. Neil congratulated me on a masterly piece of work. Hitting the tanker was a masterstroke, according to him. It obliterated any evidence and got rid of her full team in one fell swoop. He was actually laughing when he said it. I thought I was going to be sick. I had to hide my feelings. He can be such an asshole at times. The next day I was sent to her London flat to search for anything interesting. I found, among other things, a folder with all the information about this place. I was pissed off with Neil, so I handed in the other documents I found, but the folder containing all the legal documents and spare keys for this place I took home. I took some time off and headed up here.

"The day I arrived, I stood on the balcony and looked out over a stunning September evening. The sun was setting behind the three little islands, and my heart melted. I knew then I would never hand Neil the keys to this place. It was the first time in my life I had fallen in love with anything."

She drained her glass, stood up, and grabbed my hand. "Come on. I have something I want to show you." We headed down to the basement, and Sam produced a key that she used to unlock the heavy, leather-clad door to her office. The door opened, revealing a large oak desk and green-leather reclining office chair. On the wall was an oak-framed glass cabinet, and on display were various types of handgun. Sam explained, in her line of work she sometimes fell heir to the occasional gun, and she kept the nicest examples for her collection. She strolled across the office to a walk-in cupboard on the far wall. She opened the door and put on the interior light. The wall-to-wall shelves were stacked with bundles of new bank notes.

"I forgot to tell Neil about this little lot as well. This is where the gang stored their cash."

Once more, I was speechless. "My god, Sam, how much money is here?"

Sam looked me straight in the eye, her red-rimmed eyes waiting for my reaction. "When I arrived here, this room had twenty-five million pounds in it. Today, it has twenty-two million, three hundred thousand, give or take a few hundred. I sent the tanker driver's wife two million pounds. It can never replace her family, but I hope it has helped ease the pain a little."

As she spoke, a tear rolled down her cheek. She wiped it away and closed the door of the cupboard. "Anyway, I need another drink." She marched out of the office, not bothering to lock the door. I found her in the lounge, pouring two rather large vodkas. She handed me one. I was about to refuse it as I was already feeling the effects, but then she said sternly, "A nightcap, Adam."

I took the drink reluctantly and sat down, sipping at the glass. Sam sat next to me, a foot or so away, sitting sideways on the couch and watching me.

"Sam, why do you do it? You have a stunning house and more money than you will ever need. Why put yourself in harm's way? You are still young, or at least, you look young. I never did ask your age. You could still have a family and a life. Have you never thought about settling down?"

Sam was looking into her drink again, deep in thought. She took a large gulp of vodka and looked away as she started speaking. "I am thirty-two years old, or at least, that is what they tell me. I am not sure of my birthday. I was found at the door of a maternity unit. I am an orphan. As for a family, I already told you, the only thing I have ever fallen in love with is this house. In my line of work it is hard to make friends. The work is hard enough without having to lie to someone you have feelings for. It's better to stay single." She was back looking into her glass again.

"Sam, don't you ever get lonely?"

She turned and looked at me, and her eyes were filling up again. "Of course I get lonely. I'm not a machine. I have feelings you know. I just can't show them all the time. I know you hate me for being a cow to you when we first met, but I could see your head wasn't in the game, and I had to take charge. I had to get you off the island before the Americans got to you. If bullying got the job done, so be it."

"Sam, I will admit you got under my skin to start with, but hate is too strong a word. I still don't know why you risked your life to save me when you were ordered not to, but I appreciate everything you have done for me. There is only one thing I am having trouble forgiving you for."

Sam stared at me, wondering what was coming next. I was having trouble keeping a serious face. "You set fire to my new Land Rover, which was bad enough, but then you had the cheek to replace it with that stinking pile of rust in the garage."

Sam wasn't sure whether to take me seriously or not, but then my composure failed, and I started to smile. She hit me playfully in the ribs, and I grabbed her to stop the blows. We both fell over on the couch, our balance helped by the amount of alcohol consumed. We lay on the couch, not moving, both deep in thought. It only took a few seconds before Sam was fast asleep.

I watched her through vodka-hazed eyes. It was hard to believe this girl in my arms was the same person who could be so violent. She felt so soft and warm next to me. It was only when she moved or twitched that I felt the hard, toned muscle beneath her feminine curves.

The next morning was not good. I awoke to a very sore head. The blinds had been opened, but there was no sign of Sam. After a tour of the premises, I found my rucksack in the second bedroom. Sam had laid my last set of clean clothes on the bed, along with a clean towel. The power shower brought me back to life, and after two pints of water and some paracetemol, I was back in the land of the living, if somewhat delicate. Sam was still missing, but a peek into the garage showed both vehicles were present, so she couldn't be far away. I made myself a strong coffee and headed out on the balcony to study the view. The morning was cold, but the view as I stood on the balcony was stunning.

The low sun glinted on the calm surface of the sea. The three little islands seemed to float on top of the sparkling waves, and the pale blue sky was spoiled only by the jet wash from an airliner. Further to my right, I could see in the misty distance the Isle of Skye, its jagged mountains cast in miniature against the blue sky. Then a voice behind me startled me. Sam had been watching me for a few seconds while I had been lost in the scenery.

"It doesn't matter what time of year you come out here. It is always different, but always beautiful, don't you think?"

Sam was decked out in running gear and had been working hard. She was drenched with sweat. Even her hair, which had been tied up in a ponytail, was soaking wet. She turned and went back into the kitchen. She pulled a pad and pen from a drawer. "Here. I am heading into town. It isn't a good idea for us both to go. You have been promoted to head chef. Have a look round and see what we need, and I will pick it up. After I shower."

Sam was back to I'm-in-charge mode. I put together a list of food and clothing and a few other bits and pieces while Sam bathed. When she reappeared, she had dressed. Her hair was back in a ponytail, and she was decked out in black designer jeans, a white polo-neck sweater, a black leather jacket, and matching black leather shoulder bag. She took a quick look at the list and remarked on the battery charger. I explained it was for the big BMW that had obviously sat for some time, as the battery was flat.

She was not one for hanging about. She grabbed the old Land Rover keys and a bottle of water and headed for the door, reminding me on the way past to stay in. She had put my Glock in the bedside cabinet, just in case I was looking for it. I had no doubt that her Glock would be in the bottom of her bag—she was that type of girl. I smiled to myself, thinking heaven help any shoppers who picked a fight with Sam over the last loaf of bread. They would get more than they bargained for. Without a goodbye, Sam was gone. I got the impression Sam wasn't in the mood to talk today. I had a feeling that she had opened up too much to me, and it was almost as if in her eyes, it had made her look weak. Until that moment, I hadn't noticed that the house had no radio, television, computer, or even telephone. It was completely isolated from the outside world. I found this quite refreshing. I had become sick of switching the telly on and being bombarded with doom and gloom.

I went to my room, grabbed the Glock, and headed for Sam's firing range. After a bit of mucking about to get the range working, I was off. The range was set out for five distances. The closest was ten metres, then rising in ten-metre increments, with the furthest distance being fifty metres—the full length of the house. I set my first target at twenty metres and fired five rounds, then examined my shots. The grouping was wide but not in any direction, all slightly low. I put this down to the weight of the weapon. It was lighter than I had expected, and I was overcompensating for this. Another five rounds saw some slight improvement. I willed myself to loosen my arms slightly, and my last five rounds were within the outer markers of the target.

I loaded another clip and moved the target to the thirty-metre mark. By my third set of five-round bursts, again at this further distance, I was within the outer markers. I left the target at thirty metres and emptied two more full clips into the target. On my second clip, I scored two bulls, but I pulled my last shot, and it just caught the corner of the target. I noted, because of the lightness of the weapon, when you pulled a shot, it could be way off target. I was glad I had decided to practice. I was rusty and also had little experience with handguns. Most of my training and combat had been with rifles or machine guns, a very different discipline.

***

Aron Fletcher was not in a good mood as Ed pushed the big Range Rover through the tight, twisty Scottish back roads. He rolled from side to side as Ed flung it into corners like a sports car. This did not bother him. He had instructed Ed to get to Campbeltown "like, yesterday." What was bothering him was one of his team had gone AWOL. Marcus Laine had had enough sitting watching the Arran ferry. He had called Fletcher and informed him he was going to play the game his way, and that he would call when he had a lead. He had not been seen since. Fletcher was not used to working with mavericks. He had come from one of the world's elite fighting units. Delta had no room for mavericks; they worked as a team. He had not planned for this and was not a happy bunny.

Marcus Laine was a clever cookie. He had not achieved his reputation by watching ferries, and after calling Fletcher, he had set up base at what he regarded as the most central part of Scotland. He had set up headquarters in a Travel Inn near Stirling. He had made up a poster with the photo from the Americans and stated on the poster that this man was missing while hill walking. He also stated that the gentleman had dementia and that there was a reward for any information leading to his safe return. He then placed his cell phone number as the contact number. He had contacted a printing and distribution company, and they were at the moment posting fifty thousand flyers all over Scotland. All Laine had to do was wait for the calls, then sort out the fake sightings from the genuine ones. Why use one pair of eyes at a ferry when you could use thousands of eyes all over the country?

Fletcher, Holts, and Richter met up with Areli Benesch at the harbour. She had booked bed and breakfast for them at various locations in the town and had drawn up a street plan with designated areas for each of them to check. She had not been told that Laine was AWOL, but she quickly took his share of areas to check when she found out. Fletcher, although he didn't say anything, was uncomfortable with this situation, as it seemed Benesch was taking over the running of the operation. He decided to keep his mouth shut for the moment because he was already one team member down, and he did not want another stomping off in a huff because she had been put in her place.

On the second day of knocking on doors, Benesch arrived at the outskirts of town and walked up the drive to a big, white house. The chubby woman who answered the door to Areli recognized the picture right away. Areli was thinking on her feet and advised the woman she was after two confidence tricksters. She asked to see any credit card transactions but was told that everything had been paid in cash. Areli managed to get a good description of the girl from the shocked woman, who told her the story of the broken-down car. She knew already this was a red herring, but she noted that the pair had left to get the Glasgow bus. She left, telling the woman that if they reappeared, she was not to let them in and to contact the local police as they wanted to speak to them—a lot of rubbish, but it made her story sound better.

Next stop was the bus depot. It didn't take long before she found a driver who recognized them. He said he had seen them getting on

Bill's bus to Glasgow. She tried to contact this Bill guy, but he was not working that day. His next shift was tomorrow morning, and she would have to come back then. Areli decided not to share this information with her colleagues just yet.

Next morning Areli was up sharp and down to the bus station. Bill had just clocked in and fired up his bus. He was busy scraping ice from his windscreen when a petite, dark-haired woman approached him. She had dark, piercing eyes, and her olive skin and strange accent gave her away as a visitor to Scotland. Her English was perfect, and from tip to toe, there was not as much as a hair out of place. She introduced herself as an investigator working for a law firm who were trying to trace the whereabouts of a gentleman. She explained that his mother had just passed away, and they were trying to find him before the funeral. Bill studied the photo, but he was not sure until the woman described his partner. Bill had paid more attention to her and recognized the description of her clothing. He told the woman that they had traveled as far as Tyndrum, where he had dropped them off.

Areli contacted Fletcher and gave him a vague outline of the story, adding that she did not hold out much hope of the lead going anywhere, but she would check it out anyway. She suggested that the rest of the team stay in town and keep knocking on doors. Fletcher agreed but told her to keep him posted. Areli put the phone down, smiling to herself. She was a natural loner and preferred to work by herself. She would keep Fletcher informed but was happy to be one step ahead of him now. Next stop was this town called Tyndrum.

Sam arrived home from the shopping and was immediately aware of the faint smell of cordite. To her relief, it came from the shooting range. She entered and put the light on. Half a dozen used targets lay in a pile by the wastepaper bin. Sam picked them up and studied them. She took them with her to the kitchen, poured herself a vodka and coke, and wandered into the lounge area.

*****

I was on the balcony watching the winter sun set over Rum, a sight that I don't think anyone could grow tired of. I envied Sam, for this might not be her house by law, but she had the privilege of watching some of the best scenery in Europe every morning when she woke up. I had seen the old Land Rover return and was expecting Sam to appear at any moment. I was still surprised when I turned to find her by my side, watching the sunset.

There had been no sounds or sharp movement. She had moved with the stealth of a panther stalking its prey. We watched as the last rays of sun were extinguished by the skyline of the islands, and it was dusk before either of us spoke. It was as if we were milking the last drops of beauty from the scenery.

We both headed back inside and proceeded to empty the shopping from the Land Rover into the kitchen via the lift. Sam stored away the shopping while I prepared a Spanish omelet for our evening meal. During the meal, Sam poked fun at me over my targets and my shooting skills. "Adam, I wasn't dreaming when they told me you were a member of the Special Air Service? Was somebody winding me up, or are these targets from a fun fair?" She held up my targets and waved them at me.

"In my defense, I am now retired, I have been dragged all over Scotland by a madwoman and I haven't recovered yet, a handgun is not my preferred weapon, and finally, if you had taken time to find out, you would have known that I was drafted into the SAS as a munitions specialist and not as Billy the Kid."

Sam had got under my skin, and she knew it. She wasn't nasty about it. She was just finding out how far she could push. "Adam, let's go through to the lounge. We need to decide what to do now."

We both topped up our vodka rations and headed for the comfy seats. It was my turn to see how far to push. "Steady with that vodka. You might end up like last night if you're not careful. I wonder what revelations we can get you to divulge tonight after the vodka kicks in." Sam's eyes gave away a flash of anger, but she controlled it and sat down, quietly sipping her vodka. I had evened the score.

"Adam, I have decided to contact Neil. We can't stay here forever. I need to know if you have any evidence from the air base. Neil will need proof before he will agree to stick his head on the chopping board. We can't sit here knowing people are in danger and do nothing."

I reached into my jeans pocket and produced the memory card from the camera that Kay and I had used at the air base. Sam lent across the couch to take it, but I moved my hand away, shaking my head. "Not so fast, Sam. This is my get-out-of-jail-free card, and it will stay with me until it is needed. I'm not about to let some politician accidentally lose it so he can score big with his American buddies while I go to jail on some trumped-up charge. No, Sam, if Neil won't play ball, the memory card will be handed to the newspapers. Neil wasn't about to save me before. What makes you think he will now?"

Sam was quiet for a few seconds before replying. "You are probably right to keep the memory card. Still, as I have already stated, I don't know why Neil called off the mission, but I'm sure he wouldn't deliberately try to harm you. It's not like him. It's just if he has the memory card, it will add more weight to his argument."

Sam popped into the kitchen and topped up her vodka again. "I am going to go to Edinburgh in the morning and get in touch with Neil. It's too dangerous to contact him from around here, and if I'm in Edinburgh, I can pop on a plane to London. I've got you provisions for a few days until I get back. You will be safe here as long as you stay at the house."

I got up and headed into the kitchen. "I better get the battery charger on the BMW so you can get it started in the morning."

"No, Adam, come back and sit down. I will take the old Land Rover." I smiled at this comment. "You are a madwoman. There is a perfectly good BMW in the garage, and you want to use the Land Rover to drive all the way to Edinburgh? You will have to book yourself in for physiotherapy after you get there."

"I don't know the history of that car. I always meant to get it checked but knowing my luck, it will have been used by the gang for a hit-and-run or something. I don't want to try and explain it to your local plod, thank you very much."

I sat next to Sam and made eye contact with her. "Listen to me. I know you think you are the female version of Chuck Norris, but please be careful. There are probably going to be some nasty bastards looking for us. You have no idea what Neil is up to. Watch him. Power has gone to his head. He is not the same person I went to school with, and there is also a traitor in the government code-named Merlin, so watch yourself, madam."

I had been looking into Sam's eyes as I spoke. She had been paying attention to me up until I said the name Merlin. The change in Sam was worrying. Her whole body tensed, and her eyes burned through me as if I weren't there. It felt like I was sitting next to a cobra just about to strike.

"Tell me about Merlin. Why have you mentioned him now?" Her words were a demand, not a question. It appeared Neil had been economical with the truth. Sam knew nothing of Merlin's involvement in the agent's death in Nevada. Sam finished her vodka in one gulp, retired to the kitchen, and returned with her glass filled to the brim. Something had rattled her badly. She was trying not to show it, but she was as white as a sheet.

"What is wrong? You look as if you have seen a ghost."

She sat next to me, staring out the window. After a notable silence, she replied, "Sorry. I just don't like to go on a job and not be told the whole story. I'm fine." She was far from fine, and her answer was a poor attempt at a cover-up.

I changed the subject. "Anyway, just be careful. I don't know what I would do with the twenty-two million if you didn't come back." She broke into a smile at last and handed me her empty glass for refilling. "You better be careful if you are driving tomorrow. Keep going at this rate, and I will have to put you to bed." I filled both our glasses and sat down opposite Sam.

"Adam, tell me something. Did you fancy Mary?" Sam's tongue was starting to loosen with the drink again.

"Why are you asking me that when you know she was engaged to Neil?"

Sam shrugged her shoulders. "I know, but you didn't know that at the time, and Mary had a thing for you, I know that. She loved Neil, but it was you she never stopped talking about. She cancelled her leave when she found out the IRA were after you. I'm sure she died protecting your identity." Sam took another huge swig at the glass and emptied it again.

"Sam, be careful. You will be in some state tomorrow if you don't stop. Sam, how do you know so much about Mary? You must have been very close friends. It's funny, I can never recall her mentioning your name."

Sam crossed the room, taking her shoes off on the way across, then took one step forward and two back. The vodka time bomb had hit home with a bang. Sam stumbled forward and landed on the couch next to me on her knees. She laughed hysterically and slumped back, trying to regain her balance. She stopped laughing and with some difficulty sat up next to me, staring into my eyes. She was about to say something then stopped. She lunged forward and kissed me full on the lips.

I was so surprised, I almost fell off the couch. Sam sat back and did fall off the couch, giggling as she fell.

"What was that for, you madwoman?"

Sam sat up straight and stopped giggling. "Don't you know, Adam? It's for killing those bastards in Ireland. All I wanted to do at Mary's funeral was to run up and give you a big hug. I could see how hurt you were, but you got the bastards, Adam. You got them." Her voice trailed off, and she was asleep or passed out, I wasn't sure which.

I carried Sam to her room, dropped her unceremoniously on the bed, removed her socks, and undid the top two buttons on her blouse. I placed the quilt over her and headed for my own room. I might not have had the same amount as Sam, but I was still feeling the effects of the extra strong Russian vodka.

I awakened the next morning to find Sam and the Land Rover missing. A pink Post-it note stuck to the fridge door informed me she would be back in a day or two and to stay at the house.

CHAPTER SEVEN

Taken

Sam made good time in the old Land Rover. She had left at six and had not stopped for breakfast. She pulled into the Edinburgh Airport Hilton hotel at ten forty-two and remembered Adam's words of wisdom about driving the old Land Rover long distances. Her ankles and back had seized up driving that distance in the old boneshaker. It was not helped by her severe hangover. Her last recollection of the previous night was the mention of Merlin's name. After that it was a blur. There was something in her mind that she had fallen of the couch, but she wasn't sure if she had dreamt that.

Sam booked in for a week, then headed across to the airport. She called a number and asked to be put through to Neil. After some time, Neil answered at the other end of the line.

"Sam, are you OK? How is Mr. M?"

Sam had already rehearsed her lines. "Not over the phone. Get your boffins to put a message on the UK arrivals board with my national insurance number as the flight number and the time to meet as the arrival time. I will see you at the coffee shop, Edinburgh Airport. I will check the board every morning for three days. I hear nothing, and I am into the wind." Sam hung up and left the airport. Food and sleep were her only priorities now.

***

My first task of the day proved to be rather a large surprise. I had decided to get the BMW in the garage up and running. Opening the bonnet proved fruitless and rather dusty. The BMW designers had obviously wanted to distribute the weight evenly, as there was no battery fitted under the bonnet. A trip to the boot found it locked. Luckily there was just enough in the battery to open it. The boot lid sprang open at the touch of the switch.

The boot was packed from the top to the bottom with packets of white powder. Knowing who the previous owner was made me quite sure it was not a delivery of flour for the bakery. An attaché case tucked down the side of the packs of powder backed up my theory.

I opened it to find it packed with new one hundred dollar bills. I was no expert on drugs, but comparing it to finds shown on TV by police, I reckoned that there had to be twenty to fifty million pounds worth of heroin in the boot of the BMW, and the case contained ten million US dollars.

I spent until lunchtime unloading the stash to get the battery out for charging. Then I spent the afternoon well wrapped-up, exploring the surrounding areas of the house. There was a forty-metre area in front of the house that was grass. In the left corner of this area, there was a steep, zigzag path that led down the hill to a variety of little sandy bays below the glass house. It was while exploring one of these bays that I came across a wooden sign and signpost that had at one time belonged to the Russians. It had Russian writing on it, almost worn off by the action of the sea. I decided to reclaim it and give it a good Scottish name, not some Russian nonsense.

The rest of the day I spent removing the original writing. A hunt through the library in the house found only a few books that were not written in Russian, but among the English books was a Gaelic reference book. I pored over the pages, trying to find something that was apt and that also rolled off the tongue nicely. I turned a page, and it caught my eye immediately. The next morning, I started carving out the new name with a kitchen paring knife.

Once the letters were cut, I found a workman's chest in one of the outbuildings. It contained some gold leaf for the carved-out areas, and I topped off the whole thing with a coat of varnish. It had barely dried, and I had it dug into the ground at the back corner of the house, facing back down the hill toward the main road so it could be seen on arrival. I stood and surveyed my new creation. The sign boldly announced, "Comriach," or to the non-Gaelic-speaking world, "Sanctuary," particularly apt given the circumstances.

***

Sam had woken early, taken breakfast in her room, then headed for the airport. To her dismay, there was no message on the arrivals board for her. It was not going to be today for the meeting. Sam was not the type of person who would let grass grow under her feet, and she decided not to waste the day hanging about the hotel room. She visited the airport again and raided WH Smith's for any current auto magazines. Next stop was the gadget shop, where she bought a satnav. A further check of the arrivals board on the way to the coffee shop proved fruitless. Sam had decided that it was time to offload the Land Rover for something a bit faster and a lot more comfortable. She had no idea what she was looking for, so she was checking everything that had a local phone number.

Her knowledge of cars was a bit sketchy. The only cars she had owned were a Volkswagen Polo when she passed her test and recently, a Porsche 911 Turbo. She had finally grown tired of having to have it repainted after mindless morons had taken their frustrations out on her pride and joy. London was not the best place to leave your ego trip parked in the street unguarded, so she sold it back to the Porsche salesman who had sold it to her—at a thirty-thousand-pound loss. Taxis were a cheaper and hassle-free option.

Sam had brought a sizable amount of the Russian cash with her but had decided to stay well clear of garages, as they were duty bound to inform the authorities if anyone turned up with large amounts of cash. No, Sam was going to buy a car from a private seller who would ask no awkward questions and might even be talked into taking the old Land Rover as a part exchange. She had called five possibles on the airport payphone, but the cars were sold, or there was no reply, or the owner was not interested in a part exchange. Sam was running out of options when she got to her last pencil-circled ad. The phone was answered by a young-sounding bloke who was selling his eight-year-old Beetle. When Sam brought up the subject of the Land Rover part-exchange, he seemed open to the idea. Sam took his name and address and agreed to meet him in a couple of hours.

Sam arrived at the address and sat staring at the sight in front of her. Her head said to drive away, but her mischievous nature pictured Adam's face when she drove up to the glass house in this icon. In front of her sat a mark-two version of Herbie, its white paint emblazoned with the red and blue speed stripes and the obligatory number fifty-three on the doors.

Sam knocked on the door, which was immediately opened by a spotty youth called Gavin. Sam doubted if he were old enough to drive. "You didn't say in your advert you were selling Herbie, did you?"

The youth smiled sheepishly. "No, but I don't want any extra money for the paint job. You still want it lady? 'Cos I will need to take out ma sounds if you do."

Sam wandered round the Beetle as if she knew what she was look-ing for. The youth was getting nervous. "It's just been MOT'd, and ma dad put a new clutch in it last week. Ma dad says am an idiot sellin' it. You still want it then?"

Sam made a decision. "Gavin, you had it advertised for two thou-sand pounds, is that right? I can't wait for you to take the stereo out, so if you leave it in, I will give you two thousand pounds, and you keep the Land Rover. You can sell that and buy three new stereos. Do we have a deal, Gavin?"

Sam parked Herbie at the back of the hotel car park. She was pleased with her purchase. It drove along beautifully. It was not the most invisible car in the world, but then again, who would expect somebody trying to hide would drive a Herbie?

Sam arrived at the airport the next day to find her national insur-ance number displayed with an arrival time of 1430 hours next to it. Sam left the hotel at two. As she left, she had a second thought and headed for Herbie. She took the envelope with the remaining money and placed it under the passenger seat. She was not sure what was going to happen today, but the last thing she needed was Neil sniffing about her affairs if he found the unexplained cash.

Sam walked across to the airport. She was playing a dangerous game. In her shoulder bag was her loaded and silenced Glock. If she was stopped and searched, her feet wouldn't touch the ground. She wore a long tweed jacket, knitted beret, and false glasses. She was twenty minutes early, but she wanted to sweep all areas for unexpected surprises. Eventually, happy nothing was out of place and with ten minutes to go, she placed herself at the luggage carousels by the coffee shop. To her relief, the luggage delivery was very slow, and there were a number of passengers hanging about waiting for their cases.

She caught a glimpse of herself in a polished surface. She was happy with what she saw. She had sucked her cheeks in and was wearing no makeup. She stood with a slight stoop, and her dress and stance had aged her twenty years.

Neil's bodyguards swept into the coffee shop with typical male bravado. Sam watched as Neil followed twenty paces behind them, making it very clear he was the big "I am." Sam smiled inwardly. If this had been a hit, she would have dropped both the peacocks with two shots and moved in for the kill shot on Neil while he was still wondering why his men's knees were buckling. She would have shot him between the eyes on the way past heading for the first exit. She would have picked up the first taxi as the screams from the coffee shops just started. She would have hit the motorway as the first police officer arrived at the three dead bodies. Sam was not daydreaming. She knew that is exactly what would have happened, and she knew this because she was the best assassin that the British secret service had.

Sam walked toward Neil, watching his every move as she came. The closer she got, the more her temper rose. At one time she had been good friends with him, but over time, they had drifted apart. She was not happy he had turned his back on his friend, but the thing that burned into her was he had told her nothing about Merlin's involvement in this case. He had had plenty of opportunity to do so.

Sam sat down next to Neil. His monkeys still hadn't noticed. Neil turned and was about to tell the woman who had just sat down that the seat was taken when it clicked.

"Sam, my god, how long have you been here? Are you both OK?"

Sam's guard was immediately up. Neil was far more rattled than he should have been. "I don't know what you are worried about Adam for. You were quite happy to let him be screwed by the CIA, weren't you?"

Neil was thinking on his feet now. "So you think it is definitely the CIA behind all this."

Sam was finding it hard to keep her temper in check. "Well, it was two CIA agents we killed, yes, and it was a CIA computer I planted our bug in, so yes, I think it safe to say it was a CIA job. So what the hell do you think you were playing at, hiding the fact that Adam Macdonald is a civilian and that Merlin is involved in this job. Just as well I have friends in the department who whispered in my ear, or I might have missed the chance to kill the traitor. You of all people keeping that little cracker to yourself, knowing what catching that bastard means to me."

Sam's temper had overflowed. Neil could not hold her stare. He looked away, knowing to look into those eyes was like staring down a black mamba. "Sam, has it escaped your notice that you are still working for Her Majesty's government, and that you are speaking to a superior? My men will escort you to pick up Adam and then debrief you both. That is an order."

Neil nodded to one of the gorillas, who started to move toward them.

Sam leaned close to Neil's ear. "Neil, if that monkey as much as breathes on me, I swear he will never walk without a stick again."

Neil knew she was not kidding and raised a hand to stop his agent's progress. He put his arm around Sam's shoulder in a friendly gesture. "I know, Sam, and you would do it without even breaking sweat." Neil's right hand gripped Sam's upper arm. He squeezed tightly, and she started to jump up, but he held her tight. The nerve agent from the hypodermic needle on the back of his ring acted almost instantly. She was wide awake and knew everything that was going on, but she could do nothing about it. She was a living tailor's dummy. "Sorry, Sam, but

I can't afford to take no for an answer. Get the van to the front door now."

With meticulous precision, Plan B sprang into action. A pair of paramedics arrived to check on the woman who had taken a stroke. No one noticed that the ambulance was a City of London patient transfer. Twelve hours later, Sam was dropped off at an MI6 safe house in Croydon. Two rookie MI6 agents were left to guard and look after their new visitor.

Sam had used the NLB 7 nerve agent before and knew that depending on the individual it could take up to three days to wear off. There was also one case where the victim had ended up paralyzed for life after taking an allergic reaction to the drug

Nathan Alderton and Peter Lyons were the two young agents charged with the care and protection of Sam.

Peter was quiet and kept himself to himself, not natural MI6 material. Nathan was his alter ego. Loud and brash, he thought babysitting was beneath him. Sam was taken to the main bedroom where the agents stripped her clothes off, checking for tracking devices. Sam was to be kitted out in pajamas. When she recovered her mobility, she would find it harder to escape in pj's. Peter was finding it difficult to hide his embarrassment at having to deal with a naked female and left Nathan to dress her. After they had finished their search, he went to make coffee, returning twenty minutes later to find Sam still naked, and Nathan standing at the end of the bed staring at her. "What the hell are you playing at, Nathan? Get her clothes on before someone comes to see her. You do know that with NLB 7, the recipient retains all mental capabilities. That means that she knows you are watching her. When she comes to, she will be able to put a complaint in about us, for God's sake."

Nathan continued to stare at Sam, and then he took the pajamas and flung them at Peter. "If you are so worried about your ass, you dress her. I am sure you have had plenty of practice at dressing dollies from your youth." Nathan marched out and headed to the kitchen. Peter dressed Sam, fumbling badly and going very red in the face in the process.

His shift was finished, and he had a dinner date with his uncle in town. Peter pulled up ten minutes late and dashed into the restaurant to find his uncle waiting patiently for him. He did not like letting his uncle down. After all, it was his uncle who had pulled a few strings and got him into MI6.

"Merlin" stood up and shook hands with Peter before inviting him to sit and tell him what he had been up to lately. Peter told him he was guarding a woman agent who had been brought back from Scotland for debrief by the assistant director. Merlin had placed his young nephew in MI6 so that in future years, he would be there to help Merlin keep his finger on the pulse.

Peter had no idea his uncle was about to betray his trust. He was more worried what he would find when he got back. He did not trust the woman's safety with Nathan the pervert. Merlin's late arrival at the US embassy was not planned, but after a few minutes, he was ushered into the communications room. Brad Whiteford was already on the line. Within five minutes of telling Whiteford the story, a message was sent to Fletcher's team telling Fletcher to get to Croydon and eliminate the woman agent.

Fletcher and his second-in-command, Holts, left immediately, leaving Lucas Richter to meet up with Benesch in Tyndrum and continue the search for the second target.

Benesch and Richter found no more clues in Tyndrum, but Benesch had already decided to head north. That could have been the only reason they did not continue south with the bus. Benesch had studied the map and decided to head for the next big town north of Tyndrum. She had called ahead and booked rooms in Fort William.

They had booked in at one of the town's many hotels. After arriving and parking the car, Benesch noticed the flyer tied to the lamppost next to the hotel reception. She was amused to see the picture and details of the man they were hunting.

Richter was furious, but Benesch was not worried. On the contrary, she was pleased. She rummaged around in her handbag and, coming up with a black marker pen, she altered the contact number at the bottom of the flyer, replacing the current number with her own.

She and Richter spent the next day combing the area for flyers and altering the contact number.

In Stirling, Marcus Laine was methodically working his way through the sightings that had just started flowing into his answer-phone service. His target was undoubtedly on the west coast of Scotland, as that was where most of the sightings were from, but there was not a consensus of opinion as to the exact location. There was one call that intrigued Laine. The caller claimed to know where this man's home was, and he did say that he had been missing for some time.

Laine called this gentleman back. He explained he was the closest neighbour to the man in the photo. He gave the man's address, which turned out to be the back of beyond, north of Crieff on a back road. The closest village was called Amulree. He explained the man was a loner and that he had not realized that he had dementia. Laine thanked the man, then sat thinking, but it took no more than a few seconds to decide. He would visit this man's house. He was not there, but it would give an insight into the man, and it might shed some light on his current location.

***

Sam had been gone for over a week now, and provisions were getting low. I had made the decision that if Sam wasn't back that morning, orders or no orders, I was going to have to hike it to Malaig for some provisions and some type of transport as the big BMW's fuel tank was bone dry. The morning had started with fog. Then, as the wind picked up, the fog lifted enough to chance hiking.

By lunchtime, I was in Malaig. I had borrowed some of the Russian drug money and had a look round the same garage where Sam had bought the old Land Rover. There was little to choose from, but the one that caught my eye was an old silver BMW 518. After inquiring about it, I found that it was for sale, and after a bit of tyre-kicking, the six-hundred-and-fifty price tag dropped to five hundred.

It was a bonus that the old car still had a cherished number plate. My plan was to use the old BMW to knock about here, but when it became time to head south, the number plate and tax could be swapped to the Russians' BMW in the garage, giving it a new, clean identity. Wild horses would not make me sit in that old Defender all the way to London. I parked my new transport outside the store-cum-post office. I had two things left to do. First, I posted the camera chip and a letter to my house. The letter asked whoever opened it to hand the chip to Neil Andrews at Vauxhall Cross in London. The letter was addressed to myself at my home address. If nothing happened to me, I could pick it up on the way to London. I filled three carrier bags with provisions and headed back to the glass house to await Sam's arrival.

***

In the safe house in Croydon, Sam was still struggling to overcome the effects of the drug she had been injected with. She could feel pins and needles in her toes but try as she might, she could not move them at all. She vowed to herself if she ever became paralyzed, she would ask somebody to end her torture. During the night, she had wet the bed. She knew she had done it but could do nothing about it. Even worse than wetting the bed was the indignity of having to let the two clowns that were guarding her wash her and change her clothes and bedding.

The loud, perverted guard called Nathan had taken great pleasure in smacking her bare backside after cleaning her, telling her she was a naughty girl. Sam fumed inside her drug-frozen body. She knew once the drug wore off, she would take great delight in breaking both his arms. Nathan passed the time by telling Peter all about his latest acquisition, which was parked in the next street. His father had just bought him a new Porsche Carrera 4. He boasted to Peter that, armed with that car and his looks, there was no woman who could withstand his advances. "It's the money, Peter. These birds can smell money. The Porsche just confirms it. They will do anything to get their hands on a good-looking bloke with cash. I tell you, Peter, they can smell it."

Peter shook his head and headed for the kitchen. "Nathan, I can definitely smell something, but I don't think it's the money!"

Sam had been listening to this intellectual conversation and chuckled inwardly when Peter brought Nathan down to size with his latest comment. Sam tried her toes again, and her right toe twitched. She studied her two captors to see if either of them had noticed, but they were oblivious to the act. Sam listened to her captor's conversation again, just in case she could use anything that was said to her advantage.

Peter was talking this time. "Nathan, don't you think it's funny that we are holding one of our own agents? I mean, what does that say about our organization if we do that to our own people?"

Nathan was half-listening and half-watching the teatime news. "Doesn't bother me, mate. She has obviously crossed the line at some point and is paying the price now. When she was dropped off, the others told me to watch her like a hawk. She is meant to be a real bad bitch. Hard to believe—she can't be that good, or they wouldn't have caught the silly cow."

By eight that evening, Sam's legs were fully mobile, and the feeling in her arms was coming back rapidly. She had terrible cramps in her limbs and was having problems disguising the pain. Sam knew she had to make a move sooner rather than later before the clowns decided it was about time she was tied up. She had checked out her surroundings. Although she couldn't confirm it, she was sure the windows were bulletproof and bolted shut. She would have to try and negotiate the hall and wherever that led to. Sam had been monitoring the conversations, but nothing had yet been said about securing her. Sam had just found out that Peter was about to go off shift, and she knew this would be her best chance of escape.

As Peter opened the front door to leave, he was hit with a hail of bullets, and he was dead before he hit the ground. Nathan hit the panic alarm, then had the good sense to stay clear of his fallen comrade and fire through the plasterboard wall from the lounge into the hall.

The last shot missed the top of Fletcher's head by millimeters, forcing him to dive on top of the dead MI6 agent. Merlin had called

Fletcher and asked him to spare the life of the agent called Peter. Fletcher had agreed, saying he would look after the lad, but he lied. He had no intention of leaving any witnesses alive to put him in jail at a later date. Everybody in this house must die.

When Sam heard the shooting, she tried to jump off the bed, but her legs were weak, and she went down like a ton of bricks on the floor. She crawled to the door. She could feel the adrenaline coursing through her veins, clearing away the last effects of the drug, but was it too late. She was unarmed and little more than a quivering jelly.

Nathan decided he was too exposed in the lounge. He had to hang on for ten minutes, then help would arrive, but before then, he needed to get into the back hall. From the hall, he could stop the attackers from reaching the bedroom with the woman in it. All he had to do was vault the couch. The door was already open behind the couch. He lunged for the couch, but as they picked up the movement, Fletcher and Holts opened fire at the same time.

The devastation two M16s made at close quarters to a living room had to be seen to be believed. Nathan fired as he moved, but his shots were way off target, so much so that two rounds took out the light fitting, plunging the living room into darkness. The same could not be said for Fletcher and company. Their short, sharp, deliberate bursts sprayed the room to maximum effect. Nathan was hit by two shells. One smashed his ankle to pieces while the other entered under his right rib cage, passing through his lung and exiting just below his shoulder. Nathan landed halfway through the doorway just as Sam crawled up to it.

She could tell from one look that he was finished. Sam grabbed his pistol and fired twice toward the door to give the effect that the MI6 agent was still a threat. Nathan was trying to breathe and was coughing up blood and lung tissue. Sam checked his trouser pockets and took only a second to find his car keys. She picked up the pistol again and fired the two remaining shots at the doorway, then got to her feet like a newborn calf and staggered down the hall, heading for the moonlight that was streaming through the back-door window.

Fletcher and Holts reloaded and charged the living room. This time they found no resistance, and a quick search of the room revealed Nathan's dead body in the doorway.

It had taken Sam what seemed like an hour to turn the lock on the back door. Her hands were still not doing completely what they were told. Sam knew she needed to get the door closed and locked so it would not give away her position. Sam had ducked down while locking the door so not to be seen from the inside. Finally, it was locked, and Sam climbed into the large bush that was next to the back door. Sam found loose panels in the boundary fence and slipped into the next-door garden. She crawled slowly across the garden and continued this for four gardens until she felt safe enough to curl up in a bush. She could hear the screech of tyres, shouting, then sirens.

They were too late. The attackers were pros, and they would be long gone. She was cold, but this was nothing to the cramp in her limbs. She lay quietly sobbing for two hours, knowing how close she had come to the end of her life.

Fletcher was in a rage again. The girl wasn't here. He had not slept, and what looked like a walk-in-the-park job had turned into a wild-goose chase. They destroyed all CCTV footage and left in a hurry before the cavalry arrived.

Sam stopped herself falling asleep and hobbled through two gardens using the opportunity to pick up a dress that had been left on the drying line. She was wearing mud-spattered pajamas, so the dress would come in handy.

Sam changed into the dress and composed herself. She stumbled into the next street and pressed the remote. Indicators flashed halfway down the street. Sam had found Nathan's Porsche. She bundled herself into the Porsche and headed for the motorway. She knew it would be only a matter of time until someone noticed that the agent's car was missing. She knew she had to put as much distance as possible between her and London to give herself a fighting chance of escape. She was glad to see that the car had three-quarters of a tank of fuel, which would get her clear of the area. She had escaped with nothing but the dress and the Porsche. She had twelve pounds in change that she had found in the glove box, and that was it. Sam pushed on through the night, not speeding as the last thing she needed was to be stopped by the police. If she were stopped by the police, she knew within four hours she would be back in Neil's hands.

Her feeling had fully returned, but she was ill. The after-effects of the drug were worse than even the worst hangover. Her head was pounding, and at times she retched violently. Even the thought of food made her want to vomit. The sun was just starting to peek over the hills of the Lake District as Sam took the turn-off for the motorway services. She pulled the Porsche into the car park and sat quietly for a few seconds, watching the sun rise.

She was covered in a cold sweat, having endured one of the worst nights of her life. Sam grabbed the change from the glove box and headed into the shop. First stop was a barefooted visit to the ladies, where she freshened herself up. Even just washing the sweat away from her face was an improvement. Next stop was the shop. Sam found what she was looking for in a basket at the door—plastic flip-flops on special offer. Her right foot was red and swollen. Porsche designers had never meant for their cars to be driven barefoot obviously, and Sam's accelerator foot had paid the price over the long night. The flip-flops cost her seven ninety-nine, which at motorway prices left her just enough for a mug of coffee. She filled it with sugar, much more than she would normally use, just to give her a boost and sat at a table looking out at the red morning sky as the sun's rays danced over the pond outside the window.

Her hands cupped the mug of coffee as she sat guarding it jealously. Halfway through her mug of coffee, she could feel the energy returning to her body. She sat looking at her own reflection in the window. She looked forty-two, not thirty-two. She used an elastic band from the flip-flop purchase to tie her hair back in the obligatory ponytail then set about the remains of her coffee.

Sam was in deep thought about what to do next. She could try and hitch a lift, which was the safer option, or she could fill the Porsche with fuel and do a runner. This was a risky option because it brought her to the attention of the authorities. Sam was still weighing up the options when she heard the voice. "OK darling, you can put as much bacon on top as you want. Am a hard workin' man wi' a long way tae go, so a wee bit extra would be appreciated." The accent was unmistakably Scottish, and from the man's dress, he was a driver of some description. He was in his late fifties and sported a belly that said he should have been asking for less bacon, not more.

Sam wandered over to where he had sat down and broke the ice with, "Did she give you any extra? Sorry to bother you, but I couldn't trouble you for a lift? Only I heard the accent, Glaswegian right, and I need to get back up to Scotland. I wondered if you were heading back that way?"

The driver looked at her and seemed to be making a decision. "Pet, am no supposed tae take passengers, but seen as it's almost Christmas, an' am a good Samaritan, y'can come wi' me, lass."

Sam waited patently while Wull, the driver, polished of the rest of his big breakfast, mopping up the last of the egg yolk with two slices of bread while telling Sam the virtues of starting the day with a good meal.

Sam's luck had started to change for the better. It turned out that Wull was heading back to his depot in Bathgate, which was not far from Edinburgh Airport. Wull agreed to drop Sam at the airport. He was a joker and proceeded to entertain Sam for the whole journey, making her feel very welcome.

He dropped Sam off at the Hilton just after lunchtime, and she was glad to see Herbie still parked where she had left him. Her room was on its last day of booking, and she headed there for a shower and change of clothes. Then she realized she had only one slight problem. Her car keys were in London somewhere. She checked out of her room and asked reception if she could use the phone.

She called the AA and had lunch in the restaurant while waiting for the AA to arrive. The AA patrol man who arrived listened to Sam's story about losing her keys but was happy when she explained she had a spare set in a box in the boot, half an hour later he handed her the spare keys and left saying that was the first time he had been asked to work on Herbie. Sam was back in business. She had her clothes, her new car, and the remainder of the cash she had left in the car. She needed to sleep but not yet. She had a call to make, and she wanted to get away from the airport in case any of Neil's friends were hanging about.

Neil Andrews had just returned to his office after having endured a verbal beating-up from the MI6 director. He knew he was skating on thin ice on this one. He had withheld most of the information about the deaths of the two MI6 agents at the safe house, and when the director asked for answers, he had none to give. He was sent away like a naughty schoolboy and told to find some answers.

Neil had just sat down when his secretary informed him there was a call for him from Sam. He had the call put through on a scrambled line. "Samantha, good to hear you are still in the land of the living."

Sam had bought a pay-as-you-go mobile phone and was standing in the airport car park so as not to be overheard. "Now listen to me, dickhead. This is what is going to happen. You are going to get the government to open a public inquiry into the American air base at Machrihanish. Only when I hear it on the news will I come out of hiding and bring Adam and evidence of wrongdoing at the base to the hearing."

There was silence for a second as Neil worked out the best approach to the situation. "And what if I say no to this and report you for dereliction of duty?"

Sam would have loved to have put her hand down the phone and slapped him. "You do that, and you are finished. I will hand over the evidence together with Adam's sworn statement to the press, and the nation will find out its secret service—namely you—sent two civilians to do their dirty work, and when it went wrong, you turned your back on them and left them to die. It's your choice—dare to be a hero, and challenge the world's only superpower. Or explain to the director and the government how you have been involved in a case where three MI6 agents and one civilian have been murdered. Also you know there is something happening at a British location, but you have turned the other way to cover your own backside."

Sam took a deep breath. "Oh and one other thing. Don't ever call me Samantha. Only friends get to call me that, and after our last meeting you can forget that. Neil, if you send people after us, as god is my witness, MI6 or not, I will shoot them dead where they stand." Sam did not wait for some smug reply from Neil. She hung up, pulled the battery from the phone, and flung them into the bin by the ticket machine for the car park.

When Neil came off the phone, he was pale. His shirt collar seemed to tighten on his neck. He had no option. He had to inform the director before he found out from other sources. He had no doubt if he sent more agents after Sam, it would result in a bloodbath. He was having trouble believing that the Americans would actually launch an attack on MI6. Only the director himself would have sufficient clout with the PM to organize an inquiry. He thought to himself that he would be lucky to have his job by the end of this disaster. He reluctantly called his secretary and asked her to schedule an hour's appointment with the director at the first opportunity.

Areli Benesch was just finishing her lunch when her mobile rang. It was a report of another sighting. This was the third call she had received, thanks to the modified flyers. The first two she and Richter had followed up but they proved to be false alarms. The woman on the phone was adamant the man in the photo had been in her shop and that a trip by her to Fort William on a Christmas shopping spree had resulted in her seeing a flyer. Areli could sense she was onto something here. The woman explained the man in the photo had been in her shop buying provisions. She also told Areli he drove a silver BMW, and she thought he might be back soon as the provisions that he bought must be starting to run out. Areli thanked the woman but informed her that it would be dangerous to approach the man. She was a psychologist with the police, and it would be better if she approached him herself. Areli took details of the grocer's shop in Malaig, then called Richter. He agreed he would wait in Fort William for the return of Fletcher and Holts while Areli checked this lead out herself. Areli smiled to herself. She was alone again to get on with the job.

Sam woke early the next day. She had stayed at a bed and breakfast in the town of Callander. She came down the stairs to find the landlady fussing around in the dining room. The smell of cooked bacon and freshly brewed coffee went round Sam's heart.

The last effects of the drug had left Sam's body overnight while she slept, and she was firing on all cylinders and ravenous after her ordeal. Sam devoured a full cooked breakfast. She was anxious to get back to the glass house. She had been missing for over a week and was not sure what Adam would have done in that time. After breakfast, she thanked the landlady then asked if there were a petrol station nearby. After following the landlady's directions, she filled Herbie to the brim, then pointed him northward, and set sail for the glass house.

***

The morning started much the same as previous mornings. I toasted the last of the bread and covered it in marmalade, washed down with a mug of coffee, then headed for the gym. I spent two hours in the gym, then showered and changed. I was starting to worry. There was still no sign of Sam.

I wandered down the zigzag path to the beach, but the bitterly cold wind drove me back to the glass house within a few minutes. I cleaned the kitchen and lounge and put in a wash with the last of the washing powder. It was afternoon, and it looked like Sam wasn't coming home today. I was bored and lonely. Time for another shopping trip. I toyed with the idea of driving to Fort William but decided against that just in case I was spotted. Better to stick to the same shop I had used before. The chances of bumping into a nasty were much less there.

I fired up the old BMW and headed out to Malaig. There was a parking space right outside the grocer's shop. Inside the girl serving was too busy talking to one of her mates to be interested in me. I wandered around filling my wire basket to the brim. I wanted to get back quickly just in case Sam had arrived. I paid for my groceries and headed back home.

Areli Benesch was parked in the main street in Malaig. This was her second day here. Frozen to the bone, she cursed herself for taking a job in this cold, god-forsaken country. She wished she were back in her beloved Israel, drinking wine in the warm sun at her favorite roadside café. She was just about to give up the will to live when the old silver BMW pulled up outside the shop.

It was like an electric charge surging through her. She was instantly awake and no longer cold. Her target had arrived at last. It was unmistakably him. He was probably between five feet eleven and six feet, built like an American football player, dark, very short hair. Areli noted that he moved effortlessly. He looked very fit, only his weather-beaten complexion gave a clue to his age. Areli reckoned he was mid to late thirties. She noted all this in a blink of an eye, and she had already made a mental note not to engage this man physically. He had the neck and shoulders of a prizefighter, so she must never let him get within arm's reach. She would make sure he was dead long before he got that close.

Areli phoned Fletcher, and he answered immediately. She told him what she had found and advised him she was going to follow her target to his hideout, and she would contact him again when she had confirmed the location of the hideout.

Fletcher advised her they had just left Fort William ten minutes ago, and that they would be with her as soon as possible. He then asked what she thought was a strange question—was the female with him? Areli didn't pick up on it, but obviously things had not gone according to plan in London. It did not matter to Areli. Even if Fletcher flew up the coast road, he would never be here before she eliminated this man. Then she would hunt down the female and terminate her as well. She would prove to the American that her Mossad training was superior to his. Then the icing on the cake would be taking his money. She would go somewhere hot, away from this accursed island.

***

The trip back to the glass house was uneventful. The roads were quiet, and the car behind me turned off to the village of Morar. I hoped that in my absence Sam had returned. I longed for some company, in particular one of Sam's vodka-fueled chats. On arrival there was no old Defender in sight. It looked like an early tea, then bed again.

***

Benesch turned off at Morar, turned her side lamps off, waited a few seconds, then followed at a greater distance. She missed the BMW turning off, but luckily as she passed, she caught the car in her peripheral vision climbing the road on the right. There was no right turnoff but on further investigation, the road on the left doubled back on itself and continued through a tunnel under the main road, then climbed steadily up the hill toward the sea.

Areli knew this would probably lead to a house. She stopped in the tunnel and called Fletcher. She gave him directions, and he told her to wait for them and they would storm the house in force. He would call her when they were close. Areli agreed, hung up, and smiled to herself. She had heard in the background the engine of the big Range Rover screaming. Fletcher was moving heaven and earth to get there, but he would still be too late. This was her kill.

***

I had just unloaded the shopping and had shut the garage door when I heard the engine coming up the hill. At first, I was jubilant. Sam was home at last. Doubt started to grow as I listened. This was no Land Rover engine; it was a small car.

A Ford Focus pulled up at the front of the house, and a smallish woman stepped out. She wore sunglasses and was dressed in black— black slacks, black shirt, and black leather jacket. Her hair was jet black and pulled back tightly into a long black mane of a ponytail. She carried a large black shoulder bag. She stood and studied the front of the building. She was unaware that I was standing behind the black privacy glass studying her.

CHAPTER EIGHT

The Assault

Eventually she found the front door. The German engineers had done a fabulous job of making the front door fuse into the glass front. It took a few seconds to register where it was. You needed to follow the path up to the glass to give you a clue where to start looking. The doorbell rang, and I actually jumped back. I watched her press the button, but the noise was so alien it startled me. I stood behind the door, debating what to do next. The woman was trying to look in through the glass. Her expression told me she thought she could see things, but I was sure that the reflection of the sea behind her in the glass spoiled her view. Then, for a fraction of a second, the low winter sun broke through the cloud. It sent shadows across the interior of the house, and for a fleeting second, I realized too late, it allowed the woman to see at least the outline of me looking back at her. What happened next was breathtaking.

Faster than a flash of lightening, the woman drew a silenced gun from her bag. I had not even noticed that her hand had been inside the bag. I had only time to blink. She fired three times at point blank range—two shots to my chest and one to my head.

It took a few seconds to register that I was still alive. The woman stood outside equally stunned. Then it clicked—those beautiful Russian drug dealers had specified that the builders use bulletproof glass, and their self-preservation instincts had saved my life.

Looking at the bullet marks on the glass, it was clear I would have been hit twice in the heart and once in the forehead. For sure, I was a lucky laddie.

The woman's hesitation only lasted for a split second. I watched in horror as she removed the silencer and forced her arm and gun through the letterbox. She could no doubt see little but she started firing in an arc, emptying a full clip in the process. I dived behind the old BMW just in the nick of time as two shells smashed into the old girl's bodywork, sending sparks flying across the open plan hall come garage. She pulled her arm back out and started to reload.

It was time to move. I charged to the back of the house, to the firing range where I had left my Glock. I grabbed the gun and three clips of ammo and headed back for the garage. I could hear an engine outside and wondered if the woman was leaving. The look in her eye as she fired at me told me that would be unlikely. She had come here to do a job, and I did not think she would give in so easily. A strange sight awaited me as I reentered the garage.

***

Sam was halfway up the road to the glass house when she heard the gunfire. She changed down a gear and floored Herbie. She appeared over the rise by the side of the house at speed. A dark-haired woman stood in front of the house, in the process of reloading her gun. Sam recognized the weapon, a SIG Sauer nine mil. Sam knew how deadly a weapon it was and did not fancy being at the receiving end of it. She headed straight for the woman, but the woman was faster. Before Sam could get there, she had the gun loaded and had spun round to meet the new threat.

Sam realized that she would not hit the woman before she had peppered the windscreen with shots. At the last second, she spun the steering wheel and pulled the handbrake, causing the back end of Herbie to break away. The car now headed sideways for the woman. Sam flung herself flat across the seats just in time. A hail of bullets hit the side of Herbie, all his side windows exploded in a shower of glass. Areli was forced to stop firing and leap into the air. She was just too slow, and Herbie's bonnet clipped her foot as she tried to vault over it. The force of hitting the car sent her spinning into the air. She lost her shoes and her bag, and crucially, her gun flew from her grip. She hit the ground with her shoulder in a cartwheeling motion. As fast as she went down, she was back on her feet and heading for the driver's door of the Beetle. Sam lay still across the seat, watching her progress out of the corner of her eye. She was about a foot away from the door when Sam pulled the handle then kicked the door with all her might. The door flew open and hit Areli with a sickening crunch on both her kneecaps.

Areli didn't have time to hit the ground before Sam was out of the car. Areli staggered back and looked up as Sam launched a spinning back kick at her head. Areli flung herself backward away from the kick. Sam made contact with Areli's head but the woman's backward movement had taken the power out of the kick, and Areli lived to fight on. As Sam landed from the kick, Areli counterattacked. She spun round, her back to the ground, and she caught Sam on the ankle and knocked the legs from her. Sam hit the ground and rolled sideways, away from this dangerous woman. Areli was back on her feet and assessing her next move. The man she had tried to shoot had appeared from the house armed with a Glock but was keeping his distance. Areli needed to keep the bitch with the Volkswagen between her and the man so he could not get a clear shot at her. She scanned the ground for her gun but could not see it. Areli decided that the two of them would expect her to try get away, so she would take them by surprise. As Sam got to her feet, Areli ran straight for her. She threw a half-turning kick with her back foot. Sam moved to block her but in midair she changed feet and hit Sam hard across the chest on her unprotected side. Sam was shocked at the power the woman had for her size. She was badly winded, but Sam knew the follow-up kick was on the way. Sam saw the flying-axe kick coming for her head.

She ducked under it and caught the woman's ankle. She forced Areli's ankle upward and outward and dived down. Punching upward with her free hand, she hit Areli hard between the legs. Both women collapsed on the ground. Sam was struggling for breath, and Areli was curled up in a ball. Sam recovered first and stood up. As she stood up,

Areli went from the curled-up ball to kneeling in one fluid action. She pulled the knife from her belt and threw it at the same time.

Sam saw the movement in the nick of time and jinked to the side. The knife sailed past her head so close she felt the draught of the blade as it passed. Sam saw Areli reach for another blade on her belt. Sam charged her down, and by the time Sam got to her, she had changed her throwing position. This time she was going to throw over arm.

Sam grabbed her arm before she launched the blade, forcing her hand back. The razor-sharp blade made contact with Areli's shoulder. Sam forced all her weight onto the woman's arm, feeling the blade cutting through skin and muscle as it went. Areli released her grip on the blade and Sam fell on her shoulder, forcing the blade further home. Areli kicked for her life, making contact with Sam's thigh. Sam lost her balance and crashed to one side as Areli squirmed out from underneath her.

Areli made a run for the cliff edge and found the zigzag path to the beach. She flung herself down the path. She was no fool. She knew the fight was lost and escape was her only hope.

***

I had been watching the fight from the sidelines. At no point had the dark-haired assassin presented me with a clear shot, and when she fled down the zigzag path, I approached Sam who was still winded from the blow to her chest. Sam refused point blank to let me follow the woman. She grabbed my Glock and headed for the beach.

Ten minutes passed, then Sam reappeared. She told me the woman had dived into the sea and was swimming north, which in itself was a miracle as she was swimming with a knife in her shoulder. Sam and I were standing, debating our next move when a phone started ringing. It was coming from the woman's bag. Sam picked up the bag and answered the phone. She didn't get a chance to speak. An American voice on the other end of the line barked down the phone.

"Benesch, we are five minutes away from you. We will be at the turn-off in the next two minutes. What is your position?"

Sam was thinking on her feet, and she answered with one word. "Busy." She did not want the woman's friends thinking she was out of action and putting them on their guard. Sam shouted, "Adam, make sure that slippery bitch doesn't turn back."

I watched as she set off at a sprint down the hill, Glock in one hand, spare clips in the other, following the track toward the main road.

***

Fletcher was in a rage. They were slowing down looking for the turn-off. "That stupid Israeli bitch couldn't just wait. No, she has to be the hero and start something. She screws this up, and I will wring her Mossad neck. Busy! I'll give her busy."

Ed Holts was driving and was having to deal with a raging boss and a navigation system that said there were no turnoffs for miles. Lucas Richter spotted the turn and bellowed over his boss's rants to turn off now. No sooner had they turned off than the road turned left into a tunnel under the main road. The big Range Rover was half-way through the tunnel when a silhouette of a woman framed against a grey, stormy sky appeared from the side of the tunnel. For a fleeting second, Fletcher thought it was Benesch. Holts slowed the Range Rover just as the woman brought her Glock up in a two-handed stance. She started firing into the cabin of the Range Rover.

Only the speed of superbly trained men saved their lives. All three flattened themselves against the seats. Holts fared the worst. As the driver, he was Sam's primary target. He took a flesh wound in the upper arm, and another bullet took off the bottom part of his ear lobe. The Range Rover lurched to the right, hitting the exit wall of the tunnel, and coming to rest at a forty-five-degree angle on the embankment.

Fletcher and Richter spilled out of the doors, laying down covering fire until they cleared the stricken Range Rover. As the Range Rover crashed, Sam had climbed the north embankment. She saw from the disciplined way the men exited the Range Rover, they were well trained and well armed. There were three against one. If she stood and fought, she was finished. She wished she had brought Adam with her, but there was only one thing she could do—a planned retreat back toward the house, hopefully picking one of them off on the way. Already there were shots kicking up the ground around her. To her northwest, about one hundred metres away, were gorse bushes and then woodland after a further fifty metres. Sam reckoned if she could get to the bushes, she could then pick off anybody crossing the dead ground. Sam fired a volley of shots down the slope to the tunnel then set off at a sprint toward the bushes.

Richter was the first to the top of the embankment. He arrived to see Sam vanish into the gorse bush, and he fired, but at that distance, in the fading light, his chances of a hit were poor. He shouted down to Fletcher where she was. Fletcher's leader qualities kicked in, and after checking Holts and patching up his arm, he sent Holts up the road toward the house. They got their comms gear and battle gear on. Holts loaded his sniper's rifle and set off. His target was the man. Fletcher told Richter to hold station and keep an eye on the woman.

Fletcher was going to continue along the foot of the embankment for two hundred metres, where the slope became gentler. He would be out of sight of Richter, so he would contact him when he was in position; Richter would keep her attention while Fletcher flanked her and attacked from the trees behind her.

***

I was halfway down the cliff path, and there was no sign of the woman. I made a split-second decision. I reckoned Sam might need backup. She had already been in action and was now facing the unknown alone. I charged back up the path. The Beetle still had its keys in it. I could hear gunfire in the distance. I pointed the Beetle back down the hill. I decided to take the scenic route. Who knew what was coming up the road? The old Beetle bounced and bucked uncontrollably, but I kept the power on, broken glass flying everywhere. Suddenly, there was a man with a M16 in front of me. He looked up as I charged over the crest of a hump. He started to remove the M16 from his shoulder, but it was too late. I crashed into him, sending him flying up into the air.

The Beetle stalled, and I was out in a flash. There was no hurry. He was either dead or unconscious. His left leg turned outward, clearly badly broken. Either way, he was going nowhere.

I stripped off his vest, gun, knife belt, US Army-issue boots, his throat mic, and receiver. I was checking out the M16 when the ground at my right foot exploded. Luckily, I had been sitting with my back against the Beetle's front bumper, and the sniper had aimed for the only thing he had in his sights—my foot. I rolled over on my stomach and surveyed the surrounding area from the underside of the Beetle. There was no cover for him to hide. The only place he could be was on the track up to the house. He would be tucked into the foot of the incline, if I was correct. If I stayed on the far side of the crest, he would not have a shot. I moved slowly, always keeping the crest between myself and the track up to the house. The comms crackled into life. "Richter, Fletcher is down. I repeat, Fletcher is down." Seconds went past. "Holts, take care of the man. I will take care of the woman."

So there were two of them left. We now had a fighting chance. I continued to work my way along behind the crest of the rise back toward the house. After a few minutes, I came across a small sapling growing on the edge of the crest. It had a good view of the road and would be a good vantage point from which to view the track below.

***

Holts was not in a good frame of mind. He had taken a gamble on hitting the man's foot, which was visible at the front of the Volkswagen. The wound on his arm had made it difficult to steady his rifle. He had pulled the shot and alerted his target to his presence.

The man had vanished over the rise, but some sixth sense told Holts that this was not the end. He reckoned the man would try to get back to the house. Holts stayed tight into the foot of the incline and moved slowly and deliberately up the track in the direction of the house, watching the top of the embankment as he went for any movement. He had been moving for a few minutes now, and on the skyline, there was a small, spindly tree. Holts paid particular attention to it.

It would make a perfect ambush point. He knew if he had the high ground, that was the place he would have chosen to launch an attack.

He was just about to start moving on when he saw it. As he stared at the object it became clearer to him what it was. It was unmistakably the end of a barrel of an M16. As he watched, it moved slightly. He had him!

Holts moved back slightly. It was getting dark now. If he moved slowly and hugged the incline, he could reach the top of the slope and attack from the crest while his target was watching for him on the track below. His body was aching. It seemed like hours since he had started his crawl to the top of the rise. He was almost at the top. To his left, he could just barely make out the shape of a man lying on his belly watching the track below.

Holts moved through the tall grass until he was only twenty feet from his target. Slowly, slowly, he moved his rifle round from his side. His wounded arm was stiff, and he wondered if he would be able to fire with any accuracy. He steadied the weapon, took in a sharp breath, and held it. The rifle kicked once. Holts need not have worried at that distance. It hit the target perfectly. Suddenly Holts saw movement to his right, but it was too late.

***

I had watched the sniper's slow, deliberate movements up the hill. He was a careful and dangerous man. I waited until his full attention was on my body armour and jacket. He was six feet in front of me when I stood up and fired five shots at point blank range—four into his chest and one to his forehead. His face still wore a look of shock as he lay on his back, his sightless eyes staring at me in disbelief. I loaded another clip into the Beretta and placed it back into the holster. The hunting knife I had used to cut the grass I had hidden under went back into its sheath.

I wandered across to my body armour and studied it before pulling it on. If I had been in it, I would be dead. The bullet had entered just under the armpit and exited through the right-hand chest plate.

The relief of tension was like a drug. I felt like I was floating in the air, and a primitive emotion struck me. I had won in an even fight to the death. I now knew how the gladiators must have felt, that sudden rush of adrenalin. I walked over to the dead body and started lecturing him. "So you thought you could teach your granny to suck eggs, did you? Who dares, wins, mate. Who dares, wins."

I suddenly realized I was standing in the open countryside shouting at a dead body. The sound of four gunshots in the trees behind me brought me back to my senses. "Sam."

***

Sam was in trouble. Her pursuer was relentless. She had just fired her last rounds, and she had set a trap, waiting under a felled tree. She had been spot-on the money. The big guy following her had stepped through the gap, and she fired her last four shots, but his reactions were incredible. Not one shot hit him as he dived for cover. Even worse than that, he had closed the gap to a few feet. Sam had no idea at that point who she was dealing with. Lukas Richter was probably Europe's top hand-to-hand combat expert. Sam dropped the empty weapon and ran. She headed in the direction of the glass house, and she was halfway across a small clearing when Richter dived, catching her ankle and sending her sprawling in a pile of wet leaves. She got up to find Richter blocking her path. He never took his eyes off her as he undid his gun belt and placed it on a fallen tree by his side. He removed the throat mic and wires until he stood with only his stab vest on. Sam knew she had little chance of winning in a fight, but if she could distract him and get to the gun belt it would be a different story.

Richter would have shot her but he was out of ammo. He was very confident this woman would not put up much of a fight. It would be nothing difficult, no more challenging than wringing the Christmas turkey's neck.

First, she had to turn him so she could get to the gun belt. Sam took a run at the big German and spun round as if to hit him with a back kick, but at the last moment she changed her target and brought her leg down with all her might on his right shin, a blow that her trainer had promised her would floor any mortal man. Richter stumbled backward, but at the same time hit Sam across the side of the face with a mighty forearm. The blow took Sam completely off her feet, and she landed facedown in the wet leaves, her head ringing with the blow. She started to get up but was grabbed by the neck of her top and pulled backward with incredible force. She was once again flying through the air, this time backward. She crashed into the big German's chest, and he released the torn neck of her top, ready to grab her throat. Sam thrust her head back with every bit of strength left in her body. The crunch was sickening as she made contact with the German's nose. She tried to break away, but the German held onto her arm with a vice-like grip. The strength in her legs had gone. Again, she kicked backward at his shins. He used her arm to spin her round while his other hand came up in a clenched fist and hit her square in the jaw. She was thrown backward into the wet leaves. She stumbled to her feet, not sure where she was.

Richter was behind her again. He had one hand round her waist, and his second hand was round her throat, crushing her airway. She tried to head butt him again, but Richter was wise to this move and kept out of distance. She could feel the hot blood from Richter's broken nose running down her neck. She could also feel the darkness of unconsciousness descending upon her. She had nothing left. This was it, this was the end, she would die here in unnamed woods on the Scottish coast. Everything was becoming warm, she had no pain, and the darkness was being replaced with a brilliant white light.

***

I had seen what I thought was movement just at the edge of the woods, in roughly the same area from which the shots had come. As I entered the edge of the woods and my eyes adjusted to the semi-darkness, I could see there was a big guy with his back to me. He was in the process of strangling Sam; there was no time to lose. I could not shoot him. The M16 round would have passed through both of them. From the look of Sam, she was finished. The big guy had some sort of bloodlust, and he was still flinging Sam about by the neck, even though she was unconscious or dead. He was so busy with his gruesome task, he was unaware of my presence. I charged him from the back. I used the big hunting knife, ramming it up and under the stab vest he was wearing. It slid in with only slight resistance. Pushing it up to its hilt, I twisted it violently, doing the maximum damage possible.

The big German dropped Sam. What happened next was a shock to me. Instead of collapsing in a heap as I expected, he spun round, hitting me in the face with a serious elbow smash. The force took me off my feet. The big German staggered toward me, removing the hunting knife from his stomach. I pulled the Beretta from its holster, firing into the German's stomach first, then aiming properly—three rounds in his chest. He swayed like a leaf in the wind, but he raised an arm to throw the knife. I shot him again, this time between the eyes. He fell forward as he threw the knife. It landed with a thud, a foot from my head.

He landed with an even bigger thud, his head resting on my feet. I kicked his head out of the road and scrambled to where Sam was lying in a heap. She was pale, too pale. I couldn't find a pulse. I started mouth-to-mouth and heart massage. I checked for her pulse again, trying the side of her neck this time. Nothing at first, then there it was for a second. I shifted my fingers slightly. There it was, very faint, but she was alive. I wanted to shout for joy, but she wasn't out of the woods yet. She had taken a terrible beating, and by the looks of the big German, she had given him a good run for his money. I whipped off my stab vest and top, covering Sam to keep her warm. There was some slight colour returning to her face. She needed to be warm at home.

I set sail across the field to see if I could get any sort of transport to the edge of the woods. As I approached the track, I could hear the sound of an engine bursting into life.

I ran over the crest at full speed to see the dark-haired woman helping the man I had mowed down with the Beetle get into the passenger seat of the big Range Rover. At the sight of me running toward them, she shot round to the driver's seat and gunned the big beast through the tunnel. By the time I stopped and got the Beretta out, I only had time for one shot before the Range Rover vanished round the bend. The right tail lamp exploded, but this was little consolation to me. I was actually aiming for the driver.

It was pitch black when I pulled up next to the woods. To my relief, Sam was still breathing. I carried her to Herbie then struggled to negotiate all the bumps with only one head lamp. At the house, I carried her up to her room. I stripped Sam down to her underpants. I needed to know if she had been shot. She was covered from head to toe in blood, but luckily most of it was not hers. She was black and blue from head to toe. Her left eye worried me. It was purple and starting to close. She had no holes in her, which was a huge relief, but the lady was going to be in agony for a while. If her eye wasn't damaged, she was a lucky girl. There was no more I could do here for the moment. Sleep would be the best medicine.

I flung some clean clothes on and headed out. The big Guy was first. I had listened to him on the comms and was almost certain his accent was German this puzzled me. Why would the CIA use a German? On arriving at the edge of the woods, I was horrified to see through the woods about half a mile away the lights of a crofter's cottage. I concluded they must have been out, or there would have been a police car here to investigate before now.

I could hardly move the big German. I eventually put him across the bonnet, strapping him to the mirrors to stop him falling off. The sniper was lighter, but by now, it was starting to snow heavily. Back at the glass house, I wrapped the two bodies in some polythene that I found in the storeroom and transferred them to the boot of the Focus the dark-haired woman had arrived in. I checked on Sam. She was still out cold, but her colour had returned. Her eye was completely closed. Boy, was she going to get a fright when she looked in the mirror.

I needed to get rid of the two corpses. I left with the intention of dropping the car in a car park in Fort William and getting the train back when an idea struck me. I parked opposite the local cemetery. My luck was in. There was no one about, and the cemetery gate was open. I wandered around the graves until I found what I was looking for,—a new grave that had just been dug. Even better, the diggers had left their shovels under the imitation grass covering the pile of earth.

I carried the corpses in one at a time and unceremoniously flung them in the open grave, I covered them with a layer of soil and let the snow do the rest. It was three in the morning, and the adrenalin had long since vanished. I was so tired I could hardly walk.

I awoke the next morning with a start. I had been having a bad dream. I was covered in a cold sweat. The Beretta nine millimeter lay on the pillow next to my head. I pulled a dressing gown on and went straight to Sam's room. During the night, her nose had been bleeding. I returned a few minutes later with a basin, a sponge, and some warm water. I cleaned the congealed blood away from her swollen face and continued with her neck and chest. By the time I got to her stomach, the water was blood red. I left, cleaned the basin, and returned with fresh water. Sam's nose had started to bleed again. I dabbed at it with the sponge. As I was doing this, Sam opened her good eye.

"What happened? Where am I? Is Mac here." Sam was confused. I made her drink water and take painkillers, and a few minutes later, she was asleep again. I finished washing her legs and feet, then moved her to one side so I could change the bed sheets. At least the road to recovery had started and I had managed to get fluids and anti-inflammatory medicine into her.

Downstairs, it looked like a bomb had struck. There was splintered glass everywhere, bullet holes in the walls, even part of the banister had been shot away. Outside, it was snowing. I cleaned up downstairs, then checked on Sam again. She was still asleep. I left a note to say I would be back shortly and headed for the cemetery.

To my relief as I pulled up, the funeral party was breaking up. No one wanted to hang about with the snow coming down. Thankfully, the gravediggers were of the same opinion and were working at breakneck speed to fill in the grave. I sat in the Focus and watched for ten minutes while the three diggers worked like Trojans to get the grave filled in. I had seen enough; my secret was safe. I headed back to the glass house, stopping on the track to check for anything left last night.

The snow had done a wonderful job of hiding the evidence of any struggle, but on entering the wood, I found the big German's gun belt, gun, and knife. They obviously had a job lot—it was the same belt and Beretta that I had taken from the bloke I had knocked down. Back at the house, the first thing I did was check on Sam.

As I entered the room, she opened her eyes. "Adam, what happened to me?" She had no recollection of the previous day's events.

"You take these pills and drink the water, and I will go and make you some soup. Then and only then will I fill you in on what you have missed."

To my huge surprise, Sam walked into the kitchen as I was heating the soup. "Adam, who was the dark-haired woman I was fighting with?" Sam had a lost look on her face. Things were starting to come back to her but in flashes that she could make no sense of.

"I am not 100 percent sure who sent them, but she was part of a team sent to eliminate us. Luckily for us, they screwed up. If they had coordinated their attack, we would not be sitting here talking about it, that's for sure."

Sam crossed to a bar stool at the raised breakfast bar section of the kitchen worktop and eased herself onto it gently. She was trying hard to make it look like she was OK, but the pain etched on her face told the real story. "Do you think it was a CIA hit? I remember being chased in the woods. How many were in the kill squad?"

I pushed a bowl of steaming hot tomato soup under her nose and joined her on the adjacent bar stool with my soup. "There were four of them. Two were American. The one that got you in the woods was German, I think. I'm not sure about the nationality of the woman, but as for it being CIA, why use a German? And if that was a CIA mission, they are getting sloppy. No, I have a gut feeling there is something strange going on here."

Sam pushed her soup about the plate, deep in thought. I was getting used to these quiet moments with Sam. She never spoke until she had it clear what she was going to say.

"We need to get back in contact with Neil. He must have an idea what is going on."

"Adam, when we last met, he had me drugged and taken to a MI6 safe house for debrief. His men were attacked in the safe house by a hit team. They were organized and pros, and both the MI6 officers bought it. In the confusion, I managed to escape. Adam, they had only one goal, and that was to execute me. Who has the power and the balls to attack a MI6 safe house? They have somebody in MI6. Merlin has an inside line at MI6. Nobody in government knows any safe houses." She took a spoonful of soup and then continued. "I demanded that Neil get a government inquiry into the air base under way. I told him we would come in from the cold if he did, but I don't know how safe we would be if they have a handle on MI6 operations."

Sam sipped her soup, watching me for a reaction. The fact that Neil by his own admission had drugged and imprisoned his best agent shocked me. He was a changed man since he had joined the secret service, but this latest episode was a new depth of desperation.

"Adam, we need to get out of here. Our cover is blown, and we need to get to some place that we can get in contact with Neil but still be safe. We need to know if the government has set a date for an inquiry."

I emptied the rest of the soup into Sam's bowl. "We are going nowhere until you are better. For one, the government has broken up for Christmas, so there is no hurry for that, and second, the bad guys took a hell of a beating. I don't think they will be back for a while, if at all. And third, I have the perfect place to go, my house, so you concentrate on getting that pretty face of yours better, and then we will head for my house. We will be able to contact Neil from there."

Sam gingerly climbed off the bar stool and slowly wandered across to the living area, lowering herself to lie on one of the couches. "Well then, you said they took a hell of a beating. Care to enlighten me on that."

I walked into the living area and handed Sam a pack of frozen peas. "Here, put this on your eye. It will help reduce the swelling. The German who attacked you is dead. One of the Americans, a sniper, is dead. The other American has a broken leg and possibly a broken arm and pelvis. The woman has a severe stab wound to her shoulder, courtesy of you. On our side, you have a black eye and a bruised ego, but I have to report that our biggest casualty is Herbie. I don't think the poor old guy will pull through. He fought bravely, but his wounds will send him to the big scrap yard in the sky, I'm afraid."

***

The air-base doctor at Machrihanish checked over his two new arrivals. The base commander had woken him the previous day in the small hours of the morning to attend two people with serious injuries. There had been no explanation as to who they were or what had happened to them, only that they needed urgent medical attention. The man looked to have been in a road accident. His left side had taken the main impact. After various X-rays, the doctor determined that he was suffering from a broken leg and a fractured wrist. Most of his other injuries were tissue or muscular damage. The woman was a different affair. She had been in a street brawl. The stab wound had missed her arteries by millimeters, but her more serious problem was blood loss. Her heart was close to failure due to massive blood loss. Another hour untreated and she would have died. An armed guard had been posted outside their rooms. The doctor wasn't sure if it was protection or imprisonment.

***

I left early the next morning. Sam was on the mend, and I had no worries about leaving her for a few hours. My intention was to dump the Focus we had acquired when the dark-haired woman came to visit. It was a hire car. This fact was given away by the name on the number plates and subtle badging on the boot. I wasn't sure, but I had heard that some hire companies used tracker devices on their cars, and the last thing we needed was the hire car leading anybody else to our glass hideout on the hill. It had to go, and I had decided to drop it off in Malaig and hike back via the grocer's for some provisions.

The first part of my plan worked, and I deposited the car in an unusually quiet ferry car park. As I walked back toward the town, it was eerily quiet. There was no one to be seen. On arrival at the grocer's, I found it shut. I studied the sign on the door with amusement. It read "Closed for Christmas Day, open again tomorrow as usual." I had been so wrapped up in looking after Sam and cleaning up after the attack at the glass house that it completely skipped my mind that today was Christmas Day. We didn't have so much as a Christmas cracker in the house, never mind a turkey. It was the same story on the way back down the road.

I used the peace and quiet to help me concentrate on my running. My PT trainer at Hereford had drummed into me running is only half the task. You need to concentrate on your technique and most importantly your breathing. If you don't feed your muscles with oxygen, you won't run far. Usually, I found running a chore. I had been glad that my entry into the Special Forces had been fast-tracked, so to speak. I had missed out a lot of the running and all of the jungle training. I smiled to myself as I ran. If the lads I had been in charge of over the years knew how I got into the SAS, they might not have been so keen to follow me into battle. Today was unusual. I had set a good pace and was actually enjoying the run. It was a crisp, cold, but sunny Christmas morning.

I seemed to be the only person on the planet.

***

The turning to the left under the main road arrived surprisingly quickly. I decided to go for one last push and set off through the tunnel and up the hill at a sprint-finish pace. The morning was still young when I arrived at the front door and let myself in. A quick glance into Sam's room found her still asleep. Although I wasn't out of breath, my clothing told the tale. I was soaked to the skin with sweat. My old PT instructor would have had great pleasure telling me it was all my badness coming out of me. There was no point kidding myself. I wasn't super fit. There were more than a few guys in my old unit who wouldn't have even broken sweat on the same type of run I had just completed. I didn't even know why I was comparing myself to them anyway. I was out of it, just a very fit civilian now. It was just somebody needed to tell the bad guys I was a civilian so they would stop trying to kill me.

Sam arrived in the kitchen, admitting that the smell of the cooking bacon had awakened her from her slumber. Her face had improved dramatically over the last couple of days. I had been very worried about the state of her left eye, but the swelling had gone down, and although the eyes was still bloodshot, Sam assured me she could see out of it with no double vision. She had a bad cut on her top lip that really should have been stitched, but apart from that, Sam was well on the way to a good recovery. This was borne out by her change in mood.

She was far more upbeat and was attempting to give out orders again. Her movement was back to normal, and I could tell it wouldn't be long until she would be attempting her early morning runs again. After a hearty breakfast of bacon rolls and coffee, Sam asked if we could go for a walk on the beach as it was a beautiful morning. I agreed but told her to wait in the living room for me. I grabbed two coats and both the captured Berettas and headed back to the living room. I handed Sam the coat then the Beretta. She looked at me quizzically. "I thought you said they wouldn't be back. Not telling me something?"

Sam followed me down to the garage area, this was the first time she had been down here since the shoot out, and she was shocked. "Oh my God, what have you done to my house, you bad man." She looked around with her mouth open.

"Hey, I was too busy trying not to get my arse shot off, thank you very much, to worry about the décor."

We headed out the door and down the zigzag path toward the beach. I continued the conversation we had started in the garage. "Anyway, I thought you were supposed to be protecting me, not going on a week's jolly to London. No wonder you got your house shot up."

Sam gave me a withering stare. "You wouldn't have thought it was a jolly if you had been drugged, abducted, then ended up in the middle of gun fight at the OK Corral, and on top of that, forced to find your way back to Scotland with no money."

The tide was out, so we walked among the rocks, studying the trapped sea life in the rock pools. "You have had a bad few weeks, arriving back home to find your hideaway under attack. Has your memory recovered as well as your body, or is it still a bit hazy?"

Sam studied the horizon before answering me. "It is getting there, but my self-esteem is wrecked, beaten by a man, then rescued by the man I was sent to save. It hasn't been my finest hour, I'm afraid. You, on the other hand, are a revelation. That is more like the "Mac" all the stories talk about. I believe I owe you one." Sam shivered noticeably then suggested we head back to the glass house.

"Did you see my new name for your house?"

"Yes, what does it mean?" Sam picked up speed as we talked.

"It's Gaelic. *Comriach* means sanctuary in English."

Sam smiled. "Not a bad choice at all." We were halfway along the beach when I remembered I hadn't told Sam it was Christmas Day. She had also lost track of time and was as surprised as I was. At the foot of the zigzag path, Sam called me back. She had stopped for a moment. As I approached her, she had a strange expression on her face. She reached out and pulled me toward her with one arm while holding up a sprig of seaweed in the other hand. "Sorry, Adam. Seaweed will have to do, no mistletoe here, I'm afraid."

She pulled me toward her, kissing me full on the lips, then wincing. She had forgotten about the cut on her top lip.

"That will teach you, madam, for sneaking that one up on me."

Sam let go of me, smiling. "Merry Christmas. Ouch, that was nice, but it hurt like hell. Time for some vodka pain relief I think." On the way to the front door, Sam spotted Herbie. I had moved him to the far side of the house, out of eyesight. She walked round him and, to my amazement, started to sob. "Adam, look at the state of my Herbie? The poor old guy needs a car doctor."

His passenger side had been riddled with bullet holes, and it was a miracle Sam had not been hit. There was no glass left in Herbie, and his front bumper, bonnet, and passenger head lamp were broken.

I refrained from telling Sam her Beetle was dead. After all it was Christmas, and the bad news could wait for another day.

Back in the house, I poured out two vodkas. Sam had vanished for the moment. As quickly as she had vanished, she reappeared. We sat in the living area, and Sam handed me a brown-paper bag. "Sorry, there is no Christmas paper, but I hope you like it." The brown paper bag contained a new Land Rover key ring. "Sorry, it's not the Land Rover yet, but I will replace your Land Rover, I promise."

There was an awkward silence for a second. "Sam, I don't have anything to give you in return. Wait, how about a story? How about the one about the Gulf, the story you have been pestering me for, my memoirs from Iraq."

Sam clapped her hands in anticipation, got up, and vanished into the kitchen, reappearing with a new bottle of vodka. "OK, Adam, I'm ready. Fire away."

CHAPTER NINE

Kuwait

I set the scene with some background information that Sam needed to know then with a deep breath began telling her the story. My story started back in Australia. I had only been in Oz for a few months when the shit hit the fan, and Iraq invaded Kuwait. Things went from bad to worse, and the Americans seemed hell-bent on confrontation. Within two weeks of this, I was informed my presence was requested in Riyadh, Saudi Arabia, where I was to report to a Major Henderson.

Our first meeting did not go well. Major Henderson informed me that I would be leading a four-man team in the coming conflict. We would be heading off to recon an Iraqi air base. I informed Henderson that I was not trained in this particular field and that my talents would be better put to use in a different role.

Major Henderson was old school. He had been given control of all British Special Forces in the Gulf, and the power had gone to his head. He was having none of my nonsense, as he put it. I was a captain in the Special Air Service, and he expected me to act like one. I decided to keep my thoughts to myself and left to meet up with my new team who were stationed in a tented city that was building up nicely in the Saudi wastelands.

My second-in-command was Sergeant Ferris, a fellow Scot. He had been due to be returned to his unit but had been asked to stay on because of the present situation. Ian Ferris was a true Special Forces hero. He had served in the Falklands with great distinction, and his men had nothing but good words for him. He had been flown out from Hereford where he had been standing in as a weapons trainer. Corporal Robert Hunter had been with 22 SAS for nine months. He was a giant of a man, hence his nickname, "Big Bob." He was Royal Marine from tip to toe, and he had not yet got used to the more relaxed atmosphere of the Special Forces and spent his spare time cleaning everything. The last member of the team was Private Nigel Daws. He was our comms specialist and had just returned from jungle training and looked as if he badly needed a good feeding. He had originated from the Royal Engineers. This was his first taste of real warfare. He was dedicated and clever, but I decided he needed to be watched carefully. You never can tell how somebody will react to war until he is in a real war, no matter how hard he trains.

My first meeting with my new team did not go down well. Sergeant Ferris and his team had been together for three weeks and had time to gel. The arrival of a "Rupert" to take command was not to their liking. Although they were courteous, there was a look of rebellion in all their eyes. I decided to nip the problems in the bud right there and then. I asked Sergeant Ferris to accompany me on a stroll around the tented village. "Sergeant, this is off the record, so feel free to speak your mind. It doesn't take a brain surgeon to work out I am not flavour of the month with your team."

The sergeant stopped walking and came to attention. "Sir, if a man steps out of line in my unit, he will have me to deal with, sir."

I shook my head. "Sergeant, please hear me out, and don't interrupt. I have been transferred here from Australia. I was sent there to keep me out of trouble. Let's just say our Irish friends would take a very great interest in finding me. I have already talked with Major Henderson and told him this is not the field for which I was recruited into the Special Forces. I requested he reassign me but to no avail. So here we are. Sergeant, you are the true professional at this, and you have been told to take orders from a Rupert who has not a baldy clue about infiltrating air bases."

Ferris was thinking through what I had just told him. I was looking at him closely to gauge his reaction when the penny dropped. "Bloody hell, sir, I mean, Macdonald? I mean, Mac? Am I right, sir? That is who you are." Ferris looked like his head was about to explode.

"Yes, sergeant, you are right. I would appreciate it if you kept that between you and me. The secret service have moved heaven and earth to keep me a secret, and I don't want to spoil their party, if you know what I mean."

The sergeant was a changed man. He couldn't stop patting me on the back, an act that in a camp full of soldiers felt quite disconcerting. "Don't worry about your team, sir. We will be behind you 100 percent. If you need an opinion, sir, it would be my honour to assist you."

Within the week, we were moved to a forward staging point at the village of Umm Al Jamajm to the north of Riyadh half way to the Iraq border. We changed to local dress, although the bitterly cold nights had us all wearing our uniforms under the local garb for warmth. It all happened too quickly. One minute we were playing cards, the next we were marching up the gangplank at the rear of a Chinook.

I watched as my team boarded. The last few days had gone well. The sergeant had obviously had a word because the men looked on me as a team member now, not the dreaded "Rupert" tag that so many officers have to live with. The three of them looked like extras from Laurence of Arabia. I had to stifle a smile. Bob complained bitterly about the temperature. "Hunter, shut it. You are worse than a whining donkey." Big Bob trudged past the sergeant. "It's all right for you, Scotch. You are used to this weather."

The remark had been aimed at both the sergeant and me, but Sergeant Ferris got in there before I came up with a response. "Laddie, it's Scots, not Scotch, and if you don't button it, I'm sure our good Scots captain will take great delight in putting you on point for the whole of this fabulous mission." Bob shaped up. We all knew when the sarge called you "laddie," you were not his favourite person.

The Chinook dropped us twenty-five miles from our target. It arrived at zero feet and left at zero feet. I marveled at the control and the reactions of the RAF pilot who practiced this death-defying stunt regularly. It had to be done to get under the radar and to make sure we arrived unnoticed. The pick-up was forty-eight hours from now, five miles to the west. We watched the big Chinook skim over the sand and vanish into the distance. It was time to get down to business. We plotted a course northeast, and I told Hunter to take point.

A quick look over to Sergeant Ferris resulted in a wink, which I took as confirmation I had started OK. After an hour, I rotated the point man, and the less experienced Daws took over. I was leaving the sergeant until last for point duty. I wanted my best man on point as we approached the airfield. After an hour, I took point from Daws.

We continued doggedly fighting against the brutal desert conditions. Light was fast approaching when Sergeant Ferris appeared by my side.

"Want to take a breather, sir, and let me take point for a bit? I reckon our target lies just over that ridge on the horizon. Might be better to rest up now."

He was trying to tell me enough was enough. "I hear you, sergeant, but I would rather have eyes on the target before we stop. Do you think we can make that ridge before sun up?"

"No problem, sir." Ferris probably thought I was nuts, but he knew never to question an officer in front of his men. Ferris was a hard taskmaster and took off at a jog, leaving the rest of the team to try and close the gap. We arrived at the top of the crest just as the first rays of sun were warming the frozen desert. From our vantage point, we could clearly make out the two runways of the airfield.

It was a strange design and looked almost as if two air bases had been built next to each other. Sergeant Ferris was not sweating and had not a hair out of place. Considering he was by far the oldest member of the team, it was a remarkable achievement. On the other hand, Big Bob looked like he was about to die. Sweat was pouring out of his every pore, so much so that the sergeant asked him if he were still feeling the cold. Big Bob gave him a hard stare but couldn't summon up the energy to answer him.

We set about our makeshift camp. We all had places to hide if any aircraft came our way. Strangely, for an air base that was in the middle of a conflict, there was very little movement, and not one plane ventured into the sky.

After some rations and a good drink of water, we all settled down for a sleep, the sergeant gave Big Bob the first watch. Unfortunately the only person who could sleep was Big Bob. He fell asleep instantly after being relieved of his watch duties. Sergeant Ferris and I sat making plans. We agreed that I would take Big Bob and check out the southernmost part of the base, while Ferris would take Daws and check out the northern part of the base. Ferris had the furthest to cover, but the southern approach looked to be protected by a minefield. This was more my cup of tea, hence why I had picked it. We would gather the intel requested, then head back here where we would contact the headquarters for Operation Granby, and then head back to the pickup point and home.

We were ready to move as soon as dusk started to fall. We were all keen to get on with the tasks we had been set, and then get the hell out of there as quickly as humanly possible.

There was an unspoken feeling in the British forces that we had been dragged into this unprepared and totally underequipped. Our government seemed to forget that they had been cutting away at the defense budget for years. When I picked up my kit at the quartermaster's tents, the soldier handing me my kit had summed it up in a nutshell.

"Sorry, sir, but its Yankee kit for officers. Our leaders sold our desert kit six months ago to the Iraqi army. Makes you wonder who has any brains upstairs, sir. I mean, did they think the Iraqis were throwing a fancy dress ball or something? Then shock horror, they invade Kuwait. Well, slap my face, is it me, or are we ruled by a bunch of monkeys, or what?"

As an officer, I should have pulled him up for his attitude, but I didn't have the heart. In my mind, he was right on the money. I cautioned him about expressing himself this way with other officers as they might not hold the same views. I had arrived at my rank by a strange route. Discipline had been drummed into me at Sandhurst, but my time in Australia as a captain had been a much more laid-back affair.

About a mile from our target, our little force split in two, both heading in our own directions. Twenty minutes later we arrived at the edge of the minefield. It was signified by the universal language of the red skull and crossbones.

A pathetic single roll of barbed wire signified the start of the mine-field. At first glance, it did not look too daunting. There was only a thirty-metre distance between the minefield and the back of a large hangar. Take five metres off for foot patrols, and I only had to negoti-ate twenty-five metres of mines. Bob cut a section of barbed wire out of the way, and we waited to see if the area had a foot patrol. After twenty minutes, I made the decision to start crossing the minefield.

Night-vision mask on, I started cautiously. I was three metres in before I came across my first mine. After a bit of work, I uncovered the mine.

I didn't like the look of it. It was of Chinese origin and had been laid a long time ago, not on anyone's list of favorite things to dig up. Chinese mines were unstable at the best of times, never mind ones that were old and corroded. I spent a long time removing it and studying it. I had originally decided to dig up the mines in our path but now changed my mind. They were too unstable, so instead, I would use markers to mark the position of the mines. I reached for my bag of angel dust.

This was a powder that to the naked eye was invisible but when viewed through night-vision goggles left a luminous trail that could be followed, perfect for marking a minefield. It had the added bonus that a second team could use it if required. My initial slow pace changed as I got used to my task. An hour later I only had three metres left to check. Then disaster struck.

A door a few feet away opened, and an Iraqi soldier stepped from the light of the hangar into the darkness. I was frozen to the spot. The game wasn't up just yet. His eyes had not yet adjusted to the dark, and there was a chance if I froze, he might not pick up my shape on the uneven ground. I slid my knife, which was already in my hand, up to my chest.

The guard had picked a bad time to relieve himself. At first he searched for his fly, but then I watched his head turn and stare in my direction. I had been waiting for any signs of recognition from him.

He froze, then went for his rifle strap on his right shoulder. That was my cue. There was no option but to take my chances over the last few metres and try to strike first. My blade was aimed in an upper stroke, an attempt to kill him and silence him in the same move. As I started to rise, a shot from behind me rang out. Bob had been looking for the same reaction as me. His shot was good and took out the Iraqi cleanly through the heart. My brain instantaneously flooded with hundreds of outcomes but none that would let us complete our mission. That one shot had blown our chances of any sightseeing. Our priority now was to get out of here alive. As my brain registered this, I was still heading out of my crouched position. I could see the Iraqi in slow motion, falling, falling toward the minefield.

I shouted a warning to Bob and continued my leap past the doomed Iraqi and onto the safe ground behind the hangar. The Iraqi soldier fell with full force, chest first onto a land mine. There was a fraction of a second delay as I landed behind the Iraqi soldier, the vibration from the first blast set off the rest of the very old ordinance.

The concussion waves were huge that close to the blast area. My brain seemed to be thrown about inside my head. It was like having my head inside Big Ben when it struck midnight. My brain was racing again. I came to, and I could hear gunfire in the distance, but it took a second for it to register that it had to be Sergeant Ferris. He was either compromised or was laying down fire to confuse the Iraqi defenses. I stood up, swaying like a tree in the wind. I had to get away. I walked straight across the minefield. It felt like I had walked for miles before I lost my footing, fell, and promptly passed out.

When I regained consciousness, the sun had started to show its first tentative rays of the day. My head was exploding, and the ringing in my ears was as if I had just stepped out of an AC/DC concert. I groped round my limbs to make sure they were all still with me. The victims of mine blasts had told me that you still feel like your legs are there. It's when you try to stand that the bad news hits you. That thought had haunted me since Ireland. Thank God, they seemed OK.

Then I heard the groan. I staggered to my feet to investigate and found that I was only one hundred metres from the minefield. I dropped to my knees and cursed my stupidity. It was then that I noticed Big Bob. I crawled over to him. At first glance, I thought he looked like he was in a bad way. I must have had the luck of the devil to avoid being hit. Bob had no such luck, and he had caught a chunk of mine casing just below the left shoulder. I got him, sat up against a bush, and broke out the medical kit. The morphine kicked in and brought him back to this planet. I had a dilemma—try to take the chunk of metal out now while the morphine was working, and risk Bob bleeding out on me if it had nicked an artery, or leave it in place.

I was no doctor but reckoned that the shrapnel was too low for an artery. I decided to take it out and try to patch up the hole. The amount of traveling we were going to do, leaving it in the wound would cut him to pieces. My final thought was to set off a flare and let the Iraqis look after him. That thought was a nonstarter. There was no way I was going to leave one of my team to be tortured. I knew that I had not missed my vocation as a doctor. The shrapnel came out of Bob's chest with a disgusting slurping noise that reminded me of when you get your Wellie stuck in mud and have to break the suction.

I had a dressing waiting for the inevitable fountain of blood that followed. To Big Bob's credit, he took it like a true soldier. He was shaking like a leaf, but not a noise crossed his lips while I applied pressure and waited to see if the bleeding had slowed. While I waited, I studied the shrapnel I had removed from Bob's chest. If I had managed to get it all out, it had only penetrated around an inch and a half, so it looked to me like if Bob survived the shock and the blood loss, he had a fighting chance. I removed all visible dirt and covered the wound with antibacterial solution then glued the jagged flaps of skin together then applied a field dressing round his chest, then a sling to hold it in place. Luckily for us, because Daws was carrying the radio gear, we had taken the medical gear and most of the spare ammo. Bob's colour already looked better.

I let Bob rest for half an hour while I tried to devise some sort of plan. There was a road to our left, which, after checking my maps, I figured would head south into Kuwait. We had missed our ride, and with no radio equipment, we had no way of contacting anyone. Our best bet was heading down the road to Kuwait, and hopefully, we'd bump into some friendly forces coming our way. It wasn't foolproof. We had a long way to go, and there was a good chance that we would meet Iraqi forces rather than coalition troops, but in the circumstances, it was our best shot. We needed to put some distance between the air base and ourselves. It was a miracle we had not been discovered already. I gave Bob a good drink of water and got him on his feet.

We transferred as much as we could to my Bergen. Bob just about had a fit when I suggested we dump some of the spare ammo. To keep him happy, I loaded it into my Bergen, this was going to be a sore march.

We cut across by some loose scrub and hit the dirt road at a forty-five-degree angle. For the first time since being dropped in Iraq, we got lucky. Lying against a bush was an old step-through moped. I told Bob to wait by the scooter, and I slowly moved through the bush, looking for the scooter's owner. My luck was still in. On a slight slope just below where we had set our camp the previous night, was a small flock of sheep, and there was a young lad about twelve putting down feed for the skinny-looking beasts.

I estimated even if he heard the bike start and sprinted, he would not reach the road for at least five minutes. I retraced my steps and reported my findings to Bob. We had a quick look over our new mode of transport and were happy to find that the jerry can tied with twine to the back was also full of fuel. Loading the scooter up was a task in itself. I jammed my Bergen between my legs in front of me while Bob climbed on the back and laid both our M16s across his knees. It was the moment of truth. Could this old girl actually take both of us? I turned on the ignition and the fuel and kick-started the scooter. It fired first time. There were no gears. It was simply twist the throttle and hope for the best.

I told Bob to hang on and gave the throttle a half-turn. The engine revved, and the poor old thing strained but would not move.

I gave it everything it had, and it started to crawl forward. I put my feet down and gave the old girl a helping push, and she started to pick up. In a cloud of blue smoke, we were off. It was only running pace, but at least we were away. As the road leveled out, the old girl picked up more speed. I throttled back slightly and gave the burdened machine a bit of a breather. We were probably cruising along at about fifteen miles an hour. If we could keep the old thing going for a bit, it would help our journey enormously. All day we stayed on the road and never came across a single person. I had abandoned map reading. There was no need. The Iraqi soldiers had shown us the way. In the distance, we could see the oil wells of Kuwait set on fire by its captors. They were obviously working on the plan that if they couldn't have it, you couldn't have it either.

We found a hollow and set up camp for the night far enough away from the road not to be spotted, but close enough to flag down a friendly face if we spotted any. I redressed Bob's wound. Then we got stuck into some rations and a good helping of water.

We bedded down for the night. "Are you still awake, Adam?" I half-turned in Bob's direction to see if he needed any help. "Sorry to bother you, sir, but I was thinking. I owe you an apology. I screwed the mission up good and proper, sir. I should have let you deal with the rag-head back at the base. If I hadn't shot him, we could have finished the mission proper."

I sat up and yawned. "Bob, if I hadn't got to him on time, we both could be dead. The only thing that went wrong with the mission was the guard needing to empty his bladder at that time and in that place. It was nobody's fault. It was bad luck. Just in case you are worried, I will be filling in my report when we get back to say that we had to neutralize the guard when challenged and had no option but to open fire. You get a good sleep. We may have a very busy day tomorrow. Night, Bob."

***

The next morning we emptied the rest of the petrol into the scooter and set sail again. All day the burning wells got closer, and the little scooter chugged on. Just after lunchtime we passed what looked like a burned-out checkpoint.

There were no signs, but we were very close to the burning wells. I reckoned this was the border between Iraq and Kuwait. As if on cue, the scooter started to splutter. It picked away again, then died. The irony was not lost on me that in one of the world's most fuel-rich nations, we had just run out of petrol. It was time for a stroll in Kuwait. For an hour or so we walked. We were fast approaching the burning wells, and I wondered if any of our guys were around.

About two miles away was the biggest and closest of the oil fields. Strangely, it had not been touched and seemed from this distance completely intact. A look at Bob confirmed my fears. Although putting a brave face on it, he was stumbling and sweating badly. His dressing showed the telltale signs of bleeding again. The walking was literally killing him. He needed some encouragement. We agreed when we walked up to the oil field, we would stop for the day, put our feet up, and wait for help. It took Bob an hour and a half to walk the two miles. It was clear to me, for the moment at least, he could go no further. The last one hundred metres as we turned off to the oil field was a medium hill, and it knocked the stuffing out of Bob. The perimeter fence was just about intact, and the first entrance we came to was a works entrance. In the area where there should have been gates stood an old wooden gatehouse. Continuing up the hill would have taken us to the main concrete office block, but Bob was done. I sat him down in the old wooden gatehouse and gave him a good drink of water, then fed him my last Mars bar. I told him I would be back shortly and headed off to explore the offices. Although the wells were untouched, the staff had left in a hurry, and the buildings had since been looted, so much so that the only things of any use I could find were three bottles of cola and a packet of aspirin. On the plus side, I did find more transport of a sort.

I arrived back at the wooden shack with a rear-wheel-steer dump truck. Bob had still not recovered from his exertions yet but brightened up when I pointed out that the shack contained four big gas bottles, which were full, and a heating panel. At least we would be warm tonight, if nothing else. The instillation at one time had been well guarded. About twenty metres behind the shack on either side of the road sat two gun emplacements. The guns had long since disappeared, but the sand bags and gun mounts still stood. Between the service road and the offices was a watchtower. I made a mental note that after I had sorted out Bob and had eaten the last of the rations, I would explore the tower on the off chance there was anything useful up there.

Bob's dressing was a mess. It took most of the medical provisions I had left to tidy it up. I was not happy about the colour of the wound—it was dark purple and red hot to the touch.

Bob was putting a brave face on it, but I knew he was in trouble. I left Bob sorting out what was left of our kit and took a wander over to the tower. I climbed the wooden ladder slowly; I had forgotten how tired I was. The tower gave a commanding view of the oil field and surrounding countryside. It seemed strange to me that during a conflict like this, we had seen very little enemy activity and, for that fact, no coalition forces. The only telltale was the burning oil wells and the sound of aircraft in the distance.

I concluded that the war was obviously taking place in another part of the country. My heart skipped a beat. I looked again. To the north, on the road we had just followed, dust was being kicked up. I cursed—one of the things I had lost in the madness of the last few days was my binoculars. I screwed up my eyes and stared hard at the approaching dust cloud. After a few seconds, I could just make out the shape of the lead truck. It was military and had a canvas back, which meant it was probably a troop carrier. It looked like two trucks were coming this way, probably with troops on board. Coming from that direction put the chances of them being our boys at very slim indeed. My mind was racing as I flew down from the tower. We couldn't run; Bob wouldn't survive. We could hide and hope the trucks didn't turn up off the main road and head here, or we could fight.

Bob was wounded, so it would have been acceptable to duck out this one if it happened. "Adam, you're the boss. I'll go with whatever you decide, mate. We have all got to die sooner or later."

There was no time to dither. The trucks would be here in minutes. My head was pounding, but the stubborn Scotsman came out again.

"Right. If the trucks turn up here, we fight. Let's just hope they drive right past." It was time for some seat-of-the-pants planning.

"Bob, take the two M16s and put one in each bunker with half the ammo each. I need to block the access road to the offices so they can't flank us." I grabbed the belt of grenades and headed to the dump truck. Just outside where the gate should have been, I parked the dumper downhill toward the main road with its bucket up and dug into the dirt. I ripped out the ignition wiring and placed a grenade next to the right front wheel. If they tried to move it, they were in for a wee surprise. Next stop was the old wooden shed, where I placed a grenade on the top of each of the gas cylinders. It was going to get hot tonight if they stopped. I sprinted back to the left gun bunker, the one closer to the main road. There was no sign of our trucks yet. Bob gave me a thumbs-up but said nothing.

My mind was racing again. How many troops in each truck? They must not flank us. I let that happen, and it would be over. A real captain would have been trained for this. What was I doing here? I reached down to take off the safety catch, and my hand was shaking so badly I was worried I was going to discharge the weapon right there. I left the safety on and started taking deep breaths.

The noise of the trucks slowing down and turning up the road to the oil field stopped my deep breaths instantly. To my absolute horror, three trucks appeared in view. On each front door was the insignia of the Republican Guard. I was aware that I was close to being physically sick. The lead truck, seeing its path to the offices blocked, turned up toward the old gatehouse. My hand steadied. Fuck it. If we were going to die, we were going to do it in style. The lead truck was almost level with the old gatehouse when I opened up with rapid fire into the gatehouse. The explosion was massive, much worse than I had expected. Bob fired into the cab of the stricken truck, killing its driver and both officers instantly. The back of the truck was destroyed in the explosion, so I concentrated on the second truck. Again the driver and both officers were my first target. Men were starting to pour from the back of the truck right into my line of fire. The M16 carved them to pieces. I sent a grenade over the back of the second truck and ducked down while I slammed a second clip in and opened up again. The third truck had started to reverse so I took out the driver then sprayed the canvas back before turning my attention back to the second truck. So far things had gone better than I had expected, but the officers from the third truck had rallied from the initial shock and started to organize a counterattack. Most of the troops from the third truck were unharmed and had formed a line next to the boundary fence.

If left unattended, they would work their way round from the main roadside. Out of the corner of my eye, I noticed three heading for the dump truck. I thumped in another clip and opened up on the dump truck. There was a *crump* as the grenade, muffled by the wheel, went off, and one off the three men's legs were blown off. The other two decided to make a run for it, but I was ready for it. One took five rounds in the chest while the man behind took a head shot as my M16 lifted as I fired. I ran across the road, which was being increasingly peppered with shells, and dived into Bob's gun emplacement. Bob was barely conscious but managed a wink. I grabbed his last two clips and shouted to him to cover me. I banged in another clip and set off down the left side of the burning truck appearing at the back, level with the perimeter fence, here the remainder of the second truck had joined up with the third truck's troops.

My movement had thrown them off guard. The first man in the line was an officer, and he took six rounds in the chest. The man behind him went to throw a grenade as he took a round in the stomach. The grenade fell at his feet, decapitating him and blowing the arm off the soldier behind him. I emptied the rest of the clip into the mass of troops along the fence and then dived back behind the burning truck.

What I had just witnessed shocked me. I estimated that there were at least forty enemy casualties, and there must have been the same number still waiting for their chance to counterattack. I had one clip left. I looked back to the gun emplacement. Bob was not firing anymore. Things were starting to happen in slow motion. I was aware I had started reciting the Lord's prayer to myself. For a second, the sunlight faded, which caused me to look up. Appearing from behind

Bob's position was a chopper. The noise was unmistakable—it was an Apache gunship.

The Iraqi Republican Guard made the biggest mistake of their lives and opened up with everything they had. The Apache was taking some serious hits, but then its awesome chain gun burst into life. The perimeter fence disappeared before my very eyes. Chain link, barbed wire, posts, and various parts of the human anatomy were thrown into the air as the chain gun did its gruesome work. The Iraqi troops fought on doggedly. The Apache turned its attention to the second truck, which is when I decided to get out of it. I was too close to the second truck for comfort. I dived headlong into Bob's gun emplacement as the Apache turned the second truck into Swiss cheese.

The remaining Iraqis saw their opportunity and made a run for it in the third truck. It had just made the junction with the main road when the missile from the Apache hit it on the rear axle. The blast sent the remains of the truck twenty feet in the air, and it came down on the far side of the main road in a ball of fire.

I was a physical and mental wreck. I sat looking into the floor of the gun emplacement, and I was weeping openly. I could not believe I was still alive. How could I have survived when all around me lay the dead—a full platoon of Iraq's best soldiers? I had been saved when fifteen minutes ago, I was preparing for my last suicidal charge and certain death. The joy of still being alive mixed with the anger of why I was here, and the bitter sorrow I felt for the deaths I had caused. I grabbed the two M16s and threw them as far as I could muster.

My temporary insanity lifted, and I realized Bob was lying next to me. I pulled myself together and started checking out Bob. It looked like he had a graze on his forehead, but that was the only new wound I found. The first Apache touched down as three more Apaches arrived. The gunner remained in the cockpit while the pilot approached, handgun at the ready. I had just found a very weak pulse when the pilot arrived. "Major Lee Tribby, of the 101st Airborne out of Fort Campbell, Kentucky. May I have the pleasure of your details, sir?"

He spoke in a friendly tone, but his side arm was pointed at me, and his stare never left me. The last thing I needed was an itchy trigger finger.

I stood up slowly and kept my hands where Tribby could see them. "Captain Adam Macdonald of Her Majesty's Special Air Service. This is my colleague, Corporal Robert Hunter, also Special Air Service."

The major relaxed visibly, but the gun remained poised. "Captain, could you let me know the nature of your mission?"

I relaxed my arms. "Major, I should not be giving out that information, but as you have just saved our lives, I will run the risk of falling out with my superiors. We were part of a team carrying out reconnaissance on Ar Rumaylah Air Base. We were split up, and the corporal and I were making our own way back to Kuwait."

Tribby put his side arm away. I had said the magic words. The major stepped past me and took a look at Bob. He pulled out a hand radio and talked to his gunner. "Air medevac requested urgently. We have a man down. Repeat, we have a man down. Contact the rest of the tribe and advise friendly aircraft is en route to pick up casualty."

Tribby walked around looking at the devastation. I was content to stay by Bob's side. You just never knew whether there might be a wounded hero who fancied his last chance at vengeance.

"Captain, you certainly did a job here, boy. I'm a bit pissed I missed the start of it all. So are you telling me it was just you and your buddy? You didn't lose any of your unit."

I shook my head and sat down. "Major, when you arrived, I had just loaded my last magazine and was contemplating my last charge, so all I can do is thank you. It was certain death on the menu for us until you arrived."

The Chinook arrived a few seconds later, and we were soon on our way back to an American medical unit, escorted by Major Tribby and his four helicopter gunships. Bob and I were treated for our wounds. It was only when my adrenaline returned to a normal level that I realized that I had a few problems of my own. I had been shot through the left foot, my left hand and the left side of my face had third degree burns, and my right eardrum was perforated. Bob was suffering from concussion, and his shrapnel wound had become infected.

It was another two weeks before Big Bob was stable enough to be moved. In that time, Major Tribby and the rest of his flying circus visited us regularly, and during that time, I concluded none of the 101st Airborne came with volume control, although I must admit they were good fun and great company.

It was on one of these visits that Tribby, seeing my sullen mood, pulled me to one side. "Hey, buddy, I've got some good news for you. You're gonna be a real-time, goddamn war hero. Those turkeys you took out at the oil field were responsible for most of the oil fires, and my boss, Colonel Ness, has sent a dispatch to the White House asking that you be decorated for your defense of Kuwait resulting in the death of eighty-nine Republican Guard. We checked them out for you, bud—eighty soldiers, six officers, and three drivers. Way to go, pal. With a little help from the 101st Airborne of course." Tribby was a little dismayed that this information did not hit the spot intended.

The next day brought an unexpected guest. We had just got lunch by, and Bob had just returned from having his wound dressed, when Zoë, one of the American nurses, came rushing up to Bob and me. "Guys, you better stand by your beds. You've got company." The way she spoke, it sounded like the president had arrived. I sat up on the edge of the bed, and as I did so, the flaps at the far end of the tent were pulled back. Thirty patients and their nurses all turned and stared at the same time as three figures in full regimental dress uniform marched into the tent. Major Henderson led the way, followed on his right by Sergeant Ferris and on his left by Private Daws. They marched up the tent as though they were on the parade ground, wheeled round at the end of our beds, and came to attention, all three saluting at the same time.

Bob and I came to attention, which must have looked quite funny as we were sporting striped pajamas. I was frightened to look at Bob. I was having enough problems keeping my face straight.

Henderson gave the order to stand at ease and received a round of applause from his captive audience. It was like water off a duck's back to Henderson. "Well, Captain Macdonald, we meet again. Good to see you pulled through. Thought we would give the Yanks a bit of a show. Let them see how it should be done. I am going to speak to the doctors about your release. Sergeant Ferris will answer any questions in my absence."

Henderson marched off to find his target. Ferris watched him go, then sat on my bed while Daws sat by Bob. "Well, laddie, I take it you didnae fancy our company on the way back."

For the first time since arriving in hospital, I had a grin from ear to ear. "Thank God you made it back OK. I've been asking everybody to find out about you. What happened about the air base?"

Ferris looked at Daws, then shook his head. "What a bloody waste of time. We got back and reported that the mission had been compromised to find out the Americans hadn't waited anyway, and as we spoke were carpet bombing the base. Anyway, hardly important, are you two Muppets going to be OK?"

It was at that point that I noticed the row of medals on the sergeant's chest. "Jesus, Sergeant, is that the VC?"

Ferris blushed. "Son, it's a bit of tin. They are so proud of us, we don't even get to wear them in public. It's only Henderson's playacting for the Yanks that has allowed me to blow the dust off it."

"But surely you are proud to own it."

Ferris wiped a speck of dust from his polished shoe as he formed his reply. "Adam, one day they may pin medals on Bob and you. When you look at the medal, try and think of the men you helped get home safely. You can wear it with pride for that. Try not to think what you had to do to achieve your goal, because if you do, it will be like wearing a ball and chain round your neck. People will ask you how you got it, and it will drag the terrible past back to haunt you."

Ferris jumped off the bed. "Stand by your beds, gentlemen. Here comes Major Muppet." Henderson marched back in, said his good-byes, and marched the three of them back out to the waiting Lynx helicopter.

***

Sam was sitting cross-legged on the floor in front of me, nursing her glass of vodka. She had been hanging on every word and was still on her original glass of vodka, which was a record for Sam. My storytelling had lasted for the best part of two hours. Apart from the official report, this was the first time I had told anybody the full story from start to finish.

Sergeant Ferris was right. It had done nothing for me but drag up emotions that had taken me a long time to bury. Sam sensed that my head was not in a good place after the story and refrained from asking too many further questions about the Gulf.

I went to the kitchen to top up the cola in my vodka, and Sam followed me. She came up to me at the breakfast bar and gave me a hug. "Thanks, Adam. I can see it still gets to you."

Sam went to move away, but I held onto her. "Sam, you're the only person I have told the full story to. You will probably be the last. I hope you can understand why."

Sam smiled and pulled me back into the lounge. We sat together, staring at the view, just enjoying each other's company. Sam decided to change the subject. "Adam, I am going for a run tomorrow morning. Do you fancy being my bodyguard and joining me?"

I gave Sam a hard stare. "Oh my God, here we go again, Mrs. Bloody Rambo."

Sam smiled. "Well, I'm not getting any younger, and I can't have my image ruined by being upstaged by an old retiree like yourself."

I gave Sam a playful slap on the knee. "Why can't you just stay the way you are at the moment? I like quiet and vulnerable. It makes for an easy life."

Sam cuddled into my side. "OK, Adam. Tonight, I will be quiet and vulnerable, but tomorrow morning at six, I will be back to bossy and brilliant."

Six o'clock arrived far too fast. Sam was up and out the door as I was still trying to tie my laces. She was at the bottom of the road before I managed to catch her up. As we ran, Sam chatted away to me. "I take it you bought the old BMW in the garage for a reason." Sam was not slow to catch onto things.

"I thought we might steal its identity and swap it over onto the drug dealers' M5 and start to use that." After turning left at the road end we ran on the main road for a mile then turned left again onto a little back road that followed the coast north past the sands of Morar.

"How long will it take to swap the parts over, Adam?"

"Not long. It's just number plates and tax disc. I have already charged the battery and put some fuel from the old car into it. Sam, did you ever check the BMW out?"

Sam glanced across at me as we ran. She had noted the change in my voice as I asked the question. "No, now that I think about it. I never was going to use it, so—no, I never gave it much thought. Why, what did you find?"

"Well apart from the battery, there is a very, very large quantity of white powder, which I take to be heroin, and a case filled with hundred-dollar bills. So as well as the twenty-two million pounds, you now have ten million dollars and millions of pounds' worth of drugs."

Sam shook her head in disbelief. "What the hell are we going to do with that little lot?"

As we ran a car had started to catch us from behind. We both were aware of its presence. After the last fiasco, we were a bit jumpy.

"I have a confession, Sam. As your bodyguard, I have failed miserably. If the car behind us turns out to be hostile, I didn't bring a weapon."

Sam glanced back as the car drew closer. "Don't worry, Adam. I have enough firepower for both of us."

Sam was smiling at me, making it clear to the driver that we were unaware of his presence and enjoying each other's company. The driver was keeping his distance and had been following us for far too long. I was starting to get worried. "Adam, if the shit hits the fan, I have a Beretta taped to each ankle."

If the situation had not been so serious, I would have burst out laughing at that statement, but at this moment, it seemed to be the most sensible thing imaginable, to strap a gun to both your feet and go for a run. Sam had done a good job of hiding them. She wore pink Nike trainers and scrunched-up leg warmers at her ankles to conceal the weapons, followed by white, skintight leggings. Any red-blooded male would pay far too much attention to her shapely legs to notice the leggings at her ankles. Sam knew it and used it to her advantage. The car seemed to close in on us. Both Sam and I turned at the same time. Sam stopped and bent down as if to check her laces. The car closed to a few feet, then swung hard right into a walled drive. As it turned in, we both caught a glimpse of the driver. It was none other than the local clergy, who smiled from ear to ear while giving us a friendly wave.

Sam and I waited until he was out of sight, then collapsed in a heap, laughing until our sides were sore. The tension had been unbearable, and the sight of the wave and the dog collar had just been too much. "Oh my God, Adam, I almost shot a vicar."

I was busy wiping away tears while Sam reattached the sticky tape she had torn off her leg in the rush to defend herself. "Two things—I don't know who is the bigger nervous wreck, you or me, and there are no vicars in Scotland. He was either a priest or a minister."

We pulled ourselves together and continued our run with no further scary moments. We agreed on the run back to the house that I would work on the car with a view to using it tomorrow. Sam did not volunteer what we were going to do, but I knew in her own good time, she would tell me.

CHAPTER TEN

The Cleanup

In a room on the Machrihanish air base, Areli Benesch watched from a window as the C130 transport plane touched down. She watched as a number of nonmilitary types exited the plane and headed for the main building complex. Benesch had already decided to leave, but this new development strengthened her resolve. She was under no illusion that when the time came, the US authorities would have no problem complying with a request from Israel asking for their wayward agent to be sent back to them for sentencing.

Her wounded shoulder was healing well, and she had just had the stitches removed. It was time to leave.

Dinner arrived from the kitchen as usual. The guard took the food from the kitchen staff and unlocked the door. Areli was at the sink washing her face. Over the last few days, she had been building a relationship with the guard. "Hi, Billy. Sorry, I have soap in my eyes. Honey, can you stick the tray down on my bed for me?"

Billy obliged and was in the process of putting the tray down when she struck. Areli had spent the last four nights digging out one of the support bars that held the sink to the wall. To her surprise, when she examined it she had found it was made from wrought iron. The bar hit Billy across the base of the skull, fracturing his skull and knocking him out in the process. Areli stripped his holster and side arm and removed his clothing. She tied his arms behind his back with the gun belt and stuffed a pillowcase in his mouth, then tucked him up in bed with the covers over his head.

She pulled on his uniform and made some turnups in the legs before tucking them into the boots. She tucked the handgun into her boot and pulled the cap down to cover her face.

Her last task was to lock the door, which she did before snapping the key in the lock. Areli did not hang about; she headed straight for the kitchen where she found the locker room empty. There, she swapped her boots for a pair of trainers and her shirt for a pullover and heavy winter jacket. The local butcher's van was parked unattended at the back loading bay.

Areli seized the chance and climbed in the back, hiding between two carcasses. She didn't have to wait long before the door was closed and the van was on its way. She was free from the base. She knew she needed to put as much distance as possible between herself and the American base. The butcher's van made its next stop in Campbeltown, and the driver left the back door open while he made the next delivery. Areli made her escape and headed to the local supermarket.

The small, dark-haired woman was too busy loading her groceries into the boot of her car to notice Areli studying her. When she went to get in the car, Areli made her move.

She placed the gun in the small of the woman's back and whispered in her ear to open the rear door. The woman did as she was told, and Areli climbed into the back seat, making sure the woman could see the gun in the rearview mirror. Areli instructed the woman to drive to her home. On the way, Areli quizzed the sobbing woman about her work, her home, and her family. The woman was single, a schoolteacher who lived alone with her cats. When they arrived at her house, Benesch instructed her to pack a travel bag, including her passport.

The woman did as she was told. Then Benesch told her to go to the bathroom and pack her toothbrush and soap. As she entered the bathroom, Benesch hit her over the back of the head with the butt of the gun. The woman collapsed on the bathroom floor. Benesch wasted no time. She stripped the clothes from the woman and with some difficulty, hoisted her unconscious body into the bath. She proceeded to fill the bath, and her task was almost complete when the woman started to come round. Areli held her head under the water for a full ten minutes, which she timed by the woman's wristwatch. Only when she was sure the woman was dead did she release her grip on the woman's head. With any luck, the local police would put her death down to a tragic accident. The woman had slipped on the wet floor and banged her head as she fell into the bath. Benesch decided to get out of the country and put this assignment down as a failure.

***

Master Chief John Steiner came to attention as the three men walked into the control room. He had received a direct order from the director of the CIA that anything these men asked for, they must have. From that moment on, all communications were to be through the CIA agent in charge, Special Agent John Zelenski. The tall man led the other two across the room. He was tall enough to have played basketball in his youth, but his athletic frame had started to stoop slightly as age had taken its toll. His hair was thinning and almost nonexistent in places. He walked over to Steiner and introduced himself as Zelenski. Steiner knew his career was on the line and this elderly gentleman had the power to make or break him. Zelenski introduced his two colleagues: Tim Cortez of the FBI, and Colonel David Southern, Pentagon and NASA Liaison officer.

The colour drained from Steiner's face. Colonel Southern's reputation was legendary. If he was here, this was far more serious than he had suspected. "Master Chief, Colonel Southern will be taking over from you for the moment. All officers will be suspended and confined to their rooms until this investigation is complete. Please be aware that this is a very serious situation and your cooperation would be appreciated. Furthermore there is to be no contact with Deputy Director Whiteford or anybody from his office. Failure to comply with this request will be met with the gravest consequences. Do I make myself clear?" Steiner called his second-in-command over, introduced him to Colonel Southern, and advised him he had been relieved of duty and that the colonel would be replacing him. Zelenski wasted no time and started his interrogations. Steiner was first on the list. Zelenski was intrigued to hear that a member of a team sent here by Whiteford had returned injured and with a woman he claimed was part of his team.

They had been placed under observation in the medical wing. Zelenski asked to see them right away. To Steiner's horror, the woman was found to be missing. Southern ordered the base to be closed down and every available man was sent to search for the woman in every part of the base. Southern and Zelenski watched as six soldiers dressed in some type of chemical suits, headed past the control room along the runway, to the west end of the runway by the beach. Southern asked Steiner what they were wearing, and why.

The reply shocked him. "Colonel, they have to wear the radiation suits. I take it you are aware of the SR3000 prototype based here? Therefore you must know about the radioactive pollution it emits on return from space." By the horrified looks on Zelenski's and Southern's faces, it was obvious he had disclosed a hidden truth. "My God, you mean you don't know about the radiation?"

Zelenski was almost afraid to ask the next question. "How bad is the radiation, and where does it effect? Please remember, I am not a scientist so if you don't mind, for our benefit, laymen's terms."

Steiner shuffled about the papers on his desk, then crossed the room and spread a map of the Scottish coastline on a big table in the centre of the room. "The area marked in red is the worst area affected. It is relatively small, and for twenty-four hours after landing, is contaminated by 10 percent less radiation than was produced at Chernobyl. As the radiation spreads out, it drops to 50 percent of its original reading. The yellow area is more or less constant and is more than fifty times the recommended safe level of radiation. The white areas show a constant radiation level 10 percent above safe levels." Steiner stood quietly as the three new arrivals studied the map. The red area was the runway, the coastline to the west of the base, and the large hangar that housed the SR3000. The yellow area covered the rest of the air base and the surrounding fields, and the white area stretched out over the whole peninsula. Colonel Southern recovered first from the horrific news. He ordered the SR3000 grounded and the building containing it sealed.

Zelenski headed for the hospital wing while Tim Cortez quizzed Steiner about his involvement in the project when it had been based in Nevada. Colonel Southern contacted the situation room in the White House. He relayed what he had found out so far to the chairman of the NSA and the president's chief of staff. Faced with the facts, Fletcher told everything he knew about Whiteford and his operation. Zelenski was shocked to hear there was one assassin still unaccounted for and the second one had escaped their clutches.

They had to be stopped before they tried to kill the British agents again. America was already on the brink of causing a major incident between the two countries, without pouring more petrol on the fire by having their agents killed. The report was compiled hurriedly and sent directly to the White House.

An hour later Colonel Southern was in the control room when the message came through from the White House marked top secret, for his eyes only. The message read, "Return SR3000 to Area 51 urgently. Deploy all personnel to Afghanistan and Iraq with immediate effect. Terminate all nonmilitary persons deployed by Whiteford in the UK. Cleanup team and security arriving within the next eight hours."

Merlin collapsed into the big wingback leather armchair. It had been a busy day in London, and he wasn't getting any younger. He sat in the chair, looking out over his manicured lawns and hedges, his estate spread out in the distance. It had been a bad winter in England, and he was looking forward to gazing out once more over sun-ripened fields. He clutched his glass of malt whisky jealously. He undid his collar and switched on the TV to catch the news. At first he was not paying much attention. The news seemed to be focusing on a plane crash in America, and by the look of the pictures, it was a small jet.

The newsflash band appeared at the bottom of the screen. There was a crash as the crystal whisky glass smashed into a million pieces on the polished floor. Merlin sat looking at the screen, trying to take in what he was seeing. He read it again. "Today Deputy Director Whiteford of the CIA was killed when his plane lost control and ploughed into a hillside in Virginia. The president has expressed his sympathy to

Mr. Whiteford's next of kin, praising him for his contribution to the smooth running of the intelligence community."

Merlin didn't know whether to laugh or cry. The man had been a thorn in his side, but he was his contact with the CIA. It was Whiteford and the CIA that were paying for his wife's treatment at the drug addiction clinic. They had suppressed this fact to keep his career on track. It was Whiteford who had found out from his Irish informer that the IRA were blackmailing him over his wife's drug habit, and Whiteford who had arranged for her removal and treatment in America. Merlin mulled over the different scenarios in his head. In the end, he decided to do nothing and wait for somebody else to make the first move.

Fletcher was mentally and physically drained. He had spent the last three hours being grilled by Zelenski and his two buddies. In the end, he had told the whole story with every detail about his team, right down to how he was paid and how Whiteford had funded the operation. At the end of the interrogation, he was told to get some sleep. He would be flown back to Washington where, in return for testifying against Whiteford, he would be given immunity against prosecution.

Fletcher was woken the next morning at five thirty, given a full cooked breakfast, and told to be dressed and ready to leave for six thirty. He finished the breakfast, trying to work out a plan to salvage his shattered career. He drained the last of the orange juice and sat back, checking the clock to make sure he had time to dress and shave. The pain in his chest appeared suddenly. The more he tried to breathe, the worse the pain. He tried to call out to the guard, but the strain of trying to speak caused the pain to double. He tried to stand but collapsed on the stone floor. The saliva in his mouth started to foam, and the room darkened.

The official story was that Aron Fletcher died from a heart attack at 6:31 a.m., while working abroad on a government contract. When Zelenski quizzed Colonel Southern about Fletcher's untimely death, he was advised by Southern that he and Cortez had finished the investigation and that they would leave for America, returning with the plane that was bringing in a cleanup team. He thanked them for their assistance but warned them against any further involvement in the situation, as it had now become a military matter. He also advised them against leaving the base. Because of the situation, anybody attempting to leave would be shot on sight.

Southern and Zelenski stood outside the control room and watched as the four Apache helicopters stationed at the base left, heading northwest.

Zelenski made sure there was nobody around before speaking. "Colonel, I take it you are aware that the Apache helicopters were stored in the same hangar as the SR3000. They must be contaminated with radiation. Surely you are taking a risk sending them into service."

There was an uncomfortable silence. For a second, Southern looked weary; then some kind of inner strength took over. "Special Agent Zelenski, I am going to take a risk here and disobey a direct order from our commander and chief. You are a clever man, so I will do you the honour of telling you the whole truth, because I am sure if I don't, you will figure it out for yourself. The Apaches have been sent to the North Sea, between Greenland and Iceland, supposedly to rendezvous with a carrier group bound for the Mediterranean. There is no carrier group in the area. The choppers and crew have been sent to their deaths. The radios have been altered to give out no signal, as have the distress beacons. The survival gear has been removed or tampered with, and the fuel range calculated so that no return is possible. Agent Zelenski, the crews were doomed. Three were exhibiting signs of radiation sickness, and they and the others would have died a terrible death in hospital. The average life expectancy in Arctic water is around five minutes."

Zelenski was shocked but tried not to show it. "And if that shocked you, Zelenski, this next one will blow your goddamn socks off. I have been ordered to terminate any nonmilitary involved with this case. Which brings us to your good self and Agent Cortez. Luckily there are some grey areas in this matter, so get on the plane and get the hell out of here before somebody tells me to kill you both. Don't ever breathe a word of this conversation to anybody, or I will come for you, and don't think you are safe in the CIA. Whiteford thought that, and now he is pushing up daisies."

Zelenski was too shocked by what he had just been told to continue the conversation. He nodded, turned, and started to leave. "Zelenski, I am sorry it had to end like this. If you hadn't contacted your director about your suspicions, who knows how bad this could have got. Go home to your wife, put your feet up, and try to forget any of this ever happened."

***

I changed over the number plates and tax disc on the big BMW, and now I was running it outside to let it warm up and charge the battery. Sam emerged from upstairs with two holdalls and a large shoulder bag. She announced she was ready.

As I drove down the hill, away from the glass house, I took one last look in the rearview mirror. The winter sun glinted on its surfaces, magnifying the sunset effect. I wondered if I would ever see the big house again. Sam had booked a hotel in Inverness. We were back to being a honeymoon couple.

"So, Mrs. Ann Hunter, are you going to tell me what the plan is?"

Sam was busy applying makeup using the mirror on the sun visor to hide the last of her bruising. "Well, for a start, Mr. Hunter, watch the road and not me. I thought it was about time we gave Neil Andrews a call to see how he is getting on with my demands, and if there is no progress, we need to give him a deadline before we call Rupert Murdoch's papers."

The drive up the Caledonian Canal was not pleasant. It was a sullen, misty January day. The rain came in fits and starts and blotted out the highland scenery. The roads were quiet. It seemed nobody wanted to venture out in this weather. Sam had decided she was back in charge mode and took the BMW keys from me at Fort William. Our relationship over the weeks had changed—confrontation had given way to more playfulness. We tested each other just to see how much we could get away with before the other retaliated or said enough was enough.

I had my first dig at Sam for taking the keys as we left Fort William. I asked Sam if she were sure a wee English girl like her would be able to find Inverness all by herself. Sam took the bait and retaliated with a strange answer. "And what, Mr. Hunter, makes you think that I am actually English in real life?" Sam smiled to herself but kept her eyes glued to the winding road ahead. "You must remember, Adam, that I am MI6. They go to great lengths to hide our true identity, but I am flattered that my portrayal of an English rose has worked for you."

That remark had taken me by surprise, but I couldn't let her win so easily. "Not so much of an English rose, more of an English tomboy." Sam took a swipe at me with her fist but I had half-expected it and got out of the road before it landed.

I decided to change the subject, as I was on the losing side so far. "So are you going to tell me why we have brought the drugs and the suitcase of dollars with us? We get stopped by the police, and they will throw away the key."

Sam rolled her eyes and shook her head in mock disbelief. "Adam, Adam, what are we going to do with you? Have you no imagination? If we get stopped, all I have to do is give them my ID number and tell them we have just carried out a drug bust and are heading back to London with the evidence. We won't be in jail. We will be heroes. To answer your question, I don't want that stuff lying about the glass house. I would be in enough trouble if they found out about the house without bringing the drugs into the equation. I am sure if we put our heads together we can find something original to do with the contents of the boot."

We sat in silence for the next few miles, both deep in our own thoughts. Sam was probably planning what to do next, but my mind had wandered back to Sam's last comment. It had made me think just how little I knew about my MI6 friend. It stood to reason doing the job she did, she would have more than a few skeletons in her closet. If we were to remain friends, I would have to brace myself for a few surprises. I studied Sam as she drove. My remark to her in jest had been right on the money. Although she could become very feminine when she wanted to, it was not her natural state. She was wearing makeup today, but it was more to cover up the last of her injuries than it was a normal thing for her to do. Sam was more at home challenging her male counterparts than she was competing with other women. I reckoned the only time you would catch Sam in Tesco's was if they had a buy-one-get-one-free offer on handguns.

We arrived at Dovecote Manor in the early evening. The big country hotel sat back from the main road, set in its own large grounds a few miles from the outskirts of Inverness. Sam maneuvered the big BMW up the winding gravel drive. Looking at the country hotel's clientele, I was glad we had used the M5. Even the drug dealer's big BMW was outclassed by some of the machinery parked in the car park. Pride of the car park was a new Bentley, which was parked at the door and obviously belonged to the owner of the establishment. Aston Martins, Ferraris, and the odd Lamborghini were the order of the day, with some other guests slumming it in Jags, Mercs, and BMWs.

As we walked through the car park with our holdalls, I took time to study the lovely green Aston Martin Vanquish parked at the end of one of the rows.

"Oh my God, look at you. Most men look at women the way you look at cars. Come on. Put your tongue back in, and let's go. We will be late for dinner." We booked into our room and were given the grand tour by the lady proprietor of the hotel. She was a very attentive host, and I couldn't make my mind up if this was because we were alleged newlyweds, or if every one of her six-hundred-pounds-a-night guests was treated this way. From her designer dress and her diamond-encrusted jewelry, it was obvious business was booming. Sam played the part of the new Mrs. Hunter perfectly again, but this time I sensed a change. She wasn't as tense as during our last honeymoon scene. As she put her arm around my back and gave me a hug, it was far more natural than on the previous occasion. We stood for ten minutes while our host explained every contraption known to mankind fitted in the bathroom. I was trying my hardest not to yawn as the tour finished. The owner left, explaining dinner would be served in forty-five minutes.

I showered and changed for dinner, emerging to find Sam nowhere in the suite. I checked my watch. Half an hour to dinner. It was then I noticed the fan arrangement of newspapers on the coffee table.

My time spent at the glass house had starved me of any news, so within seconds, I was wading through them. Sam reappeared, but I was too busy reading to take a lot of notice. Noises from the bathroom told me Sam was in the shower. I continued with my news overdose. The hotel obviously catered for visitors from abroad, as there were French, German, and American papers among the pile. The French and German I discarded, but a quick thumb-through the American paper out of curiosity brought me to a page about the conflict in Afghanistan. At the bottom of the article were pictures of two American soldiers. The paragraph below the pictures stated the two men were the latest casualties on the growing list of US troops killed in action in Helmand province, Afghanistan, assisting British and Afghan troops maintain law and order. They were named as Petty Officer Howie and Seaman Fernandez, both Navy SEALs deployed in an advisory capacity. They were killed when their vehicle detonated a roadside bomb. At first I continued reading, but a strange feeling of déjà vu came over me.

I was still thinking about it when Sam made her grand entrance. Sam had raided the in-house boutique and had put a lot of effort into her appearance. Her blond hair was plaited tightly in a single plait, showing off her sculpted neck, which was amplified by her new low-cut dress, which also showed her toned shoulders and a fair bit of cleavage to match.

The pale blue dress was set off by a matching clutch bag and blue stiletto heels. A sapphire necklace and earrings completed the transformation. Sam's makeup was slightly on the heavy side. This still masked some of the old bruising on her face.

Sam was standing, waiting for my verdict. "Well, Adam, will I pass inspection?" It took me a few seconds to realize how nervous Sam was. Her beating had obviously knocked her confidence.

"Hmm, I can't call you Sam. Tonight you are definitely Samantha, and so much for keeping a low profile. Tonight, I will have to fight off every single male in the hotel. You look lovely, Sam."

As I had predicted, the minute Sam walked into the dining room, every set of eyes in the room studied her. The owner met us at the door and escorted us to a corner table, complimenting me on marrying such a beautiful wife. She was having a ball showing off her new model for the boutique and asked me if I liked my wife's new dress, adding that it was made in the finest Italian design houses. I agreed that the dress made my wife even more beautiful than she already was. The owner left, undoubtedly pleased her sales pitch to the rest of the dining room had worked. Her boutique would be booming in the morning, I had no doubt.

Sam and I ordered dinner and while we waited on its arrival, the talk turned first to Sam's outfit. "Well, spill the beans, Mrs. Hunter. How much did that little lot cost?"

Sam caught my eye and immediately knew I was attempting to wind her up. "Not that it is any of your business, Mr. Hunter, but as you are aware, our Russian friends left us a rather large wedding present, so here is some of it."

I smiled and poured Sam a glass of Champagne, which the hotel owner had delivered to our table, compliments of the hotel. "Nice try, Samantha. You didn't tell me you were in training to be a politician. You gave me an answer, just not the one I asked for."

Sam drew closer to me and whispered in my ear. To anyone watching, it just looked like an innocent moment between two newlyweds unable to keep away from each other. "Well, Mr. Allan Hunter, you would have failed spy academy with that little cockup. I am Ann, not Samantha, remember? By the way, try not to swallow your glass when I tell you this. The dress, shoes, and handbag cost seven thousand, and the jewelry, eleven thousand-ish."

Sam returned to her original seating position, smiling, just in time for dinner to be served. We ate dinner not saying much. Then Sam broke the silence "What is the matter, Allan? You are very quiet. Did that last bit of information shock you?"

It was Sam's turn to try and wind me up, but I was not taking the bait. Instead, I answered truthfully, maybe a little too truthfully.

I leaned across and whispered in Sam's ear. "I was just thinking if I ever end up getting married for real, I will be a lucky man if on my real honeymoon, my bride is as lovely as you are tonight."

Although it was not a windup, it was game, set, and match to me. Although Sam was a trained professional at hiding her feelings, her lack of response and glowing cheeks gave the game away. Sam reached for her Champagne glass and drained it in one go. She asked me to refill her glass and watched me intently while I did so. "Adam, are you serious, or trying to wind me up? Be honest because I can't tell. You are too good at this game."

I got up and moved my chair next to hers so I didn't need to lean across to whisper in her ear. "Who would have failed spy school now, Mrs. Hunter? My name is Allan, not Adam, and by the way, that was the windup. This is not. I almost lost you in the woods that day. I was worried sick, and here you are today looking fabulous. I will wager there is not one man in this room who does not envy me. Looking at you tonight, I am a little sad that we are only playacting, and that is the honest truth, no windup."

Sam stood up, took my hand, and nodded toward the exit.

She said nothing as we made our way to the room but held on tightly to my hand. I wasn't sure what Sam's game plan was. Had she seen something or somebody that looked out of place? I wasn't sure, but I knew Sam would tell me in her own good time.

We entered the room, and Sam shut the door behind me. I was about to ask what was happening when Sam pinned me to the door. Her kiss was warm and passionate, her body warm and inviting. At first I was taken by surprise but relaxed quickly, helping Sam unzip her dress while we kissed. It looked like the playacting was going to continue in the bedroom, only we both knew the playacting was over. We both had secretly wanted what was about to happen next for a long time. The sexual tension had been growing from day one. Sam was about to unbutton the last button on my shirt when she stopped.

"Adam I can't do this. Please forgive me." I was caught off guard by Sam's sudden change of heart. Her emotions were evidently in turmoil for some reason that eluded me. "I'm sorry. The Champagne went to my head, and you charmed me, and I was so tempted, but we can't. I mean, I can't, not now." Sam was in tears. I tried to comfort her, but it only seemed to make her worse. "Don't hate me. I'm so sorry. I need to keep you as my mission, not my lover. I won't be able to do my job and protect you. I need to be professional. It can't happen this way. There are things you don't know, things you need to know."

I sat on the bed bewildered, trying to make sense of her rambling statements. "Sam, if you need to tell me something, tell me now, and get it off your chest. It is obviously bothering you, so tell me."

Sam wiped her eyes with a tissue from the bedside cabinet. "No, Adam. I have made a fool of myself tonight. We need to talk, but if you have any feelings for me, let me do this my own way. We need to see this through to the end. God knows how many agents the CIA have sent after us. When it is over, we will sit down and sort out this thing between us."

I was still none the wiser to what she was on about. "Sam, if that is the way it has to be, so be it. I will respect your wishes, but do one thing for me in return. Please don't get yourself killed trying to protect me. I don't have a good track record when it comes to women, so please be careful because we really need to have that talk."

Sam put out the light and climbed into the bed. She leaned across and kissed me on the lips. "It's a done deal, Mr. Hunter. Thank you. Now get some sleep because I have an important job for you tomorrow."

I was still awake long after Sam had fallen asleep. Things were just going round and round in my head. Sam's strange behavior and her occasional strange comments puzzled me, but for the life of me, I couldn't make any sense of them. Then for some reason, the names of the two soldiers kept popping into my head. I lay awake wondering why my life had ended up the way it had. I wondered what type of future I had in store. Sam woke me at eight thirty. She had been up for some time and had showered and ordered breakfast from room service.

Sam nipped down and paid the bill while I ate breakfast and showered. We were back on the road and heading into Inverness by ten o'clock.

CHAPTER ELEVEN
The Inquiry

The prime minister finished his morning cup of tea as he studied the letter from the head of MI6. He was not in a good mood, and the more he studied the letter, the angrier he became. Who did this man think he was, demanding the government open an investigation into the operations at the Machrihanish Air Base in Scotland? The letter had put him in an intolerable position, stuck between a rock and a hard place. Both he and his predecessors had spent a long time cultivating the relationship between the UK and the United States, and he did not want to rock the political boat between the two countries. On the other hand, the head of MI6 was not a man to be taken lightly, and anyone who ignored that fact was in a dangerous position.

The prime minister knew if he did nothing, the director of MI6 would be true to his word—he would resign and publish all his findings on the Internet. As he pondered the problem, his secretary phoned to tell him that Sir Antony Carrington had arrived and was waiting to see the prime minister. The prime minister had picked Carrington to hold the public inquiry for two reasons: one, he was a Conservative, which would ensure that the government could not be accused of a whitewash, having picked a member of the opposition to chair the inquiry; and two, Carrington was a personal friend and well respected by his fellow members of the House of Lords, where he now presided. The two men shook hands and the prime minister suggested Carrington make himself comfortable in the big leather chesterfield opposite his desk. The usual coffee or drinks were offered to Carrington, but he refused, getting right to the point and asking the PM why he had been asked to attend at such short notice.

"Tony, I have a dilemma, and I am hoping that you can help me out here. The head of MI6 has demanded that I authorize a public inquiry into the American air base at Machrihanish. He has some sort of evidence of wrongdoing at the base and wants it investigated. He is so sure of his facts that he has given me an ultimatum—investigate it, or he will resign. As you know, if I charge in, the Americans will not be happy."

Tony Carrington was deep in thought. He could not disguise the frown that had formed on his face. His old boss Thatcher had worked hard at Anglo-American relations, a feat that had benefited the current Labour government greatly when it came to negotiations. "May I ask the prime minister what he thinks is going on at the air base, and can he prove it? The Yanks will not take kindly to us poking our nose into their business. I'll tell you that for nothing." The prime minister shifted in his chair and rearranged some papers on his desk before meeting Carrington's stare. He had the reaction he was looking for. He knew now Carrington would be opposed to any outcome that would jeopardize the two countries' relationship.

"Tony, if I knew, I would tell you. MI6 are playing their cards close to their chest. They have told me they will present two witnesses at the public inquiry, and that the witnesses have been placed in protective custody until the inquiry, as MI6 fear an attempt on their lives. The whole thing is a political nightmare. What I propose is that you chair the inquiry, which will be for all military bases in the UK. This will limit the time spent on Machrihanish and keep the spotlight off the base, but at the same time will appease MI6. Tony, I am relying on you to steer the investigation the right way for me. We cannot afford to fall out with our friends in America."

Carrington was about to launch into a number of questions, but the PM was on his feet and making for the office door. "I'm sorry, Tony, but I am late for an appointment with Her Majesty. Must dash. My press secretary will set up the inquiry and keep you in the loop. It will be soon, so don't make any plans for the near future, I will be in touch."

Two hours later, Sir Antony Carrington was at his gentleman's club in London. He had just ordered lunch and was working his way through his second brandy while studying the *Financial Times* when his train of thought was interrupted by the arrival of a small, portly man who sat down in the large leather highback chair opposite him.

"So Antony, I hear you will be chairing the inquiry into British military bases."

Carrington drained the last drops from his brandy glass before replying. "Well, well, director, we are well informed. It took you only two hours to find out who is chairing your little fiasco."

The director smiled and stared into the big roaring fire beside them. "My dear Carrington, I knew five minutes after the PM left for the palace. They didn't make me head of MI6 for my good looks you know, old boy." The director turned his attention from the fire back to Carrington, making eye contact. "I am well aware no one wants to rock the boat with the Americans, but if I suspect for one minute that you are trying to brush this under the carpet, by the time I have finished with you, your glittering political career will be in ruins. Do we understand each other, Sir Antony?"

Carrington held eye contact, smiling. "My dear director, as usual you have the manners of a pit bull, and yes, we understand each other, but hear this. If your witnesses don't turn up or your evidence is flawed, then when I am finished with you, your shabby little career will be over, and you can go back to your council house where you belong."

The director was rattled by this, but did not let it show. "Well 'Tony,' as long as we understand each other, we won't need to keep having these cozy little chitchats. I bid you good day."

***

We arrived in Inverness around lunchtime. Sam drove around Inverness for some time, crossing and recrossing the River Ness, looking for a good place to contact Neil from. Eventually she decided on the caravan park on the south side of the town. Sam explained that it would give us good exits in the event of an emergency, and it had no

CCTV within half a mile. It had pay-phone facilities in the reception area and at this time of year was quiet. Sam parked the BMW on one side of the Ness and accessed the caravan park by a series of footpaths and bridges over the river.

"Sam, do you really think MI6 has a team in Inverness? Don't you think this planning is overkill?"

Sam gave me a withering stare and shook her head. "Adam, that is why you are a soldier, and I am a field agent. If I didn't plan every op down to the last detail, I wouldn't be here talking to you today. Humour me, and do exactly as I tell you. Neil may or may not have manpower in this area, but all he needs to do is pick up the phone to the local chief constable and have us held on some trumped-up charge until his men get here."

As we arrived at the entrance to the caravan park, Sam issued her instructions. "Take this white hanky. If something doesn't look right, blow your nose with your left hand and walk away. Cross the bridges, watch for someone tailing you, head for the town centre, then get a cab to the Eden Court Theatre. I will meet you there." Sam didn't wait for the inevitable barrage of questions I was thinking up. She crossed the road and entered the reception area for the caravan park. I watched as Sam picked up a phone next to the window, slotted in a credit card, and punched in a series of numbers.

***

Neil almost shouted with joy when his receptionist told him who was on the phone for him. "Samantha, I can't tell you how good it is to hear your voice. You have put me under a bit of pressure with the boss. How are Adam and yourself getting on?"

Sam knew right away this was not the normal Neil. "For a start, Neil, cut the crap. Let's get down to business. We are in Inverness, so don't bother with the trace, in an hour's time it will have done you no good. Just to jog your memory, if you send anybody after us, you will get that person back in a body bag. Do I make myself clear?"

Neil loosened his tie. He wanted to scream down the phone at her, but he knew he had to keep the peace like never before. His future depended on it. "Sam, calm down, girl. It's all sorted. Your inquiry is about to happen, thanks to the director. You need to lay low for a little longer. Then you can give your evidence to the inquiry, and things will be back to normal."

Sam's eyes were everywhere. "I don't think things will ever be back to normal, Neil. You and I both know that. By the way, Adam and I were attacked by what seemed to have been a CIA hit team. It looks like our special relationship is dead in the water."

Neil sat up. The hairs on the back of his neck were standing on end. "Sam, we are pretty sure the team that hit the safe house in London were CIA or American Special Forces. Are you both OK?"

Again Sam scanned the surrounding area and checked across the street for signs of a hanky, but all was well. "Adam proved to be a bit of a revelation. He killed two and wounded two. They were last seen hotfooting it away with their tails between their legs."

There was a pause. "Sam, I have had to make Adam a MI6 asset. It was the only way his evidence would stand up in a court of law. We have back dated a year's salary into his account."

Sam's grip on the phone tightened. "Neil, you are a true piece of work. You don't care whose life you fuck up, do you?"

Neil knew he was on dangerous ground. "Sam, both I and the director have put our jobs on the line to get this inquiry started, which by the way, will be announced on the evening news. We can't afford any mistakes, so you need to get you and your new boyfriend with his evidence to that inquiry intact. Do you want additional protection?"

Sam had tears in her eyes. "Go to hell, Neil. I've seen what happened to your last so-called protection. I will call you when the time is right."

Neil knew he had rattled her and couldn't resist one last dig. "Say hello to your new boyfriend for me. Does he know who you are yet? Remember to tell him he now works for MI6."

Sam slammed the phone down, ripped the credit card out, and marched out of the reception.

I watched Sam march across the road to where I was standing. She walked past without stopping. Her face was cast in stone. Something she had been discussing had really bothered her. "Adam, let's move, please."

I followed her. We were setting a fast pace as we crossed the main road and headed for the footpath that led out to the little islands in the middle of the River Ness. We walked for some time until we found a park bench. Sam plonked herself down and sat staring into the fast-flowing waters of the Ness. I sat down next to her, not quite sure how to treat the mood Sam was obviously in.

After a moment, Sam spoke first. "We need to stay under the cover of the trees for at least an hour. There may be a satellite in the area, and I don't want anyone finding out about the BMW or where we are going. We will wait for an hour. Then you will put your specs on, put your jacket in my backpack, leave by the north side of the river, and head for the town centre. We will meet in the Irish pub in the town centre. I will leave by the south side of the river. Don't go near the car. Try to change your style of walking. Eight out of ten suspects give themselves away by their stance you know."

We both sat watching the dark waters of the River Ness flow by at great speed. There had been a lot of snow and rain in the area, and the river was in full flow. It was my turn to break the silence. "Where did you get the credit card from?"

Sam smiled but did not look away from the water. "Remember the little fat Canadian woman in the hotel lobby this morning? She had more credit cards than you could shake a stick at. I was pretty sure she wouldn't miss one for a long time, so I borrowed it for my phone call." Sam reached into her pocket and removed the credit card. She launched it like a skimming stone into the deepest, darkest part of the river.

"Your good friend Neil says hi. He has arranged the inquiry soon. He said that it would be on the news tonight." Sam continued to stare into the depths of the river.

"So if the inquiry is arranged, and we haven't been found yet, why the sudden change in mood since the phone call? If you don't mind me asking."

Sam stopped looking at the river and changed her attention to the ground in front of her feet. "It's Neil Andrews. He knows how to push all my wrong buttons, and he has dragged you into this, right up to your neck."

I was at a loss about how to make any sense of what Sam had just told me. "I am already up to my neck. I don't understand how he could drag me into it any further if he tried."

Sam turned her attention from the ground to me. She was pale and obviously not relishing the next part of the conversation. "Adam, Neil has had you drafted into the service and has backdated a year's salary, in case anybody checks. He says for your evidence to stand up, you need to be a fully operational agent."

I started to laugh. "You mean I'm a real-life James Bond? When do I get my license to kill? We can go to the casinos in Monaco and spend my salary on vodka martinis."

Sam was frowning at me. "You have no idea what this means, Adam. Even if we get through this, you will be on a leash for the rest of your life. Now that Neil has his talons hooked in you, he will never leave you alone. Trust me, I know. I've got the T-shirt."

The sound of a siren caused us both to stop talking and look for the source of the noise. After a few nervous moments, Sam spotted the ambulance crossing a road bridge in the city centre. We both relaxed visibly. I decided to change the subject, as I could see that my joking about the situation wound Sam up.

"So once we leave Inverness, what is the plan of attack? Where do we go next?"

Sam stifled a yawn and then half-turned on the seat and looked across at me. "I thought we would stay in the Inverness area for the night, then tomorrow head south for your house—that is, if you think it would be safe to stay there." Sam was staring at me and waiting for my reaction.

I had no problems with this. I was sure we would be safe as I had already installed a few security measures just in case I received a call from my Irish friends. I was pretty sure Sam was curious about my house, as I had never talked much about it. "That wouldn't be a bad idea. We can pick up the camera chip. I posted it to myself when you went missing for a week, just in case it fell into the wrong hands."

Sam stared at me in disbelief. "Let's hope it made it there, or this inquiry will be a short one. I can't believe you did that just before Christmas. Have you any idea how much mail goes missing over the Christmas period?"

Sam was right, but I still felt the need to defend my actions. "I know, but at the time I had lost all track of time. Being chased all over the country by assassins and being ordered about by a madwoman will do that to you."

Sam made a face and looked at her watch. "Right. Time to head off. Remember, stay away from the car, and don't go into the pub if you are being tailed. Head for the theatre if that happens, and wait for me, OK?"

Sam pulled on a foldaway raincoat and dropped her bag into a carrier bag along with my jacket. I put on my specs and Kay's baseball cap under the supervision of Sam's watchful eye.

Sam decided to make a few adjustments to my dress, pulling my T-shirt out of my trousers and turning the baseball cap with the skip to the rear. Finally happy, she left, first telling me to give it a few minutes before I left. I watched Sam with admiration as she made her way up the river footpath. Her whole body language had changed. If I hadn't known it was Sam, I would have said I was watching a sixty-year-old woman returning from a trip to the supermarket.

It was my turn now, and I was desperate to get moving. With no coat and a T-shirt open to the elements, I was freezing. I was not sure if I was convincing anybody with my moves, but I shortened my step and increased my rate of movement, checking regularly to make sure no one was behind me. The trip to the pub in the town centre should have taken me fifteen minutes but a loop of the shopping centre first made the trip last half an hour. I entered the pub to find Sam already there, sitting in a corner table with a clear view of the front and side doors of the bar.

The bar was quiet. Two men stood at the bar, one giving me a hard stare as I entered, the other deep in conversation with the barman.

Sam already had two coffees sitting on the table. As I sat down, the barman appeared with toasties.

"Well done, Sam, that was judged well. I am absolutely freezing." Sam gave the young barman a big smile and asked him if he minded us putting on the TV that was positioned above us. He returned a few seconds later with the remote for Sam, as well as a plate of biscuits, which he also handed to Sam. He had fallen for Sam's feminine charm. Sam watched him as he returned to the bar. I found this quite amusing as Sam obviously liked what she was looking at.

"Leave him alone, Mata Hari. He is just out of nappies, and you need to keep your mind out of the gutter and focused on the job in hand."

Sam dragged her stare from the retiring barman back to me. "Do I detect a little jealousy in your voice, captain?"

Sam had done it again. My little attempt at winding her up had backfired on me. I decided to change the subject. "The man at the end of the bar was giving me the once-over as I walked in. Did you notice?"

"Yes, but it is nothing to worry about. When I came in, he came over and was trying to chat me up, so I got rid of him by telling him my boyfriend was about to arrive, and could he send the barman over so we could order some drinks and food. He was just checking out the opposition when you arrived, I'm sure."

***

Neil Andrews had checked but there were no satellites anywhere near the Scottish Highlands, and his closest agent was in Manchester at the moment. There were a few cameras, but nothing like London, and he gave up on tracking the pair as a bad joke. After a few minutes thinking out the situation, he lifted the phone and called his PA. "Make arrangements for Peter Kent and Robin Alder to be stationed at the safe house in Edinburgh. Tell them I need them there for tomorrow evening at the latest. Make sure they are armed, and tell them to await further instruction."

Next to Sam, Peter Kent was the best operative Neil had on his books. Sam had worked with him before and had once been his understudy until she found her feet. If anybody alive knew Sam, it would be Peter.

***

"Tell me about your house. No, wait. Let me guess. Then you can tell me if I'm close. Is it in the country, a small bungalow miles from human habitation, set in an overgrown garden full of trees that need cutting?"

I laughed at Sam's observations. She was close, and if my gardener hadn't been, she could be spot-on about the garden. "Well done. You are close, but you will just have to wait and see for yourself just how close."

Sam protested bitterly that this was not fair, and that I wasn't playing the game. Her objections were silenced by the early evening news. I turned the volume up, drowning out Sam's argument.

We listened to the headlines, and then the broadcaster brought up the subject we had been waiting for. It was buried between a heat wave in Australia and the latest food that was found to be bad for you. The newsreader said that the government had announced today that, as part of the ongoing strategic defense review, all military bases in Britain would undergo a public inquiry to evaluate their uses. The inquiry would be chaired by the Conservative peer Sir Antony Carrington, a former advisor to the secretary of defense. The date had been set for February the twentieth.

Sam turned away from the screen as the subject changed, switching her attention back to me. "Well, what are we going to do until February the twentieth? Any ideas?"

I sat back in the chair, smiling. "Well, according to you, probably my garden."

Sam stood up, shaking her head at my last comment. "Funny man. Right, get your jacket out of my bag while I pay the bill, and then let's get out of here."

Outside, Sam hailed a cab, and five minutes later, it dropped us off outside the theatre. A quick ten-minute walk back across the River Ness brought us back to the BMW. Sam set the satnav to hotels and places of interest, and ten minutes later we pulled up at a Travel Inn-type hotel. Sam was back in I'm-the-boss mode again.

"OK, Adam, I will go, and check in first. You give it a few minutes, and then you check in separately. We will meet back here at the car at nine tomorrow morning, OK?"

Sam's dark mood was back again. "OK, so that's it for tonight, then? I suppose I can take a visit over the road until you get checked in."

Sam looked across the road to where I was pointing. "A burger joint? You really need to start watching your diet. At your age you can't be too careful, and to answer your first question, yes, that is it for tonight. You have the night off."

Sam handed me a bundle of notes to pay for my room and burger, then got out and headed for the hotel. As she walked, she looked back at me pointing across the road making a gesture with her mouth as if she were throwing up. It didn't take a brain surgeon to work out she was not impressed by my eating habits. I watched Sam at the reception desk, then my taste buds got the better of me, and I headed across the road at speed. It had been months since my last fast-food burger, and wild horses, never mind Sam's disapproval, were not going to stop me.

Back at the Travel Inn, I booked in. After giving my room the once-over and finding it exactly the same as any other modern, quick-turn-around hotel room on the planet, I decided it was early yet and headed out for a stroll around the surrounding area. As I left, in the reception I came across my partner in crime on the phone, standing with her back to me. I found this a bit strange, and as I got closer, it got even stranger. She was not speaking in English. Her voice was low, and it was difficult to say for sure, but it sounded like possibly German.

I continued past without her seeing me. Outside I walked along, not paying particular attention to anything that was going on around me. I was far too busy thinking about Sam. Had she given me the night off so she could make that call? And who the hell was she phoning? It made no sense. After turning a corner into a poorly lit side street, I chanced upon a little outdoor shop that by the look of its window display, specialized in shooting and fishing. I was scrutinizing a lovely over-and-under shotgun in the window when an old man appeared by my side.

"That's a beauty, isn't it, sir?" I turned my attention from the gun to the elderly gentleman who was talking to me. He was small but immaculately turned out. His shoes sparkled in the street lights. He wore a green apron over a white shirt, finished off with gold cufflinks. He was obviously the proprietor of the establishment. "Please, sir, go in and have a look around. I am shutting up for the evening, but I will be a while with these damned shutters."

I was already sure that the old gent was ex-military, and as I walked round the shop, my hunch was proved correct, on the wall in the back of the shop was picture of a group of officers from the Gordon Highlanders, and the owner of the shop was pictured on the right of the group. As I looked at the picture the old gent entered the shop somewhat red in the face from his exertions closing the shutters. "Now, sir, is there anything I can get for you?"

I dragged my attention from the picture back to the owner. "Well, I was actually just window-shopping, but if you have a gun-cleaning kit, I will take one." No sooner were the words out of my mouth, and he was off, returning in seconds with a choice of two kits. "Here we are, sir. If you don't mind me asking, I would be interested to know which regiment you are serving in, sir."

I smiled at the old gent. "Is it that obvious? The Royal Engineers, but I am retired now."

The owner returned my smile. "Dear me, they must be getting rid of men early these days. You don't look nearly old enough to be retired. Still, it will give you plenty of time to go shooting I suppose."

I decided to cut the conversation short. The old guy still had all his marbles, and it would only take one slip-up in my story for him to become suspicious. I paid for the kit and left, thanking the old man for his help. Back at the Travel Inn, there was no sign of Sam in the reception area, so I headed for my room. After making a cup of coffee and putting the safety chain on the door, I set about stripping down my Beretta. As I worked, I tried to remember why I now had a Beretta when I had started off with a Glock. The madness of the last couple of months was obviously catching up with me. I concluded that the Glock must be somewhere in the firing range at the glass house. The Beretta I was now carrying had belonged to one of the assassins who had been sent to eliminate me. At some point, both Sam and I had carried the Berettas. This one Sam had used as I could still smell Sam's perfume on the weapon.

The Beretta was in bad need of some TLC. The gun had seen a bit of action, and I doubted if it had ever been stripped and cleaned before. Half an hour and I was ready to reassemble it when there was a knock at the door.

"Adam, it's OK. It's just me. You can open up."

I removed the safety chain and let Sam into the room. "How did you know which room I was in?"

Sam shook her head as she strolled over to the bed and plonked herself down. "Gee, I don't know. Maybe it's because I am a spy or something. Adam Smith? I mean come on, a bit more imagination. I had a sneak peak at the register while the receptionist was on the phone."

I continued to reassemble the Beretta while Sam spoke to me. "So what brings you here? I thought that was it for the evening."

Sam sat watching my reassembly. "I see we are in a bit of a mood tonight are we not, what has brought this on?" The gun was back in one piece. I checked its action a few times, then set it down on the bedside table next to its fully loaded magazine.

"I didn't know you could speak German." Sam watched me as I crossed the room and sat opposite her on the only chair in the room.

"There are lots of things you don't know about me. I take it you are referring to my phone call tonight." Sam stood up and walked toward the door. "I think we had better continue this conversation when we are both in better moods." Sam had opened the door and started to leave when she changed her mind and turned around in the doorway. "Just to put your mind at rest, my phone call was to the builder from Germany who built the glass house. I was arranging for him to send a team across to repair the damage." Sam left before anything else could be said.

***

In a small, unmarked office in the Pentagon, David Southern sat buried in a pile of folders and paperwork. He had refused the use of a secretary due to the confidential and sometimes incriminating work that he carried out for the powers that be. He was studying one particular file with great care. He checked his watch; it was time. He picked the phone up and dialed the number from the folder.

Areli Benesch sat looking out the window of her Monaco apartment. Her shoulder still ached, but the warm sun streaming through the open window helped, along with the glass of Teva Muscato wine. She was in a good mood. Not only did she have her favorite flowery wine from her homeland, but that morning her bank had received her payment for the Chinese job, and she was now two million Euros better off.

Her phone started to ring. Areli was in two minds about whether to let it ring or answer it and find someone trying to sell her something. After a few seconds, she reluctantly picked up the phone. Instantly, an American voice started to speak.

"Miss Benesch, if you value your life, don't hang up until you have listened to me. Please go to your door, the one that opens out onto the lane. Do it now, then come back to the phone please."

Areli put the phone down and walked to the door. Her heart sank as she looked outside. Standing outside the door were two large, black men dressed in business suits. As she looked out, one gave her a smile and a little wave. She could tell from the way their jackets lay that they were armed. She knew right away she was in trouble, and she was not looking forward to the rest of her conversation.

"Miss Benesch, I have a little task for you and your special talents. I am looking at your file right now. I believe your little holiday in Scotland did not go as planned. Unfortunately, I have been tasked with cleaning up your previous employer's mess. I read in your file that you were to be paid one million dollars on the completion of your mission. You did not get a single cent, as the mission failed miserably. Here is my offer to you. Go back and eliminate both targets before they can testify at a government hearing in London on February the twentieth, and you can collect the million dollars, and we will leave you in peace. Refuse, and my two friends outside will escort you to the Israeli embassy. Do we have a deal?"

Areli sat for a moment, thinking things through. "I alone have made contact with your targets, and I have the wounds to prove how dangerous they are. I must ask you for two million dollars, a million for each target, and if we agree on that, I will not kill the monkeys that you have placed by my door."

Southern was taken aback by the cheek of the woman but also impressed by her calmness considering the position she was in. "Miss Benesch, I for one would not like to play you at poker. Here is the deal. Complete the mission, and there is a NASA account earmarked by your previous employer for payment to your whole team, six million dollars in all. I will transfer it all to your Monaco bank account if you are successful. If you refuse or fail, I will use it as a bounty on your head, payable dead or alive. I don't play poker, but I know when someone is bluffing, and I always win." The phone went dead.

Areli walked to the door and checked for her black friends, but they were gone. Areli returned to her seat and sat sipping her wine thoughtfully. She smiled to herself. She was going to get a second chance to kill the bitch who stabbed her, and this time she would be ready for her. She picked up the phone and dialed a number. After only a few seconds the phone was answered. "Hi, Paul. It's Areli. Paul, I need you to help me get fit in a hurry. How soon can you see me, honey?"

Areli listened for a second, then cut Paul off midconversation. "Darling, I am sure your gym is busy with all the budding Michael Schumachers, but it would be a special favour for me, and I will pay you just as much as they do, and I am far better to look at in shorts." There was a short silence, and Areli held her breath. "Paul, you are a darling, I will see you tomorrow morning at nine thirty. Ciao."

Colonel Southern only waited a few seconds after speaking to Benesch, and then he dialed the number he had been given for the White House. It was answered instantly. "I have some news on the SR 3000 problem. I have checked with Whiteford's agent in London.

Unfortunately, despite our best efforts, the Brits are going ahead with an inquiry into Machrihanish. As we have already agreed, we must do everything we can to stop this before it becomes an international incident. I have been in contact with the Israeli woman, and she has agreed to eliminate the witnesses, and this Merlin character says he will try and stop the hearing going ahead. Should any of this go wrong, there are no US nationals involved, so we can deny any involvement. The cleaners have finished with the base and have managed to reduce the amount of radiation present. I have ordered that the main hangar, which housed the SR3000, be sealed permanently as it poses a major health hazard. Our radiation experts have calculated that the surrounding area will show higher health problems, but this can be blamed on an aging British nuclear submarine fleet and fallout from Chernobyl. I believe if we can stop the hearing or prove its evidence incorrect, we can put this problem to bed. I will keep you informed of any developments." Southern hung up and closed the file in front of him.

***

In the morning, I entered the breakfast room to find Sam already sitting in a corner booth, watching the comings and goings of the staff and clientele as she ate her breakfast. It was clear to see why Sam had survived for so long in her profession. There was not one person entering that room whom Sam had not checked out. No doubt her handgun was no more than a fingertip away at any given time. Luckily, breakfast was uneventful. There seemed to be no killers in the room today. After breakfast, I took the chance to call my old colleague, Ian Ferris. Ian had retired from the army well before me and was working as a gamekeeper in Perthshire. It was Ian who had loaned me his time-share on Arran, and it was Ian who was responsible for getting me the house I now owned. When Ian had found out I had left the service, he had spoken to his employer who agreed to sell me the western lodge house on the outskirts of the Menamar estate.

Ian was a good friend although he knew of my military history, he never brought it up. It was always reassuring to know Ian was in the area and looking out for me. It had been this way since we had served together in Iraq. I waited for him to answer my call. "Hello you old git, how are you doing?"

There was silence for a fraction of a second. "Stand by your beds, lads. It's the wandering captain, if I'm not mistaken. Where the hell have you been hiding?"

No matter what the situation, you never got Ian Ferris any different. He was straight to the point, and you knew exactly where you stood with him.

"Ian, I am sorry I didn't call. I got myself into a bit of a situation. Tell me, has there been anybody looking for me?" Silence again for a second.

"I'm not going to ask. Knowing you as I do, you can find trouble in an empty house. You do remember you were going to Arran for a bit of R and R. That would be just before you vanished off the face of the Earth, young man. To answer your question, there was a stranger wandering about. When I stopped and pulled him up about what he was doing, he gave me some bullshit about looking for a house to buy and buggered off pretty damned smartish."

I was somewhat concerned at this revelation. "Ian, watch your back, old son. If he reappears, keep out of his way, and that goes for any other interested parties that are looking for me. I know you are a pretty handy guy in a brawl but these guys will play dirty if you get my drift. I will be back over the next couple of days, and then we can have a proper chin wag about things."

Sam had appeared in the reception and was hovering. "Adam, I will see you soon. Look after yourself, lad, and remember, you can only cheat death so many times. If you play with fire, you are going to end up with burnt fingers at some point. Speak to you soon."

Sam was somewhat concerned about my phone call, in the car she proceeded to interrogate me about it. "Adam, why did you need to make the call. If it were monitored, you could have given our next movements to our hunters." Sam had taken the wheel of the big BMW and was gunning it down the side of Loch Ness at motorway speeds.

"Madam, if you keep driving like Jackie Stewart, when we hit the tractor pulling out, it won't matter who knows where we are. Can we wind the speed down a bit before my breakfast makes a bid for freedom?"

Sam complied with my request and brought the car down to a more sensible speed. "Can I ask who you were on the phone with? Family, friend, girlfriend?" Sam glanced across at me as she said the last one, checking for my reaction.

I shook my head at her last comment. "You really think any woman would want to hang about with me after they found out about my track record with female company. No, if you must know, it was my sergeant from the Gulf War story I told you about, Ian Ferris. It was by pure coincidence that when Neil Andrews started looking for the next place to hide me away, Ian Ferris's position as an instructor at Hereford came up. When the doctors declared that Bob and I were fit to be returned to our unit, we found ourselves heading back to Hereford. Bob had been promoted to sergeant and was now also an instructor. When Ian found out that I had been given his old job, he was pleased for me. Ian contacted me to offer some words of wisdom and before long we were best friends. He is still a good friend and lives not far from me. I was letting him know I was still alive and just checking, before we headed into a trap, that everything was OK back at the house." I watched Sam's reaction to this news. It was clear that Sam was trying very hard not to show her displeasure with me. "Sam, I'm sorry if I was out of line. I know I should have run it past you before I called Ian. It won't happen again, I promise."

I decided that throwing Sam the olive branch was far better than us falling out with each other for a second day. Sam's facial expression relaxed visibly. She was busy thinking of something to say. I studied her face as she drove.

Her face had all but recovered from the pounding that it had taken. The only telltale was the slightly overdone lip gloss that hid her damaged lip and gave her mouth the appearance of being larger than it actually was. Sam clocked me staring at her. "What is so fascinating about my head this morning?"

I thought for a second. "I was just checking out the lip gloss you used to cover up the scar on your lip. It makes your mouth look larger, not in a bad way, I hasten to add."

Sam was grimacing. "Yeah, right. Lips like Miss Piggy." Sam was clearly very conscious of her scar.

"No, I was thinking with your hair in a ponytail and your lips done that way, you are not unlike Cameron Diaz."

Sam almost put the BMW in a ditch. She was too busy staring at me to see if I was taking the piss to notice the car heading for the verge. She noticed at the last moment and corrected the steering before any damage was done.

"Would you like me to drive? You seem to be having a bit of a problem there."

Sam regained her composure. "After that last comment, you are not getting to drive until you have had your eyes checked."

"Sam, like it or not, no matter how hard you try to be a tomboy, you can't stop the girl from coming out."

Sam changed the subject quickly. "You do know, if somebody has put two and two together about you still being friends with your old army buddy, they could have tapped his phone and be waiting for us to arrive."

I shook my head. "Ian's no dummy. If anybody were up to no good, he would have spotted them."

It was early afternoon when Sam's mouth fell open in astonishment. At first I didn't notice. I was too busy studying road maps, looking for someplace to stop for lunch. Sam had just seen Glen Coe in all its glory for the first time. We had passed through it already, but all the other times, the clouds had been low and it had been raining heavily.

Today was different. There was hardly a cloud in the sky, and the snow on the three sisters that formed one side of the mountain pass was pure white and sparkled as if encrusted with diamonds. Sam pulled in halfway through the mountain pass in a lay-by that in the summer would be overflowing with tourists. She stepped out of the BMW. I followed suit, and we both took in huge vistas of Scottish scenery. We stood in silence for minutes, not daring to break the spell that the Highland scenery had cast upon us.

Sam eventually spoke first. "My God, we have passed through here before, but I never knew how awesome Glen Coe was until today. There is nothing in Britain that even comes close to this. Even Canada would be hard pushed to match this little lot."

It only took a few seconds for the cold air to penetrate our clothing, and as beautiful as the scenery was, we could only stand it for so long. It may have been just below freezing, but the thing that catches out so many unprepared climbers in Scotland was the wind-chill factor. Taking this into account, I reckoned that the temperature in the valley this morning was minus twelve. A few seconds later, we were thankfully back in the big BMW with the heater on full blast.

CHAPTER TWELVE

Menamar

Ian Ferris pulled up in the drive of the old stone lodge house. He was in a good mood this morning. For some time, he had been worried about his friend. It was not like Adam to go AWOL without a word. He was still somewhat concerned as to the situation Adam had seemingly got himself into, but he knew Adam well, and he was sure if anybody could look after himself, it was Adam Macdonald. He had more lives than a cat.

Ian unlocked the big wooden outer door and entered the inner hall. On his left was a key pad that was blinking at him. He entered the six-digit code to disarm Adam's alarm, then leaned over behind the coat stand. Here was a second switch that Adam had installed himself. Although it looked like an innocent light switch, it controlled a series of infrared light beams on the ground floor that triggered a silent alarm upstairs if broken. If it was not deactivated within five minutes, the system dialed an emergency number in London and alerted the local bobbies as well. Ian had laughed at this when Adam had shown him his creation. He had told Adam it only needed a member of the local wildlife to get in and break one of the beams to trigger off the biggest farce in the history of the security services. Ian had changed his mind in light of Adam's latest comments. It didn't seem so stupid now, especially after he had found the stranger wandering about the area.

The house needed to be lived in. Although the heating had been left on, the old house still had that damp smell. Ian resisted the temptation to leave a window open and went straight to the kitchen where he deposited fresh milk, bread, butter, a few tins of soup, and a six-pack of lager. He left a note on the kitchen table advising Adam that he had put some provisions in the fridge and larder and telling Adam to call him when he arrived if he needed a hand with the lager.

Ian left, retracing his steps, switching the beams on, and entering a second code into the alarm system before pulling the big storm door shut and locking it.

He had no idea his every movement had been watched. Marcus Laine had learned from his earlier mistake when the old gamekeeper had stopped and questioned him about his intentions. In the woods that bordered the grounds of the house, Marcus had built a hideout where he could watch the comings and goings at the lodge house undetected, and today it looked like his patience was about to pay off. Through his powerful Zeiss binoculars, he was able to see the old gamekeeper punch in the access code for the alarm and just as he was about to put the glasses down to make a note of the number, he saw the gamekeeper switch off a light switch. After a few minutes inside, the game keeper reemerged, and Laine watched him reset the switch and alarm. Laine made a mental note to remember to use the switch before entering the house.

After the Gulf War, Ian Ferris had decided enough was enough. His body had told him on the long trek back to base that he was too old for this work anymore. The government was looking for cuts in the defense budget again, and Ian was given permission to leave within weeks of returning to Hereford. He wasted no time, and one month later, he started on the Perthshire estate as head gamekeeper.

***

Ian was thinking about the imminent return of his friend as he drove along the rutted farm track to the flight pond. This was Ian Ferris's little secret. He guarded this area with his life. High up in the pine tree that overshadowed the flight pond was a secret Ian had guarded for the last two years. Ian switched off the old Land Rover and let it coast for the last few yards until it hit a pothole and ground to a halt.

Ian took his binoculars and headed quietly down the track to the edge of the pond. It only took Ian a few seconds for his eyes to pick out the large nest high up in the tallest branches of the tree. As he watched, the male golden eagle arrived. Ian could just make out the female's head in the nest. Ian was sure she was busy trying to hatch their latest offspring. It was early in the year for it, but last year she had produced a chick at about the same time. Ian had high hopes for the breeding pair.

Then, just two months ago, he had come across the young male bird they had raised. It lay by the roadside; it had been hit by a car.

The ex-SAS soldier had seen terrible things in his career, and very few times had he shed a tear, but the sight of the young eagle had been too much for him. He had watched every day as the parent birds took turns looking after and feeding the young bird. It was almost family to Ian, and he had wept openly on finding the bird dead.

Ian moved into position by the pond and watched as the male bird used his talons to dissect an unfortunate rabbit that was not fast enough to escape the dive of the powerful male bird. As Ian watched, something in the corner of his eye made him turn and look. To the normal human being it would have been nothing, but to Ian, it started alarm bells ringing. The holly bush to his right had a branch broken where it joined the stem, and on further examination, he saw the grass at its base had been trampled into the ground. Someone had been here very recently. The spell had been broken. Ian forgot about the eagles and headed back to the Land Rover.

As he approached it, Laine stepped out from behind the back of the 4x4 and fired at point-blank range into Ian Ferris's chest.

Laine had not used a gun. Instead he had fired a Taser. The shock incapacitated Ferris, who dropped to his knees as his muscles began to spasm uncontrollably.

Laine was a self-confessed sadist, and he had no intention of just killing. He wanted his victims to die but on his terms. He walked behind the frozen gamekeeper, looping piano wire round his neck all in the same movement. He placed his foot in the small of Ferris's back and gradually increased the pressure until he could feel the wire start to cut skin and tissue on the way to the bone. The wire cut into the jugular vein, spraying blood out on the grass, Laine released the pressure, removed the wire, and stood in front of Ferris watching the doomed man's last movements before his death. The last thing Ian Ferris saw as he started to slip into darkness was the golden eagle as it launched from the branch.

Ian fell backward and came to rest on the grass. Laine stood watching the dead body. He had a warm glow and a warped sense of achievement, but he was somewhat puzzled by the peaceful expression on the gamekeeper's blood-covered face. Now that the gamekeeper was out of the way, he could explore the house without worry of being found out.

He knew from day one the gamekeeper was trouble. He had had to go to extraordinary lengths to avoid being detected. He got away with his story the first time, but if he had been stopped again by the gamekeeper, he knew his cover would be blown. Now he was free to get ready for the arrival of his real targets. Laine had listened into the gamekeeper's call from his friend using a scanner. He was now ready for the finale.

***

Sam followed my directions as she threw the big German car along the narrow, twisty country roads. We had left Crieff twenty minutes ago and were well on the way to Aberfeldy when the turning on the right came into view. I instructed Sam to turn off and head for the old stone house. We parked in the drive, and I headed for the big wooden door. The key turned effortlessly, and the big door swung inward, revealing the keypad on the wall. A few seconds later, we were both in the hallway, studying our surroundings. Sam walked through the hall, studying the pictures on the walls, which consisted mostly of old army photos. Sam stopped and looked at the last picture, which hung next to the step that led down to the open-plan living room.

The picture Sam looked at was of Mary O'Conner and me, taken in the poolroom of a Belfast pub three weeks before Mary's death. "I haven't seen that one before. Mary looks very happy." Sam broke her trance-like stare and continued her examination of the lodge house.

After showing Sam the rest of the house, I made the mistake of asking Sam what she thought. Sam was deep in thought for a second. "Well, it is obvious you didn't use an interior designer. It looks like a typical bachelor pad. It reminds me of an officer's mess, no womanly touches at all."

Sam continued to wander round the house exploring while I brought in the bags and checked the rest of the house. To my relief, the camera chip I had posted to myself was in the mail. Ian's note in the kitchen made me smile.

I had missed my old mate and was looking forward to a chat with him about the situation I had ended up in. Sam was already upstairs in the guest bedroom when I entered carrying her bag. "Sorry it doesn't have an en suite. The only bathroom in the house is the one downstairs between the hall and the lounge. It has a cracking power shower though."

Sam was only half-paying attention. She was busy staring out of the bedroom window, which overlooked the drive up to the house. "Is this the only entrance to the house, or is there a back way in?" Sam had finished studying the house and was now working out her strategic options just in case the shit hit the fan.

"There is a farm track behind the garage, but it only leads to the estate roads. There is no direct access from the main road."

Sam was still studying the surrounding countryside from her vantage point. "I don't like it, Adam. A sniper could sit back in the woods and pick us off at his leisure."

I took Sam's hand and led her away from the window. "Well, don't stand in front of the window giving away your position. Come on. I will make the coffee, and you can decide where you want to eat for dinner. We will need to go out unless you want to slum it with a pot noodle."

A flyer for a new Chinese restaurant in Crieff was among the pile of mail that was left on the living room table. Sam called it while I made the coffee and booked a table for eight o'clock. In the car on the way to the Chinese, Sam quizzed me to see if there was another way to get to Crieff. "Adam, this is no good. One way in and out from Crieff is bad. I take it you are still carrying?"

It wasn't until that moment that I realized that the Beretta was lying on my bed next to my discarded clothes. Sam could tell from the look on my face what the answer was. "Oh, that's just great, Adam. What if we were to be attacked? What would you do?"

I glanced back over my shoulder at the road snaking away behind us in the moonlight. "Calm down, Sam. There is not another car on the road for ten miles behind us. There is more chance of dying of food poisoning tonight than anything else."

***

Marcus Laine waited for a few minutes just in case the BMW turned back for some reason, then made his way to the house. He input the code and switched off the dummy light switch, then entered cautiously, taking great care not to disturb anything.

In the main bedroom he found Adam's handgun. He smiled to himself. He was going to have some fun with this pair. Taking great care, he removed the Beretta without disturbing the clothing lying on top of the gun, which partially obscured its presence. He rummaged around in the rucksack he was carrying until he found what he was looking for. He slid the magazine out of the handgrip and inserted a similar clip of ammunition. He knew since he had entered the house and studied the old photos that Macdonald was nothing more than an army builder. He doubted if he could even fire a handgun, but the blanks he had just loaded would make sure he was no threat at all. He returned the gun to its original position and left the room. Downstairs, he installed a micro camera inside the smoke alarm so he could see what was happening inside the lodge house.

***

During the meal at the Chinese restaurant, Sam made it clear she was not happy about our latest port of call. "Adam, you know yourself you could hide an army in the woodland around your house. If the CIA found us, we wouldn't stand a snowdrop's chance in hell of surviving. We need to move on." Sam had already made up her mind. There was going to be no changing it.

"For one, we don't know if it was the CIA, and secondly, they took a beating the last time we met. I doubt if they are in any fit state to try anything again."

Sam was not for turning. She continued her lecture. "So you think that a group who found you at a house with no links to the outside world and registered in a third-party name can't find your home, which is registered to you. Do you think that an agent who swam fifteen hundred metres with a knife in her shoulder, then ran two miles to help her colleagues won't try again? Have you lost your marbles, man?"

Sam's eyes were burning into me. She was absolutely right, and I had no defense left. "I know, I know. You win."

Sam continued to stare at me. "So why argue with me, you idiot!" Sam sat back, raising her hands in exasperation.

"Sam, has anyone told you that you look like Cameron Diaz when you're angry?"

Sam shook her head in disbelief. "Just get the bill before I switch sides and shoot you myself."

On the way back we did not speak much. We were both in our own little worlds. Sam broke the silence first. "So you have a Cameron Diaz fetish then."

I smiled inwardly. "No, not at all. You just look like her in some lights."

Sam half-turned in the passenger seat and was studying me intently. "So are you saying you don't fancy Cameron Diaz?"

I had a rough idea where Sam was going with this but played along. "No, not really. It's hard to say until I met her in the flesh if she would be my type or not."

Sam thought for a second. "So what is your type?"

I thought about my reply. Here was my chance at a great chat-up line, but I decided to just tell the truth instead. "Good question, Sam.

The way things are going with female friends, just breathing would be a good start. As you know from my history, I've never really settled after my wife died. All the women I have been close to since then are no longer with us, apart from you, of course."

Sam turned her stare back to the road again. "Don't worry about me, Adam. I have no intention of expiring any time soon. Pull over before the next bend and let me out."

Sam bent down and undid her high heels pushing them into the foot well. She reached into her handbag and retrieved the Beretta, checking its action, and making sure the safety was still on.

"And where do you think you are off to, madam?"

Sam opened the door and stepped out, leaning back in through the doorframe. "I am just going to check we don't have a reception committee waiting for us when we get home. Wait here for ten minutes before heading home. I need to get my hearing and night vision working before I get to the house, so I will run the next couple of miles. Keep your window open. If you hear gunfire, come in on foot and be careful."

Sam didn't wait for a reply. Her barefooted shadowy figure was already past the reach of the BMW's head lamps and vanishing into the drizzle of the Scottish winter's night. Ten minutes felt like ten hours. I cursed myself for leaving my gun in the house.

This was a quiet backwater area of Scotland. In the ten minutes I waited, not one car passed. I told myself Sam was paranoid. If there had been a threat, Ian would have been there to warn me. When the ten minutes were up, I continued at a sedate pace with the window open, but the only noise I could hear was the rumble of tyres on wet tarmac and the soft throb of the big BMW engine working just above idle.

***

Markus Laine could hear the low rumble of a car approaching at slow speed. He was about to move a low branch out of the way for a better view when he froze to the spot. Right in front of him, the shadowy figure of a woman moved noiselessly, with the stealth of a panther. Laine was no more than ten feet from her. He was frozen like a statue. Rainwater from the branch he was just about to move ran down his wrist into his clothing. Water dripped onto his head and ran down his neck. He knew watching this woman that one muscle twitch would be fatal. The woman moved in a slightly crouched position, right hand holding an automatic pistol, her left arm supporting her right wrist. A bird broke cover far to her left. With one movement, she fell to her knee and brought the gun to bear on the bird. Laine watched her return to her sweep of the perimeter. He was impressed with what he was watching, so much so that he decided to change his plans. He had originally planned to kill the man first, then have some fun with the woman before finishing her off. Watching her, he knew she was far too dangerous to be left forewarned. He would have to deal with her first.

Sam was spooked. she couldn't put her finger on it but her sixth sense told her all was not well. The hairs on the back of her neck were standing on end, and her eyes felt as if they were out on stalks.

***

I pulled the big German car off the road and accelerated hard up the drive just in case there was a boogeyman waiting to take a potshot at me. I pulled the car up right in front of the door, blocking a clear shot at the front door. As I stepped out, Sam appeared by my side, stepping out of the undergrowth and covering me as I opened the door. Inside, the door bolted and the outside flood lamps switched on, we both breathed a sigh of relief. Sam was soaked through to the skin but insisted on checking all the windows and doors before finally heading to the bathroom for a hot shower. By the time she reappeared wrapped up in one of my bathrobes, I had started the big open fire and was sitting watching the flames. Sam plonked herself down on the hearthrug, propping her back against the big Chesterfield couch. "Adam, we need to get out of here, no joking. We need to go in the morning."

I handed Sam a large tumbler. "Here. It's not up to the standards of the vodka in the glass house, but it's not bad. It's blue label. Cheers."

Sam took a sip and pulled her knees up to her chest. "I know, Sam. We will leave tomorrow, but I want to see my old mate before I vanish again. I have a good idea where I will find him. I will pop across and see him in the morning, and we will be out of here by lunchtime."

Sam seemed more relaxed at this news and sat quietly staring into the flames, mesmerized. I broke the spell. "We will need to get a picture of you to put next to the others on my wall."

Sam smiled. "Spies don't like their pictures taken. It's not good for business. Anyway, I can't help notice you have no recent pictures of you in the Special Forces. I would imagine now you have retired you would be showing those off to everybody."

Sam was watching me as I shook my head. "You haven't got it yet, have you? I never joined the army to kill people. That just happened. Although it was my destiny, it was not my intention. I do not feel that I am part of the regiment. I did not do the proper training, and even my rank was contrived. It is hard to explain. The Special Air Service is a very elite club, and I feel that I sneaked in the back door, and I am not proud of that." I dragged the vodka bottle off the couch and refilled my glass, topping up Sam's in the process.

"One thing is for sure, Adam. I have never seen anybody like you who can get himself in so much trouble without even trying. Don't be so hard on yourself. Correct me if I am wrong, but you will be thirty-seven at your next birthday. Since you left school, you have devoted your life to the defense of your country and because most of your work was covert, you never got as much as a thank you. Put the bloody pictures up, and be proud of them. You have already paid your way in whatever regiment."

I flung a cushion on the floor next to Sam and joined her on the hearthrug. "So you have heard my life story. You have seen my house, so it is your turn tonight to tell me all about yourself." Sam took a large mouthful of vodka while continuing to look into the flames. "Has the cat got your tongue? It's OK to tell me. I have already signed the Official Secrets Act, and now it would appear that I am working for MI6. That would make me your partner, and partners don't keep secrets."

Sam finished her glass and was about to put it down when I filled it to the brim again. "Adam Macdonald, anybody would think you were trying to get me drunk and take advantage of me." Sam had a twinkle in her eye, and her cheeks were starting to glow.

"The thought had never crossed my mind. I'm just trying to slacken that tongue of yours to find out a bit more about you."

Sam leaned across and kissed me on the cheek before standing up. "Nice try, partner, but I'm off to bed. See you in the morning."

I couldn't help feeling that it was my interrogation of Sam that had brought on her retreat to the bedroom. I sat alone watching the fire slowly die—one last glass of vodka and the bottle was dry.

***

Colonel David Southern was still not happy with his arrangements for London. He needed someone close to the action to keep him up to date with developments. He picked up the phone and dialed the number he had written down on a sheet of paper. "Hello, may I speak to Neil Andrews please." Neil came on the phone a few seconds later. Southern introduced himself and immediately launched into his story "Neil, I gather from my sources you are heading up the investigation team into Machrihanish Air Base. Furthermore, it's your agents who are to give evidence at the forthcoming inquiry. I would like to offer my country's full support in the matter. It is in both our great nations' interests to make sure there has been no wrongdoing. I gather your agents have had their lives threatened over their testimony? As a result of this I am sending one of my best field agents across to liaise with you and make sure no harm comes to your people."

Neil was somewhat taken aback by Southern's comments but recovered quickly. "Well, in the spirit of cooperation, why not give us unrestricted access to the base so we can judge for ourselves if there has been any wrongdoing?"

There was silence for a second. "Neil, if it were up to me, pal, it wouldn't be a problem, but the powers that be have other ideas. I will put your suggestion to my superiors and let you know in due course. Is there anything else I can help you with?"

Neil knew he had just been brushed off and decided to throw a spanner in the American's game plan. "Well, now you ask, we are looking for a traitor in our midst, a man who goes by the code name Merlin. Have you heard of him at all?"

This time the silence was longer. The American knew he was being played but needed to act normally. He needed his agent in the UK, so if it meant playing along with the MI6 mind games, then so be it.

Zelenski had just returned to his desk after lunch, and he was looking forward to another afternoon of checking and filing reports in preparation for his imminent retirement. His phone started to ring. Zelenski was glad to answer. It broke up the chore of endless paperwork. Zelenski listened as the caller talked. "John, it is Colonel Southern. I need you to fly to London and do a little job for me before you retire. I need you to shadow the man and woman that Fletcher was sent to eliminate. They are due to give evidence at a hearing about the air base in Scotland, and we need to make it look like we are watching their backs for them. America can't be seen to be trying to kill a friendly nation's subjects. In truth, you will make sure the woman Benesch completes her mission. My office has cleared you with the Brits. They know you are coming and think you are there to watch out for any renegade CIA agents still loyal to the late deputy director, Whiteford. They have been informed of his treachery and that he was overzealous in defending US property. We think that they know most of the truth about the air base. Their mission is to get it out in the open, and our mission is to make sure that never happens. I will contact you in London with more details. Have a good flight."

Zelenski wanted to ask more questions, but he had that sinking feeling in his stomach and hung up without a word. He knew he had been selected because of his previous involvement in the case. The fewer people that knew, the better. It made it easier to tidy up loose ends at the end of the mission. In due course, an agent arrived with his papers and a letter of introduction for the Brits and one for the US embassy. Zelenski's last task before leaving the country was to make sure a copy of his will was in his top desk drawer.

***

I awoke the next morning slightly the worse for wear. I was still in the same position by the fire, only covered with a duvet. A note protruded from my empty vodka bottle. The note read, "Gone for a run to stretch my legs. Will be ready to leave at lunchtime." I grabbed some water and a couple of headache pills. I wanted to see Ian before I left and had a good idea where to find my old mate. I headed out to the shed. Since my return I had not ventured out to the old stone garage behind the house. In it lay two of my guilty pleasures. I opened the side door and switched on the strip lights that surrounded the room. In the centre of the room sat the love of my life, covered in old bed sheets. I could not resist the temptation and tugged at the sheets. They slipped off the highly polished surface as if made of silk. I stood back and admired the beauty of the bodywork that was revealed. Sitting in all her glory was my metallic-green, 1981 Aston Martin V8 Vantage. Her tan leather seats had hardly ever been used; her hand-beaten alloy panels glinted as the light reflected off her hundreds of coats of paint and lacquer, lovingly applied by craftsmen of a bygone era. She was from the eighties supercar stable and a priceless piece of motoring history, one of the last truly handmade sports cars.

She had been here waiting for me when I came with Ian to view the house, and it had been love at first sight. She belonged to the owner of the Menamar estate, and she only very occasionally came out to play when the estate owner felt the need to impress one of his guests. Ian had managed to broker a deal after I pestered him to death about the car. Finally the owner of the Menamar estate caved into pressure and did a deal for the house and the car.

Finally I tore my eyes from the car and headed for my second toy. In the corner stood a state-of-the-art, carbon-frame Trek mountain bike. This was the first thing I bought after leaving the army. I had always fancied one, just never got round to buying one. This was to be my main mode of transport when I retired; it would be the mainstay of my keep-fit campaign.

I checked the tyres and headed out the back gate onto the many tracks of the Menamar estate. I followed the northerly track, which climbed steadily to the northeast. After a couple of miles, the road cleared the treetops, giving a good view of most of the Menamar estate below in the valley. There was no sign of Ian's Defender, green with a white roof. I retraced my tracks back down the hill, then took the left junction through the trees and headed for the flight pond, a couple of miles to the south. It was a safe bet I would find Ian brooding over his eagles. As I approached, I was proven correct. The old Land Rover sat a few yards from the flight pond. I could make out Ian in the driver's seat, watching the trees. I jumped off the bike and placed it gently against a gorse bush. I opened the driver's door slowly so not to startle the big eagles if they were about.

Ian Ferris looked through me. His soul had left his body. He had been dead for some time. The shock hit me like a tidal wave, threatening to drown me. I had to fight my body to stay upright on my feet. My head spun, and my heart was trying to explode through my rib cage. Then the rage came. It made my eyes fill with tears. I was going to rip someone apart for this. I would do it with my bare hands.

Suddenly it dawned on me, the situation I had placed Sam in. My rage turned instantly to fear; my brain was now working overtime; my gun…"SHIT!" In my hurry to meet Ian, I had not changed, so I had not been in my room. The gun was still lying on the bed. "SHIT!"

I needed to get back to the house pronto and warn Sam. I was unarmed. Sam was going to kill me if she found out I had left the house again with no protection. I jumped on the bike and started to leg it along the track. After a few seconds, a thought struck me. I stopped, turned the bike round, and headed back to the Land Rover. In the centre console, I found what I was looking for. Ian was a smart man; he knew there could be trouble.

One night after a few whiskies, he had told me a little bit about the Falklands. In his story, he had run out of ammunition and had fought hand-to-hand with an Argentine sergeant. In the scuffle, he managed to shoot the soldier with his own side arm. After the battle, he kept the dead Argentine's handgun as a good luck charm. It looked like Ian's luck had finally run out, but his lucky charm was in the centre consol—an Argentinean-made Browning nine millimeter. I checked the breach. The weapon was fully loaded. I made sure the safety was on and again legged it for the house.

***

Sam returned from her run to find the house deserted. This was not a major surprise for Sam. They had talked about meeting up with Adam's friend before leaving. Sam put two and two together and decided Adam had gone in search of his friend. The BMW was still parked, so Adam couldn't be far away. Sam grabbed a towel, removed her Beretta, which she had taped to her leg, and deposited it on the table in the hall next to the bathroom. She made a final check on the front door, making sure it was locked securely, then headed for the bathroom and the shower.

From his sleeping bag, Laine watched as Sam checked the house before heading for the shower. This was his chance. He had watched twenty minutes ago as the ex-soldier left on his bike. He needed to move quickly before she left the shower. It would mask the noises of him picking the lock. Laine stood up and half-hobbled, half-ran to the front door of the house. He was making heavy weather of it due to the stiffness in his legs after being immobile for so long.

He was in the front door within a matter of seconds. He punched in the code for the alarm and made sure the switch on the wall was off. His first port of call was the hall table. The woman's gun was still there. The bathroom door was slightly ajar, and he could hear the thunder of the power shower coming from the room. He breathed a sigh of relief. The woman was still in the shower. The strength in his legs had returned. He tucked the woman's gun into the back of his trousers, well out of reach of his intended victim. He checked his pockets. In the left was his piano wire, in the right, a stainless steel knuckle-duster. He reached in and slid on the heavy steel weapon, then moved very, very slowly to the half-open door.

The shower cubicle was of an early design, with a heavy polythene curtain instead of a door. The curtain obscured the view from the cubicle. Sam was busy washing the soap from her arms when the blow hit her on the side of the temple, knocking her against the tiled back wall of the shower. Sam was trying hard to regain her senses when the shower curtain was torn away. Sam was aware of a man just outside the shower cubicle but could not focus on him. Her head was ringing and the right side of her face was numb. She was having problems just keeping her balance; her legs felt like a newly born foal. Things were just starting to come back to her when her attacker launched his second assault.

Sam felt something loop over her head and out of pure instinct raised her hands. She had been quick but not quite quick enough. The piano wire closed with a hiss as Sam managed to get one hand inside the loop. Laine used his body weight to pull Sam backward, legs flailing, out of the cubicle. Sam managed to regain her balance and stand on the bathroom floor, taking the pressure of the wire, which bit into part of her neck and her trapped hand. Laine could see the fight was not completely knocked out of the woman yet and reached for the knuckle-duster again. Sam used this brief respite to counterattack. She got her foot on the side of the shower cubicle and pushed backward with all her might. It caught Laine off balance, and they both went careering backward toward the door. The door handle caught Laine in the left kidney, and the knuckle-duster flew from his grip. Sam smashed the back of her head into his teeth. It was Laine's turn to struggle to keep his footing. The struggle continued in the hall, but the smooth tiles were now covered in water and blood from both their wounds. Sam tried to free herself but slipped on the treacherous floor, causing the wire to tighten and bite into her hand and neck again. Laine recovered first and tightened the wire, feeling it cut into flesh as he pulled. Sam winced as the wire cut into her hand. She could feel the hot blood running down her arm and across her chest before dripping in a pool at her feet. It was as if she were trapped in an animal snare. The more she struggled, the more damage she did to herself. She twisted round, heading for the hall table and her gun. It was not there. The wire pulled her back again and continued tightening. Sam slithered about in a pool of her own blood, trying to relieve the strain of the wire but to no avail. She was desperately tired and the loss of blood had increased. She could see the spray patterns on the walls and pictures as she turned. Her left hand was useless, and her legs were starting to buckle.

A voice came from behind her left ear. "Give in. Your time is up. Stop fighting, kneel down, and I promise I will finish you quickly."

Sam could not place the accent. Her head was spinning, but the last thing she would ever do was give up. She was about to attempt to kick the leg from him when the front door burst open.

***

My precious new bike went flying as I jumped off, grabbing the Browning as I landed. I hit the front door with my shoulder at full speed. The doorframe gave way with a crack, and the door flew open. Unlike movies, the shock of hitting the door rendered my right arm useless, and it dropped by my side as I half-charged, half-fell through the front door. My brain was having problems comprehending what I was seeing.

Sam stood in the hall some twenty feet in front of me, naked and covered from head to toe in blood. A large dark-haired individual was behind her, staring in disbelief at my grand entrance. His voice boomed out from behind Sam. "My good captain, you are a builder, are you not? Put the weapon down before you shoot your foot off. We both know you build bridges, not kill people. If you want your girl to live, drop the gun." Laine's eyes came to rest on the gun in my left hand. His free arm went for the gun tucked in his belt. I brought the gun up and on target all at the same time.

I aimed slightly to the left of the perfect shot, trying to avoid hitting Sam. Squeezing the trigger took what felt like hours. Then the hammer struck.

The bullet struck Laine's right eye a millisecond before he returned fire. His gun fired then jerked up, firing a second time into the roof. His grip on the wire released, and Sam fell forward onto her hands and knees. I joined her. Now both my sides were out of commission, and I went down hard on my face, the gun falling from my grip. I wanted to sleep, but my brain was screaming at me to get up. I dragged myself back from the edge of consciousness and sat up. The pain in my arm was bad, and when I drew breath, it was as if I were being stabbed. I looked down at myself in disbelief. My left side was covered in dark, sticky blood. I was not the only one who had hit his target. I got shakily to my feet. I needed to know what had happened to the assassin.

He lay on his back, a few feet from Sam. At first, I thought I had just winged him. He was twitching, and his legs were moving. Then I saw the damage the Browning had inflicted on him.

It was clear in that moment, his body was in the final throes of death, the muscles moved by rogue signals as they lost their last energy. The back of his head was gone, and his face was a ghoulish Halloween mask. There was no doubt—he was very dead.

It had not dawned on me that Sam was not moving. Only when I turned my attention to her did I see how bad the situation was. She was lying facedown in a pool of her own blood. The power seemed to return to my body as the adrenalin surged once more. I turned Sam over and found the side of her face badly swollen, a deep cut in her neck. Then I noticed her hand. She had coiled it round the piano wire in an attempt to keep it away from her neck, and it had bit in deep. The blood was pumping from an open wound in her wrist, and I could tell from previous experience it was from an artery. I lifted her ridiculously light body into a chair in the living room and charged into the bedroom, grabbing fresh pillowcases and making a tourniquet with them. There was so much blood, it was hard to tell whose it was and how much Sam had lost.

There was no time to waste. Sam needed a hospital and fast. I wrapped her in a big towel and carried her to the car. In the car, I reclined the front seat and placed her in it. I tied her damaged wrist to the roof handle with a second pillowcase. I was not sure of the nearest hospital but knew the location of the Stirling accident and emergency and headed for that.

After half an hour of hard driving on back roads, I reached the motorway and gave the BMW everything it had. Lights blazing, I passed by the town of Dunblane at fighter-jet speeds. On the downhill sections of motorway, the speedo needle touched one hundred and sixty miles per hour. The Stirling slip road arrived a few minutes later. I slowed the big car to a more sensible speed and headed for the city centre.

A few more minutes and we were in the ambulance lane outside A and E.

CHAPTER THIRTEEN
Stirling Royal

I was busy getting Sam out of the seat. My knees were like jelly, the pain in my side like a burning poker, and a cold sweat had taken hold. My head was light, and I was struggling to keep going when a small tubby nurse with attitude appeared by my side, growling at me for parking in the ambulance lane. I turned and shouted at the woman to get help. As I spoke, my mouth started to fill with blood. I spat it out and continued to get Sam out of the car. The woman reappeared a few seconds later with help in numbers. They lifted Sam onto a trolley and rushed away.

To my annoyance, two male nurses were trying to get me into a wheelchair. Only when I agreed to sit in the goddamned chair would they let me use a phone. I was sure I was about to die. I had seen men shot in the lung before, and I had all the symptoms. The blood in my mouth was starting to bubble and froth. I needed to call Neil Andrews and tell him where Sam was before I lost consciousness. I explained to the staff it was of national importance that I call London. I could see in their eyes that they thought I was mad, but after threatening bodily violence, they finally appeared with a phone. Neil answered just in the nick of time. I got out where I was and that Sam and I were in a bad way just before the darkness hit me.

My last thought was for Sam. Had I done enough? I tried to remember the last few minutes but they were swept away in the darkness.

***

Stirling Royal Infirmary had no idea what had hit it. Reception contacted police headquarters and informed them that they had a gunshot victim. This was passed around the relevant departments, and two officers were sent to investigate. Peter Kent and Robin Alder arrived fifteen minutes before the police and were waiting for them. As the officers argued about protocol, they received a message from the chief constable telling them the two gentlemen they were speaking to were now in charge of them and to follow their instructions to the letter.

Sam's heart stopped twice on the way to theatre. After being patched up, she did not regain consciousness for twenty-four hours. Neil Andrews's helicopter touched down in the Stirling transport section of the Ministry of Defense, known as ABRO. A few seconds later, a second helicopter landed, having taken a separate flight path from Hereford. Neil Andrews was taking no further risks. He had lost two men to a professional hit, and now his two key assets had been attacked. On board the second chopper was a four-man urban assault team. Neil briefed them before heading for the hospital. The team leader pored over the blueprints of the hospital and picked the location he wanted both patients moved to.

Neil Andrews convened a hastily arranged meeting with the SAS team. "Gentlemen, what I am about to tell you must go no further. There is a strong possibility that the people you are guarding will be the target of an assassination attempt. You need to know that if it comes, it will most likely be from American Special Forces."

There was complete silence in the room. These men were used to unusual instructions, but this was exceptional. They had fought alongside the Americans in many conflicts, and a mutual respect had grown between the regiments. "I take it from your silence that I have your undivided attention. I cannot go into detail, but know this—the safety of our country is in your hands."

***

The first sense that returned to me was smell—fresh paint and antiseptic; and then hearing—rain, then voices talking to me. Somebody was at the end of my bed. I came to with a bang.

"Hello, old boy. God, you gave us a fright." It was Neil Andrews, in the flesh. A doctor fussed about checking machines and drips while a man I had never seen before stood looking out of the small side window.

"Where is Sam?"

Neil sat down on the bed next to me. "You are a lucky man. The bullet broke two ribs on the way past. We think when you lifted Sam you nicked your lung with the broken rib."

I tried to sit up, but the blackness threatened to return. "Neil, what about Sam? Did she make it?"

Neil could see I was starting to lose patience with him. "She is even luckier than you, old son. She has just come round and seems to be responding well. She had lost so much blood that the doctors thought she might have brain damage. They had to postpone surgery twice because her heart stopped. They say the two things that saved her life were her incredible fitness and your quick actions. Oh by the way, I had to speak nicely to Stirling traffic police. They were looking for the driver of a BMW M5 that passed them at one hundred and fifty seven miles per hour. Not bad for somebody with a bullet in them I thought."

I started to laugh then screamed as the pain from my side stabbed me like a dagger.

"I shall leave you in peace. Get some rest. You should be safe. Steve here is part of your protection detail. You have an SAS team, two MI6 officers, six armed-response police officers, and an Apache attack helicopter sitting waiting within a mile of here. Sweet dreams, old boy. See you tomorrow."

***

Outside, Neil Andrews talked to Robin Alder. "Robin, I want you to head back up to Adam's house. There is a cleanup team on the way. I gather the place is a mess. I want to know who the dead man is, and

I do not want press. The last thing I need right now is Adam's face all over the BBC. Peter will stay here to coordinate all our assets. Call me if you need anything."

Much to the disgust of the surgeons, the two patients had been moved to a nursing home on the outskirts of the hospital complex during the middle of the night. All staff dealing with the patients had gone through rigorous MI6 checks and had to sign the Official Secrets Act before continuing with their duties.

***

I awoke with a start in the middle of the night. In the corner of the room sat a man, and in the poor light, it was hard to make out his features. The worst of the drugs had worn off, and the cotton wool that fogged my brain was starting to recede. I sat up gingerly, thinking for a minute.

My guest was watching me with one eye, his other eye on the window. "Can I get you anything sir?"

I got the impression from the way he spoke that he knew me. "I take it you are one of my protection detail?" My eyes picked out the shape of an M16 compact that straddled his legs.

"Yes, sir. Corporal Smith, sir. I will be with you for the next three hours, sir. I was on a few of your courses, sir."

I sat up and swung my legs onto the floor. "I thought so. Smithy, is it not?" I stood up, and the room started to spin.

"Sir, where are you going?"

I started to make for the door. "I need a pee, Smithy. Which way is the toilet?"

Smithy was up on his feet. "The door between the two rooms, sir."

I continued to the door. "Take the weight off your feet, soldier. I will be back in two minutes, that is, unless you want to come and hold it for me."

Smithy was unsure of what to do next but sat down uneasily to await my return.

I bypassed the toilet and headed for the second room. I needed to see for myself that Sam was OK. I knocked gently on the door. There was no reply. I opened it slowly, but as I popped my head in, a Glock was pressed against my temple. It was time to pull rank, even though I was not sure if I still had any. "Well done, soldier. Do you really think though, that the enemy would knock. Holster your weapon. That's an order."

There was a second of indecision, then the gun was removed from my head. The door opened further, and Peter Kent stepped into the hall light. "I was under the impression that you had retired from the army, Adam."

I slipped past the MI6 agent. "Just checking on my partner."

Sam was asleep. Unlike myself, she was still attached to monitors, but she looked peaceful. I retraced my steps into the hall.

"Actually, you are wrong, Adam. Sam was assigned to look after you, but she is actually my partner. I am Peter Kent, and Neil has left me in charge of the rest of this operation." Peter extended his hand, and we shook hands. I had already decided I wasn't too keen on this guy. I could tell he liked to control situations, and at that moment in time, I was not in the mood to be controlled.

"Peter, it has just dawned on me you may not know about my friend's death. His body is in his Land Rover, three miles to the west of my house by a pond. That bastard who tried to kill us murdered him before he got to us."

Peter rushed off. Obviously my news was new to him.

Back in my room, Smithy was panicking. "You all right, sir?"

I sat on the bed, my side burning. "Corporal Smith, I need you to do me a favour. Stop calling me sir for a start. Then I need you to contact Hereford and get them to tell you when Sergeant Ian Ferris will be buried and where. Then you can tell the rest of your squad to get their dress uniforms looked out because we are all going to the funeral. Don't do it until the day after tomorrow. News hasn't broken about his death yet."

Smithy pulled his chair a little closer to the bed. "I will give it my best shot, sir. May I ask who Sergeant Ferris was?"

I filled Smithy in on my old mate's adventures, adding that the regiment couldn't let a Victoria Cross-holder be put to rest without honouring him. "Sir, you can count on me. It's a done deal."

Next morning was manic: nurses, doctors, and then Peter Kent arrived. I informed him of my plan to attend the funeral.

"Adam, it's not going to happen. The bodies will be disposed of, but this has to stay under the radar, my friend."

It was red-mist time. "Do us both a favour, Peter. Go and look up the SAS history books: Ireland, the Falklands, Iraq...good God, Ian Ferris is a legend. Get your head out of your arse. You can't just sweep him under the carpet. For God's sake, man, he won the Victoria Cross, and what's more, I won't let it happen. Get Neil Andrews on the phone now." I hadn't realized until that point that I was screaming at the top of my voice, right into Peter Kent's face. "And another thing, I am not your bloody friend. I'm your worst fucking nightmare."

Peter Kent's face was flushed. He was having great difficulty controlling his temper, and he was about to respond to my threats when there was a voice from the doorway. "I would do as he asks, Peter. He is a real pain in the ass, but he grows on you." Sam stood in the doorway. She was pushing a stand with a drip on it, which was still attached to her arm.

A nurse appeared behind her. In the distance, alarms were going off. The nurse was flushed and out of breath. "Sorry, nurse, but I had to get up and come and sort out these two knuckleheads before they killed each other."

Sam entered the room with the nurse and Peter Kent fussing around her. "Guys, it's OK. I feel fine. Can you give Adam and me a few minutes alone? Then I promise I will go back to my room."

Reluctantly, they left the room, shutting the door behind them.

"Adam, you look like shit. Are you OK?" I was far from OK. My side was killing me, and my shouting had brought on a cold sweat. Sam sat on the bed next to me and lifted my hand onto her lap, holding it with both of hers. I was surprised how warm she felt next to my cold, clammy hands.

"I'm sorry, Sam. I didn't mean to disturb you. You've been through enough without this as well."

Sam squeezed my hand. "I have been worried sick about you. When they told me you had been shot, my heart almost stopped again. Are you sure you are OK?"

I pointed to the drip, changing the subject. "What's in that then, vodka?"

Sam smiled. "I wish. Better get going before they threaten to lock me in my room." Sam got up and pushed her drip to the door.

"Sam, they murdered Ian Ferris."

Sam turned in the doorway. "I gathered that from your conversation with Peter. I am truly sorry, Adam. I know you're hurting. They may have started this, but we will finish it. You have my word on that." Sam turned to leave.

"Sam, if you see your pal Peter, tell him I want the Browning from the house. It belonged to Ian, and it is the gun that saved your life."

Sam turned once more. "Funny that. Everybody I speak to says it was you who saved my life. It looks like I owe you once again. How will I ever be able to repay you?"

Sam and I made eye contact. "Just promise me that when all this is over, we will have that conversation we talked about."

Sam nodded but said nothing as she left the room.

***

Areli Benesch did not want anyone to know she had entered the country. She did not know if they were looking for her in connection with the woman's murder, but she could not take the risk, so she had elected to enter the country covertly. Areli decided to use the same route that Mossad had used in the past to sneak past British border controls when they were operating under the radar in Britain. The big cabin cruiser cut through the white horses before entering the shelter of Portpatrick harbour. The harbour was all but deserted. No one in his right mind would be out in that weather. The rain lashed the harbour wall as the big cruiser edged her way into the harbour. Areli took advantage of a lull in the downpour to secure the bow of the boat to a mooring point. She did the same with the stern and checked that her side protection was in place before tightening the moorings.

Areli had flown to Ireland using her alias Areli Antonov. She hired the cabin cruiser and made the short voyage across the ribbon of sea to the Scottish village of Portpatrick on the west coast of Scotland. She had already arranged for a car rental to be dropped off at the pier, arranging it over the Internet with a second fake Irish passport and driving license. Areli, like all other Mossad agents before her, would be in London in six hours, and the authorities would be none the wiser. If Interpol checked, they would see she was in Ireland.

In his drawing room, Merlin paced backward and forward. He was in a troubled state. He had tried every possible way to derail the MOD hearings, but it seemed the PM was going through with them. He had to be very careful. If he showed too much interest in the hearings, or was not seen to be actively supporting the inquiry, it would bring the spotlight down on him, and he could not risk that. Because of his position, he had to be seen to be all for the hearings.

Yet he needed to prove to the unnamed American who had called him that he was still a valuable asset. The American had told him the original deal would stand if he could prove to him he could stop the inquiry or the witnesses from testifying. He had done all that could be done behind the scenes to stop the inquiry to no avail, but he still had one card up his sleeve. When he found out the location of the witnesses, he knew some old friends who would help make sure they never testified.

The phone rang in the office of the freight haulage company. The transport manager answered the call. Billy Downes was reversing his rig into the loading bay when the transport manager shouted across the noise of the big Arctic's engine that Billy had a call.

He lifted the receiver to his ear. "Billy. It's Merlin here, and if you remember that name, then you must remember this name. Do you remember the Mac?"

Billy's grip on the phone tightened. "What have you brought that murderin' bastard's name up for? Geez, d'yah think I'm stupid? I'll no forget the name o'the animal who killed ma brother."

Merlin knew he had his full attention. "And what if I told you after all these years I have found him for you?"

Billy sat on the corner of the desk, taking in what he had just been told. "Well, in that case, Mr. Merlin, I think I need to come to England and pay the man a visit."

Colonel Southern had just entered his office in the Pentagon when the phone started to ring. The switchboard operator advised him she had a call from a "Merlin" character, and did he want to take it? Southern was speechless. He had not given out his name or number to this man. He accepted the call.

"Hello, old chap. How are we doing today? Or should I address you as colonel?"

Southern was beside himself with rage. How had this man gotten to him? "Merlin, what can I do for you? I don't remember arranging any meetings."

"I am sure you are wondering how I managed to track you down. It was a simple case of deduction, as Sherlock Holmes would have said. Where is the centre of operations? It had to be the Pentagon. I simply asked the switchboard to put me through to the person in charge of the investigation of Brad Whiteford's death. Now I know it was probably you who tampered with his plane, so it would be safest for you to take charge of the investigation, and here we are."

Southern was making a mental note to have the switchboard operator replaced as he replied, "Congratulations, Merlin. Carried out like a true spy."

Merlin had no idea how much danger he had just put himself in. Southern had been careful to keep his name out of anything to do with this mess, and now Merlin had become a loose end. He was the only person who could finger Southern.

"Anyway, I thought I would give you a quick call to let you know that I have failed to get the hearing stopped, but I kicked Plan B into action. I took the liberty of calling a few of my IRA friends. Mac won't be alive for much longer."

Southern thanked him and hung up. He did not like what he had just heard. From a controlled operation, this could now end in a disaster, and Merlin could tie him to it all. Something needed to be done. He did not want to be linked to a bloodbath in the centre of London.

***

The mist still swirled around the gathering on the Perthshire hillside that overlooked the Menamar estate. I, along with my protection detail, all in dress uniform, stood by the graveside. The only other two people present were Peter Kent and a local minister. The minister said a few words, and then the men from the regiment made ready to lower the coffin. I had a sudden change of heart and stopped them. Before tramping up the hillside, I had visited Ian's cottage. In the top drawer of his bedside table, I found what I was looking for—his Victoria Cross, which sat in its velvet case. I had originally planned to take custody of it for safekeeping, but standing at the graveside, I had a change of heart. I bent over the coffin and placed the case in the centre of the solitary wreath. "Here, my old friend. Wear it with pride."

I kept my voice low. It was a private moment between Ian and me, and not for other ears.

Sam had remained at the hospital with the armed police. She was still on the road to recovery. The truth be told, I was no better; the tramp up the hill had taken its toll on me. I fought back the urge to throw up as cold sweats and nausea hit me in waves. The trip back to Stirling would not be a good one I feared.

***

Neil arrived at the hospital unannounced, and when he found Sam alone, he flew off the handle. Sam watched with some amusement as he ranted and raved, but her amusement changed to dismay when he told Sam she was off the case and leaving for a convalescent break, to be followed by a medical reevaluation of her fitness and health, before being passed fit to return to duty. The waiting car took Sam to a helicopter, which ferried her to a spa resort in Oxfordshire.

CHAPTER FOURTEEN
Gleneagles

Steve drove the lead Discovery while we followed in a Jaguar. I had Peter Kent for company and Smithy as our driver, about ten minutes after leaving my house Kent's phone went off, he answered with some trepidation he had seen on the screen who was calling him. There were a lot of yes sirs, as the conversation progressed Kent's face became paler and paler, eventually the call ended and Kent immediately asked if I knew how to get to Gleneagles hotel.

The small convoy followed my directions, and within an hour, we pulled up outside a holiday cabin in the grounds of Gleneagles Hotel. Kent dispatched Steve back to the hospital to pick up everyone's kit. Then, over coffee and cakes, Kent relayed the latest orders he had received. The news that Sam had been replaced by Kent did not go down well with me.

For the moment, all I wanted to do was sleep. The day's exertions had been too much for my newly repaired lung. It took most of my remaining strength to take my kit off and get into bed.

I was awakened by someone closing a door in the next room. A quick look at the alarm clock on the bedside cabinet told me I had slept from two thirty in the afternoon through to eleven thirty the next day. My body was in full repair mode, and I was starving and thirsty. I tried to remember the last time I had eaten. It was probably the Chinese meal Sam and I had gone out for. I had so completely lost track of time that I didn't even know how long I had been out after the shooting. After an unsteady start, I found fresh clothes at the foot of my bed. Someone had raided my wardrobe at home. I found Smithy in the lounge watching daytime TV. "Good morning, Mr. Smith. What are you up to?"

Smithy switched off the TV and sat up. "Good morning, sir. How are we feeling today?" A quick recce of the kitchen found the cupboards were bare. "Right, Smithy, let's go, and for God's sake, stop calling me sir. My name is Adam."

As I headed for the door, Smithy stood up and half-started to follow me. "Sir, where are we going? Don't you think it would be better to wait for Mr. Kent?" Ignoring the last comment, I marched out of the door, heading for the main hotel entrance. I knew the area well, for I had spent two weeks here during 2005 checking for bombs before the G8 summit got underway.

Smithy was clearly not having a good time. He was probably thinking of what he was going to tell Kent when he found I was AWOL. "I really think we should let Peter Kent know where we are going, sir."

Five minutes later we were standing in the dining room, and a gentleman in a suit showed us to a table. Although it was midmorning, he gave no objection to us ordering a full cooked breakfast, coffee, and orange juice for two. Smithy tried to object. "Sir, I am here to watch your back, not dine with you."

I was already on my third slice of toast while I waited for my breakfast to arrive. "And you can't watch my back while you eat, Smithy? You need to relax, and for the last time, will you call me by the name I was given? It's Adam, not sir."

Forty-five minutes later, as Smithy and I were draining the last of our coffee, I saw Peter Kent talking to the man in the suit who had served us.

Peter Kent wasted no time with pleasantries when he approached the table. "The bill has been taken care of, gentlemen. Let's leave now, please."

It was clear to see he was not a happy camper. Out in the drive heading back to our cabin, Kent instructed Smithy to go ahead and lead the way. Then he waited until Smithy was out of earshot. "Macdonald, let's get things clear right from the start. I am here to protect you, and I can't do that if you decide to waltz off when ever you feel like it. You will do what I tell you, when I tell you. Do I make myself clear?"

My natural instinct was to break his nose. I had only met this man twice, and I already hated his guts. My head kicked into gear, and I managed to compose myself. He did have a point, but I was not about to concede the high ground to him just yet. "I take it the MI6 training manual does not have a section about manners. Sam suffered from the same problem the first time I met her."

Kent was having problems keeping his temper under control. "I don't know who you think you are, but I think you should have some respect for the people who are looking after you."

I could feel the red mist slackening my tongue again. I stopped in my tracks in the middle of the famous hotel drive. Kent stopped and stared at me. "I will tell you, sir, exactly who I think I am. I am the man that had to go into a hostile military base and rescue a civilian that your boss had sent in because MI6 were too chicken shit to do it themselves. I am the man that has just been shot while saving an MI6 agent's life, so by my reckoning, MI6 owes me big, and as for respect, you shall have it when you earn it. Until then, don't open your mouth until your brain is engaged."

Kent was about to explode when his mobile phone started ringing. He stopped and answered it. I continued onward catching up with Smithy before we reached the cabin. "Watch yourself, sir. He is a nasty piece of work." Smithy held the door open as I entered. The rest of the team was already inside. Steve was the team leader; Archie and Matt were senior members of the team; Smithy was the youngest and was treated accordingly.

"Listen guys, thanks for the support at the funeral. I would like to apologize now for being a pain in the arse, but please listen to me. Trust no one, and I do mean no one." The words had only just left my mouth when Peter Kent entered the room.

"Right, lads. I've just had an interesting conversation with my boss. It would appear we are to have a new member of the team join us today. Apparently his name is Zelenski. He is CIA, and he will help us identify any potential threats."

There was a stunned silence from everybody in the room. Steve was first to blink. "Kent, we were told that if an attack came, it could be from American Special Forces. This is madness. We have given our position and strength away to a potential enemy, and we will have him in our team. I don't like it, and I don't want it. Macdonald, what the hell have you got us into?"

***

Zelenski sat in the back of the big Range Rover as it flew up the fast lane of the motorway. He noted with interest that the speedo very rarely dipped below one hundred miles per hour. He knew if he had tried that in America, he would have had every state trooper in the country behind him. His phone vibrated in his pocket. It was a new, state-of-the-art scramble phone handed to him by Southern at the airport. He answered the call.

"Don't speak just listen. We are tracking your phone. Can you confirm you have just turned off the freeway and are heading to the Gleneagles complex. Star key once for yes, hash for no."

Zelenski pressed the star key as the sign for Gleneagles flashed past on the left.

"Pressing and holding the off key for four seconds activates video feed and microphone. You need to remember not to give the Brits too much information and keep my name out of it. Call me later."

Southern had been economical with the truth. The phone he had given Zelenski was bugged. The microphone was on constantly.

***

Steve, on hearing of the imminent arrival of our American guest, had got the finger out so to speak. He picked the lock on a holiday lodge in sight of our cabin and placed myself and Smithy in it. Smithy was busy prepping his Glock while I busied myself with the holdall I had picked up from the house.

In it was the Beretta from the bedroom and a few tricks that I had up my sleeve in case of emergencies. Also, cut into the foam base, was a Heckler and Koch MP5 with folding stock and a cutout for three clips and two grenades. Smithy smiled as I sat on the bed unloading the clip then reloading it to make sure the action was smooth and snag free.

"I picked your holdall up from the house and knew as soon as I lifted it you had some nice goodies in it. Glad to see you are ready to join the party, sir. I mean, Adam. Sorry."

Smithy was young, and I doubted he had seen a lot of action yet. He still thought this was one big adventure, a video game in the flesh, so to speak. "Smithy, I need you to pay attention to me for a second. In my top breast pocket, I have a flash drive for a camera. Whatever happens to me, my partner at MI6 has to get it. Her name is Sam, the girl from the hospital. Do not give it to anybody else. They cannot be trusted."

Smithy holstered his weapon and crossed the room. His carefree attitude was gone for the moment. "No problem, Adam. What is Sam's second name?"

For the life of me I couldn't tell Smithy. It had just occurred to me that I had never asked Sam what her real second name was. I knew plenty of her aliases, but her real name had never come up in conversation.

***

Matt had taken first shift on stag and was positioned fifty metres away high in a chestnut tree. He had picked up the approaching Range Rover in his L96 sniper rifle sights long before it pulled up outside the cabin. Kent, Steve, and Archie met Zelenski in front of the cabin. Although Peter Kent was pleasant, Steve insisted Zelenski was searched before he moved another inch.

Zelenski handed over his Glock without a quarrel but insisted he keep his phone at hand. Kent wanted to know more, so when they were in the cabin, he pressed Zelenski about his presence here. "Can you tell us what your mission parameters are, and who has sent you here, Mr. Zelenski?"

Zelenski removed his coat and sat down in the corner with one eye on the door. "Listen guys, I am sure you don't want me here, and I can assure you, I don't want to be here either. I have been sent here to assist you by my boss. He feels I may be able to point out any unfriendly agents who might have an axe to grind."

Kent sat opposite him and tried to make eye contact with the CIA man. "You're making little sense, man. Why should American agents want to kill British citizens?"

Zelenski knew he had to mix a little truth with his cover story to make it believable. "I won't lie to you. I don't know all the facts. Here is what I do know. The deputy director of the CIA went rogue. For some reason that we don't know, he targeted two civilians. We found out too late, and he has now been eliminated, but not before he sent a kill team to the UK. Unfortunately, he has some agents who are still loyal to his memory. We think they might be hell-bent on revenge for his death and would be willing to stir things up between our two great nations."

***

I had come in the back door and was standing quietly while Zelenski went through his spiel. "So we are to believe that this was all caused by one man, and that America has no hidden agenda?"

Together, Zelenski and Kent turned to face me. Kent was furious. "I thought I told you to stay put, Macdonald."

"You did, but as I am not your dog, I chose to ignore the request. If this story is correct, Agent Zelenski, then you should have no problems letting us examine the base at Machrihanish."

"Mr. Macdonald, I have no problems with that, but it is out of CIA jurisdiction. The base is the property of the US Air Force. However, I am sure if you followed the correct protocol that the US Air Force would allow an inspection."

My temper was on the rise again. I walked across the room to Zelenski. "Stand up, look me in the eye, and tell me you don't know that your own people are being killed because of some lunatic plane! Not because of one man."

Kent tried to step in between us, but I closed the gap before he could step in. I was standing six inches from Zelenski's nose.

"Those are serious accusations, Mr. Macdonald. I hope you can back them up with facts."

I reached into my pocket and produced the flash drive from the camera. "You can bet your last dollar on that, Zelenski, and I will do it legally, in public, where the facts can't be squirreled away by politicians trying to cover their own backsides."

I had had enough. Bad memories were starting to flood my head. I needed some space and some peace and quiet. I announced I was going for a walk and if anybody tried to stop me, I would probably shoot him. Kent thought about stopping me but backed off when he saw the look in my eye and the Beretta tucked into my waistband.

A few yards through the trees brought me to the edge of the golf course. It was a frosty, clear day, and I watched as two rabbits made the most of a deserted fairway to catch up on some food gathering. It was clear to me that emotionally I was not in a good way. Images of Kay Miller and Ian Ferris dominated my thoughts. I had become a natural loner over the years. I had few friends and losing Kay, then Ian, had been hard to take. I found myself wishing Sam were here to speak to. It came as a bit of a surprise how much I was missing her company, even after such a short time.

A voice startled me. "'A penny for your thoughts' is the English expression, I think." Zelenski was only a few feet behind me. Who knew how long he had been standing there.

Over his shoulder, I could see some distance away. Steve watched on with some concern. "They thought I was nuts coming after you, but we did not get off on a good footing, so I would like to offer my apologies and see if we can try again." The lanky American leaned forward and shook my hand.

"Can I be honest, Zelenski? I don't trust you, and that crap you told them in the cabin didn't help your cause."

The big American smiled and released my hand. "Point taken. Now it's my turn to be honest. I don't know why I was picked for this job, but I have a gut feeling it might not be good for my health. You are right and wrong at the same time. A lot of what I said back there was bullshit, but a lot was truth. I was sent to the island called Arran to investigate the murder of two agents. I take it from your previous comments you may know something about that."

I turned my gaze from the rabbits to Zelenski. "I know that Dr. Kay Miller was murdered by two scumbags calling themselves agents, and at the hearing, it will be revealed that Her Majesty's secret service killed them in the line of duty."

Zelenski was not expecting this answer, and it took him a few seconds to regroup. "Adam, please listen to me. This is a matter that should be sorted out behind closed doors. If you try to go public with this, for sure both countries will try and stop you. You will put yourself in an impossible position. Adam, I have three weeks until I retire, and I don't want to spend them dodging bullets. Listen, Adam, look at me. Do I look like Dirty Harry to you? No, that's right. There is a reason they sent a desk jockey who is about to retire to help protect you. They don't want you to win. I am window dressing so they can say in their press statement it was a joint operation. Adam, there are things I know that I will not tell you, but if I can help, I will, if only because my country has hung me out to dry, and after forty years in the service, that pisses me off."

I started to walk, and Zelenski walked with me. For some reason there was something about this big guy that I liked. "It's John, isn't it? If you want to help, let's start with the bastards who have already tried to kill me. Do you know who they were and who sent them?"

Zelenski ambled along by my side. He was obviously deciding whether to spill the beans. "OK, Adam, the truth, no bullshit. They were sent by Deputy Director Whiteford. They were a team of mercenaries employed by a man called Fletcher, who led the team. His second-in-command was Ed Holts. There was also a German called Lucas Richter, a Finn, Marcus Laine, and an Israeli woman called Areli Benesch. Does that answer your question?"

The names all tied up with the events of the past. "John, do you know what happened to them?"

Zelenski smiled. "Oh, I think you know what happened to a couple of them. From what I hear, they returned from their first attempt on your life with two dead and two wounded. Laine is unaccounted for, and the woman is missing. Fletcher died, and the other two bodies have never turned up." Zelenski was watching my reaction to this news very closely. It was clear to see that he was an accomplished investigator, not a bodyguard.

"Well, John, I have a sneaking suspicion you can score Laine off the list as well. I shot and killed a man who broke into my house, and on later examination, it was found most of his gear was Finnish."

We had walked for a mile or so round the perimeter of the golf course. My side was starting to ache, so we did an about turn and started to head back to the hotel and cabins. Steve and Smithy appeared from the undergrowth and took up flanking positions, keeping a reasonable distance. John Zelenski was quiet for some time. He was deep in thought, and I sensed he was having some sort of dilemma. I decided to remain silent and wait for him to make the next move.

We were almost at the cabins when he stopped me. "Adam, I am going to give you two very good pieces of advice, and you would do well to heed them. The Israeli woman who is missing is a very dangerous person. She is ex-Mossad, and mark my words—she is not one to give in. Don't ask me any more about her. I cannot tell you. Secondly, I have left my phone in my coat pocket in the hall. I was given this phone at the start of the operation. Please be careful what you and the others say in its vicinity. I have a hunch it is bugged."

***

Sam had stayed at her flat overnight. She had been up since four in the morning, and now she sat in a corner of the office with files all around her. The computer was working overtime, and she was busy looking through a police report of the Brighton bombing when she realized someone was standing by her side.

"Sam, what the hell are you doing here?"

Sam put down the file "Good morning, Neil."

Neil Andrews pulled up a chair and sat in front of the desk. "Sam, you are suspended. You shouldn't be here until you are passed by the doctors."

Sam made a face. "The bloody horse doctor won't even give me an appointment until next week."

Neil leaned closer, dropping his voice. "Sam, you can't keep going around bending the rules to suit yourself. I can't keep covering for you."

Sam shook her head in disbelief. "Well, after your little stunt in Edinburgh Airport, bending the rules is going to continue, like it or not. We may be work colleagues, but our friendship is over, so you better get used to me telling you what I will be doing, and at the moment, that is looking for leads that will tell us who Merlin is."

Neil stood up. "In that case, knock yourself out. You won't be reading anything that our analysts haven't already checked a dozen times. One day, Merlin will make a mistake, and when he does, I will be there to put the cuffs on him."

Sam looked into Neil's eyes, and the look sent a shiver down Neil's spine. "If I find him first, he won't need the handcuffs."

Neil started to walk away. "If we are not friends, you won't want to hear the latest news fresh off the jungle drums then." Neil kept walking, waiting for Sam to take the bait.

Sam got up and followed Neil into the hall. "Oh, you don't want to be my friend, but you expect me to keep you informed?" Sam fought the overwhelming urge to strangle him with his own tie. "OK, I've seen that look before. Three of Adam's old adversaries just landed at Heathrow this morning. It's too much of a coincidence that Adam is due to arrive soon, and we suspect Merlin may have tipped them off about Adam's schedule. Don't worry. We have them under surveillance. I contacted Peter Kent this morning and informed him. As an extra precaution, I have instructed Peter not to use the planned safe house. We will put decoys there, and Peter is taking Adam to my house for the moment." Sam was looking through Neil, her mind elsewhere. "Don't worry, Sam. We will look after Adam. Even the director has no knowledge of the switch."

Sam snapped back out of her dream-like state. "If the rumour is true that the Americans have sent an agent to help protect Adam, you need to get rid of him. If the Americans have got Merlin to bring his old pals from Ireland to do their dirty work, the agent could give away Adam's position. He is in great danger."

***

The trip from Gleneagles was a long, drawn-out affair. Peter Kent received a call over breakfast, and forty minutes later we were on the move. Kent refused to tell anybody where we were headed. The three-vehicle convoy was headed by Steve in the lead Discovery; we followed in the Jaguar; and Zelenski and his driver brought up the rear in the big Range Rover.

My two companions were again Smithy and Kent, which gave me the opportunity to run an idea past Kent. "Peter, I have an idea that I think you should consider carefully. We both know we can't trust the American. Although I don't think he is here to attempt anything himself, I am sure he is here to shadow us and give our position away. My BMW is hopefully still parked in the hospital car park, and we are headed that way, so why not swing past and pick up the BMW. Smithy and I can take the Beemer and tail you at a distance. Steve's car and Zelenski's car can continue, and you can catch them after dropping us off. That way Zelenski will be in the dark, and if he has a tracking device, it will be rendered useless. Also, if you come under attack, you won't need to worry about me. You can concentrate on the enemy. Come on, Peter. You know it makes sense. It keeps us one step in front."

Kent sat thinking for a few minutes, then called the lead car. "Steve, we are going to take the Stirling cutoff. I have some unfinished business at the hospital. You call Zelenski's driver and tell him to follow you. We will meet you at the Southwaite services on the M6 if we don't catch you before then."

Steve could be heard complaining bitterly but complied with Kent's orders. Kent turned to me and handed me a piece of paper. "This is the address we are headed for. Don't get too far behind, call if you need us, and for God's sake, do as you are told. That last stunt you talked me into almost got me fired. Neil Andrews would have buried me with your friend that day if he had the chance."

Kent dropped us by the BMW and waited for a few seconds until we got the car running and bags swapped over from car to car. He left quickly so he could catch the other two cars. Smithy went to drop the bags in the boot, but I stopped him. He blushed when I pointed out he was making a schoolboy error. His spare clips for his handgun were in his holdall. If it came down to a gun battle, how was he going to reload?

My second reason for stopping him was because the boot was filled with illegal drugs and lots of money. The fewer people who knew about this, the better. Unfortunately, I had forgotten that the BMW had been used as a high-speed ambulance. The driver's seat was covered in dried blood, and the passenger door had been sprayed with Sam's blood. A full tin of deicer later, with one of my old shirts for a duster, and the cabin was habitable. A quick stop for fuel and we were on our way.

Smithy elected to drive with me giving directions. For a while, I watched Smithy. His eyes were everywhere, and he drove with his Glock tucked between his legs. He may have been young, but I knew he did not get into this team without being a very special talent. I pointed to his Glock. "I hope for your family-planning-unit's sake that you have the safety on."

Smithy chuckled while checking the rearview mirror. "Sir, do you really think the Yanks are mixed up in this thing?"

I frowned at him before replying. "Smithy, for God's sake, if you can't call me Adam, call me Mac. To answer your question, it is definitely an American problem, but it is hard to tell if it is rogue individuals or state-sponsored. You need to keep me alive until I can put this whole thing on the table at the hearing. Then the pressure will be on the two governments to sort this bloody mess out, and I can go home without looking over my shoulder."

Once on the M6, Smithy needed little direction, and we lapsed into a mutual silence. Smithy was busy studying the surrounding traffic for potential threats, and my mind had wandered back to previous events. I wondered about the camera memory card in my top pocket. It had never been checked out. For all I knew, there might be nothing on the card that could be used in evidence. I needed to check it out sooner rather than later. I found myself thinking about Sam again. No one had any news of her. She was a tough cookie, but I was sure the last episode had taken a lot out of her.

***

Sam had been at the firing range for the last hour. With the right hand, her marksmanship was passable, but her left hand was another story. The wire had cut deep into her wrist, damaging muscle and nerves. She had enough trouble holding the Glock when it kicked, never mind getting it on target. As she tried, her arm became weaker. She was losing all feeling in her hand. She was frustrated. She needed to get back to work, and her left hand was going to keep her from passing the medical.

She had just decided to try one last clip and was working her hand to try and get some feeling back in it when she became aware Neil was standing behind her. "Good morning Neil, how are we today?"

Neil Andrews stepped from the shadows into the light above the firing station. "Samantha, I see you still have eyes in the back of your head."

Sam swapped the Glock to her good hand deliberately and fired two shots at the paper soldier at the end of the range. "I told you before, Neil. Only my friends get to call me Samantha." Sam fired another three shots checking out the target for grouping.

"Come on, Sam. You and I go way back. You have a short memory." Sam ignored the comment and fired two more rounds at the target. "Sam, I hear from the grapevine that you have been asking about the location of Adam's friends who have arrived in Britain. I thought it would be worthwhile reminding you that you are on medical leave."

Sam put the safety catch on, placed the Glock on the bench, and turned, removing her safety glasses as she did.

"Before you go off on me, madam, here is the situation. I have just read your latest medical report. It says, and I quote, 'The subject has severe nerve damage to her left arm and may never regain full use of her arm. If no further improvement is achieved, we recommend the subject be removed from field operations.' I think you are going to need all the friends possible in high places if you don't want to be stuck behind a desk for the rest of your career. Now, were you going to say something to me, or have you changed your mind?"

Sam was trying to keep it cool, but the urge to pick up the Glock and empty the rest of the clip into Neil was very real. "You do know that our Irish guests may know the identity or location of Merlin. We can't let an opportunity like that slip through our fingers."

"Sam, you need to get this obsession with Merlin out of your head. It will be the undoing of your career. You have already crossed the line and got away with it, but you won't be so lucky the next time."

Sam removed the clip and checked the breech of her gun, then holstered it before making eye contact with Neil. "You are right, Neil. It is an obsession, and no matter what you say or do, I will only stop when that bastard is dead. If you try to stop me, you will fail. It's as simple as that."

Sam started to leave, but Neil reached down and grabbed her left arm. Sam wanted to scream but managed to keep a lid on the pain that burst into her head. "Remember this, Sam. You may have joined this mission with your own agenda, but you were told to baby-sit Macdonald, nothing more. I will catch Merlin in my own good time, not when you decide, so back off, or you will end up sorting letters in the mail room."

Sam pulled her arm free and pushed past Neil, heading for the exit. "One last thought, Sam—have you told your new-found boyfriend why you joined the team? I wonder, does he know you really have no interest in saving him? Does he know you are using him as bait?"

Sam left without turning or replying to this last statement. She was not sure if her emotions would belie her outward calm.

The little convoy of vehicles rendezvoused at the Southwaite services just south of Carlisle. Zelenski noted that they had shed two of their company, one of whom was Adam Macdonald. He was not surprised by this new arrangement. The men he was with were no fools. They had to figure that he could give away the position of their star witness and had obviously taken steps to wrong-foot anybody tracking them. It also came as no shock that they had found an excuse to get him away from the protection detail.

Zelenski's presence had been requested at Vauxhall Cross by Neil Andrews, on the pretense that he had some mug shots of suspects he wanted Zelenski to look at. Neil Andrews put together a mass of pictures that had nothing to do with the incident, but they would keep Zelenski out of harm's way and both agencies sweet.

CHAPTER FIFTEEN
Aylesbury

S mithy pulled up in the late evening. The other cars had been here for some time. I had not expected this destination. I was expecting a secluded cottage far from human habitation, and I couldn't have been more wrong if I had tried. Our travels had taken us to the town of Aylesbury, a few miles to the north of London. We had arrived at the north end of the town in a modern, very up market housing estate situated on the banks of the very large village pond. The houses were large and mainly detached villas. It looked like the company who had built the estate had attended a fire sale for cream and white paint. The estate was spotless but lacked character as every second house was the same as its neighbours. Smithy carried the bags into the house while I studied my new surroundings. The house we were staying in was at the end of the estate, and the access road went to the house and no further. It was more than likely the most sought-after house in the estate. It sported a huge conservatory and its own pier out onto the corner of the pond. As I studied the surrounding houses, I noted that the next-door neighbour was none other than Steve, who gave me a little mock salute from the living room window, which looked out onto the pond. As I watched, Archie appeared and moved the Range Rover from the drive into the access road, parking it and effectively making a road block to the house at the end of the lane. Anybody that wanted to get to me would have to get past Steve and the guys in the house next door.

Smithy shouted to me from the front door of the end house. "Mac, the guys are sending out for a munch. You game? Oh and there is a call for you in the front room."

I headed for the front room, secretly hoping that the caller was Sam. I gave Smithy my pizza order on the way, but as I lifted the phone and listened to the voice, my heart sank. "I trust that you had a good journey down. Peter tells me that you improvised, good for you, but I already had that one covered. Well, what do you think of my pad? You are a lucky laddie. I don't normally let anybody know where I stay, let alone hand them the keys to the front door."

As Neil spoke to me, my eyes fixed on the picture on the phone table. Mary smiled out of the frame at me. The picture had been taken at a polo match; behind Mary stood Neil in a blazer and Panama hat. He was deep in conversation with an important-looking elderly gentleman dressed in similar fashion. For a split second, I forgot Neil was on the phone. An image of poor Mary in the bath flashed through my head. I leaned over and placed the picture facedown. Then Neil's voice came back to me.

"Sorry, Neil, I missed that last bit. I think I need my bed." I was about to end the conversation prematurely when a thought entered my head. "Neil, do you have a computer in the house? I need to look at the pictures from the base."

There was silence. "Good God man, you mean you haven't checked them before now?" Neil was flapping big style. He knew his arse was on the line.

"Sorry, mate, I don't carry a laptop when I am on the run from God knows who. If you haven't noticed, I have been rather busy staying alive."

Silence again. "OK, there is a laptop in my bedroom. The password is MI6MI6. Call me in the morning after you have checked them. Just lift the receiver of this phone, and it will dial here automatically. Anything else?"

I chuckled to myself. One of the top security people in the country, and he had a really crap password. "Only one thing, Neil. Have you heard from Sam? How is she doing?"

There was that silence again. "No, Adam, I haven't seen her. I suspect she is sunning herself on a faraway beach while some bronzed Adonis rubs suntan oil into her back. Back to business. Get some sleep, then call me in the morning as soon as you have checked the pictures."

That night, sleep would not come. My shoulders ached, my foot ached from my old wound, my side was as stiff as a board. It felt as though my body was on the point of saying enough was enough. I sat up and pulled Neil's laptop across the bed to me. If I could not sleep, at least I could take my mind off it.

I punched in Neil's password and popped the camera chip in the reader port. In all there were twelve pictures that were of importance to the inquiry. I studied them with interest. I was no lawyer, but it looked to me like a good lawyer could shoot them down in flames if used as evidence.

I could almost hear the lawyer now, discounting each picture one by one. I was sitting on the bed looking at two pictures in particular. Then it clicked. I scrambled off the bed and raked around in the side pocket of my holdall. At first I thought I had lost it, then my fingertips found it. I pulled out the newspaper article from the hotel in Inverness. Back on the bed I spread it out, ironing out the creases as I went. There they were—HOWIE and FERNANDEZ—the two names that had been spinning around in my head for weeks.

The article stated that Howie and Fernandez were killed in Afghanistan. I was looking at pictures of the two SEALs I had killed in the dunes. Their tunics were labeled as Howie and Fernandez. It was far too much of a coincidence. I picked up the phone and was connected immediately to Vauxhall Cross. After explaining to the duty officer who I was, he reluctantly patched me through to my requested number. My first call was to Fort Campbell, Kentucky. It was a bit of a long shot but worth a try. "Hello, Lee, is that you? It's Mac. Listen, buddy, I really need your help. It's life or death."

"Captain Mac, how are you doin' pal? You getting yourself in the shit again? Don't worry. I've got your back, just like old times, buddy.

What do you need?" It was as if time had stood still. Lee Tribby had not forgotten me, and he was still as large as life.

"Lee, I am reading an article that says the bodies of two Navy SEALs were flown back to your base in Kentucky. I was wondering if you could recall that happening. The flight was from Afghanistan around November."

Tribby was chuckling away down the phone. "Did they shoot you in the head in Kuwait, buddy? The bodies did arrive here, but they came from the UK. Either you read it wrong, or someone wrote it wrong. Not every day SEALs get sent home in body bags to the wrong base, so I remember it well."

Bingo. I had hit the jackpot, but I needed proof. "Lee, I know this is asking a lot, but could you get me the flight log? It is crucial I know where it came from and can prove it."

"Oh, I think I can manage that old bubby, but it will cost you. I am about to go on leave next week. Say I pop across the water to see you—will you buy me a beer if I bring the flight log with me?"

My mind was working overtime. "Lee, I will pay for your trip if you bring the log. Lee, don't tell anyone what you are doing. It might shorten your life expectancy if anyone found out."

Tribby laughed. "Many have tried, buddy, many have tried. I'll be fine. I will call you from the airport. Get the beers racked up. Speak to you soon."

My second call was to the offices of the paper that had run the story. My first attempt to talk to the journalist whose name was on the report failed. The secretary I talked to knew of no one by the name of Ricky Freeman who worked for the paper. I was put through to the editor's secretary, and it turned out that Freeman was, as his name suggested, a freelance journalist who had sent the piece into the editor. After a ten-minute wait, Chloe, the secretary, came back with a mobile number for Ricky Freeman. I thanked Chloe for all her help, hung up, and redialed the mobile number. My luck finally ran out. The mobile was switched off. I left a voice mail and sent a text message. Then all I could do was wait for him to call back.

***

Areli Benesch sat in the cinema that she had been told to go to. She had picked a seat high up above the entrance tunnel and next to the emergency exit. The call had come from the agent called Merlin. Although she knew of him, she had never worked with him, so she was taking extra precautions. The film showing was a kids' cartoon, and Areli watched as the cinema filled up with kids and their parents. No one remotely fitting Merlin's profile was present. The film had started before Merlin made his appearance. He spotted Benesch high up next to the emergency exit and sat one row below her. He said nothing to start with, only making eye contact. Then, after a few minutes of scanning the audience, he spoke first.

"Good afternoon, Miss Benesch. Or should I call you Areli Antonov, or even Anna Kowalski?"

Benesch was shocked but tried not to show it. Merlin had just given her real name, her name in Monaco, and the name she was currently traveling under. Merlin was well informed and was using it to wrong-foot Benesch from the word go.

"I take it from your face, my dear, you were not expecting that. You must remember you are dealing with the largest and most sophisticated intelligence agency in the world. You can run, but you can't hide. I suggest that you do what you are told, and you may remain useful to them. Cross them, and they will swat you like a fly." Areli's face was cast in stone, but she remained calm. "Well, enough of the chit-chat, I have been asked to give you this bag. It contains a silenced Sig Sauer, ammunition, a mobile phone with my number in the memory, spare ID, and a file on the two targets. It also contains a press pass for the forthcoming hearings. Happy hunting, my girl."

Merlin wasted no more time. Areli watched him leave. His face was familiar to Areli, she had seen him before but could not for the life of her place him. He was not her idea of a spy, but this had obviously worked well for him over the years.

Sam was woken up by the rain lashing against her windscreen. She had spent the night in the car park of a Croydon Travel Inn. Four cars away was the first of a two-team surveillance squad. Sam had one eye on them and one eye on the hotel. She had managed to acquire photos of her Irish targets. She checked her watch. She had been asleep for fifty minutes. She was mad with herself but decided the reason was that she was still on medication and not fully recovered from her attack.

A little after eight, two men left the hotel. Sam consulted her photos, confirming the two men were Billy Downes and Shaun Malone. As she watched, Downes jumped into the driving seat of a battered old white Transit and left the car park, trailing a plume of blue smoke behind him. Ten seconds later, a Vauxhall Astra followed with half of the surveillance team. Sam watched the other unit, but there was no movement. They had obviously decided to wait for the third member of the team. The big people carrier had tinted windows, but Sam watched as the vehicle moved from side to side slightly, giving away the fact that it had occupants who were moving around. Sam had no doubts that the people carrier was decked out with directional mics and all the latest video technology. She was going to have to be very careful. If Neil found out what she was about to do, he would freak out.

Sam took one last look at the third member of the team's photo and headed for the on-site restaurant. She found the man she was looking for in the corner booth. Andy O'Neil was studying page three of the *Sun* while waiting for his breakfast to arrive. Sam apologized to the waitress who had come across to seat her, saying she would wait for her husband, and she headed back out the door, heading to reception. By the time she arrived at the reception desk, she had pulled on a knitted hat and was wearing specs. The receptionist was appalled to hear her story that she had just been sideswiped in the car park by two men in a white transit van. Sam gave the registration to the receptionist, adding that it was her husband's new car, and he would kill her. The receptionist checked her records and felt like Sherlock Holmes when she found the culprits' van on the hotel records. Sam talked the receptionist into giving her the room number (Room 201) so she could pop a note under the door for the driver to contact her with his insurance details. It was like taking candy from a baby. She thanked the receptionist and headed off to deliver her note. A few feet down the corridor, and she found the staff area. There, she paused and pulled on a pair of tan-coloured latex gloves before entering the room. Inside, she found an overall complete with master key and a trolley with cleaning equipment. Sam swapped her hat and glasses for a burka and pulled the overall on top of her coat. A quick check in the mirror and she was off to Room 201 before O'Neil finished breakfast. Sam had used the Asian dress before. It was perfect for getting by camera technology, and Croydon had a large Asian population, so it did not look out of place. In the room, Sam wandered about pretending to dust. She was very aware she was probably the star act on the video screens in the van outside. Brushing against the jacket hanging up, Sam felt something heavy in the coat pocket. On the desk was an opened envelope. Sam made a sweeping motion with the duster and accidentally on purpose knocked the envelope and documents onto the ground, then made heavy weather of gathering them up and putting them back in the envelope. Sam read them one by one as she put them back.

It was time to get the hell out of there before O'Neil came back or the team outside got suspicious and came for a look. Sam replaced the trolley, pulled off the burka, unzipped the hood inside her jacket collar, and pulled a scarf from the pocket, wrapping it around her face. She left via the fire exit, which backed onto a new housing estate. Sam was glad that the boundary fence was only three feet high as her arm was still in no state to lift her body weight. Sam appeared between two houses and walked to the main road where she managed to flag down a taxi. The hire car in the Travel Inn car park could be picked up by the hire firm at a later date.

Sam's adrenalin pumped round her body. She felt alive again. She had missed the feeling. She wanted to tell someone about her exploits, and suddenly she felt very lonely. She missed having Adam to speak to, but she was sure it was just a side effect of the drugs. She had done this job for years and had never felt the urge to confide in someone. It had to be the drugs.

***

It was three in the afternoon when Smithy summoned me from the kitchen. There was a call waiting for me in the lounge. It was Freeman, the journalist. He apologized for missing me, and after hearing my request, he thought for a minute, then admitted his story had been put together from an official press release by the Pentagon and not, as you would have expected, by the US Navy press department. Freeman promised to dig out the press release and send it recorded delivery. I returned to the kitchen and finished making a coffee. Then I wandered out of the house and headed to the pier. I sat by the water, deep in thought. Why had the director not just ordered a team to go and check out the area around the air base? Why all the cloak-and-dagger stuff? The director was no fool, so he must have his reasons.

I was tired of it all. I just wanted to go home and sort my life out. "A penny for your thoughts." I turned and looked in the direction of the voice. There was only a silhouette against the low winter sun, but I knew instinctively it was Sam.

"Hello, stranger. Boy, am I glad to see you." I stood up and met Sam halfway down the pier. It was as if we had not seen each other for months. Sam wrapped her arms around me, giving me a lingering hug and a peck on the cheek for good measure. It was as if neither of us wanted to let go. Sam drew away first, looking back over her shoulder.

Steve was eyeballing us from the front room of the neighbouring house. "I see we have company. I suppose we better act in a professional manner." We both sat down, dangling our legs over the edge like a couple of school kids. There was silence for a few seconds while we both gathered our thoughts. It was as if we didn't need to speak, both of us just happy to be in each other's company.

I broke the silence first. "How did you find us?"

Sam sighed and rolled her eyes. "I don't know how many times I have to tell you. I am a spy. It's what I do, Adam."

I changed the subject. "Hey, I bet you will never guess who stays here."

Sam smiled back at me. "Neil bloody Andrews stays here, scumbag that he is."

Sam had taken the wind out of my sails. "Wow, how do you know that? I didn't know that."

The smile was no longer evident. It was clear Sam was thinking of something. "I've been here before, Adam. I knew Neil socially before I joined the service." I watched Sam's face. She was attempting to read my thoughts as I digested the last statement.

"Sam, there is a hell of a lot I don't seem to know about you."

Sam looked at the rowing boat tethered to the pier. "Let's see if the boat works, Adam." I was about to object, but Sam stopped me. "Adam, get in the boat, I want to talk to you, and I don't want Rambo and his mates butting in until I have finished." Sam was back to her old self again.

"OK, but if they shoot me for desertion, it's your fault, madam."

Sam stepped into the boat and untied the rope while I clambered about, freeing the oars from under the seat. I could see Steve and Smithy getting edgy, so I gave them the thumbs-up and signaled with my fingers that I would be ten minutes. To my surprise, Sam asked me to row as her hand was still sore. For Sam to admit a weakness was a rare event indeed.

Out in the middle of the pond, I stopped rowing. "Will this do here?"

Sam nodded and shivered noticeably. She pulled up the zip of her coat and wrapped the collar round her ears.

"I thought after your visit to Scotland, the weather down here would be a walk in the park to you."

Sam ignored the comment and sat looking at me in a strange, detached way. "Adam, this is the talk we were going to have. Are you OK with that?"

I sat back, trying to get more comfortable. "Fine by me, but I thought we were going to talk once this was all over."

Sam was still watching me. "Adam, there have been a few things that make me think you need to know now. If anything happened to either of us, and we hadn't talked, I would never forgive myself. Please let me tell the whole thing before you say anything." Sam was looking more worried by the second. She was obviously having problems with what she was going to tell me.

I steeled myself for whatever that might be. "I will keep it zipped until you have finished. Please continue."

Sam took a deep breath. "I think we need to start with me. I need to tell you this. I don't want you to hear it from anybody else." Sam took another deep breath and continued. She was examining her fingers instead of looking at me. "My full name is Samantha Jane O'Conner; my big sister was Mary O'Conner."

If it were not for the water gently lapping against the side of the boat, you could have heard a pin drop. With some difficulty, I managed to refrain from saying anything. "Our parents were killed in a bomb blast in Belfast, and our foster parents moved to England to escape the troubles. Mary was older and had already acquired a strong Irish accent. I on the other hand did not. Mary was hell bent on getting revenge for the death of our parents and applied for the RUC. She came to the attention of the British secret services, and the rest is history."

Sam swallowed as if her throat had gone dry. "Mary had just got me an admin job in MI6 when she was murdered. I talked Neil into training me as an operative, and to his surprise, I was rather good at it. But I have only ever had one goal. Between yourself and Neil, you killed the men who murdered my sister, but the turncoat bastard who betrayed her is still out there. As God is my witness, I will not rest until he burns in hell. And I will kill anyone who tries to stop me." I watched as the tears welled up in the corner of Sam's eyes before escaping down her pale cheeks. "When I flew back from Argentina and studied the file on this case and found out that Merlin was active again, wild horses could not have dragged me away from the case. Neil tried to call me off, but he knew that would never happen. I am sorry, Adam. I did not stay on the case to protect you. I was using you to get to Merlin. And you needed to hear that from me and not Neil Andrews, who would undoubtedly put his own spin on it." Sam wiped away the tears and blew her nose. She looked utterly miserable but she was not staring at her fingers anymore. "I am sorry for keeping you in the dark. I hope we can still be friends. I have missed you. The things that have happened have made me realize life is too short to wait until everything is sorted. Now is the time to sort it. I'm officially off the case, so if you don't want to see me again I will understand." There was a silence. I didn't know what to say. "Adam, I need to know where I stand."

The emotions running through me were in the hundreds. I wanted to laugh, I wanted to cry, I wanted to slap her, I wanted shake her, but most of all, I wanted to hug her. She looked like a frightened kid waiting to hear what punishment the teacher was going to dole out. "Sam, I almost lost you in the woods. Then I almost lost you at my house. I will be damned if I lose you again. You had your reasons for keeping your secrets to yourself, and yes, we are still friends, and yes, I want to see you again. I would like to be more than friends, if that is OK with you."

There was a bump, and the boat lurched as it came to rest in the reeds at the side of the pond. We had both been so intent on our conversation, we had not noticed the little boat drift into the reeds out of view of the houses. I started to use the oar to push the boat off the reed bank, but Sam stopped me. She leaned across and pulled me toward her. She was a lady who would not take no for an answer, so resistance was futile. Her kiss was long and passionate, and it left me in no doubt about her feelings for me.

Then Sam pulled away and sat up. "OK Mr. Macdonald, enough of that. We better get back before they send out the search parties. There will be plenty of time later to continue where we left off."

I pushed us out of the reeds and got underway again, heading for the pier on the right of the pond. "OK Miss O'Conner. I will take a rain check on that one and cash it in soon, hopefully."

Darkness was descending as we tied up at the pier. "Adam, go and get the rest of your team and meet me in Neil's lounge. We need to have a talk. It is important the rest of your protection detail is present."

I had no idea what Sam was up to but carried out her instructions. Ten minutes later we were all standing in the lounge. Peter Kent had a worried expression on his face. He knew what Sam was capable of, and he also knew she flew by the seat of her pants. He had already had a bollocking from Neil, and I'm sure the last thing he needed was Sam rocking the boat.

"Right, guys, I'm going to tell you something that will get me into big trouble if it gets back to my boss, but you need to know this, so here goes. Earlier today, I got into the rooms of three Irish men who were under surveillance by MI5. I found out they are carrying weapons and that they have someone on the inside. They have been supplied with press passes and site information for the Central Hall in Westminster, the scene of the hearings. They have floor plans, and the plans have been marked to show security points."

Peter Kent was the first to react. "How the hell did you get access to the room if it was under surveillance? If MI5 find out you have been snooping about, there will be hell to pay."

Sam chewed her lip. "As I stated earlier, Peter, I know I will be in trouble, but it will be worth it if we know what they are up to."

Steve was the next to speak up. "Sam, can you tell us what weapons they have?"

Sam seemed relieved to change the subject. "All I came across were handguns. I am sure if there were anything more, MI5 would have spotted it."

After the meeting broke up, Peter Kent made a beeline for Sam and me standing in the hall. Luckily for us, he was intercepted by Steve.

"Peter, did you know about the Irish men?"

Kent looked like a rabbit caught in the headlights. "Well, yes, but MI5 had not confirmed the intentions of the trio, so I thought it better to wait until it was proved that Adam was their target before I let you know."

Steve glared at Kent. He must have been well pissed off. "Any more pearls of wisdom you have neglected to tell us about, or should we consult our crystal ball?"

Sam and I left them arguing and slipped outside onto the front steps of the house. I informed Sam about the pictures and my conversation with Tribby and the journalist.

"That's good news, Adam. It may help at the inquiry. If I were you, though, I wouldn't get my hopes up. I've seen what happens when you get politicians involved too many times. The main thing is you give your evidence and get the hell out of London as fast as you can. Let Neil worry about the outcome. That's what he's paid for."

Peter Kent swept past us and headed for his car. It didn't take a rocket scientist to work out he was in a foul mood. "Sam, what about you? Are you going to get into trouble? Kent was not happy with you."

Sam smiled as she looked out over the shimmering surface of the pond. "Peter likes to be in complete control. He can't handle it when that doesn't happen, but he'll be fine. He wouldn't dare tell Neil he has lost control again. It would hurt his male ego too much, and anyway, I'm on sick leave, so I will do what I please."

She checked her watch. "I better get going. Neil wants me in the office tomorrow to babysit the CIA guy they sent across to help us." Sam started to move down the steps. "Are you going to be a gentleman and see me to my car?"

We walked slowly to the car, which was parked round the corner from the house. "Sam, you need to quiz Zelenski about Merlin when you meet him tomorrow. He seems to be a genuine guy. I think, like me, he has been caught up in this whole mess by mistake. He has already warned me that his phone is bugged. Sam, someone at the CIA knows the identity of Merlin, and Zelenski works for the CIA. It's time for you to go back into spy mode."

Sam stood for a few seconds by her car. "Well, are you going to give me a goodnight kiss or not, you big Scottish idiot?" Sam was about to continue, but something over my shoulder caught her eye. "Steve, you can come out from behind the bush now. You have just ruined the mood."

Steve appeared somewhat sheepishly from behind the shrubbery at the corner of the house. "Sorry, guys. Just doing my job."

Sam gave me a quick peck on the cheek and jumped into her latest acquisition from the hire car firm. "Call the office, and ask for me tomorrow. Speak to you then." Sam glared at Steve as she pulled away in the Astra.

Steve and I walked back to the house together. "Mac, I am sorry I spoiled your goodnight kiss, but I have to do my job. Mac, if your girl finds out any more, I need to know. Kent is a typical spook—he will tell you only what he wants to. I want to be one step ahead, not one step behind. Do you understand, mate?"

I was about to pull Steve up on the "your girl" comment but decided against it as it was getting harder to say we weren't an item. As for Kent, I was in the same frame of mind as Steve.

***

Zelenski was already on his second coffee when Sam arrived. He had been digging around the office for some information about Sam but had failed miserably.

It seemed no one knew her very well, or they were trained not to say anything. "Good morning. You must be Samantha. My name is John Zelenski, although I am sure you have studied a file on me at some point."

Sam smiled and shook hands with the tall American. "Hi, John. It's nice to meet you, and no, I have never seen your file, that is, if there is one."

The ice broken, they picked out a corner desk and sat opposite each other like two prizefighters weighing up the opposition.

Sam offered Zelenski more coffee, but he refused politely. Zelenski decided to test Sam first before she got too comfortable. "Samantha, if you don't mind, I think we should get right to the point here. Let's not kid ourselves. I have been studying every mug shot the British secret service has, just to keep me out of the way. Now that they've run out of mug shots, they have given you the job of keeping me amused. Tell me if I'm wrong."

Sam smiled inwardly, then took a deep breath. "First of all, John, it's Sam. Samantha is my Sunday name. Nobody calls me that, and yes, you are absolutely correct. We don't know the full story on this incident, so we are treating everybody with caution, even our friends."

As Sam spoke, she noticed the phone in the chest pocket of Zelenski's shirt. It was covered by his suit jacket, but as he leaned forward on the desk, it became visible. Sam puzzled over why the detectors in the building had not picked up the phone. In this part of the building, no electrical devices were permitted, and scans were carried out every thirty seconds, so it was a mystery that the alarms had not been triggered. Sam was sure that this was no ordinary phone. Sam caught Zelenski's eye and made a gesture for him to look behind him. Zelenski half-turned to see who or what Sam was making a reference to.

As soon as Zelenski started to turn, Sam went for the phone. The first thing Zelenski knew about it was when he heard the plink as the phone made contact with the bottom of the coffee mug. "Oops, it looks like your phone has had a small accident. Maybe that's just as well, John. I take it nobody told you phones were banned in here." Zelenski stared in disbelief as bubbles rose through the steaming coffee. "It must be some phone. Our scanners never picked it up. Do you think they designed it to work underwater as well? Looks like James Bond isn't the only one with cool gadgets."

Zelenski regarded Sam carefully, seeing her in a new light. She might look like the girl next door, but he was starting to respect her. He would have to be very careful with this woman. Sam pressed a button on the underside of the desk, and forty seconds later, security arrived. Sam asked them to take the phone to the lab to see if they could revive it for Zelenski. Meanwhile, Zelenski sat quietly studying Sam. He had comprehensively lost round one.

"Sorry, Sam. That was stupid of me. So are we going to sit and stare at each other all day? Or what do you have planned?"

Sam wiped down the desk with a hankie where the coffee had spilled. "Well, John, we could go through mug shots to see who attacked us. That was the official line for today, but I think you already know who attacked us, so you can ask me something that will help your investigation, and I will ask you things that might help our investigation. Or we can sit and stare at each other over a cup of coffee. It's up to you."

Zelenski thought for a moment. "So you will answer any questions, Sam?"

"I have been given no guidelines as where to go with this, but I am prepared to use my own judgment on the question."

Again Zelenski thought for a moment. "What involvements have you with the incident that is to be heard in your court?"

It was Sam's turn to think before answering. "John, it's not a court case as such, just an inquiry. I was sent to guard the lives of two agents who were sent to gather evidence of wrongdoing at the US Air Force base at Machrihanish. I was already tied up in a case on the other side of the globe, and by the time I arrived, one agent was dead, and the other was on the run from what appeared to be CIA agents. During the past two months, we have had to fight off three attacks by, again, assassins who we suspect were CIA agents. So forgive me for being paranoid, but it does not feel right when the CIA offers to help in a case that involves American air bases and CIA clandestine operations."

Zelenski pulled out a note pad and scribbled down a few thoughts. "Sorry, Sam, the old mind isn't as good as it used to be. Can I ask another couple of questions?" Sam nodded. "You said air bases, not air base. Do you have evidence that involves other air bases? That's one. The second question is, did you see any of the alleged wrongdoing or the evidence that is to be produced?"

Sam had slipped up, and she knew it. She did not want the Americans to know how much they knew about the Area 51 incident. "No, just one base, a slip of the tongue, and no, I was not present when any evidence was being gathered, nor have I seen the evidence. I was only there to make sure our team made it back alive." Sam checked her watch. "If you don't mind, John, can I ask my questions over lunch? I know a nice little place a couple of blocks from here, as you Americans would say, but we will need to be quick to get a good table."

Franco, the owner of the café, beamed from ear to ear when he saw Sam arriving. "Good afternoon, Sam. Would you like your usual table?" Sam followed Franco to the table and made sure Zelenski was comfortable before seating herself and ordering for them both.

"Sam, let's cut the bullshit. We are out of the office, and it's just you and me. Was it you who put a bullet in the agent we found in the burnt-out car? Because if it was, you better watch your back. You know too much. Do you really think they will let anyone who knows about this balls-up walk away? If our governments do a deal—and they will—the fewer people who know about it the better, so having you and your buddy deported and locked up will be a get-out-of-jail-free card for your government."

Sam frowned at the comments. "OK, John, it's time for you to cut the bullshit. What is your story? Adam thinks that you, like himself, have been dragged into this against your will. Is he right?"

"Sam, I should have retired this week. I have bought an apartment in Miami with its own pool looking out onto the beach, so forgive me if I am treading water. I want to live to enjoy it with my wife. I am quite happy to look at twenty-year-old mug shots until all this crap blows by. The truth is, I was sent by my old boss Brad Whiteford as window dressing to make it look like we were investigating the shootings of two agents. In time, I discovered both I and the CIA had been duped by Whiteford. He had his own agenda and had dispatched a private hit team to take out your two people. I managed to get word back through a family member who works in the FBI, and the CIA regained control of the situation. I know of the problems at the air base. I was sent back to help with damage limitation, as it was described to me." Zelenski stopped for a few minutes while the meal was served. He was sweating badly although it was not that warm.

Sam sensed he was on the edge of saying something and remained quiet. "Sam, Whiteford was a lunatic, and he alone has caused all the problems. I need to be careful what I say here. I may commit treason if I am not careful. The man who arrived at Machrihanish with me has been tasked with sorting this mess out. I will not tell you anything about him except to say that he is the most ruthless opponent I have ever seen. He is from the Cold War era, and his methods have not changed. The KGB couldn't stop him, so beware. This is not over yet, not by a long way."

Sam ate quietly, thinking over what she had just heard. It could be spin, but she doubted it. Adam was right; the whole situation stank to high heaven. There was only a week until the start of the hearings. She had to keep Adam alive and find Merlin at the same time before he vanished for another decade. No pressure there then.

After finishing the meal, they both sat sipping wine. "John, I have only one question for you, but it is of vital importance. Do you know the identity of an agent called Merlin, or can you tell me anything about him? He is a CIA asset. I won't ask you any more about your mission here, as I don't want to get you in trouble, but if you can tell me anything, I would be grateful."

Zelenski was thinking, and the silence was unbearable. Sam needed to know, and she needed to know now.

"The name rings a bell, Sam. I have heard it or seen it someplace, but I can't get a handle on it at the moment. Give me a few seconds to get this old brain working."

At the far side of the restaurant, a person sitting in the shadows ordered a glass of Teva Muscato. As the glass was placed in front of her, she thanked the waiter, but at no point did she take her eyes off the bitch who sat with the tall, elderly American gentleman at the window seat. She would die, and Areli would pick the time and the place. Areli's pocket vibrated. It was the phone from the bag Merlin had given her. It was the exact same phone that had ended up in the coffee cup at Vauxhall House, and it had all the same toys.

"Benesch, have you made contact with the targets yet?"

The voice was demanding. Benesch wanted to hang up, but she knew better. "I have the woman and your agent in my sights as we speak. There is no sign of the man yet, but I am sure the woman will lead me to him soon enough."

The caller waited to see if Areli was finished her report. "Good. You have my permission to eliminate the CIA agent if he gets in your way. In fact, it would look better if he died trying to protect the British agents. I will leave the fine detail to you." The phone went dead.

Areli placed the phone in her pocket and continued her surveillance. She had short black hair and large specs. She dressed and acted like a student and carried a pile of folders and books as part of her disguise.

Sam sat patiently while John muttered away to himself. Then he sat up straight in his chair. "Sam, it was years ago, but I can remember rechecking the accounts at an internal audit. That name was written in pen on the bottom of an invoice."

Sam tried to encourage John further. "That's brilliant. Well done. Can you remember what the invoice was for?"

Zelenski frowned. "Sam, I'm sorry, but it was years ago, and it was only a quick glance to check the figures were right. Whatever it was he got, it was bought in America. It was definitely dollars, and if my memory serves me correctly, it was quite a lot of cash."

Merlin had just finished his rounds of the estate and was in the middle of pulling his Wellingtons off when the phone in the lounge started to ring. He rushed across the room in his stocking feet to make sure he got to the phone before the caller rang off.

"Please listen to what I have to say. A courier will drop off a package with you tomorrow. The package will contain a tracking device and instructions. Find the signal. It will be an airmail envelope. Use your Irish friends to take control of the package and deliver it to the address on the envelope. It will lead you to Adam Macdonald. Do this correctly, and we will have taken a major step in removing a threat to peace between our great countries. By the way, I hear that your MI6 have increased their hunt for Merlin. They believe you are the key to finding out who is attacking their agents. It would appear you are public enemy number one again, so for your own sake, this had better work." The phone went dead.

Southern looked down the columns until he came across what he was looking for—a small article that had been squeezed in at the last minute. It stated that Ricky Freeman, a freelance journalist who had done some work for the paper, had died of a massive heart attack. Southern stopped. He had read enough. Freeman's death had not been investigated further. Southern reached across his desk and read the press release Freeman had died for.

The fool had tried to get another bigger story by contacting the authorities about Macdonald's interest in the document. At least he had made the paper himself, and more to the point, he had sealed Macdonald's fate when he disclosed that he had his address and was sending him the press release. Southern tore up the press release and binned it before leaving his office for the evening.

The next morning Billy Downes returned from the trip that Merlin had set for him. On picking up his key, he found a note attached to it saying simply, "Contact your old mum." Downes popped next door to the restaurant, and to his relief, the corner table that O'Neil normally sat at was free.

He ordered an all-day breakfast and slipped his hand under the table where he found the envelope taped to the underside. It contained a note and the tracking device, along with a letter on how the device worked. Downes smiled to himself as he ate his breakfast. He was sick of playacting for the spooks in the car park. The time had come to show these idiots that the Real IRA had lost none of its cunning or skill over the last years of peace. Even better, he would get to even a score that had burned in him for years, and in doing so he would become the hero of the brigade, the man who killed the "Mac."

Zelenski had been up for a good part of the night as he tried to make contact with Southern. Eventually Southern phoned him. Zelenski kept it brief, explaining what had happened to his phone and also that he believed the woman agent was no threat as she had not seen nor had access to evidence. Zelenski lied when he told Southern that Sam had no direct contact with any CIA agents. All he wanted was Southern off his back, and he saw no need to volunteer any details that would complicate matters further. Southern told him to pick up another phone at the US embassy and let him know if anything came up with the case.

***

I had not had a chance to call Sam as arranged since I had spent the day on the phone—first to Neil going over the evidence, and then to Lee Tribby and the airlines to arrange for his arrival. Neil had wanted Tribby picked up by MI5 and taken to Neil's home. I refused. Lee was coming here to see me, not be picked up at the airport like some petty criminal. Neil had backed down when I said that I and three of the protection team would pick him up from Heathrow.

Peter Kent had arrived and was boring everybody to death with his plan for our arrival at the hearings. After breakfast the last thing anyone needed was two hours of planning. I called a halt to the meeting, and Smithy headed for the kitchen to make the tea and coffee for the team. I wandered outside and called the office on Peter Kent's mobile. The operator told me Sam was not in the office but would patch me through to her mobile number. After a few rings, Sam answered. "Hello, Peter. What can I do for you?"

I decided against a phone prank. "It's me, the big Scottish idiot. How are we doing today, Miss O'Conner?"

"I'm sitting in the car park at Zelenski's hotel, waiting on our friend for forty minutes now. The hire car I am driving because someone shot up my Beetle has no heater, and my left arm is about as much use as a chocolate fireguard, so you can understand why I am a bit touchy today. On the other hand, it is good to hear your voice, even if it is a day late."

I cringed at the last comment. "Sorry, Sam. I was tied up in phone calls all day. How did you get on with our American friend?"

Sam checked her mirrors for any sign of Zelenski. "Yes, I think you are right. He is either a very good actor, or he really doesn't want to be here. I like him, but I still don't know about trusting him. He is a clever man, so we need to keep tabs on him. Neil wants me to partner him until the inquiry is over." She paused. "I better go, Neil has been trying to call me, and our American friend has just appeared. Speak to you later."

I checked Peter Kent's phone. He had two missed calls from Neil. I wandered back to the house to find Kent. I found him in the kitchen with Smithy, tucking into a plate of gorgeous-smelling bacon rolls. I handed him his phone back just as it started to ring again. Kent discarded the roll in his hand and wandered through to the lounge with his phone. I made the most of his absence and attacked the rolls with gusto. I was just tucking into my second roll when Kent reappeared. It was obvious from his expression all was not well. He called the rest of the team, and they crowded into the kitchen with us to hear what Kent had to say.

"Gentlemen, we may have a situation on our hands, I have just spoken to my boss, Neil Andrews. They have just found the bodies of two MI5 officers who were on surveillance duty outside the hotel where the three Irishmen were staying. There is no sign of the Irishmen; they managed to lose the officers who were tailing them this morning. When the officers returned to tell their colleagues what had happened, they discovered their dead colleagues. Steve, do you need backup? Or are you happy with the situation?"

Steve was already on the move. "No, we will be fine. Bring more men in, and it will only draw attention to ourselves. Right, guys. Take up perimeter positions, and remember to use comms if you see anything out of the ordinary. Kent, I want you to get mug shots of these jokers and give a copy of them to each of my men. Adam, stay away from the perimeter area. I want you carrying as well, just in case, Smithy, you stay glued to Adam. If he goes for a pee, you go for a pee. Got it?"

***

Sam had not called Neil back. On Zelenski's arrival, he had asked Sam if she could take him to the US embassy. The thought of trying to get to Grosvenor Square did nothing for Sam's mood, but in the spirit of cooperation, she agreed to drop Zelenski at the embassy.

For the moment, she had forgotten about Neil's missed call. She was busy planning her route into central London. Sam's mood had not improved when she got to Grosvenor Square. Zelenski promised to be back in a few minutes, so Sam decided to chance it and wait in the square. It was not long before an armed police officer asked her to move on. Sam flashed her ID at the officer and told him she would not be long. He backed down but could not resist poking fun at Sam. He looked the hired Astra up and down. "Not what you would expect one of you lot to be running about in. Where's your ejector seat button?"

Sam was spared having to answer him as just then, Zelenski reappeared, true to his word. Sam pulled away and gave the policeman a hard stare on the way past. Once they were on the move, Zelenski pulled out his note pad and started scribbling down something. At the next set of lights, Zelenski put the note pad in front of Sam. It read, "Just picked up new phone. Don't say anything you don't want the Pentagon to hear."

Sam read the note, then nodded to Zelenski. "Well, John, what are we going to get up to today?" Just as Sam finished speaking, her phone rang. A quick look at the screen showed it was Peter Kent. She fought off a London cab for the lane she was in and answered the phone at the same time.

"Hello, is it Peter or the Scottish idiot calling?" Peter was somewhat taken aback at Sam's response to his call.

"It's Peter. Listen, Sam, did Neil call you?"

Sam listened while Peter explained the situation, and the hairs on her neck started to stand up. She did not like what she was hearing. "Sam, we have it tied up pretty tight here, but I could do with an extra pair of eyes further out—an early warning system, if you like." Sam cursed inwardly. She had been dumped with Zelenski.

"Peter, I have John Zelenski with me. Neil wanted me to show him around."

Peter Kent cursed silently. "Don't worry, Sam. We can handle it here. Better get back to base in case Neil needs you."

Sam hung up and continued in silence. She was weighing up the situation. How safe was Zelenski? Could she trust him? Was it worth the risk?

Zelenski was watching her closely. "Problems, Sam?"

Sam did not answer. She was still thinking through the situation. How could the IRA know where Adam was? Then another thought popped into her head—that was exactly the argument at MI6 the night Merlin betrayed her sister.

This whole thing pointed to Merlin again. There was no way Sam was going to let Merlin get away with another act of treason, and Sam had made her mind up, rightly or wrongly.

Sam pulled on the handbrake and got out at the lights. In front of the Astra was a courier on a motorbike. Sam talked to him then marched back to the car. "John, phone please."

Zelenski was surprised, but he could see Sam was in no mood to take no for an answer. He handed Sam the phone. Sam handed it to the courier together with a roll of bank notes. The lights had turned to green, and the traffic was starting to blast their horns as Sam jumped in and sped away from the lights as fast as the Astra could carry them.

Sam talked as she drove. "The courier will take your phone back to the US embassy. You can pick it up later. We are going to the area where Adam's safe house is. It would appear MI5 have lost the Irish suspects, so we need to have a nose around the area to see if we can see them. You better hold your breath because the driving is going to get a bit scary."

"You have lost me, Sam. What Irish suspects? What are you talking about?"

Sam continued to thread her way through the London traffic at suicidal speeds. "Oh my, we have been kept in the dark, haven't we? You had better pin your ears back. Some of this you may know; some of it you will not." Sam filled Zelenski in on the arrival of the Irish and their connection to Adam. She also gave him a brief account of Adam's exploits in Ireland and the part Merlin played during that period.

By the time Sam had briefed Zelenski, they were out of the London area and heading north. "John, I know Merlin is behind this. He is the link that ties the American problem and the Irish together. He has worked for them both. It can't be just a coincidence they have arrived here at this time." Sam pulled up opposite the entrance to the housing estate on the pond. She bumped up on the pavement and switched the little Astra off. Sam raked about in her bag and produced three pictures of the suspects. She handed them to Zelenski, then removed her phone and her Glock. She checked the clip and made sure the safety was on. She rang Kent's number, and he answered instantly. "Peter, we are in position. I will ring you if we see anything."

Kent didn't know why he was surprised that Sam had once again done her own thing. "So 'Head back to the office' wasn't a big enough hint to keep Zelenski out of this? I hope you know what you're doing, Sam, because if you are not careful, Neil Andrews is going to kick your backside out the door." The phone went dead.

Billy Downes watched as the post office LDV van turned into the lane beside an office block. They had followed the van for four miles from its depot. His handheld scanner was bleeping away quietly, and he was in no doubt that he had found the van that was carrying the package.

A quick sortie of the alley showed that it was deserted and had no CCTV. It only took minutes to overpower the postman, tie him up, and bundle him into one of his own mailbags. Another few seconds and they had located the package. The scanner had gone from a bleep to a constant tone. Downes tossed it into a nearby skip while Malone and O'Neil opened the heavy case they had picked up earlier. In the case was a stand, ammunition, and a British army-issue general purpose machine gun, or GPMG, as it was known.

Merlin had had these toys stashed in a remote outbuilding for years. They were first placed there for the IRA's planned assault on Downing Street, but the plan never came to fruition. As the years passed, Merlin had thought about getting rid of them, but he never had because he was worried that he might be caught doing so. Now he was glad he had kept them. He would kill two birds with one stone—get rid of the munitions and supply the hit team with the equipment to deliver a knockout blow and keep him sweet with the Americans.

Downes studied the GPMG with interest, and he made the other two study it closely. None of them had ever fired this type of weapon, and there could be no mistakes, so they needed to have a good idea of what to do. They practiced with the belt-fed ammo. The handguns were Brownings, four in total, and there were four hand grenades.

Downes knew if used properly they could inflict massive damage. He just was not sure, with no training, how effective they would be. Merlin's note said they would be up against a four-man team, as well as a member of MI6. He had to be smart about this. His men were no match for soldiers who trained regularly for this situation. He had to make the most of a surprise attack.

Downes entered the address on the package into a satnav that he had brought for just that purpose. According to the satnav, they were less than ten miles from the delivery address on the package. The post van loaded, Downes took the bag off the postie. The man was chalk white and shaking like a leaf.

"Right, me old son, we are going to let you drive to the address, and all you have to do is deliver the parcel. What could be easier than that, mate? You're just doin' yer job." Downes patted the terrified postie on the back like he was his best friend. "Now you do a good job, and you can walk away from this with a good story to tell your mates in the pub. You do what I tell ye, mate, and you will have no worries, OK?"

The postie nodded and followed Downes's instruction to get in and drive the post van. Downes sat behind the driver's seat and made sure the postie could see the Browning in his hand.

Kent had just relayed the story about Sam to me. I persuaded him to let me call Sam. I knew there was no way to talk Sam out of it—when she made up her mind, there was no changing it. She answered the phone on the second ring.

"Hi, Sam. It's me, Adam. I hear you have been a naughty girl again. I take it all is quiet on the western front?"

"It's very quiet here. Has Peter calmed down yet?"

I walked to the end of the jetty and plonked myself down. It looked like it was going to be a lovely day, and I had been cooped up in the house making plans. "Oh, I am sure he will forgive you. I think he is secretly happy you are around, just in case the shit does hit the fan. Got to go. That's the postie just arrived. It will be the press release from the journalist, I would imagine."

CHAPTER SIXTEEN

Carnage

I stood up and started to make my way back along the jetty. Steve was on his way from the front door to intercept the postie, who had just reversed down between the two houses.

I shouted to Steve that I was expecting a parcel, and he relaxed noticeably. The postie ambled toward Steve. Smithy met me at the bottom of the jetty, and together, we headed for the postie as well.

Steve signed the delivery note and thanked the postie. I thought Steve looked a little worried, as if he sensed something was wrong. He popped back up the steps and dropped the package in the porch, and as he came down the steps he called Smithy on the comms. On his command, Smithy grabbed my arm and started pulling me back to the jetty. Not having the comms, I was not sure what was going on, but for now I let myself be dragged away.

***

Steve shouted to the postie, who was making a beeline back to his van. Steve had noticed the state of the postie—pure white and shaking like a leaf in the wind. Either he was unwell, or something had shaken him up badly. Steve wanted another word with the postie, just to put his mind at rest.

Unknown to Steve, the poor postie had been forced to carry an armed grenade in his left hand. Downes had warned him to keep his hand and grenade in his trouser pocket and to carry the package in his right hand. Downes had warned him, if he tried to warn anyone of their presence, he would shoot him in the arm, which in turn would mean he would release the grenade in his pocket, and the end result would not be pretty. Downes watched as the postie walked back. He could see three men, two of whom were soldier types. He could not get the van any closer because of the parked Range Rover in the lane. It was show time.

Steve had almost caught up with the postie when the back doors of the van flew open. Almost instantly, the machine gun kicked into life. O'Neil fired a burst at the postie, and the ground around the postie exploded. Shells hit him in the chest, knocking him backward. Steve dived to the ground and rolled to his left, using the big Range Rover for cover from the deadly hail of bullets. He was in the middle of telling everybody on the comms that the bastards had a "gimpy," when the grenade went off under the postie. Mercifully, he was already dead, and his body absorbed the majority of the blast. Steve was by far the closest, and the comms went dead. Downes guided the ammunition belt into the GPMG, and O'Neil continued to fire the machine gun. They turned their attention to the Range Rover, and at close range, the firepower was devastating. The tyres and the suspension on the big 4x4 exploded, and the stricken vehicle lurched heavily to one side.

Malone was just getting into the driver's seat of the van, intending to move it into a better position, when Archie appeared down the steps from next door, MP5 in hand. The two men spotted each other at the same time. Archie fired, hitting the door of the post-office van. Malone returned fire, hitting Archie in the stomach. He went down hard, and the MP5 flew from his hand along the road. Malone bent down to pick up Archie's weapon, and the blood started trickling down his arm and pooling on the monobloc surface. The metal of the van door had not saved him, only deflected the bullets upward. He had been shot in the shoulder. He reached for the MP5. He could hold it, but with his shattered shoulder, he could not lift it. Suddenly the machine gun went silent. It was jammed. Matt rushed from the house, firing a burst of covering fire as he covered the dead ground to where Steve lay facedown on the monobloc.

I stood up and started to run to Steve's aid but was brought down with a resounding crash by Smithy, who was screaming at me to get back. Smithy fired a burst in the direction of the post-office van and pulled me, kicking and struggling, back down toward the jetty. Downes changed plans and bailed out. The machine gun was a lost cause. O'Neil grabbed a Browning and a grenade and jumped out of the van.

He came level with the stricken Range Rover and was about to launch the grenade when Matt hit him six or seven times in the torso with a burst from his M16. He was dead before he hit the ground. The grenade fell from his grasp and rolled under the Range Rover. Matt saw it roll and took off like a springhare. The blast was contained by the big 4x4, but it caught fire, and thick, acrid smoke started billowing from its stricken interior.

Malone had had enough. He had just watched O'Neil being gunned down. It was time to leave. He gunned the post-office van out from between the two houses and vanished round the corner in a cloud of tyre smoke. There was an eerie silence apart from the crackling and popping of the burning vehicle. Matt ran back to Steve and turned him over while Smithy and Adam approached cautiously from the jetty. Suddenly there was the crack of two gunshots in quick succession, and the bushes to the left of the house exploded as a body fell through them. It was Downes, and a large red stain appeared on the grass underneath him. Peter Kent stepped over him, bent down, and removed the Browning from his hand. He strolled across to where everyone had gathered around Steve. "I believe you missed that one, chaps. I think we need to call for some assistance. Do you still have my phone, Adam?"

Sam had heard the gunfire only a few seconds after Adam had said the post had arrived. She put two and two together and called Zelenski, who was stretching his legs. The Astra shot off the pavement, and Sam gave it everything down the main road. She turned into the estate and gunned it through the houses, cursing as she overshot the turning and had to reverse. Every second was vital, and she was wasting time. She got back on the correct street just as a post-office van appeared at the end of the street. She flashed her lights at the driver but he was in no mood to take heed of some stupid woman in an Astra.

He went straight for her, assuming that his superior size would force her out of the way. Sam shouted to Zelenski to hold on. The two vehicles met head on. There was a sickening crunch as the pair collided. Zelenski's seat belt held him, while Sam was hit in the face by the exploding airbag. She was trying to recover from the impact when a blood-covered body appeared by her door. She tried to open the door, but it was jammed shut. Her vision was slowly coming back, but she was still half-deaf from the explosion of the airbag.

A hand with a Browning appeared by the window, and the voice started to make sense in Sam's head. "You stupid bitch, I'm going to kill you." There was a loud bang, and Sam was floating. She was still dazed from the impact and wasn't sure if she was dreaming or whether this was really happening. She turned her head to see Zelenski lowering her Glock. The barrel was still smoking, and outside on the grass lay the dead body of Malone.

Southern sat alone in the satellite viewing room. He had watched from space as the action in Aylesbury had taken its course. Just as things were reaching a climax, the area was covered by cloud. Between that and the satellite reaching its maximum working distance, contact was lost. Southern weighed up the situation, then took out his cell phone and dialed a number.

*****

Matt and Kent were heading indoors. Kent went to the lounge to make some calls. Smithy and I waited with Steve for the ambulance. Smithy left me with Steve and headed across to see if he could do anything for Archie.

I watched as Matt picked up the parcel. Suddenly, I was filled with dread. Up until that moment, I had not paid any attention to the parcel, but it was far too big for just some memos. I shouted to Matt to put it down. He did as he was told and placed it back in the hall. I breathed a sigh of relief just as the world erupted around me. The force of the blast threw me into the pond. The parcel must have had state of the art explosives, because it flattened the whole front of the house. Matt was killed instantly by the blast.

I came to as I was being dragged back to the shore. Smithy was cursing and swearing as he laboured to get me on the grass embankment. He looked glad to see me coming round. I was still dazed as I watched him look around. Suddenly, he grabbed me and started pulling me to my feet. I wasn't sure what he was up to. He started swearing again as I struggled to keep my footing. He dragged me along the jetty and then, with some difficulty, pushed me into the rowing boat.

Smithy rowed round the outskirts of the pond, keeping to the reed beds. "Are you OK, sir?"

My senses were returning. My head was exploding but I was glad just to be alive. "Smithy, if you call me sir just one more time, I swear to God…"

Smithy started to laugh, just a bit at first, then splitting his sides. It was so infectious, I joined in. It was as much the relief that we were both alive as it was because I'd said something funny.

"What the hell are we doing out here in the boat?"

Smithy stopped laughing and wiped the tears from his eyes. "Mac, I was ordered to protect you. There was not one man left standing. What if more bad guys showed up, dressed as police this time? I wasn't taking the chance. Better we sneak away and get to a safe house some place—don't ask me how, but it was a split-second decision, and one I will stand by."

We watched from the safety of the reed beds as police, ambulance, and fire crews arrived. The whole of the estate was a sea of sirens and flashing lights.

***

As Sam's senses returned she found Zelenski beside her. He was a pale shade of blue and was struggling to breathe. Sam pulled herself out of the driver's window and was surprised to find that she had survived the impact with very little damage. The air bag had done its job well. Sam rushed round to the passenger door and yanked it open. Zelenski was still struggling to breathe. Sam loosened his shirt collar and found that his neck was swollen and almost black.

This model had only one airbag, and the seat belt had dug into his neck during the collision.

His airway was closing, and he needed help fast. Sam dug around in the carnage of the Astra and found her gun, then her bag. She was relieved to find her phone intact and was in the process of calling 999 when a police car and a paramedic pulled up. Sam showed her ID and hitched a ride in the police car, leaving the paramedic to help Zelenski. They arrived at Neil's house to find a scene from hell. Bodies lay where they had fallen, and only remains of the house stood. The Range Rover looked like it had been in a fight with a tank and lost. The two police officers had seen some sights but even they were shocked. Sam could not speak. An icy-cold dagger stabbed at her heart. She blinked away tears. She could sit and look at this no longer. She had to find out for herself what had become of Adam and his team. She was full of dread. There was no one standing, only bodies.

Sam leapt from the car and made for the nearest body. It was Archie, curled up in a ball, holding his stomach, but he was gone. Sam could see from his wound that he had bled out. The next two bodies were also dead. They were both Irish hit men. Sam saw movement in her peripheral vision and spun round to find Steve attempting to get off the ground. Sam rushed across to him. He had been hit in the head by a piece of shrapnel, but he was a lucky guy. It was just above his left eye—any lower and it would have killed him. Sam had a good look. He would live, but he needed help now. Sam turned round to find the two police officers looking round in disbelief.

"This man needs help. Get on the blower now, and get someone here, pronto." Sam didn't realize it, but she was screaming at the policemen. There was no sign of Adam. She looked toward the shell of the house with some trepidation. Could anyone have survived the blast? She made Steve comfortable, telling him to lie still, that help was on its way. Then Sam headed for the house. Almost immediately she saw the outline of a body in the rubble of the house, but the body was so badly damaged it was impossible to tell who it was.

Sam was weeping openly as she checked the body for any ID. She found a tattoo on the left arm, the name of a wife or girlfriend. Sam's heart was heavy for that woman's loss, but it gave her hope—it was not Adam. One of the policemen shouted at Sam to get out of the ruin until it was made safe. Sam ignored him and continued her search. Near the back of the house, Sam's heart leapt as she heard a groan. Under a dust-covered painting, Sam found what she was looking for, just not who she was looking for. Peter Kent lay facedown, a roof beam trapping his legs and pinning him to the floor. Sam made it back to the front of the house and shouted for help.

An ambulance and two more police cars had just arrived and at Sam's shouts, the men scrambled over the rubble to help her. Half an hour later, Sam had searched the house from top to bottom. There was no sign of Adam.

***

Neil Andrews got the news of the Aylesbury attack about four minutes before the news broke on the BBC. He was powerless to cover up the attack and phoned the director's secretary, telling her he was on his way to see the director. He needed a few minutes as it was an emergency.

The director was watching SKY news when Neil Andrews entered his office. The director was neither up nor down, but as cool as a cucumber. "Neil, do you know anything I can't find out on TV? Don't bother to answer that. I already know the answer. Bill Mathews from MI5 is waiting with a chopper at the Oval. I have a letter here from the deputy prime minister giving you full powers over the police. Don't just stand there, man. Get on that chopper, and for God's sake, don't let the police speak to the press, or we will all be selling papers on the street corner. Go."

On the flight up to Aylesbury, Mathews tried his best to take charge of the situation. "Neil, you know MI5 have the jurisdiction here. This is a matter of national security. When we land, I will take charge."

Neil wished he had a pound for every time that old argument was brought to the surface, but he was not about to be upstaged. He needed to control things to ensure the correct story got out, not MI5's version of it. "Bill, you do not know what you are stepping into here. Trust me—you do not want a piece of this. It has the potential to ruin careers. What are you going to tell them, anyway? That two of your men are dead and the other two lost track of terrorists ending in God only knows what we will find in Aylesbury?"

Mathews thought for a minute. Andrews was not far off the mark. MI5 was not covered in glory over this one. "OK, Neil, have it your way, but if I take a step back, you will put a good word in for MI5 with the press, understood?"

Andrews smiled to himself. Game, set, and match, he thought. "But of course, Bill. We work as a team."

The chopper landed at a road junction in the estate, and the two men were ferried by police car to the site of the attack. On arrival, Neil Andrews made a beeline for the press, who were being kept at some distance from the investigation. He was subjected to a barrage of questions, which he answered with one of his own. "Good evening, guys. Can you tell me if anyone has given an official account of events yet?" There was a second barrage of voices. "I take it that is a resounding no, then. My name is Neil Andrews, and I am part of an antiterrorist unit. If you give me a few minutes to find out the situation, I promise I will return and bring you up to date on events here."

Neil turned and walked away before anyone could fling more questions at him. The local chief inspector had taken charge of the situation and was directing operations. Neil walked over and introduced himself. He handed the chief inspector the letter and looked with dismay at the state of his house while the inspector read the note. "OK, Mr. Andrews, you are now the head man. What do you have in mind?"

Neil folded up the letter and placed it in his breast pocket. "I think we should start with you telling me what you know happened here, and who is dead and who isn't." Neil listened intently as the officer relayed what he knew. Neil already knew a lot of what he was told, but he gave no indication to the police. Two soldiers had died in the firefight, and Peter Kent had been taken to the Royal Buckinghamshire Hospital with a suspected fractured pelvis and two broken legs. Neil had to hide his surprise when the inspector told him that John Zelenski had also been admitted to the hospital with a crushed larynx, and Sergeant Steve Hawkings had a head wound. Neil looked around and spotted Sam leaning on the rail at the jetty, her mind elsewhere. There was no sign of Adam, and if his maths were correct, there was a missing soldier as well. He cross-examined the police officer about his head count but said nothing.

Sam did not hear Neil approach. She was far away. "How the hell did you end up here? Have you any idea what would have happened if you had got the CIA guy killed? Good God, Sam, they would have said we planned it to get him away from Adam."

Sam was sick with worry, and she had had enough. "Neil, I didn't get him killed, and Peter needed help. Adam is missing, so button it. Some of us have had a worse day than you, pal."

Neil knew the mood Sam was in. He was wasting his breath. He took a moment to gaze at the shell of his house, which was all that was left. "I just hope I remembered to pay the house insurance last time." He turned and stared at the pond. "Even my boat is missing." Sam and Neil looked at each other; they had come to the same conclusion at the same time.

"Sam, you stay here for the moment. I need to talk to the press. Then we will take the helicopter and search for Adam. He can't have gone far."

Neil had the full attention of the press as he read out a rapidly prepared statement. "This afternoon, our joint task force, consisting of operatives from MI5, MI6, the CIA, and SAS, engaged a Real IRA hit team who were intent on bringing death and destruction to our capital. They were lured here, and a gun battle broke out. After killing an unarmed postman, the terrorists attacked with mortars, hand grenades, and a heavy-caliber machine gun. Unfortunately, two soldiers from the Special Air Service were killed in action, and a third member was wounded. Also wounded were a CIA agent and an MI6 officer. They are not critical and are expected to make a full recovery. All the terrorists were shot and killed. Because of the bravery of these men, our streets are safe again. Finally, I would like to thank MI5 for supplying the information that led to a successful operation today. Thank you." Again Neil walked away before he could be cross-examined by members of the press.

***

Smithy and I had skirted round the edge of the pond, discovering, as we found a sign, that this was Watermead Lake, and not a pond as I had thought. Once we were clear of the estate, we abandoned the boat and set off on foot. A few hundred feet further on, we came upon a road sign stating we were now on the A413. We followed this road for a mile or so into the town centre of Aylesbury. All the way, we were being passed by police cars and ambulances. Thankfully for us, they were not looking for anybody, so we were largely ignored.

We arrived at a large roundabout to find we had stumbled upon the hospital. The hospital entrance was surrounded by police and a crowd of what we took to be press. Smithy and I debated for some time if we should try to get in, to see if Steve were there. Smithy wasn't for it, but I was sure he had to be here.

Our debate was cut short as a helicopter passed low overhead. It had to be either police or possibly press. It banked sharply and came back for another pass, and then it vanished behind an office block. A few seconds later, a figure appeared, running toward the hospital. To my amazement, as the figure drew closer, it started waving like mad at Smithy and me.

It took me a few seconds to realize that the figure was Sam. My legs filled with adrenalin, and I was off, Smithy close on my tail. We met in the middle of the roundabout, and Sam leapt into my arms at the last minute. Anyone watching would have thought we had been kept apart for years. Sam regained her composure quickly when she realized she had an audience.

Everybody outside the hospital was staring. Sam lowered herself to the ground, wiped away a tear, took my hand, and started to run back the way she had come. Two minutes later, we were airborne. Neil sat in the front while Sam, Smithy, and I sat in the back. The chopper was too noisy for conversation, so Sam said nothing but held onto my hand with a grip of steel, as if I were a naughty schoolboy about to try and run away again. The helicopter touched down in the dark in central London, landing in some sort of sports stadium. Twenty seconds after flinging us out, the chopper was off into the dark sky, only its landing lights visible after a few seconds. We were picked up and dropped off at Vauxhall Cross, where Neil dispatched Smithy to the canteen. Then he directed us to his office deep in the bowels of the building.

He got right down to business. "Adam, do you still have the evidence for the hearing? Or do we need to start sifting through the wreckage of my house in the morning?"

Sam and I sat in the square leather chairs facing his desk. It felt as if we were being given a dressing down by the headmaster. I confirmed I still had the film. I was tired and sore. My wound ached, and I needed to sleep. I wanted this interview to end, but Neil had other ideas.

"Sam, what in God's name were you thinking? You were meant to be babysitting the Yank, and you ended up in the middle of a gun battle with him. Have you taken leave of your senses, woman?"

"Neil, if it weren't for us, one of those nutters would have gotten away. For what it is worth, I trust Zelenski, and he saved my life today."

Neil got up and paced back and forth. "I have two choices here. I can't believe I am even contemplating this—it's either you or Robin Alder to replace Kent. Are you up to it, or do I call in Alder?"

"I am back to full fitness, and Alder is OK as a wingman, but he has little experience of being in charge. I will do it." Sam glanced at me, and I knew she was hoping that Neil Andrews did not see through her lie. She was far from fully fit, and even as she spoke, she looked about ready to drop.

"OK, Sam. You need to keep this man alive for another week at least. Do you need assistance?"

I smiled inwardly. I knew what her answer would be. Sam was a loner, and she did not work well in a group. "I will sort it out myself, thank you."

Neil frowned. "OK, I will sign you in as active, but there are two conditions. One, the soldier upstairs in the canteen is his body man; he goes where Adam goes. Two, during the hearings, I have a sniper team on the roofs above Central Hall in Westminster. Make that three conditions—Adam wears a bulletproof vest at all times, even if he is going for a bath."

Sam nodded. All we wanted to do was get out of the office. We said our good-nights, and Sam and I headed for the exit. "It's late, Sam. Where are we going to bunk up tonight?"

On the ground floor, we made for the exit door. "I don't usually take in waifs and strays, but tonight I will make an exception. You can bunk up at my flat. It's not far from here."

The voice came from behind them. "Glad to hear you are taking in lodgers, but I think you may have already forgotten our deal." Sam turned to find Neil standing at the elevator doors with Smithy in tow. "Did you forget somebody, Sam?"

The taxi pulled up outside Sam's flat. Sam paid the fare while Smithy and I tumbled out and started looking around. The street was one-way with offices on one side. A majority of buildings on the left were flats, from probably the late forties. Sam's flat was in a block of three, and she had the ground-floor flat.

***

In a car parked on an adjoining street, Areli Benesch watched as the taxi pulled away, leaving the woman and two men standing outside the flat. Areli's first instinct was to pull the car up and open fire while they were occupied getting into the flat. Her professional training stopped her.

She already knew how fast the woman was, and this newcomer had an athletic build. If he turned out to be what she thought, she would be up against at least two professionals. No, she would wait.

She had been patient, and it had already paid dividends. She knew Sam lived here in Kennington. She had already checked out her flat in Chester Way, and it had been treated to some MI6 modifications, which confirmed Sam was an MI6 operative. The door and frame were of solid steel construction, and the windows were blast proof. It had a state-of-the-art alarm, and the CCTV opposite was not for the benefit of the offices. Areli was sure it had a direct feed to MI6 headquarters. She knew where Sam dined, where she exercised. She knew her route to work and her route to the gym, and best of all, she had just led Areli to her target.

***

The next day was a busy one. Sam had us up before eight, fed and watered and out the door for nine. We took a taxi to the local hire-car firm. The woman behind the desk tensed up when she saw Sam enter the office. It was not hard to read her mind. She reluctantly handed over the keys to a Ford Focus. Sam wasted no time, and we were soon on our way to Heathrow to meet Lee Tribby's flight. Sam was obviously none the worse for her accident yesterday, as she arrived with five minutes to spare, after a warp-speed effort on the motorway.

Smithy caught my eye as we exited the car, rolled his eyes, and crossed himself as Sam headed for the car park exit. "It's OK, Smithy. She is in a good mood today. You want to see her driving when she is in a bad mood."

Tribby's plane was nine minutes delayed, so as we waited, I checked out Smithy. His eyes were out on stalks. I felt for him. The last place he would want to guard somebody was in an airport. Sam was just as observant, but she was a natural at it. Although she checked everybody out, she was far better at doing it without showing she was checking everybody out. At one point, a man made a beeline toward me. Sam bumped into him and made a show of apologizing to him. In one movement, she had removed his passport and checked to see if he was armed. After checking the passport, Sam called him back and handed him his passport saying she had found it at her feet. Thirty minutes later, with Tribby's flight disembarked and Smithy's nerves at breaking point, there was still no sign of my American friend.

We headed for the British Airways desk. Sam asked to speak to the supervisor, and after showing her ID, she was shown to an office. After ten minutes, Sam reappeared, but it was not good news. Tribby had not appeared for the flight, but he had not cancelled the flight, so there was nothing left here for us to do. It was time to head back to the office and make some calls.

Sam jumped into the car, and I knew from her actions she had spotted something. Instead of heading for the exit, Sam did a return trip round the car park. I noted with interest that Sam had removed her Glock from her handbag, and it was resting between her thighs. Another tour of the car park proved fruitless.

"What is it, Sam? What are we looking for?"

Sam continued to tour the car park. "There was a girl sitting drinking coffee for the whole time we were there, and then she was behind us in the corridor as we left. She should be out here, but she has vanished." Sam sighed and headed for the exit barrier. "I need a holiday. It was probably nothing. Sorry, guys."

***

Areli Benesch watched as the trio headed down the corridor toward the exit. She had spent her time at the coffee bar, apparently looking out the window but actually watching them in the reflection. The newest arrival was jumpy but probably had lightening reactions. The woman was also very fast and very careful. Areli had no doubts that she could kill the man they were guarding, but she was not sure she would survive the aftermath of her attack. She tagged along at some distance, looking for an opportunity to carry out an attack. At the moment, it was a nonstarter. As well as the three in the corridor, two armed police officers patrolled the corridor just behind the trio. An attack now would be suicide.

Outside, Areli watched as the Ford Focus toured the car park. This was not evasive action. She had been made. She cursed under her breath—this bitch was too good. Then Areli smiled to herself. It would make it all the sweeter when she killed her and proved she was still the best in the business. Areli decided against following her. It would be far too risky. She would pick them up again later. Areli knew she was running out of time. The hearings were due to start in two days, and her targets were giving evidence on the fourth day. There would come a day when Areli could not pick and choose. It would be do or die.

***

On the way back to the office, we decided on our next course of action. We decided Sam would go back to Vauxhall Cross to see if she could find out anything about Tribby. Smithy and I would head back to Aylesbury. Smithy wanted to see how Steve was doing, and I fancied a friendly chat with Zelenski.

When we got to the hospital, I popped in and said hello to Steve. Smithy was about to follow me out of the room, but I stopped him. "Listen mate, we both need a bit of space. You stay here and have a chat with Steve. I am only two doors away, and I will shout if I need anything."

Smithy didn't look sure about this development but reluctantly let me go my own way. Zelenski seemed to be in good shape, and he said he was glad to get some company. The swelling on his throat was under control, and he had made a good recovery.

"John, we owe you one. You saved Sam's life. Well done, mate, and thanks. Anyway, how are you doing?"

Zelenski was not used to this type of praise and was blushing heavily. "Adam, it was one of those split-second decisions. I just did what had to be done. I am glad to see we are both still in the land of the living. What happened to the rest of the team?"

I went through the events of that evening. Zelenski seemed genuinely shocked at the loss of life. For a second, his face showed that his mind was elsewhere, but then he leaned over and dragged two files from beneath his pillow. "Adam, I have had to do a lot of soul-searching over this. These arrived by courier this afternoon from my brother-in-law, who works for the FBI. In light of what you have just told me, I have decided to let you have them. It may help keep you alive. I would appreciate it if you did not tell anyone where the info came from."

I opened the first envelope. It was a receipt from some sort of home for six-months care for a woman called Marie Ann Goldberg.

Zelenski explained when he saw my blank look. "Sam asked me about Merlin. I told her that I had once seen the name written on a bill. I got my brother-in-law to go through the receipts. If you look closely, you will see the word 'Merlin' in the top left corner. It was written by my late boss, Brad Whiteford. I hope this will help you in some way to stop this traitor."

I opened the second envelope and tipped the considerable contents out on John Zelenski's bed. The picture that stared up at me sent a cold shiver down my spine. "Adam, her name is Areli Benesch. You would do well to study her methods well. As you will see from her NSA file, she is a freelance assassin, and a very capable one at that. She has worked with Mossad and has done freelance work for the Russians, the Chinese, and the French. I am sure you know why I can say no more, and why I have given you the file."

I replaced all the documentation in the envelope. "John, I am just nipping out for a second. Is there anything I can get you?"

I was sure if I ran the name Marie Ann Goldberg through a computer it would turn up something.

CHAPTER SEVENTEEN
Merlin

I stopped a young nurse outside Zelenski's room and managed to sweet-talk her into letting me use a laptop.

She led me into a vacant office. My first search for "Marie Ann Goldberg" proved fruitless. My next search, for "Marie Ann at Royal garden party" was a shot in the dark but struck gold. A second and third check to confirm my suspicions left me in a state of disbelief. I had found Merlin. Marie Ann Goldberg was his wife, and various pictures showed them together at official functions.

In America, she had reverted to her maiden name.

I sat for some time in the room. I had the knowledge, but I was not sure what to do with it. I was acutely aware my next actions could and would have profound consequences. Should I tell Sam? I was certain the minute she found out who Merlin was she would not hesitate to put a bullet between his eyes. Without a doubt, he deserved everything coming to him, but shooting this person in cold blood would set off a chain reaction finishing with Sam in jail. I could not let that happen. Sam must not find out the truth, for her own sake. Should I tell the authorities? They would probably strike some deal with Merlin to blow the whistle on his associates, and he would get some tree-hugging judge who would let him walk after a short stay in one of Her Majesty's establishments. No, that would not happen. I would make sure of it. The bastard would pay for his treachery.

Smithy burst in the door. Panic was written all over his face. "Thank God! You scared the shit out of me. I thought they had grabbed you."

I switched off the computer and left the room without saying a word. I popped back to Zelenski's room to say good-bye. "John, I need to go. The info you gave me turned something up. I will take the files with me, but your secret is safe with me. Can you do me a huge favour and not mention this to Sam? It's a bit complicated at the moment, but I will come back and fill you in soon."

During our visit, Sam had called the hospital and left word with Smithy to meet her at a local restaurant for dinner. We fought our way through the rush-hour traffic and found the restaurant after a bit of hunting. Finding a parking space proved to be a much harder task, but eventually, we succeeded and legged it back to the restaurant. On arrival, we were asked by a man who seemed to be the owner if we had reservations. At the mention of Sam's name, he transformed into the perfect host and showed us to a corner table with a beaming smile. To our surprise, Sam had beaten us to the table and was already well into a bottle of wine. As we sat down, the evening news came on the TV mounted in the corner of the room high on the wall. The first story stopped us all speaking and held our undivided attention.

The BBC presenter was positioned right outside what was left of Neil Andrews's house. The Ministry of Defense had just released the names of the dead soldiers. Again the presenter went over how a major terrorist attack had been crushed by an antiterrorist team directed by MI5.

I was first to speak as the lead story finished. "Well, it looks like Neil Andrews may have a glittering career writing fiction. He seems to have turned a disaster into a triumph."

Sam returned to looking at the menu. "Adam, I thought you of all people would have known. That is one of Neil's main strong points—he is full of bullshit. It got him to where he is today. He is the director's main spin doctor."

Smithy was still watching the news. "How is that for gratitude! We never even got a mention."

I was shaking my head in disbelief at Smithy's comment. "Smithy, you better get used to that. The regiment very rarely seeks the limelight. It's the nature of the job. You would be no use in covert ops if your big ugly mug was plastered all over the six o'clock news. You can be sure if the media gets a picture of you, it will be because you're dead."

Franco arrived, took our order, and dropped off some garlic bread for us to chew on while our order was cooked. Sam changed the subject "Well what have you two been up to this afternoon? How are Steve and Zelenski doing?" We were both very quiet. Smithy probably did not want Sam to know he had left my side to speak with Steve, and I did not want Sam to know I had made a breakthrough with Zelenski.

I diverted Sam's attention by handing her the file on Areli Benesch that John Zelenski had given me. Sam leafed through the information in the file. "Sam, Zelenski was trying to warn us. She is still after us I think."

Smithy looked over Sam's shoulder at the pictures of Benesch. "Who is the woman, Mac? One of your old flames?"

Sam answered before I got a word in. "No, Smithy, much more deadly than an old flame. She is a hired assassin, and from what I am reading here, a bloody good one at that."

Smithy asked the six-million-dollar question. "Sam, do you think the woman at the airport could have been her?"

Sam sat staring into space, as if she were trying to picture the woman at the airport. "It is hard to say, Smithy. In the lounge, she never faced our way, and when she was walking behind us, she was only ever in my peripheral vision. All I can say is that if that had been me tailing us, I would have played it exactly the same. The woman acted like a spy, so it could have been her."

In the turmoil that my brain was experiencing after finding out the identity of Merlin, I had forgotten Lee Tribby. "Sam did you find out any more about Lee?"

Sam had no good news on this front. "I spoke to Lee's wife, and she is worried sick. For the last few days, Lee suspected he was being tailed. He left for the airport this morning, and she has heard nothing. She is looking into things from her side of the pond. I called Zelenski's brother-in-law at the FBI and brought him up to speed on things. He has promised to move heaven and earth to find Lee Tribby."

Sam smiled at Franco as he appeared with the meals. I noted with amusement that Sam's plate was full to overflowing while Smithy and I had more frugal servings. Sam waited until Franco had finished serving us before continuing. "I couldn't get much more done today. The place was in a bit of an uproar. The PM called an emergency meeting of COBRA over the recent events, and the director was still there when I left."

***

Areli Benesch watched Franco's restaurant from a safe distance, sitting in the passenger seat of a hired Transit van. Areli had added magnetic nameplates to the side of the van, proclaiming it to be Smith and Sons, Twenty-Four Hour Plumbing Services. Areli sported a boiler suit and skip cap and watched from behind the safety of a *Sun* newspaper.

Her targets had entered at different times. She waited for ten minutes, then headed across the street, toolbox in hand. Opposite Franco's was a Victorian block of flats. Areli noted from the whitened windows and lack of name on the intercom that the third level flat appeared to be empty. Areli buzzed one of the other occupants.

When he answered, she informed him she had a package to deliver. The door buzzed, and Areli was in. She headed straight for the third floor, and after a few minutes tinkering with the seventies lock, she was inside.

***

The apartment had a strong musky, damp smell. The previous owner had decided that leaving the place clean and tidy was a bridge too far. Areli took little notice of these facts. She had other things on her mind. She placed her toolbox to one side of the bay window. Opening it she removed her Sig Sauer and fitted the silencer. Happy with the readiness of her weapon, she turned her attention to the view of Franco's restaurant. The front door was partially obscured by a bus shelter on the left of the door, and on the right of the door was a street lamp. Areli had a dilemma on her hands. She was sure she could hit at least one of her targets from the position, and if they had been amateurs, she could probably take down two of them, but it would be pure luck if she got all three. She knew what would happen here. She would hit one, and the other two would take cover. She knew if this happened, she was in big trouble. She would be trapped in a building with two professionals hunting her down. She was not keen on the odds of surviving that scenario. Areli cursed her luck. A quick recce of the building showed that it had no good escape routes.

What was it about this job? Nothing had gone right for her. Should she cut and run while she could? Areli cursed again. She was no quitter. She would get the job done, just not here and now. Her time would come.

***

Sam's phone rang just as we were finishing our meal. Sam made a few one-word answers, then hung up. "Right, gents, we need to get moving. It seems our presence is required urgently at Vauxhall Cross, all three of us. The director has just returned from the COBRA meeting and has told Neil Andrews to round us up, so we better not keep the big boss waiting."

Sam paid the bill, and as we were about to leave, she cross-examined Smithy as to where the car was. Smithy smiled. "About half a mile to the north of here."

Sam frowned. This was clearly not the answer she wanted to hear. "I was going to give you an earful for doing that, but I suppose it would be worse if the car got towed for illegal parking. We will wait here for you to bring the car to the door."

Smithy looked a bit crestfallen at the last comment, but he knew she was right and started to leave. Sam shouted him back and when he was close, she said quietly, "Smithy, not to freak you out or anything, but you better have a look round under the car just in case. You don't know what someone might have done to an unattended car."

Sam was right. "Sam, I should go with Smithy. After all, I'm the expert in that field."

I started to follow Smithy, but Sam stopped me. "Are you totally insane? Smithy, go now. We will wait here for you. Adam, has it escaped your attention that people are trying to kill you?" Sam had that look in her eye that told me it wouldn't be a good idea to mess with her. "Smithy is a big boy. He knows the risks."

"I know, Sam, but people are dying all around me. It's not right."

Sam took my hand as we waited. "Just let's give the evidence and get the hell out of here."

I shook my head. My thoughts turned to Kay Miller, Ian Ferris, the two MI6 guys in London, the two MI5 surveillance guys, Archie and Matt from Steve's team. It struck me that I didn't even know them for long enough to know their second names. They had died saving my life, and I didn't know their names. This had to stop. It was madness.

Sam squeezed my hand. It was as if she had read my thoughts. "Come on, Adam. Cheer up. We are almost through this. By next week, you will be a free man."

I wanted to believe Sam, but what I had found out that day made me doubt this very much. "Sam, you didn't see that woman when she stood in front of me and as cool as a cucumber emptied a clip at me. She is a piece of work. If Zelenski is correct, and she is here, there could be a few more bodies before this is over."

Sam tied her hair back in her trademark ponytail. "She has to get past me first, and she didn't manage it before. You just worry how you are going to convince everybody at the hearing that our foremost allies have conspired against us."

I shook my head. "That just got a whole lot harder. We have to assume that the journalist and his evidence are no longer available after they used the package to try and kill us. Now Lee Tribby has gone AWOL. They are slamming all the doors in our faces."

Smithy arrived after a lengthy search of the hire car turned up nothing. Sam bundled me into the back and followed me in, telling Smithy to get the foot down.

***

Benesch watched from the room as the Focus sped away from the restaurant. She had been right not to attempt anything. Such was the speed of their exit, she would have been lucky to wing one of them, never mind make the kill. Back to the drawing board.

***

On arrival at Vauxhall Cross, we were ushered into Neil Andrews's office in the basement. Neil was not in residence, and the three of us sat there in silence, waiting for the top brass to arrive. We didn't have to wait long. The director and Neil arrived together. Neil said nothing and took up station at the back of his office, giving the director centre stage. "I would like to thank you all for coming, and I will cut to the chase. Today there was a meeting of COBRA, as I am sure you already know. It became clear as the meeting proceeded that it was no longer possible for MI6 to hold the high ground over the Machrihanish problem. I would have preferred it if the prime minister had not had prior warning of the incident, but ultimately it has become far too serious to continue on the route originally planned. I requested a private meeting with the PM after the COBRA meeting broke up. I laid all my cards on the table, and as a result of this, the prime minister has just finished a lengthy call with the US president. The powers that be have come to a compromise. As soon as practically possible, the Royal Air Force will retake full control of Machrihanish and will deal with any mess left by the previous tenants. As a result of this changing situation and at the request of the Americans, no questions will be brought up at the forthcoming MOD inquiry regarding the Scottish air base. In return, Britain will be given full access to the use of any further space flights for research or deployment of satellite surveillance equipment."

The silence in the room was deafening. "I must impress upon you that none of this leaves the room. I was always afraid that the politicians would talk their way round the problem, and it would appear they have again shown their true colours. It still has to be shown how they will deal with the radiation problem in the west of Scotland, but it will be covert now, and not as I had always wished—brought out in the open so it could be dealt with properly. I am truly sorry it had to end this way, but events have forced my hand. The worst-case scenario was that it could have escalated into an unrecoverable situation, with secret service personnel on both sides of the Atlantic losing their lives. Already far too much blood has been spilled over this. The only silver lining to this cloud is that the Americans have agreed to hand over any information on the people in Britain who have helped or planned to attack us, in particular the identity of Merlin and any information they have on assassins still operational in the UK."

I almost fell off my seat at the last comment. Sam was calm and collected on the surface. The only thing that gave her away was that she was gripping both arms of the chair so hard her knuckles were chalk white. I caught her eye as she turned away from the director's gaze. They were cold pools of grey ice. I had no doubt that she was already planning Merlin's death in her head.

The director cleared his throat. "I don't need to tell you of all people how much it will mean to the security services to bring this person to justice. Tomorrow the American embassy will call us when they have collected the information required. Neil and Samantha will call at the embassy and then make whatever plans are required to detain this traitor in our midst."

***

Areli had just retired to her room at the B and B for the night when her phone vibrated in her pocket.

It was the American voice again. "The mission has been aborted, I repeat, aborted. I have deposited one million US dollars in your account as a retainer and to cover costs. Good-bye."

Areli was furious. It was not just the money. She had a debt to pay this woman back. Word would get around that she had failed again, and this was not an option. Areli needed to work, and her reputation was everything. If she were seen as not reliable, her work would dry up. She would not give up. She would show this American she was her own person. She would complete the mission or die trying.

***

On the short trip back to Sam's flat, my mind was working overtime, trying to take in all the information. Nobody talked much. We were still processing what we had been told.

Smithy broke the silence. "Guys, I can see why you were told about things, but I don't know where I fit into this equation. I knew nothing about the base, and I don't want to know if it has brought you guys so much trouble. Why did I get included in the briefing?"

Sam and I looked at each other. I was first to share my opinion. "I think it is because they assumed that working in close proximity to us, you would have found out by now anyway."

Sam shook her head. "You are both so naïve, it is quite funny. MI6 and MI5 have both lost personnel that they need to replace. They don't want you going back to Hereford telling tales that will get spread about, so I will put money on it—you are about to become the next James Bond, or Bodie and Doyle, whichever takes your fancy."

My brain was still trying to find a way that would stop Sam killing Merlin in cold blood and ending up in jail. Back at the flat, I decided to test the water. "So a big day tomorrow, Sam. How are you going to handle not having to babysit me anymore, after you lock Merlin up in the Tower of London and throw away the key."

Sam kicked her shoes off while Smithy headed to the kitchen to put the kettle on. Sam double-checked the locks on the doors and windows while she waited for Smithy to get out of earshot. "Adam, it's not finished until it's finished. I am going to be away tomorrow. Smithy needs to be on his guard. This assassin the Americans talked about may not have got the message. They have not named the person yet, so it could be anybody."

I checked Smithy was still in the kitchen. "Sam, you are not going to try anything stupid tomorrow, right?"

Sam sat on the couch but she was avoiding eye contact. "Don't be daft, Adam. I will be with my boss, so I will need to go by the book."

Sam was lying through her teeth, and she knew I knew it. Our conversation stopped as Smithy appeared with three mugs of coffee.

Smithy and I spent another night in the lounge, Smithy on the carpet in a sleeping bag, while I slept on the couch.

Sleep wouldn't come. I had to think of something and fast before Sam could act. I had an idea, but I would need to lose Smithy before I could do anything.

The next morning I awoke to find Smithy in the kitchen making breakfast. Sam was nowhere to be seen. I wandered into the kitchen to see what Smithy had on the menu. I made a mental note that now this nightmare was over, I would get my body back into shape. These past weeks, exercise had been impossible, and I was feeling very lethargic.

"Morning, Mac. Did you sleep well? Oh by the way, Sam has already gone. She wanted to get to the office, just in case the US embassy calls early." I thought to myself, I bet she does. "What is up with her, Adam? Is she on a mission or what? She woke me up and pulled me in here, then gave me a lecture about not letting you out of my sight today. Man, she was wound up like a corkscrew this morning."

Smithy busied himself cooking the eggs while I studied the paper, or so I made it look. In truth, I was racking my brain as to where to start this morning. I had to get a move on before Sam found out who was Merlin.

***

Colonel David Southern contacted the US embassy in London and spoke to the US ambassador personally. He informed him that the CIA would be contacting him shortly with important information that he and he alone would pass onto the head of MI6. He also added that he would like the ambassador to visit John Zelenski, to arrange for his return to the United States, and inform him that he was to be presented with the Distinguished Intelligence Cross by the president himself.

The tide had turned in Washington, so Southern did what he always did and went with the flow. Making Zelenski a hero would keep him on side, and it would be great PR for the United States. He could read the news headlines now: "CIA agent saves MI6 female agent's life in shootout." The politicians would lap it up, and it would be more plus points for himself.

***

Breakfast had hardly touched the sides. I needed to get a move on, and luckily, Sam had taken a taxi, leaving us with the hired Focus. I was about to set foot out the door when my bodyguard stopped me and handed me the bulletproof vest. "Really? Come on, Smithy. It makes you sweat like a pig. I am a free man today. They have called off their attack dogs."

Smithy was not having any of it. "Your missus made me promise you would be wearing it, and by the look of her, she would put a bullet in me if I failed in that duty. Better sweaty than dead, sir."

I gave in and started getting the kit on. "Smithy, we are going to be doing a bit of running about today. Better you don't ask why. Get my drift?"

First stop was an Internet café. Smithy was dispatched to get the brews in while I set about finding as much as possible about Merlin. It always amazed me how much you could find out about an individual by surfing the net, and now that I knew who Merlin was, he was no different.

***

At Vauxhall Cross, Sam had just finished her third cup of coffee. The waiting around was killing her.

She visited the toilets. In the privacy of a cubicle, for the second time that morning, she removed her Glock and checked the weapon. In addition to this, Neil had asked her to pick up a capsule of NLB7 and the hypodermic ring to administer the drug. Sam sat wondering who Merlin would turn out to be.

At first she, like many others, had thought Merlin must be a politician, but this latest appearance did not make that possible. There was

301

no way Merlin could still be a politician. If not a politician, however, who else would have the knowledge to supply Britain's enemies? Sam began to wonder how much effort had been put into an internal investigation of the security services.

Sam was heading back to her office when her phone rang. It was Neil. Two minutes later, she was standing in Neil's office, trying to stop him ordering more coffee.

"No news from the Americans yet. Maybe they were playing us. I tried to speak to the director, but he has gone AWOL on us."

Alarm bells started ringing in Sam's head. "What exactly do you mean, AWOL?"

Neil had been studying some papers as he spoke to Sam, but when he heard the change in the tone of her voice, he looked up. "Just exactly what I said, Sam. He hasn't arrived at work, and his wife said he left the house this morning as usual." Sam seemed to be the only one that was particularly bothered by this. "It's OK, Sam. It's quite a routine thing that the director goes missing. He does it regularly. He will be at his gentleman's club or the Houses of Parliament. He drives his secretary wild."

Sam was still not convinced. She stood up and leaned on Neil's desk, speaking directly to his face. "I think you had better send out the search parties for him. After all, today we are about to unveil Britain's most wanted criminal. You would think he would want to be involved, unless he is the traitor?" Neil started to laugh but Sam persisted. "What's wrong? Is my suggestion so unthinkable? He has access to all the relevant information. He has been around exactly as long as Merlin, and has anybody had the guts to check on their own director?"

Neil had stopped laughing. "Not so funny when you start thinking about it, is it?" Neil was ringing a number as he spoke to Sam. His colour had paled significantly. "Sam, his mother was Irish."

There was a deathly silence as Neil waited for the phone to be picked up. "Jean, it's Neil. Listen, we have a situation here. You need to find your boss, and you need to find him fast. Call me back the minute you find him. Thank you."

Sam was starting to doubt her reasoning. "Neil, I must be wrong. Zelenski thought he had seen a bill paid by the CIA that had Merlin's name written on it, and it was paid in America. That doesn't tie up at all."

Neil was on the phone again, this time even more agitated. "Please get on the phone to the American embassy, and tell them we need that information yesterday. Also, find the director's file, and get it to my office urgently. No, I am not kidding. Just do it."

Neil put the phone down. He looked even more troubled now. "I am almost certain the director told me his first wife had moved to America for health reasons. I was pretty drunk at the time because I had just lost Mary, but I am almost sure of it." The phone rang five minutes later. Neil listened but said nothing, then put the phone down slowly. "Jesus Christ, the director's file has been removed and none of his local haunts have seen him. Also he just cancelled his membership of his club."

***

Smithy had a puzzled look on his face as he watched me exit the jewelers. It took only a few minutes on the Internet to find what I was looking for, and, as if my luck had changed, the shop was only a mile or so away.

"Bloody hell, Mac, you are a fast mover. You go for it, boy! When are you going to pop the question to her?" Smithy had put two and two together and come up with five. I let him continue with his wild speculation. It suited me that he did not know the truth.

I needed to lose Smithy at some point, and this was next on my hastily hatched plan. I suggested that we head back to Franco's for lunch, mainly because it was one of the few places in London I knew. Also, I had noted the back door next to the gents. This would be my exit strategy.

***

Areli had followed the pair about all morning, but her luck had not changed. At no point was there a chance to attempt a kill. Areli watched the pair looking for a parking space and noted they were heading to the same place they had eaten at the previous night. They drove past, still looking for a space. She knew this would take some time. This was her chance. She abandoned her hire car on double reds and headed for the restaurant, finding a wall table in a gloomy corner of the restaurant, not far from the door. She was dressed in a business suit and carried an attaché case, complete with laptop. She looked every part the businesswoman.

The only give-away was her black, rubber-soled sneakers. If she needed to move, high heels were not a good plan; running shoes were. It was a pity the woman was not here but also a blessing. She knew she could handle two of them, and they had just proved they were not as skilled as the woman. They had taken no evasive maneuvers to check if they were being followed, and they had used the same location two days in a row.

Sam was still waiting as lunchtime approached. Unknown to anybody but her, she had fitted a tracking device on the Focus, and now she checked her monitor. The car was parked two streets from Franco's restaurant. She cursed under her breath, then made a split-second decision.

She called Neil and told him she was heading for lunch. She told him to call her the minute he heard anything. Twenty minutes later she walked into Franco's.

***

Smithy and I were sitting at a table in the middle of the restaurant. Sam sat down while Franco made up another place at the table.

"Smithy, what are you doing coming back here? It's too big a risk."

I cut in before Sam could go any further. "Sam, it was my fault. I didn't know any other places to go, so it's me to blame. Sorry." My master plan was falling to pieces. Now that Sam was on the scene, there was no way I was going to be able to do a runner. There was only one good thing about the situation—Sam was here, which meant she was not hunting down Merlin. "Have you had any word from the Americans yet?"

Sam looked unsure what to say. "Nothing at the moment, so I thought I had better track you pair down, check you were OK, and see what you have been up to."

Smithy was grinning like a Cheshire cat, but a swift kick under the table from me removed the smile.

CHAPTER EIGHTEEN
Do Or Die

Benesch watched in horror as Sam arrived and sat down. She was trapped. Any movement from her would attract their attention. She quickly weighed up the situation. She had no option but to use the surprise factor to swing the tables in her favour. Benesch prepared herself for what would surely come next. She knew it was only a matter of time until the woman started to check out her surroundings and who was present.

It happened in a split second. Sam made eye contact with Benesch and instantly recognized her—in that fraction of time Benesch knew it was do-or-die time.

She launched the case and laptop out of the way with one arm, and at the same time brought the Sig Saur to bear on her intended target. Sam threw herself across the table. Benesch's first two shots were aimed and hit their target with perfect marksmanship.

All hell broke loose. Any further aiming on Areli's part was futile. She emptied the remainder of the fifteen-shot magazine into the room as she dived for the door.

Sam had not been fast enough. The first two shots hit Adam high in the chest, and whether because of the shots, or because both Sam and Smithy had knocked him to the ground, he was out cold. Sam recovered first and managed to get one shot in as Benesch fled the scene. The shot took out a plant pot just above Benesch's head, covering her in compost as she escaped into the relative calm of the street. Sam got to the door a few seconds behind her, but her conscience made her turn back.

The place was in an uproar. Benesch's bullets had done a huge amount of damage. Behind Smithy and Adam, Sam could see only carnage. Franco lay face down with a bullet wound in his lower back. The table he had just been serving had not escaped unscathed. An elderly gentleman lay facedown on the table with a bullet hole in his left temple. The blood from the wound spilled out over the white tablecloth. People were screaming and trying to get out, clambering over the prone body of Franco.

Suddenly Sam realized that Smithy was shouting at her. "Sam, go! He'll be OK. The vest saved him. Go! Get the bitch."

Benesch found to her dismay that her hire car had been towed. She was on the run with no getaway car. She sprinted along the street, looking for transport. Vital seconds were ticking away. Halfway along the one-way street, a taxi was ticking over. Benesch slipped a new clip into her Sig Saur as she ran. She had no time for an argument or scuffle with the driver. She drew level with the door, raised her weapon, and fired at point-blank range through the middle of the door, hitting the driver in the upper leg. She pulled the door open, and the driver fell on the ground with a thud and a groan. Behind her, people were spilling out of the restaurant. Benesch wasted no time checking to see if anyone were in pursuit. She jumped into the cab and took off as fast as the thing could go.

Sam was first out the door. She was still looking for Benesch when she heard the gunshot. She kicked off her high heels and took off as fast as her legs would carry her. She spotted Benesch getting into the taxi but decided against using her weapon. It was a busy street, and her confidence with the Glock was not at its usual level. She set off after the taxi, but in her heart, she knew she was fighting a losing battle.

The taxi was about to reach the end of the street. This was her last chance before she lost sight of the cab; the end of the street was quiet. She dropped to one knee, using her leg to support her shooting arm. It was now or never. She took a deep breath and held it as the taxi started to turn, moving into the sights of the wavering Glock. Sam fired.

Benesch started to pull the cab around the corner when everything exploded around her, The nine-millimeter shell burst through the interior of the cab, missing Benesch's head by millimeters, shattering the interior mirror before coming to rest in the headlining of the stricken cab. At first Benesch thought she had escaped unscathed, until a trickle of blood ran into her left eye, blurring her vision. A sliver of glass from the exploding mirror had cut deep into her head just above her eyebrow. An exploratory grope told her it would need more than a plaster. She wiped away the blood and continued to navigate her way through slow-moving traffic.

Sam watched as the taxi vanished round the corner. She was still holding her breath, hoping that the taxi would grind to a halt, but to no avail—the taxi was gone.

The Focus screeched to a halt at Sam's side just as she had given up any hope of continuing the pursuit.

Smithy screamed at her to get in. Sam jumped in and immediately started grilling Smithy. "What the hell do you think you are doing? Adam better be OK."

Smithy stopped her before she managed to break into a full-blown rant. "Sam, he is fine. He is sitting up, giving orders. He ordered me to make sure you are OK. Are we going to sit here discussing your boyfriend's health, or are we going to catch the bitch who just tried to kill him?"

Sam pulled on her seatbelt as Smithy gave the Focus hire car the beans. Using full throttle and the handbrake, he flung the Focus round the corner. The taxi had a considerable head start on them by now. Smithy used the horn on the hire car like a siren, on and off constantly to help get slow-moving traffic out of the way. Minutes went past and still there was no sign of the taxi. Suddenly Sam pointed. About one hundred meters ahead, there was a commotion in the traffic. Sam spotted the windowless cab trying to cut a path through the traffic. They were approaching the one-way traffic system at Vauxhall Bridge, just next to the office, and Sam knew there was a good chance they would catch the taxi here in the snarled-up traffic.

Benesch saw the danger ahead and charged through the one-way system the wrong way. Her gamble had almost paid off—then a big Jaguar coming the other way didn't see her until the last minute. The glancing blow sent the Jaguar careering into a signpost and also fatally wounding Benesch's taxicab, demolishing the front wing and puncturing the driver's tyre.

Areli Benesch was in no mood to give up yet and ploughed on with the stricken taxi, willing it to keep going. In the traffic madness that ensued, Sam and Smithy got snarled up at the junction. Smithy had to resort to waving his Glock at a few irate motorists before they got the message and got out of his way posthaste.

***

I had come to, and all hell was breaking loose around me. People were screaming; people were sobbing, Smithy had me propped up against the leg of a table. He was hauling at my shirt, and at first I did not understand what he was doing. It suddenly dawned on me that I had been shot, and Smithy was trying to check that the bulletproof vest had done its job.

"Where's Sam?"

Smithy continued to check me out as he spoke. "She went after the shooter, mate. You sit still for a second."

My own situation did not concern me. It was Sam I was worried about. "Smithy, for gods sake, get after her. Make sure she is safe." Smithy was shaking his head. "Smithy, I'm not asking you. I'm telling you. Get after her, and that's an order."

Smithy hesitated for only a second. "OK, sir, but you stay here and don't move." He was out the door in a flash.

I was in a bit of a state and struggling to get a breath, but I knew I needed to get out of there before the Old Bill closed everything down. With the help of a table leg, I managed to pull myself to my feet. One of the kitchen staff was standing open-mouthed, in a state of shock. I yelled at him to call 999, then staggered out into the street. The fresh air helped to revive me a little. I gathered my thoughts. Two streets further on and I had managed to rearrange my disheveled clothing. I hailed a cab. "Good afternoon. Would it be possible to take me to the Watermead estate in Aylesbury, please?"

***

Benesch continued along Vauxhall Bridge Road. She had practiced this route just in case she needed an exit strategy. She could see the Focus some distance behind her trying to cut through the traffic. The taxi was becoming more of a handful every minute as the remains of the tyre parted company with the wheel. Just before Victoria Station, she tried to turn down the inside of a bus, but the cab refused to turn, instead smashing into the bus. The bus driver stopped, but Benesch did not. Benesch smiled to herself. The bus had stopped in a tunnel under a building. Her pursuers would have a few headaches trying to get that out of the way. As she passed Victoria Station, the traffic ground to a halt. Benesch cursed. She could not wait. She twisted in the seat and watched anxiously for the Focus as she waited for the traffic to clear.

Further along Buckingham Palace Road, a bus lane opened up. Benesch roared along the lane, ignoring how the old taxi was complaining bitterly. Again, the traffic ground to a halt, but Benesch could not and would not wait. On Grosvenor Place, two police officers on foot patrol attempted to stop the careering taxi as it charged down the bus lane. As the officers stepped into the bus lane, Benesch pulled the cab with an almighty screech onto the pavement, leaving the officers open mouthed. This final act was the death knell for the taxi. It was now running on the rim, and the heat was causing the hub to seize. The cab was now almost undriveable. Benesch spotted her goal just ahead and charged through a final red light, crossing traffic to deposit what was left of the cab on the pavement outside the gates to Hyde Park. A quick look over her shoulder as she exited the stricken vehicle showed that she had not lost her tail. Benesch took off for the nearest tree line before she was spotted.

Sam and Smithy had made good time, helped by the fact that, unlike Benesch, they had four wheels left on their vehicle. Smithy spotted the abandoned taxi just as he turned right in front of Hyde Park, and he cut sharply across the traffic. The Westminster Council refuse truck could not get out of his way, and the collision spun the Focus round in a three-sixty spin, coming to rest with a sickening impact against the kerb and the flow of traffic.

Sam and Smithy clambered out, trying to regain their senses. Smithy took off first, but Sam was not so lucky. She was accosted by the driver of the truck and a well-meaning elderly gentleman who wanted to know if she was OK. Sam assured the old man she was OK and asked the truck driver to contact the police and have Hyde Park sealed off.

She could tell the truck driver thought she had banged her head or was nuts. Her argument gained momentum as he watched her scramble about the floor of the wrecked Focus, then reappear holding a Glock handgun. Sam checked the safety was on and tucked the gun into the waist of her skirt. She quizzed the old gentleman about the abandoned taxi.

"It just arrived about two minutes before you, darling. The bloody woman that was drivin' it was mad. She headed down there by the trees. I was about to call the old bill when you arrived. Take her bloody license off her, that's what I say."

Sam headed for the tree line some distance behind Smithy.

It was not by luck that Benesch had picked this route. Out of sight, behind a tree, Benesch peeled off her trousers and jacket. Underneath she wore shorts and a T-shirt. She pulled wrist and head sweatbands and a pair of sunglasses from the jacket's pockets. Now she was just one of the hundreds of joggers who frequented Hyde Park.

Three minutes later, Smithy found the pile of abandoned clothing. It was still warm. Sam arrived a few seconds later. "The crafty bitch planned this, so who are we looking for now? She can't be far away." Sam looked round for some sign of her just as two male joggers passed.

"That's it, Smithy. She is a jogger. That's what I would have done." Just as she said it, a woman appeared from the tree line, running steadily onto the main path three hundred meters in front of them. "I will put my money on it that's her. Let's go, Smithy."

What Sam did next almost made her cry. She had been dressed for a business meeting at the American embassy, not for the Commonwealth Games. She turned her dark-blue Givenchy designer skirt round until she found the seam and tore it open so she could get her legs moving. In bare feet and a torn Givenchy skirt, she and Smithy set sail after her suspected target. They were both having to sprint to make up ground as the woman in front was setting a fair pace herself.

Benesch was wearing a handmade set of sunglasses that were designed to her own specifications. On the inside of the outer frame, there were two tiny magnifying mirrors so with just a slight turn of her head, she could see what was going on behind her. She could not break into a sprint. That would give the game away. She would play it cool until she found an area where she could turn the tables on them.

Sam turned the corner. On the left was a shuttered kiosk, followed by a line of trees. The woman was no place to be seen. Either she had already cleared the trees, or they had lost her. The hairs on Sam's neck were standing to attention. This would be a good place for an ambush if she knew they were behind her. Sam said nothing to Smithy but signaled him to stop and circle the kiosk, traveling clockwise. She would travel anticlockwise.

Smithy crept off to the right, and Sam started to move but had a change of heart. The ground fell away on the far side of the building, and it was planted out in fruit trees. Sam cut down by the trees so she could look back up the slope at the far side of the circular building. "Bingo," she whispered to herself. Benesch stood at the far side of the building. She was holding her Sig Saur complete with silencer, ready for action. At first, Sam was not sure what she was doing. It was only at this close range that Sam could see the tiny mirrors on her sunglasses. If Sam had walked round behind her, she still would have been caught out. Sam marveled at Benesch's skill. Smithy was approaching, but Benesch was looking at the ground. She was watching his shadow cast by the winter sun.

Sam slipped out her Glock and tried to click off the safety catch, but it was stuck. She tried again, and then it suddenly dawned on her the gun had been retrieved from the floor of the smashed Focus. She had about a second to do something before Smithy became the assassin's next prize.

Benesch counted the steps taken by the shadow while checking her back for the shadow's partner. She would dispatch him, then fall back to safety of the trees and pick off his partner when she rushed to his assistance. Just as Areli applied pressure to the trigger, she was thrown in the air.

With no options left, Sam had dropped her damaged Glock and charged, coming in at a forty-five degree angle to give Benesch as little warning as possible. She dived and grabbed both of Benesch's ankles, pulling the woman's feet out from under her. The Sig fired into the roof of the round building, then flew from her hand as the shock of hitting the ground loosened her grip on the weapon. She was about to scrabble for the gun when a voice stopped her in her tracks.

"Go ahead. I have never missed from this range, but as a great man once said, do you feel lucky?" Smithy had been waiting all his life to say that line.

Sam dusted herself down, walked over to the Sig Saur, and picked it up, standing behind Benesch. "Have you any idea how corny that sounded, Smithy? Joking aside, don't even blink. She is pure talent. Take a step back, Smithy, just in case." Benesch watched as Smithy carefully stepped back out of kicking range.

Sam was taking no more chances. She was wearing the ring that had been earmarked for Merlin. A swift grab of Areli's neck was enough to administer the NLB7. In seconds, Benesch was lying on her back, looking up at the branches of the trees. No matter how hard her brain tried, that was all she could do.

Both Sam and Smithy had lost their phones in the crash. Sam managed to stop an old lady who was walking her dog. She gladly handed over her phone when she was told that their friend had collapsed while out jogging. She called Neil and was told to hold station while Neil organized transportation for them. There was a stony silence at the other end of the phone when Sam told Neil they had left Adam back at the restaurant. He dispatched two men to pick up Adam and congratulated Sam on managing to capture Benesch alive.

Sam wandered back to where she had left Smithy guarding the Israeli woman. Smithy watched with amusement as Sam talked to the woman. "It would seem our backroom boys are very keen to have a chat with you once the drug wears off, so as much as I would like to see you dead, you better listen to what I have to say. Don't try and fight the drug. Tests have shown the more you fight it, the more brain damage it causes." Sam bent down close to Areli's ear. "Just for the record, you were lucky. If my gun hadn't jammed, trust me—you would have been on the way to meet your maker and not my boss."

***

The taxi driver dropped me at the road end of the Watermead estate. I was about to see if the first part of my plan would work. A few minutes walk brought me to the cul-de-sac at the rear of Neil's house.

The big BMW was still parked where Smithy and I had left it, and a quick grope behind the driver's wheel proved fruitful. I had placed the spare key in a magnetic holder for emergencies. The car opened with the first press of the button. In the boot, where I had left them, were the money, the drugs, and my holdall with my MP5 and the grenades. I was in business. A quick stop to top up the BMW and pick up some bits and pieces from a motorist store and I was on my way. I programmed the satnav with the address I had found on the Internet. The satnav told me my travel time would be fifty-two minutes. I checked my watch. It would be tight, but I suspected I could get to Merlin's house before he arrived home. The address was in the countryside, south of Oxford.

En route I went over the plan I had thrown together, and doubts started to enter my head. Had I really found Merlin? What if I assassinated an innocent man? I would not be able to interrogate him, as my plan counted on stealth. I needed to be damned sure I had the right man before I signed his death warrant.

The satnav was wrong. I arrived fifty minutes later on the dot. I rolled slowly up the gravel drive. There was no sign of any cars. The big stone house looked deserted. I pulled up and put my plan into action. I pulled on a white disposable overall, the same type forensics and car painters wore, followed by rubber gloves. I loaded all my goodies into a plastic toolbox, grabbed a big plastic container, and headed to the front door.

Ten feet from the house, my heart almost stopped. An old man with a flat cap came out of the front door. I don't know who got the bigger fright, him or me. But I was thinking on my feet. "Good afternoon. Zepto Pest Control. Is the boss in?"

The old guy relaxed visibly. "Jesus, son, you almost gave me a bleedin' heart attack. I told him time and time again to get rid of that furniture. Bloody thing's riddled with woodworm, but did he listen? No. Where's the bloody woodworm this time/"

I had pulled it off. "In the living room, I believe. Is anybody home?"

The old guy shook his head. "No one, mate, and if he thinks I'm hanging about, he can think again. Here's the key, mate. He won't be back from London for a bit yet. Pop the key under the mat when you're finished, there's a good lad."

I could hardly believe my luck. I watched as the old man inspected the roses on his way down the gravel drive. A quick tour of the house proved useful. The house was old, and the kitchen was situated in the basement, harking back to the days when servants would have worked from the kitchens. The study and living room were on the ground floor to the left of the hall, with French windows leading to front and rear lawns. To the rear of the building there was an exit road that ran down the border of the garden to a country lane. The large spiral staircase led to six double bedrooms. The man's day job obviously paid well. As I toured the house, my blood began to boil at the thought of this monster sitting here in the lap of luxury while people died by his treachery.

I suddenly stopped the tour. It was time to get to work, and Merlin's luck was just about to run out—I was going to make sure of it. The lounge was my target area. I put my main plan in place, and then as a backup, I booby-trapped Merlin's phone with a C4 charge under the phone table. It would trigger if the handset was lifted. I made sure that the receiver I had fitted inside the handset worked. It did—one click of the remote and the phone rang. I was almost ready for Merlin's grand entrance. All I needed to do was hide my mode of transport.

It only took a few minutes for me to deposit the BMW behind the large shed that nestled in the trees by the rear gardens. I didn't have long to wait. I took up a position in the bushes along the border of the drive, a position that gave me a commanding view of the drive and the front of the house, including the French windows in the front of the lounge.

The gravel crackled as the big car drove up to the front of the house. Another large piece of the jigsaw just fell into place.

Merlin stepped out of the shiny, black, three-and-a-half litre Rover and headed up the steps, stopping to pull the key from under the mat. I had been right. Without a doubt, this was Merlin. His car had just given him away. It was the same car I had admired outside the Machrihanish Air Base. I wanted to step out of the bushes and scream at the traitor. How could a man in his position turn on his own people?

I watched through clenched teeth as he wandered through his front door, picking up the mail, and heading for the lounge.

*****

Merlin wandered past his high-back leather chairs and started sifting through the mail, throwing the junk mail in the bin by the fireside. He took the remaining mail and tossed it onto the coffee table. It was then that something caught his eye.

On the coffee table lay a piece of gold jewelry. Merlin was confused. There had been no women in his house for some time. He picked up the necklace and studied it closely. The blood ran cold in his veins. Someone was playing with him. The gold charm on the necklace was a tiny miniature of Merlin the magician, complete with wand. Merlin rechecked the charm. There was no doubt. Engraved on the base of the tiny figure was only one word: "Merlin."

He stepped back, dropping the necklace and tripping over the hearthrug. He stumbled to the front and then to the rear windows, half-expecting the Old Bill to be waiting for him, but there was nothing. He had been waiting for this moment for a long, long time. He needed a drink to steady what was left of his shattered nerves. He pulled open the doors of his antique cocktail cabinet, searching for a crystal tumbler to pour himself a whisky.

Two things happened. A piece of paper floated from the cabinet onto the ground. As Merlin bent down to retrieve the paper, there was a tinkle, and a piece of thread that had been attached to the door dangled against the door, held down by the weight of the two pins attached to it. The paper had only two words: "MAC'S JUSTICE."

Merlin was still reading the second word when the grenades went off. The blast threw Merlin into the middle of the room. The shrapnel from the grenades cut through the tumblers and wine glasses, sending shards of crystal in every direction. Crystal shards and shrapnel cut deeply into Merlin's shattered body. The malt whisky Merlin was so fond of soaked painfully into his wounds.

***

I was about to go to Plan B and call the house phone when the blast shook the building. The front French windows shattered. For a second there was silence. Then I heard the low moan of a man in terrible pain.

As I entered through the French windows, the smell of whisky was overpowering. Merlin lay on his back in the middle of the room. He was rocking to and fro in a pool of blood. The flying crystal had hit its mark in many places, and Merlin was leaking like a sieve.

I was not there to gloat. I needed to sort a few things and get the hell out of there. The C4 was first. I disarmed the phone and removed the plastic explosives. Forensics might have traced the C4 back to a batch bought by the British army. The note and the necklace also had to go.

Downstairs in the kitchen, I pulled the cooker away from the wall. With the assistance of an adjustable spanner, I loosened the gas-pipe coupling. I connected the plug for the electrical side of the cooker to an everyday, thirteen-amp timer for light switches, did a quick calculation for the size and number of rooms, set the timer, switched the plug on, and tapped the igniter button on the front of the cooker. In forty-seven minutes, the timer would allow electricity to the gas-ring igniters via the tapped down button. The resulting explosion and fire fueled by the whisky would hopefully erase any forensic evidence.

In under ten minutes, I was outside the doomed building. I had finished Merlin, but there was still work to do. I brought the big BMW round to the front and transferred the drugs from the boot of the BMW to the old Rover's boot. Not only was I going to take his life, but I was going to destroy his reputation into the bargain.

Time was running out, I drove the BMW into the old woodshed, and I returned its drug dealer plates and tax disc. I placed the money in an army-surplus Bergen, doused the BMW in petrol, and set it alight. I was sad. It had been a great workhorse, but it had to go. It was a forensic scientist's dream—both Sam's and my blood and DNA were all over the car.

I watched as the flames took hold. My final job was to remove the paper overalls and gloves and add them to the BMW's funeral pyre.

One final check through the French windows confirmed what I already knew—Merlin had succumbed to his wounds. I headed for the rear entrance. I checked my watch. Fifteen minutes until the timer ran out. I pulled out Kay's blue baseball cap and pulled it down to cover my face. A quick look at a map showed the lane I was on—next stop, Oxford!

***

The army Lynx helicopter touched down in Hyde Park, one hundred metres from Sam and Smithy. Smithy flung Benesch over his shoulder and set sail for the chopper.

A few joggers in Hyde Park stopped to watch the proceedings, but to them it looked as if the army were carrying out some type of rescue mission or training exercise. Benesch offered no resistance and looked as if she were being saved, not captured. When Sam reached the helicopter, the pilot handed her a phone.

Sam had to walk some distance from the chopper before she was able to hear the caller. "Sam, is that you? Let the soldier take the woman. There is a car waiting for you by the gates you entered by. Get a move on. The Americans have called."

Sam hung up and returned to the pilot and Smithy. "Looks like you got the babysitting duties. Smithy, the minute you get to where you are going, you make sure that bitch is well tethered. She has done enough damage." Sam turned to the pilot. "Where are you taking the prisoner?"

The pilot hesitated. He had been told to tell no one. He shook his head. "Need to know, ma'am."

"That's right soldier, and I need to know. Call MI6 if you need to check my clearance."

"Boscombe Down, initially, ma'am. Then the prisoner is being transported by road to Porton Down on arrival."

Sam watched as the Lynx lifted off then swung sharply to the south and vanished over the trees, only its rotor beat giving away its location. Sam couldn't believe how far she had run. It took her some time to find her way back to the gates, where a black Jaguar was waiting to pick her up. Sam got a surprise as she slipped into the rear seat. The privacy glass had hidden the fact the car had an occupant other than the driver. "About bloody time. Driver, step on it. The American embassy as quick as you like."

En route to the American embassy, Neil surveyed Sam. No shoes, skirt in tatters. "I think it would be a good idea when we get to the embassy for you to give it a miss. The driver's name is Bert, I will go and speak to the ambassador. You get Bert to take you to at least a shoe shop."

Sam ignored the last comment. She had other things on her mind. "What was the outcome at Franco's restaurant. Is Adam safe?"

Neil knew the question would come, but he had hoped they would have made the embassy before he had to answer that question. He was not sure how Sam would react. "The owner is in critical condition. There is a dead seventy-three-year-old man and a twenty-four-year-old woman with a bullet wound to her upper arm. Sam, we can't find Adam. He was last seen walking away from the restaurant, and he hasn't been seen since."

Sam had a dilemma on her hands. Should she continue on the Merlin hunt, or break it off and go looking for Adam? After dropping Neil at the US embassy, she instructed Bert to take her home to change. Sam had hoped to find Adam at the flat waiting for her, but he was nowhere to be found. She had no time to spare. After a quick change into trousers and a shirt, she was back in the car so Bert could shoot across town to the embassy to pick up Neil.

All the way back, Sam's brain was racing, trying to think where Adam had gone. They passed very close to Franco's restaurant, and police cars were buzzing about everywhere. They were obviously still looking for the lunatic who had gone on a shooting spree in a London restaurant. If they only knew the real story, Sam thought—a hired assassin caught by MI6 officers and already locked up in a MI6 safe house while the Metropolitan Police tied themselves in knots trying to find the unknown lunatic. Sam had always found it amusing when a new James Bond film hit the screens and an army of armchair experts said that it was all make-believe, a figment of the screenwriter's imagination. Sam smiled to herself. The truth was that it wasn't that far from reality, at least not today.

As they pulled up in Governor Square, Neil was waiting for them. To Sam's surprise, a police Volvo, complete with a police inspector and driver, was also waiting with Neil. Twenty seconds later, they were charging through traffic, the police car leading the way, sirens and lights blazing. "I take it we have found out who Merlin is."

Both cars screeched to a halt outside a rather grand old building. As they pulled up, Robin Alder appeared at the door. Sam had forgotten about her colleague's involvement in the case until now. Neil stepped out the car and a swift discussion with the inspector and Alder ensued. Once back in the car Neil directed Bert to follow the police again.

"What was all that about?"

Neil sat back, unbuttoned his collar, and loosened his tie. "We have a bit of a trip in front of us. Merlin left the hall some time ago."

Sam was watching Neil intently. "So Merlin is not the director?"

Neil shook his head. "No, the director turned up about an hour ago. Turns out he took a bad turn this morning and spent the day in hospital. The doctors think he is diabetic. Merlin is none other than our good friend Sir Antony Carrington, hence the police presence. We have to do this by the book, Sam. Carrington can't just disappear. He is too high profile for that."

Sam could feel her temper starting to fray. "Neil, this bastard better not walk away from this. Better to put a bullet in his head and blame someone else for it."

Neil spent the rest of the trip warning Sam of the consequences if Carrington were shot during his capture. Sam made sure she looked agreeable, but in her head, she was trying to work out some way she could get Carrington on his own.

***

I had spent the night sheltered by a small wood on the outskirts of Oxford. There I had made my plans for the next day. A change of clothing and transport were my main objectives. Although I had taken the drug money from the BMW boot, it was of no use to me as it was American currency. The money Sam and I had taken from the glass house was running low. I had about twelve hundred pounds, give or take a few quid. It looked as though my mode of transport was going to be a "budget vehicle," as the car dealers called them—what anyone else would call a "banger."

My first port of call was a Renault dealer. The salesman listened to my fabricated story that I was down from Scotland on a hiking holiday and that I had just found out that my father had been taken to hospital. I needed to get back to Scotland as soon as possible. I was escorted to the rear of the building and shown a very old Renault 5. The salesman assured me it had only been driven by an old lady, and that if I parted with five hundred pounds, it could be mine, complete with six months MOT and road tax.

An hour and three tons of paperwork later, I drove out of the dealers seven hundred pounds lighter. Five hundred for the car, two hundred for the insurance. The salesman had insisted on getting me a good deal on insurance as well.

The trip from Oxford to Aylesbury was relatively uneventful other than the little old lady that had previously owned the car had forgotten to remove her AC/DC cassette from the antique radio cassette player. I concluded this might have been because she had overdosed on the six empty tins of energy drink that were scattered around the footwells. It would appear the salesman had been economical with the truth.

CHAPTER NINETEEN

The Gamble

In Aylesbury, after a quick raid on the local supermarket to grab some food and clothes, I headed to the hospital. I found John Zelenski up and dressed and waiting for a driver from the American embassy to take him for debriefing in London. "Good morning, Adam. How are we doing this fine day?"

I sat on the bed and pulled the Bergen onto the bed with me. "John, it's good to see you up and about. I take it you have been told our superiors have arranged an amicable ending to all this nonsense."

Zelenski nodded. "I said all along it would come to this in the end."

I started to unzip the Bergen. "It's a pity so many people had to die before the powers that be got their finger out, which brings me to the reason I am here. I have two requests for you. John, I killed two Navy SEALs, Howie and Fernandez, who were doing nothing but their jobs. A good friend of mine has gone missing. I made the mistake of getting him involved in all this crap. His name is Lee Tribby, and he was an officer in the 101st Airborne. God knows where he is now."

Zelenski was about to start objecting, but I pressed on, pulling out a smaller travel bag. I started to load the money into the case. Zelenski's eyes left me and started to watch the money being transferred. "My God, Adam, how much is there?"

"That's the good bit, John. I am going to pay you in advance for your services. Your job is to deliver four million dollars to the families of each of the SEALs and then go looking for my friend. I have loaded ten million into the travel bag. The other two million is your fee."

Zelenski was speechless. I dropped the bag next to his already packed bags. "I need to go, John. Remember our previous conversation. You cannot tell anyone that I found out the identity of Merlin. Do we understand each other?" John Zelenski nodded, clearly still in shock.

"I heard on the radio that Sir Antony Carrington was killed in a gas explosion at his house yesterday!" Zelenski was watching my reaction.

I pulled my Bergen back over my shoulder and headed for the door. "Was he? You enjoy your retirement."

I had only a few things left to do before I turned tail and headed north. I ate a lonely meal at a greasy spoon café. I had been to the bank that afternoon, withdrawn every penny in it, and closed my account. Then I waited. It was after eight o'clock before I finished my second cup of coffee. My mind wandered back to Sam. What was she doing now that her main reason for getting up in the morning was dead? Would she ever speak to me again if she found out it was I who killed Merlin? What I was about to do next was pure gut feeling; I just hoped I had made the right decision.

The man at the security gate at Vauxhall Cross had seen me come and go relatively frequently over the last few weeks, so when I asked to see Neil Andrews, he let me pass without question. Three minutes later, I was standing at Neil's door. I knocked and entered. Neil had obviously received a call to say I was on my way. He walked round to the front of the desk. "Well, well! The wanderer has returned." He walked forward, his hand extended.

I aimed for a point about six inches behind his head and used the twist of my body to increase the speed of my arm. My fist made perfect contact with Neil's jaw, sending him backward over his desk. There was no way he was getting up from that one. I grabbed some paper and a pen. It did not take me long to write my note. "I promised you that if anything happened to Kay Miller, you would pay the price. That was for Kay. By the way, I resign."

I did not sign it as my left hand was beginning to swell badly. On the way out, I asked one of the security to pop down to Neil's office as he wanted a word. I had one last thing to do in London before heading for the hills.

Late that evening, I pulled the Renault up outside Sam's flat. There were no signs of life, and I was relieved. I did not want to speak to Sam until her head had calmed down, and I had time to sort out my private affairs. I posted a note through Sam's front door. It had only a few words on it, and only Sam and I would understand their meaning. That last job done, I pointed my trusty steed toward the north and set out on my epic journey. I had a feeling my trip north was not going to be as quick or as comfortable as my trip south in the BMW.

***

I had driven through the night, but I had had enough. I had originally planned to do the trip in one go, but my butt and the ringing in my ears from the screaming Renault engine told me it was time to take a well-earned break. I sat enjoying the silence of the car park while I attacked my apple. As my mind started to wander again, it always came back to the same thing—Sam. I wondered how long it would take for her to find out the truth. She was a smart cookie. She would put two and two together soon enough.

The six million dollar question was, what would she do then? I told myself I had had no option—I did what had to be done, or spend years visiting Sam in jail.

***

Sam sat by her sister's grave, still holding the bunch of flowers she had arrived with some hours earlier. Her head was in turmoil. One minute she was reliving the moment they had pulled up outside Carrington's manor house to find the local police and fire brigade trying to put out a major blaze. Then her mind flicked back to this very place, where she had vowed on her sister's grave to avenge her death. She had failed miserably. It had been confirmed that morning that the body found in the burnt-out ruin was Sir Antony Carrington. To Sam, it was as if Carrington had cheated her out of her vengeance. Sam sat in the gloom of the evening, tears rolling down her face. Everything she had lived for had been taken away. She had steeled herself to the fact that once she had killed Carrington, her career would be over, and she would spend many years in a high-security prison. She had not planned on failure, and she had no clue how to deal with it. She felt more alone than she had ever felt. She knew she should be looking for Adam, but she had nothing left to give. Her body had been battered to the edge of extinction, and now her mental state was being attacked.

***

Sam returned to her flat in the early hours of the morning. She had cried herself to sleep by her big sister's grave, only waking when drops of rain splashed on her face. Sam headed straight to bed.

In the morning, Sam made a conscious effort to pull herself together. She showered before her planned trip to the office, and on the way from the bathroom to the bedroom, she noticed the piece of paper by the front door.

Curiosity got the better of Sam, and she wandered across to investigate. On the scrap of paper were only three words. "COMRIACH. FOURTEEN DAYS." Sam's mood changed instantly. She knew exactly what it meant and who had written it. Over a bowl of cereal, Sam thought about the note. She knew what it meant, but she was at a loss to explain the fourteen-day period, or why Adam had vanished. She needed to get away and regroup. By the time Sam entered MI6, she was in a better frame of mind. She had it all planned out. She had a few calls to make, and she needed to notify Neil that she was taking some leave. She would be at the glass house before the end of the week.

***

I waited in the hall of Menamar House on the Menamar estate, a few miles from Aberfeldy. I had been lucky, and Kiron Al Ahdal was at home. He met me in the hall and escorted me into his library. I made my case to him that after Ian's death, things were not the same, that I was selling up my house, and out of courtesy, I had decided to offer it first to him so he could keep the estate intact. As I suspected, he jumped at the chance, and we came to an amicable agreement that he buy the house back for what I had paid for it. We shook hands on the deal, and Al Ahdal asked me to wait, then vanished. I walked to the window and looked up at the hillside where my old friend was buried. The voice behind me startled me. It was Al Ahdal. He was carrying a cardboard box, which, to my surprise, contained the one hundred and fifty thousand pounds we had agreed on. After I got over the initial shock of being handed the money straight away, we agreed I would have the house emptied in one week, and I would instruct my lawyer to contact the Menamar estate lawyer to sort out the paperwork. The deal done, Kiron Al Ahdal excused himself, as he was leaving for a flight to his native Saudi Arabia.

I watched from the steps of the big house as Al Ahdal sped out of the gates, the gravel spraying from the rear tyres as the big Mercedes struggled for grip as the power was applied.

I was a relatively happy man. The original deal had included the Aston Martin, so I had a free car out of the deal.

Back at the lodge house, I made some food, then busied myself removing my early-warning system before the new occupier inadvertently summoned the secret service while trying to put a light on.

In truth, I had never settled here, so it didn't take long to gather my gear. The cleanup squad had done me proud, and the main room and hall had been completely redone. Whoever moved in here would get a pleasant surprise, as I had no plans to take the furnishings. All I wanted were a few pictures and my belongings, only what would fit into the back seat and boot of the Aston Martin.

***

Sam's great plans started to fall to pieces the moment she entered the office. First, she was surprised to find out that Neil Andrews was in hospital. After speaking to a few of the staff, she was shocked to find out that it was Adam who had put him there. Sam managed to talk the director's secretary into letting her see him for a few minutes in between meetings. Sam had to use all her persuasive charms on the director, but finally he gave in and allowed Sam to take time off, providing she supplied him with a full written report on the Machrihanish case before leaving.

Sam was about to leave the office when the director stopped her. He could not resist a dig. "Samantha, it may not be a bad idea to take some time off. I believe I have some nasty bills on my desk for damage to hire cars, so it may be a good thing if you are out of earshot for a while. Remember, the report—on my desk before you leave, please."

Sam arrived back at her desk to find a police report waiting for her. Sam skipped through the first few pages. She was surprised at the speed of the report. Probably because MI6 were involved, the police had pulled out all the stops. At first, Sam was reading the report to help with her report, but things changed as Sam read the second page. For the next hour, Sam never lifted her head, and by the end of the report, Sam knew why Adam had vanished.

The report was inconclusive due to the fire that had raged through the building, but the senior officer's concluding statement meant that the case would remain open, pending any further evidence. He felt that there was a strong chance of foul play. Although the fire had started in the kitchen, there was some evidence of an explosion in the sitting room, and forensics could not say if this had happened as a consequence of the fire or not. Drugs and the remains of a car linked to known drug dealers had been found. The officer stated he had no suspects at the moment, but he strongly suspected some type of drug war had taken place. Undercover officers were following up inquiries with drug gangs in the hope of turning up new evidence.

Sam spent the rest of the afternoon at the firing range with her new Glock, which she had just picked up from the armory. It was the latest model, which had just been customized by a specialist gunsmith. Every agent who needed one had grips and balance weights added to give the weapons perfect balance. Sam had been told that it increased accuracy by 5 percent, and at that moment in time, Sam needed all the help she could get.

Sam's mind drifted as she lined up the target. She did not know how to feel. She was worried for Adam, but at the same time, she was angry. She had been cheated out of her chance to fulfill her vow to her sister, and she had been outmaneuvered. Her pride was again hurt. She focused her frustration on the target and emptied the full clip. On inspection of the target, she was pleasantly surprised. She had pulled two shots, but thirteen would have been kill shots. It was the best results she had achieved for a very long time. Sam wasn't sure if it was the anger or the new gun that had helped. She decided tomorrow she would finish her report, then head for Scotland. She wanted to get to the glass house first—she had some business to attend to.

***

It took longer than I had thought to get my gear sorted out. Eventually, I decided there was no way everything would fit in the car. I spent the next day on the phone. A removal firm came the same day and delivered my belongings to a storage company in Stirling.

My next call was to a hotel in Arisaig that was only minutes from the glass house. This was going to be my next port of call, at least until I had spoken to Sam.

My final call was an international call to America before I got into the wind. Zelenski was no longer at his desk, but he had the foreseen my call and had left a note for me. One of his old colleagues read it to me over the phone. "Your friend is safe. No harm will come to him now. Packages delivered as requested. Regards, your friend, John."

The next morning I was up bright and early. For the first time for a long time, I was looking forward to the day ahead. It was a crisp, cold March day, but the sun was warm, with the promise of spring in the air. I was going to enjoy my first long trip in the big Aston Martin. I had spent the previous evening checking tyres, oil, and charging the battery. It had been almost a year since the big beast had been let loose on the road. It was with some trepidation that I set off on the long journey. British supercars of that era were not renowned for their reliability, never mind ones that had been off the road for a long period. If I were brutally honest, the trepidation was more about Sam than the car. I had known her for some time now, and over that period, her mood swings had been staggering. What she would do now was anyone's guess.

The big Aston burbled away as I nursed it over the first few miles, letting it get up to operating temperature. My eyes darted from gauge to gauge, checking the health of the big beast. My worries were unfounded. The only worrying gauge was the fuel gauge as it headed for the red.

A fuel stop turned into a voyage of discovery. Opposite the petrol station was a Volkswagen dealer. A new white Beetle on the grass verge caught my eye, and on impulse, I wheeled the Aston into the dealer's forecourt. The salesman was horrified at what I suggested, but a forage in the cardboard box behind the driver's seat of the Aston produced bundles of notes in thousand-pound bunches.

I was suddenly the salesman's best friend and putting Herbie decals on a brand new Beetle was a great idea. I insisted that the car had to be delivered to me in two days' time at the hotel in Arisaig. We shook hands and the salesman counted the cash before handing me a receipt. An hour later, I was on my way.

Out on the open country roads, I let the big Aston off the leash. It transformed from a purring kitten into a road-devouring howling monster. I arrived in the late afternoon at the hotel in Arisaig with a grin from ear to ear. Who needed a stereo in a car like this? It came with its own soundtrack. Only the fuel gauge stopped me from turning the trip into a tour of Scotland.

I spent the next couple of days nursing my latest wounds. The bruising on my chest from the bullets that Benesch had fired into my vest was fading, and the swelling on my left hand was starting to die down. On the second day, I contemplated a run after breakfast, but two things put me off. I was not sure how well my lung had healed up. Also if the salesman was true to his word, the new Herbie should be delivered this morning. I decided on a brisk walk to burn off my breakfast. I only made it as far as the car park before Herbie and another car from the dealership pulled up. The salesman only took a few minutes to talk through the car before heading south again.

A spur-of-the-moment decision saw me driving the car north. A few minutes later, the cut off for the glass house appeared. I swung the Beetle off the main road, continuing through the underpass and up the long drive, noting the new surveillance cameras at the mouth of the underpass as I drove.

***

Sam missed the Beetle on the cameras. She was propped up on the balcony, still in her pajamas, studying the sea with a steaming mug of tea in her hand. At first, the crash of the sea drowned out the engine. Sam listened again. She was sure she had heard a car engine. She glanced at the monitor in the lounge. She had been correct. The red warning triangle was flashing—a car had just passed. Just then, a Beetle rolled up outside the house.

Sam felt like rubbing her eyes. A very shiny Herbie stood at the front door. Sam didn't wait to see who was getting out. She knew who it would be. She flew down the steps three at a time but checked herself before she got to the front door.

***

I rang the doorbell and waited. I was probably a couple of days early, but I needed to know if I had blown our friendship. There was no reply. Sam was probably standing behind the tinted glass, deciding if she should talk to me or not. My heart started to sink.

The voice from my right startled me. "You're early. You can't even get that bloody right." I spun round to find Sam leaning against the corner of the building. Her hair was like an explosion in a haystack, and her pj's were about two sizes too big for her. I was about to reply, but she cut in again. "Jesus, Adam, what the hell did you think you were up to? Neil Andrews has a broken jaw, and the Metropolitan Police are running about like headless chickens looking for an imaginary drug war." Sam's face was cast in stone.

All the way up the road, I had been thinking of what to say to Sam, but my thoughts had vanished for the moment. Sam pushed herself off the corner and started walking toward Herbie. "Where did you get the money to buy the car?" Sam was staring at me, waiting for an answer.

"I sold my house, so I thought you might like this. You seemed to miss your old one after it was shot up."

Sam pulled me toward her and gave me a long, lingering hug. In the cold breeze, her body was warm. She had softened up, and her lack of training was showing.

We held each other while Sam whispered in my ear, "Don't ever do anything like that again. You had me worried sick. Partners don't do that." Sam broke off the embrace and led me by the hand in through the new side door she had had fitted. In the garage stood a brand new Freelander, the same colour as the one she had torched. Sam laughed when she saw the expression on my face. "It's yours. Great minds think alike." Then she headed out onto the balcony.

I followed, and we watched the seals playing on the rocks. "Sam, what you said earlier about being partners, do we leave it at that?"

Sam squeezed my hand and smiled as she watched the seals. "No, Adam, it's much more than that. This is the first day of our new lives together."

***

The phone rang in the drawing room of 10 Downing Street. It was answered promptly. "The US president on the line for you, Prime Minister."

The prime minister sat back as the call was put through.

"Good evening, Prime Minister. Just a call to again apologize for the problems we have caused you."

The prime minister smiled to himself. "Mr. President, not many people can say they just had an apology from the president of the United States. Not to worry. Everything is in hand. The press has been handled, and I have instructed the Ministry of Defense to sell off the base to the private sector. I have told them to include a no-liability clause in the event of any radioactive waste being found. We live to fight another day, sir."

***

It was a beautiful August afternoon. The sun glinted off the little cottage, making its new coat of white paint look even whiter than normal. Bobby Davis arrived in a mad rush. He was late for his appointment. He did not want to mess up this sale. He had tried for months to sell the cottage, but the word had got around that the beautiful little cottage was bad luck. Its last tenant had committed suicide, not a great selling point.

All he had to do now was hand the keys over, get a signature, and the deal was in the bag, that was, if the new owners had waited, and he wasn't sure about that, as he was over an hour late. Then he breathed a sigh of relief. Mr. and Mrs. Hunter stood arm in arm on the beach, looking out over the sound to the misty blue hills of the Mull of Kintyre. "I am so sorry. My phone is dead, and I had a problem at the lawyers. I can't thank you enough for waiting."

***

I smiled at the out-of-breath estate agent. "Ann and I were just about to start pitching a tent." Davis wasted no more time. I signed for the keys using my alias, Allan Hunter. Ten minutes later, we were all alone on our own private beach.

"I still don't get it, Adam. Why did you want to buy this place? We have the glass house, so why do you need this?"

I thought about it as I looked out over the sea. "Honestly, Sam, I am not sure myself. I think part of it is to honour Kay's memory. And Ian used to love this little island. He was born here you know." My mischievous side kicked in. "Anyway when you get sick of me and kick me out, I will need my own little pad."

Sam was holding my hand and gazing into my eyes. "For a clever man, you just don't get it, do you? Adam, I used to wake up in the morning thinking of ways to catch Merlin. Now I wake up thinking about what we will do today. I've swapped torment for contentment. You keep this old cottage if you must, but if you are here, I will be with you, you big Scottish fool!"

I handed Sam the necklace I had been keeping in my pocket. It glinted in the summer sunshine as the breeze spun it round on its chain. "It is a gold charm of Merlin the magician. I left it in Carrington's house to let him know he had been found out. I thought now you might like it as a good luck charm, the beginning of a new chapter, if you like."

Addendum

In 1994, Machrihanish Air Base was refurbished at the cost of one hundred million pounds. It boasts one of the longest runways in Europe at three kilometres long and covers hundreds of acres. In May 2009, the MOD put the base up for sale. The Scottish government valuation in December 2009 stated that the base contained four separate areas of radioactive contamination due to previous use. Machrihanish Air Base was sold to the private sector on 26 May 2012 for £1.

Printed in Great Britain
by Amazon.co.uk, Ltd.,
Marston Gate.